To Carroll J. Swan
for the Advertising
Woman's Club of
Boston from his
friend

Mary Caroline Crawford

The Romance of the American Theatre

Photo by White, New York

JULIA MARLOWE AS KATHARINE IN "THE TAMING OF THE SHREW"

THE ROMANCE
OF THE
AMERICAN THEATRE

BY

MARY CAROLINE CRAWFORD

ILLUSTRATED

BOSTON

LITTLE, BROWN, AND COMPANY

1925

FOREWORD

A DOZEN years ago, when I wrote the preface for the first edition of this book, there existed no complete history of the American theatre. To be sure William Dunlap had put out in 1832 what he *called* a history of the American theatre, but this work, though honest in intent, was far from accurate in content; and it particularly failed in due recognition of the theatre in the west and in the south. About forty years ago George Seilhamer began to give to the world what promised to be an authentic history of the American theatre, the sources of information which he used being chiefly the files of Colonial and Revolutionary newspapers; three volumes had been issued and the story brought up to 1800 when Mr. Seilhamer died. No soul had been found brave enough to take up this task where it was then laid down until Arthur Hornblow, in 1919, published his "History of the Theatre in America," in two volumes. Right at this point I want to record my deep indebtedness to this careful, scholarly and interesting work.

One reason why the theatre in America so long failed to receive adequate historical treatment was because little or no care had been given to the preservation and conservation of theatrical records. Happily, there has

v

come a change in this respect during the past dozen years. Those of us especially who live and work near Boston cannot be too grateful for the priceless collection assembled, largely by Robert Gould Shaw, and now housed in the magnificent Widener library at Cambridge. I herewith acknowledge my deep indebtedness to Mrs. J. B. Hall, librarian in charge of this *Theatre Collection of Harvard University*, for her assistance in the selection of rare and interesting illustrations for my new text. The Allen A. Brown Collection in the Boston Public Library is another source of great help to workers in this field. For access to its treasures I thank its curators, and also I thank Charles Knowles Bolton and the staff of the Boston Athenæum for the use of other material.

Brander Matthews and the works of William Winter have given me much also; while to Montrose J. Moses, who has made a number of noteworthy contributions to the literature of the theatre, I am particularly indebted for counsel and helpful suggestions regarding the production of this new edition. To the J. B. Lippincott Company, the Houghton Mifflin Company, to Moffatt Yard and Company, to The Macmillan Company, who brought out Modjeska's memoirs, to the publishers of the autobiography of Madame Ristori, Ellen Terry and Tommaso Salvini, my gratitude is also due, chiefly for quotation privileges more specifically indicated in the body of the book. And in making this new edition I wish similarly to thank Brentano's, for permission to quote Oliver M. Sayler's "Our American Theatre"; Felix Isman for courtesies regarding his volume, "Weber and

Foreword

Fields"; Funk and Wagnalls Company for quotation
privileges in connection with John Ranken Towse's
"Sixty Years of the Theatre"; Miss Marian Spitzer,
author, and the *Saturday Evening Post*, publishers, for
permission to reproduce the incident about Queen
Victoria and the American minstrels; also Harper and
Brothers for permission to quote George M. Cohan's
"Twenty Years on Broadway," Arthur Hobson Quinn's
"History of the American Drama," Lawrence Hutton's
"Curiosities of the American Stage" and "Charles Froh-
man, Manager and Man," written by Isaac F. Marcos-
son and Daniel Frohman.

J. Frank Davis, who recently contributed to *Scribner's
Magazine* a delightful article on "Tom Shows," has also
been most courteous and helpful, as has Eola Willis,
whose monumental work on "The Charleston Stage in
the XVII Century" (published by the State Company of
Columbia, South Carolina) will long remain a mine of
valuable information for workers studying the history
of the theatre in the South. I am glad to thank, too,
Lyon Gardiner Tyler for an elusive bit of information
in regard to the actress-wife of his brother, — that
lady who as Mrs. Robert Tyler became briefly mistress
of the White House.

And now a word or two concerning the method I have
followed. This book was never meant to be a history
of the theatre; the utmost to which it aspired was *historical accuracy* in its somewhat eclectic survey of the whole
field. And since obviously it could not be contemporary in treatment, the fairest way to approach the subject

Foreword

of the development of the theatre in America seemed
to me to be from the standpoint of dominant personalities and general tendencies. This was also the natural
method for the reason that, for many years, the actors
were the theatre. So, more especially as I have prepared for the new edition material covering the birth
and growth of minstrelsy and its ramifications, and the
development of the theatre along our western and southern frontiers, I have let the minstrels and the managers
speak for themselves, feeling that in this way the color
and movement bound up in the very practice of the
actor's profession might be best preserved. Happily,
a number of books have recently appeared from the pens
of contemporary players, and such works have been of
immense assistance in presenting first-hand impressions
of our stage. To these actors, turned authors for the
nonce, as to those player-folk of yesterday and the day
before, who dared greatly and endured much for the sake
of the work they loved, I trust the present volume may
help to bring its quota of deserved recognition.

M. C. C.

BOSTON, MASSACHUSETTS, July, 1925

CONTENTS

CHAPTER   PAGE

FOREWORD v

I PLAYERS AND PLAYHOUSES OF THE EIGHTEENTH CENTURY 1

II EARLY UPS AND DOWNS OF THE THEATRE IN THE SOUTH 44

III RISE OF THE THEATRE AS AN AMERICAN INSTITUTION 80

IV THE CURIOUS ADVENTURES OF CERTAIN EARLY ENGLISH STARS 118

V THE ENTERTAINING OBSERVATIONS OF THE FIRST CHARLES MATHEWS 142

VI TWO GREAT ENGLISH TRAGEDIANS WHOM WE WELCOMED GLADLY 159

VII EDWIN FORREST AS ACTOR AND MAN . . . 173

VIII A PLAYER WHO INSPIRED A SONG AND ANOTHER WHO COMPOSED ONE. 210

IX FORREST'S ENEMY, MACREADY, AND SOME STARS WHO CAME AFTER HIM 226

X EARLY NINETEENTH CENTURY AUDIENCES . . 250

XI RACHEL AND FECHTER 266

XII VISITING STARS OF A LATER DAY 286

XIII EDWIN BOOTH: "HOPE OF THE LIVING DRAMA" 310

ix

Contents

CHAPTER   PAGE

XIV SOME OF BOOTH'S MORE DISTINGUISHED CONTEM-
     PORARIES 327

XV   AMERICA'S OWN "LIVELY ART" AND WHAT IT HAS
     MEANT TO OUR STAGE 355

XVI DEALING WITH DRAMA ALONG OUR FRONTIER AND
     IN THE THEATRES OF NEW YORK . . . 397

     INDEX 495

ILLUSTRATIONS

Julia Marlowe as Katharine in "The Taming of the
  Shrew" . . . . *Frontispiece*

FACING PAGE

Nance Oldfield 8

Peg Woffington 9

David Garrick and his Wife 16
  From the painting by Hogarth

An early American playbill 17

"Perdita" Robinson 60
  From the painting by Romney

John Drew and Ada Rehan in the Daly revival of "The
  Recruiting Officer" 61

Playbill for New York performance in 1750 of Otway's
  "Orphan" 80

William Dunlap, first American man of letters to make
  play-writing a profession 81

Scene from "The Contrast" 94
  From a drawing by Dunlap

Royall Tyler, author of "The Contrast" . . . 95

Thomas Wignell 95

The Federal Street Theatre, Boston 114

The Haymarket Theatre, Boston 115

Illustrations

FACING PAGE

Three Great Richards. George Frederick Cooke, Junius Brutus Booth, and Edmund Kean . . . 128

Edmund Kean as Othello 129
After a drawing from life by John William Gear

A "first night" at the second Park Theatre, New York, in 1822. The elder Charles Mathews is shown on the stage 144
From a water-color drawing by John Searle

Exterior of the Park Theatre, New York . . . 145
From a drawing by C. Burton

William Augustus Conway 160

Thomas Abthorpe Cooper 161

Drury Lane Theatre, London, in which Edwin Forrest first acted in England 192

William C. Macready as Shylock 193

Edwin Forrest as King Lear 206

Edwin Forrest 207

Mrs. Duff, whose acting Horace Greeley greatly admired 214

John Howard Payne 215
After a daguerreotype by Brady

Ellen Tree, (Mrs. Charles Kean), whose sister popularized "Home, Sweet Home" 224

Mrs. John Drew, Senior, as Mrs. Malaprop . . . 225

The mother of Edgar Allan Poe 225

William C. Macready 228

Fanny Ellsler 229
From a drawing by W. K. Hewitt

Illustrations

FACING PAGE

Master Joseph Burke 229
After a drawing by T. Wageman

Frances Anne Kemble 234
From the painting by Thomas Sully

Mrs. Siddons as Lady Macbeth 235
After the painting by Harlow

John Philip Kemble 235
After the painting by Sir Thomas Lawrence

Madame Vestris as Olivia in "John of Paris" . . 248

Lotta as The Marchioness 248

Maggie Mitchell as Fanchon 249

Tyrone Power 254
After a drawing by D'Orsay

The French Opera House, New Orleans, erected in 1860 255

Mlle. Rachel 278
After the painting by Lehmann

Rachel as Phèdre 279

Fechter as Hamlet 279

Adelaide Ristori as Mary Queen of Scots . . . 290

Tommaso Salvini as Othello 291

Eleanora Duse 294

Modjeska as Rosalind 295

Lily Langtry, the English professional beauty, and
Sarah Bernhardt, in 1887 304

Sir Henry Irving 305

Junius Brutus Booth and his young son, Edwin . . 312

Edwin Booth as Hamlet 313

xiii

Illustrations

FACING PAGE

Playbill of "Our American Cousin" on the night John
Wilkes Booth shot Lincoln 318

John Wilkes Booth 319

Edwin Booth 324

The "Royal Couch of Denmark" 325

Joseph Jefferson as Rip van Winkle 332

E. A. Sothern as Lord Dundreary 333

Matilda Heron 333

E. L. Davenport, the elder 338

Fanny Davenport 338

Charlotte Cushman 339

Mary Anderson 339

Lawrence Barrett 348

Ellen Terry as Marguerite 349

Thomas D. ("Jim Crow") Rice 376

Tony Pastor, after a caricature by W. J. Gladding . 377

Lillian Russell, "Airy, Fairy Lillian," at the height of
her radiant beauty 384

Weber and Fields in "Whirl-A-Gig" 385

Playbill of "Uncle Tom's Cabin" at the National Theatre, New York, in 1853, with the original cast . 390

Interesting copy of a lithograph poster advertising the
Morris Brothers Minstrels in 1867 . . . 391

Solomon Franklin Smith 412

Priscilla Cooper 413

Adah Isaacs Menken and Alexandre Dumas, père . 442

Interior of Niblo's Theatre 443

xiv

Illustrations

FACING PAGE

Lydia Thompson as Robinson Crusoe 450
James W. Wallack 451
Mrs. Anna Cora Mowatt 456
Dion Boucicault as Con, in "The Shaughraun" . . 457
The Daly Company in 1884 464
James H. Hackett as Colonel Nimrod Wildfire . . 465
James A. Herne in his own "Margaret Fleming" . 465
Maude Adams 472
Minnie Maddern Fiske as Becky Sharp . . . 473
E. H. Sothern as Hamlet 473
Denman Thompson as Joshua Whitcomb in "The Old
    Homestead" 482
Richard Mansfield as Cyrano de Bergerac . . . 483
Eugene O'Neill 486
Ethel Barrymore 487
Walter Hampden as Hamlet 490
John Barrymore as Hamlet 491

THE
ROMANCE OF THE AMERICAN THEATRE

———◆———

CHAPTER I

PLAYERS AND PLAYHOUSES OF THE EIGHTEENTH CENTURY

" Last week I buried Mrs. Nance Oldfield very
willingly and with much satisfaction." It was in these
somewhat equivocal words that the Reverend Dr.
Parker of the Established Church recorded his relation
to the then recent obsequies of England's best-beloved
actress. Nance Oldfield was not a virtuous woman as
we of to-day count virtue, yet Queen Caroline was on
intimate and friendly terms with her. Nance Oldfield
had no proper social standing, as do many of our pres-
ent-day actresses, yet on the terrace at Windsor she
was often to be seen walking with the respectable con-
sorts of dukes and calling countesses and the wives of
English barons by their Christian names. Moreover,
when Nance Oldfield died, she received, by burial

I

The Romance of the American Theatre

within the walls of Westminster Abbey, such honour as no actress had ever received before nor has been accorded since.[1] The public could not have thronged more eagerly to her funeral had she been a real queen instead of a mimic one, nor could she have had men of greater distinction for her pall-bearers. All of which is of interest to us, as showing that in England of the eighteenth century a great actress — who chanced to be also a lovable woman — was not held too closely to account for little lapses from the standard of Caesar's wife.

Nance Oldfield's father had been a gentleman, but she was the humble apprentice of a seamstress when Captain Farquhar, a London man-about-town, discovered her at her aunt's inn, on a quiet summer evening late in the seventeenth century, reading aloud to her mother from a rattling comedy of Beaumont and Fletcher. The smart captain promptly assured the girl that she was a born actress, and she as promptly retorted, amid blushes of delight, that to go upon the stage had long been the dream of her life. Then Farquhar talked of her to a friend who had the ear of Rich, the famous manager, and soon she found herself a member of the company at Drury Lane, with an assured salary of fifteen shillings a week. Four years later (1696) Colley Cibber himself assigned to her the rôle of

[1] The custodian of the Abbey informs me, however, that Mrs. Garrick, who was a dancer before her marriage, lies in the south transept with her husband and that in the Abbey cloisters no less than three actresses are buried: Mrs. Betterton, wife of Thomas Betterton of Drury Lane Theatre, Mrs. Bracegirdle (d. 1748), and Ann Crawford (d. 1801).

2

Lady Betty Modish in his " Careless Husband," and for the first time in the history of the English stage the part of a lady of fashion was appropriately played.

It was then not so very long since women were a startling novelty on the English-speaking stage. The female parts were always taken by boys until after the Restoration, credit being due to Sir William Davenant for opening to women, in 1662, the economic opportunity represented by the profession of the actor. The place which marked this interesting development was Sir William's Theatre in Lincoln's Inn Fields, and the " vehicle " employed, a drama called the " Siege of Rhodes," in which Mrs. Saunderson, as " the first female actress that ever played for hire before the public in England," took the part of the heroine. That the public was by no means of one mind concerning this innovation is very clear from various comments to be found in the books of the period. Tom Nash in his " Pierce Penilesse " highly commends the English stage in that it has not had " courtesans or women actors " such as were then to be found abroad. But, on the other hand, there are extant the ravings of a certain Dr. Reynolds, who had published in 1593 a foaming invective against stage plays, one reason for his objections being that the boys who wore the dress of women on the stage were wont to ape the airs of women off the stage.

A classic case which is often cited in this connection is that of Edward Kynaston, the last beautiful youth who figured in petticoats on the stage. Colley Cibber

relates that Kynaston was still playing the woman —
both off the stage and on — even after King Charles
II had begun to lend his royal support to the theatre.
Once, he tells us, his Majesty, " coming a little before
the usual time to a tragedy, became impatient that the
play did not at once begin. Whereupon the stage
manager, rightly judging that the best excuse for their
default would be the true one, fairly told his Majesty
that the queen was not *shaved* yet. The King, whose
good humour loved to laugh at a jest as well as to make
one, accepted the excuse, which served to divert him
until the male queen could be effeminated. In a word,
Kynaston at that time was so beautiful a youth that
the ladies of quality prided themselves on taking him
with them in their coaches to Hyde Park in his theatrical
habit, after the play; which, in those days, they might
have sufficient time to do, because the plays then were
used to begin at four o'clock."

The real reason why women were given parts in
the plays of the Restoration period seems to have been
not a moral one at all, however, but was attributable,
as Disraeli hints, to the fact that " the boys who had
been trained to act female characters before the Restoration had grown too masculine during the suspension of
the theatre to resume their tender office." In any case,
women were now on the stage to stay, and it was in
large measure due to their presence there that the ob-
scenity of the early English comedies gradually became
unacceptable to the public.

A beautiful girl, like Nance Oldfield, playing with

4

spirit yet without exaggeration the part of a clever, high-mettled woman, was a distinct novelty, therefore. "Who should act genteel comedy perfectly," asks Walpole, "but people of fashion who have sense? Actors and actresses can only guess at the tone of high life, and cannot be inspired with it. Why are there so few genteel comedies, but because most comedies are written by men not of that sphere. Etherege, Congreve, Vanbrugh, and Cibber wrote genteel comedy because they lived in the best company; and Mrs. Oldfield played it so well because she not only followed but often set the fashion."

Cibber had despaired, indeed, of ever finding an actress who could realize his idea of Lady Betty Modish, when good fortune threw Nance Oldfield in his way. Then he no longer had any qualms but finished the piece at once. When he brought it out, he had the almost unprecedented generosity to declare that he owed the success of the play wholly to the gay and brilliant girl who was cast for its leading part. "And not only to the uncommon excellence of her acting," as he explained, "but even to her personal manner of conversing." Many of the most effective sentiments in the play, he insisted, were Mrs. Oldfield's own, simply dressed up by him "with a little more care than when they negligently fell from her lively humour."

As time passed, Nance Oldfield became the original creator of no less than sixty-five comedy characters. Her salary at the height of her career reached three hundred guineas, exclusive of benefits, on which occasions gold was fairly showered into her lap. Tragedy parts, too, she played with pronounced success, though she never enjoyed these so much, hating, as she often said, to " have a page dragging her tail about." In private life, as well, she was averse to the rôle of tragedy queen, accepting quite simply the affection offered her by Maynwaring, a rich bachelor connected with the government, and comforting herself quite as simply with General Churchill, brother of the Duke of Marlborough, when Maynwaring died. In this latter connection marriage appears to have been at least thought of, thus causing Queen Caroline one day to remark to the actress: " I hear, Mrs. Oldfield, that you and the General are married? " To which there came from Nance the dry retort: " Madam, the General keeps his own secrets! " Yet society never rejected this its favourite, and her sons, Maynwaring and Churchill, to whom she bequeathed the bulk of a fortune — amassed, it is interesting to note, more by their mother's exertions than by any generosity of their respective fathers — mourned her earnestly and openly when she died. The distinction between Nance Oldfield's love affairs and those of certain well-known actresses who had preceded her appears to have been that they were founded on sentiment, not on interest, and society was not slow in making the distinction. Moreover, there was none of that tittle-tattle concerning this actress's relations with the gallants behind the scenes [1] that we find earlier

[1] She used to go to the playhouse in a chair attended by two footmen, and she had little or nothing to do with the others of the company and their followers.

in regard to Nell Gwyn and later with Peg Woffington as its heroine.

The delectable " Diary " of Pepys is full of snap-shots of the theatre in the seventeenth century. From few other sources, indeed, can we obtain such choice bits of information regarding the manners and customs of that day, both before and behind the curtain. Early in January, 1663, when the Duke of York and his wife honoured a play of Killigrew's by their presence, Pepys writes himself down as much shocked by " the impertinent and unnatural dalliances " of the royal pair, " there before the whole world, kissing of hands and leaning one upon another." How differently did Cromwell's daughter, Lady Mary, conduct herself in her box at Drury Lane with her husband, Viscount Falconbridge! The looks and dress of this lady elicit only praise from Pepys. " Her modest embarrassment as the house began to fill and spectators gazed too steadily upon her, causing her," he writes approvingly, to " put on her vizard . . . which of late has become a great fashion among the ladies."

No " vizard," however, was allowed to conceal the charms of Nell Gwyn when she gossiped with the diarist. The constant presence of " her kind " in the front of the house was a cherished feature of the times, as was the invasion of the green-room by the gallants of the day. Dr. Doran, whose " Annals of The Stage " present us with an incomparable description of theatrical habits of this and the succeeding century, declares that the tiring-rooms of the actresses were then open to any of

7

the fine gentlemen who frequented the house. " They stood by at the mysteries of dressing, and commented upon what they beheld and did not behold with such breadth and coarseness of wit, that the more modest or least impudent ladies sent away their little hand-maidens. The dressing over, the amateurs lounged into the house, talked loudly with the pretty orange girls, listened when it suited them, and at the termination of the piece, crowded again into the tiring-rooms of the most favourite and least scrupulous actresses. The wits loved to assemble, too, after the play was done, in the dressing-rooms of the leading actors with whom they most cared to cultivate an intimacy. Much company often congregated here, generally with the purpose of assigning meetings where further enjoyment might be pursued."

The curious intimacy between the great world and the world of the theatre is strikingly illustrated in the fact that one of the big successes of the early eighteenth century was the play " Jane Shore," the persecuted heroine of which had once condescended to be the mistress of King Edward IV. This work contains many moving passages, even when read with the eye of to-day, and its last act, in which the fair Jane is shown wandering from door to door, a starving victim of Gloster's black revenge, must have provided magnificent opportunities for the powers of a gifted actress. Though Nance Old-field did not like to play tragic parts, this character proved a great triumph for her. Rowe [1] himself trained

[1] Nicholas Rowe was a politician as well as the poet laureate of England in the reign of George I. At one time under-secretary to the

NANCE OLDFIELD
See page 1

PEG WOFFINGTON
See page 9

her in the reading of it, and she never failed to move her audience to tears by her mimic sufferings and sorrows. During the last act, bread was wont to be thrown down from the gallery as a tribute to the realism of her hunger, and no attaché of the theatre ever interfered. This was a slight interruption compared to a riot, or to that incident recorded by Pepys when " a gentleman of good habit, sitting just before us, eating some fruit in the midst of the play, did drop down as dead; but, with much ado, Orange Moll did thrust her finger down his throat, and brought him to life again."

The ability to play " Jane Shore " acceptably remained for several generations the test of a successful actress; and it is conceded by all writers of the period that in this rôle Peg Woffington " did not admit of competition with Mrs. Oldfield." But in most parts Peg Woffington shone as the bright particular star of the eighteenth century stage. Not to understand her relation to the players and plays of the time would be to fail to comprehend the hold which the theatre had on Englishmen of that day.

Margaret Woffington and David Garrick! What names to conjure with, though here we may not do more than touch very briefly on their romantic personal histories, merely mention in passing the enduring impetus that they gave to the traditions of good acting,

Duke of Queensberry, he studied Spanish in hope of obtaining a foreign appointment through Halifax. The latter, however, only congratulated him on being able to read Don Quixote in the original! " Jane Shore " was brought out February 2, 1714. Its author died in December, 1718, and was buried in the poets' corner of Westminster Abbey, opposite Chaucer.

and then cross the stormy seas — as their contemporary, Hallam, was soon to do — and devote ourselves
to the somewhat arid history of the early theatres in
America.

Peg Woffington made her stage début about 1725 at
a variety theatre of Dublin, in a basket carried by
Madame Violante, a tight-rope dancer, as she made her
perilous passage across the stage and caused delicious
cold shivers to run down the spines of her gaping auditors. Peg was the child of a journeyman bricklayer, then
dead, and of a vigorous mother, still living. The mother
took in washing for the support of the family. Between
the fair Margaret's début and a later day, when she
actually acted for Madame Violante in a Lilliputian
troupe, her profession was that of selling " halfpenny
salads " about the streets of Dublin. Thus she found it
easy to play hoyden parts, when these fell to her lot.
But, being a natural-born actress, she acquitted herself
with no less success as Ophelia when, on February 12,
1734, she first essayed this rôle at the Dublin Theatre
Royal. Though only fifteen at this time, Peg is affirmed
to have been well-grown and tall. Already, too, she
was a stunning beauty, with splendid dark eyes under
strongly marked brows, and an expression of archness
which was well set off by her unpowdered hair and the
lace cap or flat garden hat to be seen in her numerous
portraits. Moreover, she had in some way or other
learned to bear herself like a lady, and could use a fan
with great dexterity, or make in most impressive fashion
the sweeping courtesy of the " manners " comedy. In

addition to which she had a wit equal to the best of the gallants who flocked to her tiring-room.

It was Peg Woffington's wit and the dash with which she set it off that enabled her to act with tremendous success the "breeches" part of Sir Harry Wildair in Farquhar's "Constant Couple." And it was the prodigious drawing power of Woffington in the rôle of this lively rake which gained for her a hearing with the all-powerful John Rich (1740), then manager of the Covent Garden in London.[1] That season she played Sir Harry Wildair no fewer than twenty times and always to crowded houses. Which meant much more then than it would now, inasmuch as the Londoners of that day required a constantly changing bill, theatre-going at that period being confined to a comparatively small section of the population. This is the time when we find Walpole declaring Peg "much in vogue," and Conway asserting that "all the town is in love with her."

Yet it is with Drury Lane rather than with Covent Garden that we chiefly associate Peg Woffington, for

[1] A writer in the *Dublin Review* has pictured very graphically their first meeting. "The great manager, when Woffington first saw him, was lolling in ungraceful ease on a sofa, holding a play in one hand and in the other a teacup, from which he sipped frequently. Around him were seven and twenty cats of all sizes, colours and kinds. Peg Woffington was astounded at the sight. Rich, to her mind, had for years been the greatest man in the world. The menagerie of grimalkins, amid which he lay so carelessly, was so different an environment from her conception of the study of the Covent Garden theatre-manager, that she was embarrassed into silence. Rich, in his turn, was equally confused by the beauty of his visitor, and lay staring at her for a long time before he recollected his courtesy and offered her a chair. Standing before him was a woman whom he afterward declared to be the loveliest creature he had ever seen."

it was there that she fell in with David Garrick, then just rising to fame. Garrick's boyhood had been passed at Lichfield, where his mania for acting had seriously interfered with his application to school studies. His father (of French descent) was a captain in the English army, who had married the daughter of a Lichfield vicar. Because of this church connection, David's stage mania was frowned down from the first. It was considered vastly more respectable for him to go into the business of wine-selling, of which one of his uncles had made a great success. Yet the lad was not starved on his play-loving side, for his father's friends, knowing his passion for the theatre, often treated him to a journey to London on purpose that he might feast at the playhouse. Thus the lad had been enabled to see all the great players of the time from the gallery, long before he had the opportunity to mingle with them on the stage.

In time, however, that opportunity came also. For, leaving Lichfield and its cramping influences behind him, young Garrick set out, in 1737, in the company of Dr. Samuel Johnson, who had been his tutor, to try his fortune in the great city. Garrick's resources were increased about this time by the death of an uncle, who bequeathed to him a thousand pounds; but Johnson, who had only his tragedy of " Irene " as a means of advance, long worshipped comfort from afar. Later, Garrick was able to produce this tragedy for his old friend.

David's début on the professional stage was made in

12

the provinces and under an assumed name. His first London engagement was in the fall of 1741 at the theatre in unfashionable Goodman's Fields. He came on between two parts of a concert in what the playbills announced as "The Life and Death of Richard III." "Yet from the moment the new actor appeared," says Doran, "his auditors were enthralled. They saw a Richard and not an actor of that personage. Of spectators he seemed unconscious, so thoroughly did he identify himself with the character. He surrendered himself to all the requirements, was ready for every phase of passion, every change of humour, and was as wonderful in his quiet sarcasm as he was terrific in the hurricane of the battle-scenes. Above all, his audiences were delighted with his ' nature.' Garrick spoke not as an orator, but as King Richard himself might have spoken in like circumstances. The chuckling exultation of his ' So much for Buckingham! ' was long a tradition on the stage. His points, indeed, occurred in rapid succession." At the beginning Garrick drew a pound a night for all this, but soon he was sharing profits equally with the management, and his salary, when he went to Drury Lane, in May, 1742, was fixed at £600 per annum.

Garrick was twenty-six at this time and Peg Woffington two years younger. Their mutual attraction was inevitable. He had not been a month at Drury Lane, playing (among other things) Lear to her Cordelia, when he found himself deeply in love with the Irish beauty and inditing to her such verses as:

13

"Were she arrayed in rustic weed,
With her the bleating flocks I'd feed,
And pipe upon mine oaten reed
    To please my lovely Peggy.
With her a cottage would delight,
All's happy when she's in my sight,
But when she's gone 'tis endless night —
    All's dark without my Peggy."

The following June they were both in Dublin, playing in the new theatre to which they had been hastily summoned by the manager Duval, to counteract the rival attractions at the Theatre Royal of Colley Cibber's daughter-in-law and of that admirable actor, Quin, who figures in Charles Reade's novel, " Peg Woffington." Their success was so enormous — and the sanitary conditions of the time so vile — that they achieved the doubtful honour of spreading an epidemic, christened the " Garrick Fever," among the Dubliners who thronged to see them act during that sultry summer. It was at this time that Nance Oldfield's famous part, Lady Betty Modish, was added to the Woffington repertory.

The following winter found the two brilliant players back in London, frankly sharing a household and the expenses thereof. One month Peggy paid the bills, the other month Davy. During Peg's month the tea was very strong, " as red as blood " if we may trust Dr. Johnson; and it was very likely because the actress could not remember to change her recipe when Davy's pay-month came around, that her housemate soon began to grumble quite unpleasantly about the size of the

14

bills. There is considerable evidence that Garrick, though a brilliant artist, had a soul not above candle-ends.[1]

Some chroniclers of the time declare that Garrick once offered marriage to Peg Woffington. Murphy says that he had even gone so far as to buy the wedding-ring and try it on her finger, but that as the inevitable hour approached, his native caution asserted itself. Peg, rallying him on his glumness, then drew out the confession that he was " wearing the shirt of Deianira," whereupon she told him with fine spirit to put off that irritating garment and never see her more " except in the course of professional business, or in the presence of a third person." Which proposition Davy accepted with unheroic alacrity! It was agreed that the presents which she had given *him* should be returned; and they all were, with the notable exception of a pair of diamond shoe-buckles, which, Davy asserted, he kept because

[1] Samuel Rogers preserves, as coming from Foote, one story about Garrick's parsimony which is truly delicious. The actor, it appears, " had invited Hurd to dine with him at the Adelphi, and, after dinner, the evening being warm, they passed up and down in front of the house. As they passed and repassed the dining-room windows, Garrick was in perfect agony, for he saw that there was a thief in one of the candles which was burning on one of the tables; and yet Hurd was a person of such consequence that he could not run away from him to prevent the waste of his tallow." Over against this story it is only fair, however, to weigh Johnson's testimony to Boswell that " Garrick is a very liberal man, sir. He has given away more money than any man in England. There may be a little vanity mixed but he has shown that money is not his first object." The truth of the matter appears to be that, along with his artistic temperament, Garrick had an admixture of shopkeeper's thrift derived from his French ancestry. All about him he saw player-folk, who, after periods of great prosperity, had hardly a shilling to bless themselves with when the evil days descended. He did not propose to go out like that if he could prevent it by watching candle-ends!

of his sentimental attachment to them. The enemies of the actor declare, however, that he could not bear to part with anything having so much intrinsic value. The lady whom Garrick did marry was Mlle. Eva Maria Violette,[1] who worshipped him, living and dead, and to whom he appears to have been a very good husband.

To the tremendous talent of this actor all the contemporary critics bear enthusiastic record. Kitty Clive was one night seen standing in the wings, weeping and scolding alternately at his power. Angry at last at finding herself so affected, she turned on her heel, crying in the downright fashion of the day: " Damn him, he could act a gridiron! " It is said that in his King Lear, Garrick's very stick acted. Charles Dibdin asserts that the man never ceased to act whether on the stage or off, and relates that he would occasionally, for the benefit of his friends, go through what he used to call his rounds, by standing behind a chair and conveying into his face every kind of passion, blending one into the other. "At one moment you laughed, at another you cried; now he terrified you and presently you conceived yourself something horrible, he seemed so terrified at you. Afterwards he drew his features into the appearance of such dignified wisdom that Minerva might have been proud of the portrait; and then —

[1] This lady, though a dancer, was a protegée of Lord and Lady Burton, through whom the best houses were open to her. Robertson's " David Garrick " is said to have been founded on an incident of her love for Garrick. Certain it is that Lady Burton capitulated and settled £6000 upon the bride.

16

DAVID GARRICK AND HIS WIFE
From the painting by Hogarth
See page 16

New-York, November 12, 1753.

By a Company of COMEDIANS,

At the New-Theatre, in *Naſſau-Street*,

This Evening, being the 12th of *November*, will be preſented,

(By particular Deſire)

An *Hiſtorical Play*, call'd,

King RICHARD III.

CONTAINING

The Diſtreſſes and Death of King *Henry* the VIth ; the artful Acquiſition of the Crown by *Crook-back'd Richard* ; the Murder of the two young Princes in the Tower ; and the memorable Battle of *Boſworth-Field*, being the laſt that was fought between the Houſes of *York* and *Lancaſter*.

Richard,	by	Mr. Rigby.
King Henry,	by	Mr. Hallam.
Prince Edward,	by	Maſter L. Hallam.
Duke of York,	by	Maſter A. Hallam.
Earl of Richmond,	by	Mr. Clarkſon.
Duke of Buckingham,	by	Mr. Malone.,
Duke of Nerfolk,	by	Mr. Miller.
Lord Stanley,	by	Mr. Singleton.
Lieutenant,	by	Mr. Bell.
Cateſby,	by	Mr. Adcock.
Queen Elizabeth,	by	Mrs. Hallam.
Lady Anne,	by	Mrs. Adcock.
Ducheſs of York,	by	Mrs. Rigby.

To which will be added,

A Ballad F A R C E call'd,

The *DEVIL TO PAY.*

Sir John Loverule,	by	Mr. Adcock.
Jobſon,	by	Mr. Malone.
Butler,	by	Mr. Miller.
Footman,	by	Mr. Singleton.
Cook,	by	Mr. Bell.
Coachman,	by	Mr. Rigby.
Conjurer,	by	Mr. Clarkſon.
Lady Loverule,	by	Mrs. Adcock.
Nell,	by	Mrs. Becceley.
Lettice,	by	Mrs. Clarkſon.
Lucy,	by	Miſs Love.

PRICES: BOX, 6ſ. PIT, 4ſ. GALLERY, 2ſ.

No Perſons whatever to be admitted behind the Scenes.

N. B. Gentlemen and Ladies that chuſe Tickets, may have them at Mr. Parker's *and* Mr. Gaine's *Printing-Offices.*

Money will be taken at the DOOR.

To begin at 6 o'Clock.

AN EARLY AMERICAN PLAYBILL

degrading yet admirable transition — he became a driveller. In short, his face was what he obliged you to fancy it — age, youth, plenty, poverty, everything it assumed." Goldsmith goes so far as to declare of Garrick, that

"On the stage he was natural, simple, affecting,
'Twas only that when he was off he was acting."

Dr. Johnson's pronouncement about his old friend: " Here is a man who has advanced the dignity of his profession; Garrick has made a player a higher character," [1] is borne out by the honour once paid to this actor at the hands of Parliament. It happened that he was the sole occupant of the gallery in the Commons, one night of 1777, during a very fierce discussion between two members, one of whom, noticing his presence, moved that the " gallery should be cleared." Burke thereupon sprang to his feet, and appealing to the House in that strain of eloquence which Americans particularly have reason to remember, argued that Garrick, the great master of oratory, one to whom they all owed much and to whom he, Burke, felt the deepest indebtedness, be exempted from the general order that strangers leave the house. Fox and Townshend followed in similar vein, characterizing the ex-actor (for Garrick had by this time

[1] Writing of Garrick's death, Hannah More says: " I can truly bear this testimony to his memory, that I never witnessed in any family more decorum, propriety and regularity than in his; where I never saw a card, or even met (except in one instance) a person of his own profession at his table, of which Mrs. Garrick, by her elegance of taste, her correctness of manners and very original turn of humour, was the brightest ornament."

17

been many years off the stage) as their "great preceptor." Whereupon David Garrick was permitted to remain in the House of Parliament after the House had been cleared.

Garrick, of course, was a wonderful stage manager as well as an incomparable actor. And he was also a playwright of no mean ability, as Americans early discovered. His farce, "The Lying Valet," was one of the first pieces put on in the South by those confusing companies of "Virginia Comedians," for whom conflicting historians variously claim histrionic precedence in America. That Garrick was being played at Annapolis three months earlier than the date long accepted as the natal day of American drama is, however, easily demonstrable. For in the *Maryland Gazette* of June 18, 1752 may be read the following:

By Permission of his Honor, the
PRESIDENT
At the New Theatre
in Annapolis by the Company of Comedians from
Virginia, on Monday, being the 22nd of this
instant, will be performed
THE BEGGAR'S OPERA,
likewise a Farce called
THE LYING VALET
To begin precisely at 7 o'clock.
Tickets to be had at the printing office.
Box, 10s. Pit, 7s. 6d.
No person to be admitted behind the scenes.

N. B. The Company immediately intend to Upper Marlborough, as soon as they have done performing here, where they intend to play as long as they meet with encouragment and so on to Piscataway and Port Tobacco. And hope to give satisfaction to the Gentlemen and Ladies in each place, that will favor them with their company.

Dunlap, generally accepted as the historian of the American stage, from the appearance of his book [1] in 1832, until 1888, — when George O. Seilhamer in his exhaustive work on the beginnings of the drama in America came along and proved that "most of Dunlap's history was fiction," — did not realize, apparently, that Garrick was thus related to early American drama. For Dunlap was perfectly satisfied with his own firm belief that the drama was introduced into this country by William Hallam, the successor of Garrick at Goodman's Field Theatre, who in 1752 formed a joint stock company which he sent to America under the management of his brother, Lewis Hallam. The first play ever acted in America was the " Merchant of Venice," Mr. Dunlap confidently asserted, and this was given by the Hallam Company on September 5, 1752, at Williamsburg, then the capital of Virginia, in an old storehouse which had been converted into a theatre. Seilhamer proves, however, that plays were being acted in the South, as has been shown, some time before the advent

[1] " A History of The American Theatre," by William Dunlap, New York, 1832.

of the Hallams; and proves, too, that both in New York and in Philadelphia regularly established companies were performing plays at least two years before the Hallams came over.

Credit is due to an eminent jurist, the late Charles P. Daly,[1] for finding traces of even earlier theatrical performances in America than any of these. He discovered [2] evidence, from an advertisement, of the existence of some kind of theatre in New York, nineteen years before Hallam arrived in this country. This advertisement reads as follows: " To be Sold at Reasonable Rates, all Sorts of Household Goods, viz. Beds, Chairs, Tables, Chests of Drawers, Looking Glasses, Andirons and Pictures as also several sorts of Druggs and Medicines, also a Negro Girl about 16 years of age, has had the small-pox and is fit for Town or Country. Enquire of George Talbot, next Door to the Play-House." (*New York Gazette*, October 15, 1733.) That this theatre had opened December 6, 1732, with Farquhar's comedy, " The Recruiting Officer," a long overlooked paragraph in the *New England and Boston Gazette* of January 1, 1733, has since established.

Seilhamer stoutly maintains that dramatic history in America began with the production of Addison's " Cato " in Philadelphia in August, 1749, quoting in

[1] " When Was The First Play Produced in America? " by Charles P. Daly.

[2] T. Allston Brown claims to have published in the *New York Clipper*, seventeen years earlier than the appearance of Judge Daly's article, the discovery that the first theatre in America was opened in 1732.

support of his assertion the following entry in a manuscript journal left by John Smith, a son-in-law of James Logan: " Sixth month (August) 22d, 1749. — Joseph Morris and I happened in at Peacock Bigger's, and drunk tea there, and his daughter being one of the company who were going to hear the tragedy of *Cato* acted, it occasioned some conversation in which I expressed my sorrow that anything of the kind was encouraged." The background of this pioneer dramatic undertaking was " Plumstead's Store," and the company appears to have been made up, in part at least, of actors who had had some experience in England.

There is every reason to suppose that it was this same little band of Thespians who, on March 5, 1750, gave in New York the first professional performance of Shakespeare which can be indisputably ascribed to America. In the *Weekly Postboy* of February 26, the company announced their arrival from Philadelphia and stated that a room on Nassau Street had been taken for a playhouse. The play chosen for the initial program was Colley Cibber's version of " King Richard III," Thomas Kean acting the part of the humpbacked tyrant. This season was not a long one, though a variety of pieces were played, and at its close there were given a number of benefits, one of them being for the Widow Osborne, described in an advertisement as a person who had met " with divers late Hardships and Misfortunes " for which it was hoped that " all Charitable Benevolent Ladies and others will favor her with their Company." Not yet, however, was the drama to be accorded a cordial welcome in New York, and neither the Widow Osborne nor Thomas Kean found their slender purses notably fatter after this season of 1750–1751.

The Hallams had scarcely better luck when they arrived a little later.

" As our expedition to New York seems very likely to be attended with a very fatal consequence," their statement in the contemporary press sets forth, " and ourselves haply censured for undertaking it without Assurance of Success; we beg leave humbly to lay a true State of our Case before the worthy Inhabitants of this City; if possible endeavour to remove those great Obstacles which at present lie before us, and give very sufficient Reasons for our Appearance in this part of the World, where we all had the most sanguine Hopes of meeting a very different Reception; little imagining that in a City, to all Appearances so polite as this, the Muses would be banished, the works of the immortal Shakespeare, and others, the greatest Geniuses England ever produced, denied Admittance among them, and the instructive and elegant Entertainment of the Stage utterly protested against; When, without Boasting, we may venture to affirm that we are capable of supporting its Dignity with proper Decorum and Regularity.

" In the Infancy of this Scheme it was proposed to Mr. William Hallam, now of London, to collect a Company of Comedians and send them to New York and the other Colonies in America. Accordingly he assented and was at a vast expense to secure Scenes, Cloathes, People, etc. etc. And in October, 1750, sent over to this Place Mr. Robert Upton, in order to obtain

Permission to perform, erect a Building, and settle
everything against our Arrival; for which Service Mr.
Hallam advanced no inconsiderable Sum. But Mr.
Upton, on his Arrival, found here that Sett of Pretenders
with whom he joined and, unhappily for us, quite
neglected the Business he was sent about from England. For we never heard from him after.

" Being thus deceived by him the Company was at a
Stand till April, 1752 when, by the persuasions of several gentlemen in London and Virginia Captains, we
set sail on board of Mr. William Lee and arrived, after
a very expensive and tiresome Voyage at York River
on the 28th of June following; where we obtained
Leave of His Excellency the Governor and performed
with universal Applause and met with the greatest
Encouragement; for which we are bound by the strong-
est Obligations to acknowledge the many repeated In-
stances of their Spirit and Generosity. We were there
eleven Months before we thought of removing; and
then, asking Advice, we were again persuaded to come
to New York by several Gentlemen etc. whose Names
we can mention but do not think proper to publish.
They told us that we should meet of a genteel and
favorable Reception; that the Inhabitants were generous and polite, naturally fond of Diversions rational,
particularly those of the Theatre: Nay they even told
us there was a very fine Play-house Building and that
we were really expected. This was Encouragement
sufficient for us as we thought and we came firmly assured of Success; but how far our Expectations are
answered we shall leave to the Candid to determine,
and only beg leave to add, that as we are People of no
Estates, it cannot be supposed that we have a Fund
sufficient to bear up against such unexpected Repulses.
A Journey by Sea and Land, Five Hundred Miles, is not

undertaken without Money. Therefore if the worthy Magistrates would consider this in our Favor that it must rather turn out a publick Advantage and Pleasure, than a private Injury, They would, we make no Doubt, grant Permission and give an Opportunity to convince them we were not cast in the same Mould with our theatrical Predecessors; or that in private Life or publick Occupation we have the Affinity to them."

This manifesto, though inordinately long, has here been quoted entire, because it is the first known contribution to' that voluminous literature for and against the theatre which began to be written during the infancy of the American drama and did not utterly disappear until the middle of the last century. Endless variations of such titles as " The Theatre, the High Road To Hell " may be found in any library well equipped with *Americana*. Quite mild, indeed, in comparison with some of these Philippics, is the statement made by President Dwight of Yale College in his " Essay On The Stage " (1824) that " to indulge a taste for playgoing means nothing more nor less than the loss of the most valuable treasure, the immortal soul. If man be determined," he continues, " *at so great a price*, so *immense a loss*, to indulge the gratifications of his unhallowed desires, and yield obedience to the precepts of false morality, he is the *murderer of his own soul!* "

Undoubtedly the Hallams were more blamable than any other single family of the seventeenth century for encouraging this form of soul-slaughter. It would be interesting, therefore, if we could show them to have possessed a very high standard of personal morality and to have been fine artists into the bargain. But little or nothing is known about them. Hallam was a well-known name in English theatrical circles of the day, and many writers have on this account assumed that the Mrs. Hallam who came to America was the same one who played at Covent Garden and that the admirable Drury Lane [1] actor, whom Macklin accidentally killed in the course of a dispute about the ownership of a wig, rose from the dead to conduct theatrical enterprises in America years later. As a matter of fact the first generation of Hallams in this country were not at all distinguished as actors, either here or in England. But they are, of course, entitled to distinct credit for the courage and persistence with which they carried on their dramatic pioneering in a new country. Dunlap tells us that during the passage over, the pieces which had been selected, cast, and put in study before embarkation were regularly rehearsed on the deck of the *Charming Sally*, and about this he was very likely right, for he had his information from Lewis Hallam, then a lad of twelve. Rehearsals on the deck of a vessel far out at sea is the kind of a thing a lad of twelve would be likely to remember accurately, even when an old man. Not so greatly to be trusted, however, is Lewis's statement regarding the location in Williamsburg of the building his father soon fitted up as a theatre, a building " so near the woods that the manager could

---

[1] Drury Lane and Covent Garden, the two "patent theatres" of London, long had a monopoly of the serious drama.

stand in the door and shoot pigeons for his dinner, which he more than once actually did." Of the interior aspect of this theatre and of the acting that there went on we shall have more to say in the chapter treating particularly the ups and downs of the drama in the South. Suffice it here then to chronicle one interesting incident relating rather to the audience than to the players, in the course of this Williamsburg season. From a letter in the *Maryland Gazette* of November 17, we learn that the "Emperor of the Cherokee nation with his Empress and their son, the young Prince, attended by several of his Warriors and Great Men and their Ladies," adjourned from a session with the Governor to see at the theatre "the Tragedy of Othello and a Pantomime Performance which gave them great surprise as did the fighting with naked Swords on the Stage, which occasioned the Empress to order some about her to go and prevent them killing one another."

Hallam's lengthy letter about his grievances, which he circulated upon his arrival in New York, accomplished something of what its author had in mind when he indited it; that is, it succeeded in gaining for him finally the permission to perform which had been refused at first. From September 17, 1753, to March 18, 1754, the Hallam Company performed every Monday, Wednesday and Friday evening. The Shakespeare offered consisted of "Romeo and Juliet," "Richard III." and "King Lear" only; but Garrick, Cibber, Farquhar, Addison, Rowe, Steele, Fielding and Congreve were also included in the repertory, this efficient body of players evidently proving themselves as acceptable in comedy as in tragedy, and as good in farce as in both other dramatic forms. The English rule of a farce or pantomime as an afterpiece to the play was rigidly followed at this time.

When the New York season closed, in the spring of 1754, Lewis Hallam took his company to Philadelphia. With no little difficulty permission was obtained to give twenty-four performances in the Quaker City — on condition that nothing indecent or immoral should be presented — and the same warehouse which had previously been used by Thomas Kean's associates was again rented from William Plumstead. Mr. Plumstead had been born a Friend but early in life he had become an Episcopalian. Thus he was eligible for the convivialities of the famous fishing club, " the Colony in Schuylkill," and was free to subscribe to the first dancing assembly in Philadelphia, held in 1748. Moreover, he was himself a magistrate. Almost providential for the players appears to have been the unique personal equipment of William Plumstead, sole owner of a building adapted to theatrical exhibitions!

Yet it should not be supposed by this that Lewis Hallam had a very large sum of money to share with his brother William, when the projector of the company came over from England, in the middle of the Philadelphia season, to divide the spoils. America in the Hallam period had an English population of a million only — according to Dr. Franklin's estimate of 1751 — and as this was scattered from Maine to Georgia, comparatively

The Romance of the American Theatre

little of it was available for theatrical patronage in the four towns of Williamsburg, Annapolis, New York and Philadelphia, where the company had thus far played. Philadelphia in 1754, though a leading city on the American continent, was not yet any more prepared than New York to become the permanent home of the drama. Moreover, there was in Philadelphia one circumstance which militated strongly against the immediate success of the stage. This, says Seilhamer, " was the fact that Philadelphia was proud of its scientific and literary pre-eminence in the Colonies. The golden youth of the metropolis, emulating the solid attainments of Dr. Franklin, affected to regard the lectures of Professor Kinnersly on electricity and his practical experiments at the Academy as more instructive and entertaining than the exhibition of stage plays by a company of strolling players."

After Philadelphia the Hallam Company dissolved. When we meet them next, four years later, Mrs. Hallam has become Mrs. Douglass, having married the new manager after the death of her first husband during a sojourn of the family on the island of Jamaica. Young Lewis Hallam is now the company's leading man in all save the heaviest rôles; these were assigned to Mr. Harman, the husband of Colley Cibber's granddaughter, who was also a member of the Douglass Company. During the months of November and December, 1758, this company played in New York, their headquarters being a new theatre built by Douglass on what was then known as Cruger's Wharf. Again there was trouble

28

with the Magistracy, however, and it must have been with a sigh of relief that the company betook itself to Philadelphia in the spring of 1759. But here, also, there were legal difficulties as well as annoying delays over the opening of the new theatre which the indomitable Douglass had managed somehow to erect on Society Hill. By the summer and autumn of 1759, good things were none the less being presented, notably " Hamlet " and " Macbeth " for the first time in America. Another interesting bill was that put on the night of Mr. Douglass's benefit, with Lewis Hallam playing Romeo to his mother's Juliet. So far as we know this is the only instance in stage history where the immortal lovers of Verona were impersonated by mother and son.

Leaving to the Southern chapter the subsequent adventures of these players in Maryland, we come now to their invasion of New England, in the summer of 1761. Here for the first time we meet the " Moral Dialogues," under cover of which many good New Englanders of the eighteenth century long enjoyed the drama without experiencing a single prick of conscience.

A NEWPORT PLAYBILL

King's Arms Tavern, Newport, Rhode Island. On Monday, June 10, at the Public Room of the above Inn, will be delivered a Series of MORAL DIALOGUES, in Five Parts, Depicting the Evil Effects of Jealousy and other Bad Passions, and Proving that Happiness can only Spring from the Pursuit of Virtue. Mr. DOUG-

LASS will represent a noble and magnificent Moor named Othello, who loves a young lady named Desdemona, and after he has married her, harbors (as in too many cases) the dreadful passion of jealousy.

> Of Jealousy, our being's bane,
> Mark the small cause, and the most dreadful pain.

MR. ALLYN will depict the character of a specious villain, in the regiment of Othello, who is so base as to hate his commander on mere suspicion, and to impose on his best friend. Of such character, it is to be feared, there are thousands in the world, and the one in question may present to us a salutary warning.

> The man that wrongs his master and his friend,
> What can he come to but a shameful end?

MR. HALLAM will delineate a young and thoughtless officer, who is traduced by Mr. Allyn, and getting drunk, loses his situation, and his general's esteem. All young men, whatsoever, take example from Cassio.

> The ill effects of drinking would you see?
> Be warned and keep from evil company.

MR. MORRIS will represent an old gentleman, the father of Desdemona, who is not cruel, or covetous, but is foolish enough to dislike the noble Moor, his son-in-law, because his face is not white, forgetting that we all spring from one root. Such prejudices are numerous and very wrong.

> Fathers beware what sense and love ye lack,
> 'Tis crime, not color, makes the being black.

MR. QUELCH will depict a fool, who wishes to become a knave, and trusting one gets killed by him. Such is the friendship of rogues — take heed.

When fools would knaves become, how often you'll
Perceive the knave not wiser than the fool.

MRS. MORRIS will represent a young and virtuous
wife, who being wrongfully suspected, gets smothered
(in an adjoining room) by her husband.

> Reader, attend; and ere thou goest hence
> Let fall a tear to hapless innocence.

MRS. DOUGLASS will be her faithful attendant, who
will hold out a good example to all servants, male and
female, and to all people in subjection.

> Obedience and gratitude
> Are things as rare as they are good.

Various other dialogues, too numerous to mention here,
will be delivered at night, all adapted to the improvement of the mind and manners. The whole will be repeated Wednesday and Saturday. Tickets, six shillings
each, to be had within. Commencement at 7, conclusion
at half-past ten, in order that every spectator may go
home at a sober hour and reflect upon what he has seen
before he retires to rest.

> God save the king
> And long may he sway
> East, North, and South,
> And fair America.

Following the presentation of this disguised " Othello,"
the company went from Newport to Providence, en-
countering in the latter city even greater opposition than
they had met before. Immediately, indeed, there was
passed " an Act to Prevent Stage Plays and other
Theatrical entertainments within this Colony." The

reason alleged for the passage of this Act was that theatre-going occasioned " great and unnecessary expenses,"
besides discouraging industry and frugality, and tended
likewise to increase " Immorality impiety and contempt
of religion." The reasons behind the Providence Act
are almost exactly the same as were set forth that same
year as a result of an attempt to establish a playhouse
in New Hampshire. The petitions pro and con presented in the latter case make very interesting reading.

" Province of New Hampshire To His Excellency
Benning Wentworth, Esq., Governor and Commander-
in-Chief in and over His Majesty's Province of New
Hampshire — The Petition of sundry of the inhabitants
of Portsmouth, in the Province of New Hampshire —
humbly shews,

" That the subscribers understand that there has
been a proposal made by one of the actors of the plays,
sometime since at Newport, but more lately at New
York, to erect a play-house here sometime hence; and
that there is a petition presented to your Excellency
to inhibit and prevent the same:

" Now, your petitioners, being informed that the
said actors act no obscene or immoral plays, but such
as tend to the improvement of the mind and informing
the judgment in things proper to be known, in a civil
and well-regulated society: Your petitioners pray your
Excellency not to discourage, but rather forward, the
same, and your petitioners as in duty bound shall ever
pray, etc."

Signed by Matthew Livermore, George Meserve,
Theodore Atkinson, Jr., Joshua Brackett, John Wentworth (afterwards governor) and forty other persons.

To prohibit the plays there came promptly a counter-petition signed by Henry Sherburne, Eleazer Russell, John Penhallow, John Newmarch, and thirty-five others, all of whom were honestly persuaded that such " sundry entertainments of the stage," as might be given in the town " would be of very pernicious consequences, not only to the morals of the young people (even if there should be no immoral exhibitions) by dissipating their minds, and giving them an idle turn of attachment to pleasure and amusement, with other ill effects which there is the greatest reason to fear from such entertainments in a place where they are a novelty."

An even larger group, including the five selectmen, Samuel Hale, Clement Jackson, Daniel Warner, Mark H. Wentworth, George Boyd, Richard Wiburd, John Downing, Samuel Cutt, Jacob Sheafe, Thomas Chadbourn, and more than one hundred and fifty others, represented in still another petition, that the " inhabitants thereof " would lose not only their morals but their *servants* if the players were permitted to come to town. For, " as the poor will always imitate the richer," they argued, " every servant in town will soon turn player! "

To avert these many and great dangers, it was enacted in the House of Representatives on June 5, 1762, that the players be not made welcome to Portsmouth, " at least at this time." The reasons alleged were " Because when such entertainments are a novelty, they have a more peculiar influence on the minds of young people, greatly endanger their morals by giving them a turn for

33

intriguing, amusement and pleasure, even upon the best and most favorable supposition, that nothing contrary to decency and good manners is exhibited; yet the strong impressions made by the gallantries, amors, and other moving representations, with which the best players abound, will dissipate and indispose the minds of youth, not used to them, to everything important and serious; and as there is a general complaint of a prevailing turn to pleasure and idleness in most young people among us, which is too well grounded, the entertainments of the stage would inflame that temper. All young countries have much more occasion to encourage a spirit of industry and application to business, than to countenance schemes of amusement and pleasure." Which was, very likely, a perfectly valid reason for prohibiting plays in New Hampshire in June, 1762.

This early " attempt to introduce stage plays in New Hampshire " seems to have eluded the notice of both Dunbar and Seilhamer, — very likely because nothing came of it. To writers whose primary concern is the development of the theatre, Douglass succeeding was, of course, far more interesting than Douglass when he failed.

David Douglass was not a person to be easily discouraged. Between his two campaigns in Rhode Island, he had obtained permission from the lieutenant-governor of New York, Cadwallader Colden, " to build a theatre to perform in this city the ensuing winter." Thus it came about that on Beekman Street, a short distance below Nassau, on the south side of what was then called Chapel Street, was erected New York's third theatre, in which a season opened on November 19, 1761, and lasted five months, opposition being all the while bitter and determined. To-day we may follow the controversy in the columns of *Parker's Gazette.* " Philodemus " is the first contributor, charging that all ladies who attend the theatre are lacking in modesty, and declaring that the habit of play-going has often developed amorous tendencies in the hearts of good women. To which " Amanda " answers, on the fourteenth of December, that so far as she can recall, only one play, " The Fair Penitent," presented vice alluringly. And then, after the manner of woman in argument, she proceeds to call her opponent names. " Philodemus " must be an " impudent fellow," she declares, " some super-annuated animal that has past his grand climacteric, whose earlier time of life has been employed in luxury and debauchery, and now being satiated, concludes that all is vanity and every pleasure criminal." The piqued " Philodemus " thereupon queries of " Amanda " which is the best teacher, the playhouse or the Bible, going on to retort, out of his wounded self-esteem, that " Amanda " is herself a " strolling player! " So the war of words goes merrily on, the letters which attacked the drama being, however, as the publisher of the *Gazette* admitted, *very well paid for.*

No better index to the attitude of the times towards plays and players may be obtained than by perusing the files of these pre-Revolutionary papers. The advertising columns of the day offered an easy means of com-

munication between the manager and his public, and
Mr. Douglass seized with avidity upon the service they
could render him. One notice, aimed at the vice of
crowding the stage during the performance, which had
been copied in this country from the pernicious custom
then prevalent in England, reads as follows: " Complaints having been several times made that a number
of gentlemen crowd the stage and very much interrupt
the performance, and that it is impossible that the actors, when thus obstructed, could do that justice to their
parts they otherwise could, it will be taken as a particular
favor if no gentleman will be offended that he is absolutely refused admittance at the stage door, unless he
has previously secured himself a place in either the
stage or upper boxes."

Another curious advertisement printed in *Gaine's
Mercury* a few days after the close of the season of 1761–
1762, shows that the gallants who disregarded this rule
laid themselves open to unpleasant consequences; for
there may be found a card which proves that " the egg
as a vehicle of dramatic criticism came into use early in
this Continent." Seilhamer, however, declares that the
eggs referred to in the card probably expressed disapprobation not of the actors, but of the " beaus of the
period who with their powdered wigs, long, stiff-skirted
coats, and waistcoats, with flaps reaching nearly to their
knees, silk stockings, short-quartered shoes, and silver
or paste buckles," were in the habit of crowding the
stage and so interfering with the gallery's view of the
play. Now for the card: " Theatre in New York, May

3, 1762. A Pistole Reward will be given to whoever can discover the person who was so very rude as to throw Eggs from the Gallery upon the stage last Monday, by which the Cloaths of some Ladies and Gentlemen were spoiled and the performance in some measure interrupted, D. Douglass."

It was not until five years later, indeed, that New York received a play-acting company with entire cordiality. Then began the successful career of the theatre in John Street, which for a quarter of a century remained the background of all New York's most creditable dramatic efforts.

In appearance there was little that was imposing in this Temple of the Muses. It was approached from the sidewalk by a covered passage some sixty feet long, made of rough wooden materials; inside, it was constructed principally of wood, painted red. It had two rows of boxes, a pit and a gallery, and when the seats were all sold at the prices then current, could bring in as much as eight hundred dollars a night. The stage was as large as most stages of that day, and there were dressing-rooms and a greenroom in the shed adjacent to the theatre. For a description of the house as it looked when reopened after the Revolution, we turn to a passage in the first American play produced in New York and the first comedy by an American that was American in theme. This play, called "The Contrast," was written by Judge Tyler of Vermont, and in it one of the characters, the original Brother Jonathan of the stage, happens in at the theatre in John Street when " The School for Scandal " was there the bill. But let us give his experiences in his own words.

" Jenny — So, Mr. Jonathan, I hear you were at the play last night.

Jon. — At the play! Why, do you think I went to the devil's drawing-room?

Jenny — The devil's drawing-room?

Jon. — Yes, why, ain't cards and dice the devil's devices? And the playhouse, where the devil hangs out the vanities of the world on the tenter-hooks of temptation? . . . You won't catch me at a playhouse, I warrant you."

To the question, however, as to where he was at six o'clock the night before, Jonathan says that while wandering around in search of innocent diversion, he "saw a great crowd of folks going into a long entry that had lanterns over the door so I asked a man if that was the place where they played hocus pocus? " Being assured that hocus pocus tricks might there be witnessed, Jonathan " went right in, and they showed me away clean up to the garret just like meeting-house gallery. And so I saw a power of topping folks, all sitting around in little cabins, just like father's corn-crib, and then there was such a squeaking of the fiddles and such a tarnal blaze of the lights, my head was near turned. At length people that sat near me set up such a hissing — hiss like so many mad cats, and then they went thump, thump, thump, just like our Peleg thrashing wheat, and stampt away just like the nation and called out for one Mr. Langolee — I suppose he helps act the tricks." In the midst of all this, Jonathan goes on, " they lifted up a great green cloth and let us look right into the next neighbor's house. Have you a good many houses in New York made in that 'ere way?

38

Jenny — Not many. But did you see the family?

Jon. — Yes, swamp it, I seed the family.

Jenny — Well and how did you like them?

Jon. — Why, I vow, they were pretty much like other families; — there was a poor good-natured curse of a husband and a sad rantipole of a wife. . . . Yes and there was one youngster, they called him Mr. Joseph; he talked as sober and as pious as a minister; but, like some ministers I know, he was a sly tike in his heart, for all that; he was going to ask a young woman to spark it with him and — the Lord have mercy on my Soul — she was another man's wife."

For a categorical description of this 1767–1768 season at John Street the reader is referred to Seilhamer. Inasmuch as that author has devoted three large tomes to a history of the American stage in the eighteenth century, it is obvious that we can give here nothing more than a few amusing incidents connected with the stage at this period. One such was the attendance of the Indian chiefs at the playhouse when " King Richard III " was given early in the season, and their complimentary presentation of a war dance when they next came to town in April, out of appreciation for the enjoyment they had derived on their previous visit. At the bottom of the advertisement for this latter occasion may be found the following note: " The Cherokee Chiefs and Warriors, being desirous of making some return for the friendly Reception and Civilities they have received in this city, have offered to entertain the Public with the War Dance, which they will exhibit on the stage after the Pantomime. It is humbly presumed that no part of the audience will forget the proper Decorum so essential to all public Assemblies, particularly on this Occasion, as the Persons who have condescended to contribute to their entertainment are of Rank and Consequence in their own country."

Such extraordinary attractions as these notwithstanding, Mr. Douglass found himself almost bankrupt when this season in New York closed, and again he was obliged to go to Philadelphia to recoup. Nor was it very different in New York the following season, though on one night the Masons, and on another the " Friendly Brothers of St. Patrick " took blocks of seats for their membership. An advertisement to facilitate this latter indulgence may be found in the *New York Journal* of March 30. It reads: " The Friendly Brothers of St. Patrick and several Gentlemen of this City intend dining together at Bolton and Sigel's, next Monday, and from thence to go to the Play in the Evening; such Gentlemen as propose to join them will be pleased to send in their Names to the Bar of said Tavern two days before. New York, March 28, 1769."

It was at this time in the history of Mr. Douglass's players that Miss Hallam began to come to the front in leading parts as the successor of Miss Cheer, who had been for some time the leading woman of the company and who had further distinguished herself by marrying a lord in the course of one of the visits of the players to Philadelphia. In the *Pennsylvania Chronicle* of August 28, 1768, this event, which would now be good for a " front page story " at least, received the following terse treatment: "Last week was married in Maryland the Right Honorable Lord Rosehill to Miss Margaret Cheer, a young lady much admired for her theatrical performances." Lord Rosehill had just turned twenty, and it is quite probable that the lady was considerably his senior. As the first actress on the American stage to capture a lord for a husband, she is certainly entitled to extended treatment in a book claiming to deal with the "romance" of the American theatre. But there were no press agents in those days, and the scanty announcement which has been quoted is all that can be found, alas! about this interesting alliance. That Miss Cheer was a good actress is, however, certain. For during her short reign on the American stage, she is known to have played fifty of the leading characters as well as a few parts in pantomime and farce. Lord Rosehill was the son and heir of the sixth Earl of Northesk in the Scotch peerage, but his actress wife never became a countess. The old earl was still living when Lady Rosehill's still young husband died in France, without issue, in 1788.

The press of the time showed itself less niggardly toward the players when one of their number died than when a marriage into the nobility was consummated. When Colley Cibber's granddaughter, Mrs. Harman, passed away, May 27, 1773, *Rivington's Gazette* printed quite a respectful obituary notice, the first relating to an actress which ever appeared in an American newspaper. "On Thursday last," it reads, "died in the 43d year of her age, Mrs. Catherine Maria Harman, granddaughter of the celebrated Colley Cibber, Esq., poet-laureate. She was a just actress, possessed much merit in low comedy, and dressed all her characters with infinite propriety, but her figure prevented her from succeeding in tragedy and genteel comedy. In private life she was sensible, [1] humane and benevolent. Her little fortune she has left to Miss Cheer, and her obsequies were on Saturday night attended by a very genteel procession to the cemetery of the old English Church."

While we are on the sad subject of funerals, we may as well chronicle the death, in 1774, of Mrs. Douglass, who, as Mrs. Hallam, had been one of the little band of pioneers sailing on the *Charming Sally* at the very dawn of dramatic history in America. The paper which reported her death referred to her as " wife of Mr. Douglass, manager of the American Company of Comedians, mother of Mr. Lewis Hallam and of Mrs. Mattocks,

[1] That Mrs. Harman, though an actress, so lived her life as to be pronounced " sensible " by the hostile press of that day, proves that there is not nearly so much in heredity as some would have us think. For her father was a musician without character or reputation, and her mother was one of the most erratic creatures in all stage history. Married young, Charlotte Cibber soon fell out with her husband and enlisted in the profession of her father. Both at the Haymarket and at Drury Lane she held positions at a good salary, but her violent temper caused her to quarrel with the management and she then became, first, a writer, and afterwards a strolling player. Her own story of her life shows this extraordinary creature as successively a grocer, a keeper of a puppet-show, a vendor of sausages and a waiter at the King's Head Tavern in Marylebone. She also obtained employment on the stage disguised as a man and, still masquerading, secured a place as *valet-de-chambre* for a nobleman. Dibdin pronounces her " a sort of English D'Eon," evidently under the impression, as were many of his contemporaries, that D'Eon was in truth a woman and not a man, as was proved by a post-mortem examination of his remains. See my " Romantic Days In the Early Republic," p. 351.

of Covent Garden Theatre, and aunt of Miss Hallam."
It further declared her " a lady, who, by her excellent
performances upon the stage and her irreproachable
manners in private life, had recommended herself to the
friendship and affection of many of the principal families
on the Continent and in the West Indies." That this
worthy woman should have died before the outbreak
of the Revolution, in Philadelphia, where the attitude
towards players was always a comparatively friendly
one, seems a kind dispensation of Providence. It is very
pleasant to read that all the ladies in the neighborhood
of Fifth and South Streets attended her funeral, and
that she was buried with impressive ceremonies in the
grounds of the Second Presbyterian Church at Third and
Arch Streets. For she had done rather more than a
woman's part towards establishing the theatre as a
dignified institution in America.

CHAPTER II

It was in Williamsburg, then the capital of Virginia, that there occurred, in 1718, the first known representation in North America of what the purists of our time characterize as " the acted drama." Reference to this performance may be found in a letter of Governor Spottiswood dated June 24, 1718, it being therein made clear that certain members of the House of Assembly had slighted an invitation given them by the Governor for an entertainment at his house. These gentlemen, he writes, had denied him " the common compliment of a visit when, in order to solemnizing of His Majesty's birthday, I gave a public entertainment at my house, and all gentlemen that would come were admitted. These eight committeemen," he continues, " would neither come to my house nor *go to the play* which was acted on the occasion." They preferred instead, it would seem, to have a party of their own in the House of Burgesses and invite in everybody who would come there to drink the king's health!

What the play here referred to was or where it was performed, we do not know, but Judge Daly, to whose researches concerning the early theatres in America

44

allusions have previously been made, conjectures that
the performance to which the Governor graciously lent
his support was one of those given in that Williamsburg
theatre to which Graham refers as " *the first institution
of the kind in the British colonies.*" In all probability
Graham [1] was quoting, in this paragraph, from Hugh
Jones's " The Present State of Virginia " (published in
London in 1724). Jones, at any rate, makes mention in
his book of the existence of a " Play House " in Williamsburg thus early; and since Jones had been away from
Virginia for two years, when he published his book in
London, we seem to have a theatre an established fact
in Williamsburg as early as 1722.

This is not so astonishing as would at first appear when
we bear in mind that the men and women who settled
Virginia were a very different people from the Puritans
of New England. It was not for the sake of enjoying,
unmolested, " freedom to worship God " that they had
fled to America; they brought with them none of that
repugnance to stage plays which so long marked the New
England colonists. They were, indeed, in the words of
Bancroft, " a continuation of English society, who were
attached to the monarchy, with a deep reverence for
the English church and a love for England and English
institutions." That the theatre was one of the most
cherished of " English institutions " was convincingly
shown, I think, in our opening chapter.

To be sure, Williamsburg had only a small resident

[1] In his " History of the United States of North America; " London,
1736.

population at this time. But this would not necessarily imply that plays and a playhouse might not have flourished there. For it was the capital of a widely extended province. It was here that the Governor resided, here where the Legislature assembled, here that the Law Courts were held, and the prosperous planters of the day came for periods of recreation. Even at the early date when Jones's history was written, he asserts that the people of Williamsburg lived " in the same neat manner, dress after the same modes, and behave themselves exactly as the gentry of London." And Cooke, in his " History of the People of Virginia " shows the Williamsburg of only a little later to have been the centre of all that was brilliant and attractive in Virginia society.

" It was," he says, " the habit of the planters to go there with their families at this season, to enjoy the pleasures of the Capital, and one of the highways, Gloucester, was an animated spectacle of coaches and four, containing the nabobs and their dames; of maidens in silk and lace, with high-heeled shoes and clocked stockings. All these people were engaged in attending the assemblies held at the palace, in dancing at the Apollo, in snatching the pleasures of the moment, and enjoying life under a régime that seemed mad for enjoyment. . . . The violins seemed to be ever playing for the diversion of the youths and maidens; cocks were fighting, horsemen riding, students mingled in the throng in their academic dress, and his Serene Excellency went to open the House of Burgesses in his coach, drawn by six milk-white horses. It was a scene full of gaiety and *abandon*. Williamsburg was never more brilliant than at this period."

The Romance of the American Theatre

Obviously just the place to support, for many months in the year at least, so inspiriting an institution as a theatre! For in London, from which Williamsburg took its tone, the stage, it must be recalled, was at this time in high favour. The licentiousness that had long prevailed in the plays and players was rapidly passing away, and a better class of people now went to the theatre than had ever done so before. It was of this period that Addison wrote:

> "I cannot be of the opinion of the reformers of manners in their severity toward plays; but must allow that a good play, acted before a well-bred audience, must raise very proper incitement to good behaviour, and be the most quick and the most prevailing method of giving young people a turn of sense and breeding. When the character drawn by a judicious poet," he continues, "is presented by the person, the manner, the look and the motion of an accomplished player, what may not be brought to pass by seeing generous things performed before our eyes? The stage is the mirror of human life; let me, therefore, recommend the oft use of a theatre as the most agreeable and easy method of making a polite and moral gentry, which would end in rendering the rest of the people regular in their behaviour and ambitious of laudable undertakings."

Addison was highly regarded in Williamsburg, so highly regarded in fact that his "Cato" was performed by the college students on September 10, 1736. The advertisement setting forth this interesting fact may be found in the *Virginia Gazette* of that day.

"ADVERTISEMENT

"This evening will be performed at the Theatre
by the young Gentlemen of the College, the 'Tragedy
of Cato,' and on Monday, Wednesday and Friday will
be acted the following comedies by the young Gentlemen and Ladies of this country — 'The Busybody,' the
'Recruiting Officer' and the 'Beaux' Stratagem.'"

From the latter part of this notice, authority is derived for belief that Williamsburg had an organized
company of some kind acting English comedy at least
sixteen years earlier than the date given by Dunlap as
the natal day of the theatre in America. Seilhamer makes
much of this notice, and so scathingly condemns Dunlap
for not having found it, as *he* did, in the files of the
Virginia Gazette, that he has the appearance of discred-
iting quite ungenerously the first historian of the American theatre. I do not see the need of calling Dunlap
hard names; he was so very happy in his firm belief
that the Hallams, one of whom he knew well, had introduced the drama into America! And it was, in very
truth, a pretty theory. John Esten Cooke liked it so
much that he has given us, in his "Virginia Comedians,"
a picture of just what may have happened in the Williamsburg theatre when the Hallam company were playing
"Merchant of Venice" there. To be sure, he makes the
date 1763 instead of 1752, and gives Mr. Hallam, whom
he describes as "a fat little man of fifty or fifty-five with
a rubicund and somewhat sensual face," the part of
Bassanio instead of that of Launcelot Gobbo. Moreover,

48

he makes Miss Hallam, who played Jessica (" her first appearance on any stage "), take the part of Portia, which Mrs. Hallam really sustained. And in the place of Mr. Malone, who played Shylock, he introduces a fictitious Mr. Pugsby. None the less, it is a valuable service he does us in depicting Williamsburg society as it quite probably looked when enjoying this early play at its first theatre.

" The ' old theatre near the capitol,' discoursed of in the manifesto issued by Mr. Manager Hallam, was so far *old*," he writes, " that the walls were well browned by time, and the shutters to the windows of a pleasant neutral tint between rust and dust color. The building had, no doubt, been used for the present purpose in by-gone times, before the days of the *Virginia Gazette*, which is our authority for many of the facts here stated in relation to the ' Virginia Company of Comedians; ' but of the former company of ' players,' as my Lord Hamlet calls them, and their successes and misfortunes, printed words tell us nothing. . . . That there had been companies before, however, we repeat, there is some reason to believe; else why that addition ' old ' applied to the ' theatre near the capitol.'

" Within, the play-house presented a somewhat more attractive appearance. There was a ' box,' ' pit ' and ' gallery,' as in our own day; and the relative prices were arranged in much the same manner. The common mortals — gentlemen and ladies — were forced to occupy the boxes raised slightly above the level of the stage and hemmed in by velvet-cushioned railings — in front of a flower-decorated panel extending all around the house — and for this position they were moreover compelled to pay an admission fee of seven shillings and sixpence.

The demigods — so to speak — occupied a more eligible portion in the ' pit,' from which they could procure a highly excellent view of the actors' feet and ankles, just on a level with their noses; to conciliate the demigods this superior advantage had been offered, and the price for them was further still reduced to five shillings. But ' the gods,' in truth, were the real favorites of the manager. To attract them he arranged the high upper ' gallery ' and left it untouched, unencumbered by railings, velvet cushions, or any other device; all was free space and liberal as the air; there were no troublesome seats for ' the gods,' and three shillings and ninepence all that the manager would demand. The honor of their presence was enough. . . . From the boxes a stairway led down to the stage, and some rude scenes, visible at the edges of the curtain, completed the outfit."

So much for the theatre. And now let us be introduced to the *dramatis personae* of the book. One of the principal characters in the novel is a young Virginian, Mr. Effingham, who, after a visit and some stay at Oxford and in London, has returned to the paternal home, Effingham Hall, in Virginia, and while riding to visit a manorial estate on a plantation known as Riverhead, — whose owner, named Lee, has the felicity to be the father of two attractive daughters, — suddenly draws up his horse upon seeing before him in the road a young lady whom the novelist thus describes:

" The rider was a young girl of about eighteen and of rare and extraordinary beauty. Her hair — so much of it as was visible beneath her hood — seemed to be dark chestnut and her complexion was dazzling. The eyes were large, full and dark — instinct with fire and softness, feminine modesty and collected firmness, the firmness, however, predominating. But the lips were different. They were the lips of a child, — soft, guileless, tender, and confiding; they were purity and innocence itself, and seemed to say that, however much the brain might become hard and worldly, the heart of this young woman never could be other than the tender and delicately sensitive heart of a child. She was clad in a riding-dress of pearl color, and, from the uniformity of this tint, it seemed to be a favorite with her. The hood was of silk, and the delicate, gloved hand held a little ivory-handled riding whip, which now dangled at her side. The other gloved hand supported her cheek; and in this position the young lady calmly awaited Mr. Effingham's approach still nearer, though he was already nearly touching her.

" Mr. Effingham took off his hat and bowed with elegant courtesy. The lady returned the inclination by a graceful movement of the head.

" ' Would you be kind enough to point out the road to the town of Williamsburg, sir? ' she said in a calm and clear voice.

" ' With great pleasure, madam,' replied Mr. Effingham. ' You have lost your way? '

" ' Yes, sir, and very strangely; and, as the evening drew on, I was afraid of being benighted.'

" ' You have but to follow the road until you reach Effingham Hall, madam,' he said, — ' the house in the distance yonder; then turn to the left, and you are in the highway to town.'

" ' Thanks, sir,' the young girl said, with another calm inclination of her head, and she touched her horse with the whip.

" ' But cannot I accompany you? ' asked Mr. Effingham, whose curiosity was greatly aroused, and found his eyes, he knew not why, riveted to the rare beauty of his companion's face; ' do you not need me as a guide? '

" ' Indeed, I think not, sir,' she said with the same calmness. ' Your direction is very plain, and I am accustomed to ride by myself.'

" ' But really,' began Mr. Effingham, somewhat piqued, ' I know it is intrusive — I know I have not the honor — '

" She interrupted him with her immovable calmness.

" ' You would say that you do not know me and that your offer is intrusive. I believe, sir, I do not consider it so — it is very kind; but I am not a fearful girl and need not trouble you at all.'

" And so bowed.

" ' One moment, madam,' said Mr. Effingham; ' I am really dying with curiosity to know you. 'Tis very rude to say so, of course — but I am acquainted with every lady in the neighborhood, and I do not recall any former occasion upon which I had the pleasure — '

" ' It is very easily explained, sir. I do not live in the neighborhood and I am not a lady.' "

And this was all the smitten youth could find out — save that he " would not long remain in ignorance of her identity " if he were in the habit of frequently visiting Williamsburg. So, somewhat chagrined, he continues on his way to Riverhead. There he finds a copy of the *Gazette* and, looking it over, comes upon the notice that " Mr. Hallam and his Virginia company of comedians " will soon perform " The Merchant of Venice " at the " old theatre near the capitol." It is thereupon arranged that Effingham, accompanied by the old gentleman and his two daughters, will be on hand to welcome the players, one of the girls slyly insisting that Mr. Effingham will be a very useful companion, inasmuch as he could " tell them when to hiss and when to applaud — being just from London." On the appointed evening the whole party is eager for the entertainment.

" When Mr. Lee and his two daughters entered the box, which had been reserved for them next the stage, the house was nearly full and the neatness of the edifice was lost sight of in the sea of brilliant ladies' faces and showy forms of cavaliers which extended, like a sea of glittering foam, around the semicircle of the boxes. The pit was occupied by well-dressed men of the lower class, as the times had it, and from the gallery proceeded hoarse murmurs and the unforgotten slang of London. Many smiles and bows were interchanged between the parties in the different boxes, and the young gallants, following the fashion of the day, gathered at each end of the stage, and often walked across to exchange some polite speech with the smiling dames in the boxes nearest."

After the orchestra, " consisting of three or four foreign-looking gentlemen, bearded and moustached," had done what they could in the way of preliminary entertainment, the manager came forward in the costume of Bassanio and recommended himself and his company to the " aristocracy of the great and noble colony of Virginia." The curtain slowly rolled aloft, and the young gallants scattered to the corners of the stage, seating themselves on stools or chairs, or standing.

The scenes between Portia and Nerissa in the first act was omitted in the version offered by the Hallams, and thus it was not until the second act that Effingham saw again his unknown lady of the woods, whom my readers will, of course, have guessed to be Beatrice Hallam. " She was, indeed," the novelist asserts, " no gentle Virginia maiden, no ' lady,' as she had said with perfect calmness at their meeting." Yet young Effingham did not, on this account, scan her the less attentively from his wicker chair in the corner of the stage. " Her costume was faultless. It consisted of a gown and underskirt of fawn-colored silk trimmed with silver, and a single band of gold encircled each wrist, clearly relieved against the white, finely-rounded arm. Her hair, which was a beautiful chestnut, had been carried back from her temples and powdered after the fashion of the time, and around her beautiful, swan-like neck the young woman wore a necklace of pearls of rare brilliancy."

The costume of the character having thus defied criticism, Mr. Effingham passed on to the face and figure. And so favourably was the young gallant " just from London " impressed by these and by the acting of their owner that, a little later, he leaned forward and touched her sleeve.

" ' Come,' he said, with easy carelessness and scarcely moderating his voice. ' Come, fair Portia, while that tiresome fellow is making his speech, and talk to me a little. We are old acquaintances, and you are indebted to me for directing you home.'

" ' Yes, sir,' said Beatrice, turning her head slightly, ' but pardon me — I have my part to attend to.'

" ' I don't care.'

" ' Excuse me, sir, I do.'

" ' Really, madam, you are very stiff for an actress. Is it so very unusual a thing to ask a moment's conversation? '

" ' I know it is the fashion in London and elsewhere, sir, but I dislike it. It destroys my conception of the character,' she said calmly."

And though Effingham, peeved, continued to force conversation upon the young girl, she steadfastly refuses to reply — or even to listen to him. All of which is true in spirit if not in detail. For never in America were the fops and dandies of the period permitted the liberties on the stage and behind the scenes which they had, from time immemorial, claimed and obtained in London.

Another Southern city which had a theatre considerably earlier than either Dunlap or Seilhamer state, was Charleston, South Carolina, or, as it was written then, Charles-Town. A writer in the *New York Times* of December 15, 1895, gives as the result of his researches in the newspaper files of the Library Society in Charleston, the discovery that a play was acted in that city January 24, 1735. The advertisement for this occasion reads:

" On Friday, the 24 inst., in the Court Room, will be attempted a tragedy called ' The Orphan or the Unhappy Marriage.'

" Tickets will be delivered out on Tuesday next, at Mr. Shepheard's at 40s. each."

Judge Daly points out that though forty shillings seems a high price to pay for seeing " The Orphan," it really may not have been high, inasmuch as we cannot

tell what the value of a shilling then was in South Carolina, compared to the value of a pound sterling. The
price of a box ticket at Kean and Murray's Theatre in
Nassau Street, New York, fifteen years afterwards, was
only five shillings, New York currency, about the value
of two dollars at the present day. From the fact that
this Charleston performance of "The Orphan" was
repeated twice, we must conclude that the theatre-goers
of the town did not regard forty shillings as too high
to pay for a theatrical "whistle." The prologue used on
the opening night is quaint enough, I think, to warrant
reprinting.

"PROLOGUE

" When first Columbus touch'd this distant shore,
  And vainly hoped his Fears and Dangers o'er,
  One boundless Wilderness in view appear'd
  No Champain Plains or rising Cities cheered
  His wearied Eye.
  Monsters unknown travers'd the hideous Waste,
  And men more savage than the Beasts they chased.
  But mark! How soon these gloomy Prospects clear,
  And the new World's late horrors disappear.
  The Soil, obedient to the industrious swains,
  What happy Harvests crown their honest Pains,
  What various products float on every Tide?
  What numerous navies in our Harbours ride?
  Tillage and Trade conjoin their friendly aid,
  T' enrich the thriving Boy and lovely Maid,
  Hispania, 'tis true, her precious mines engross'd,
  And bore her shining Entrails to its Coast.

56

Britannia more humane supplies her wants,
The British sense and British beauty plants.
The aged Sire beholds with sweet surprise
In foreign climes a numerous offspring rise,
Sense, Virtue, Worth, and Honour stand confest
In each brave male, his prosperous hands have blessed,
While the admiring Eye improved may trace,
The Mother's Charms in each chaste Virgin's face.
Hence we presume to usher in those Arts
Which oft have warm'd the best and bravest Hearts.
Faint our Endeavours, wide as our Essays,
We strive to please, but can't pretend to Praise;
Forgiving Smiles o'erpay the grateful task,
Those all we hope and all we humbly ask."

So generously did the audience to which this perora-
tion was addressed respond in " Forgiving Smiles " —
and in admission fees — that there were presented at
Charleston that season, besides " The Orphan," a " new
Pantomime Entertainment in Grotesque Characters
called ' The Adventures of Harlequin and Scaramouch,'
with the ' Burgo-Master Trick'd; ' The Opera of Flora
or, Hob in the Well with the Dance of the two
Pierrots and a new Pantomime Entertainment and
' The Spanish Fryar,' or ' The Double Discovery.' "
That the season was a success one must conclude from
the fact that on May 3 the following advertisement
appeared:

" Any gentlemen that are disposed to encourage the
exhibition of plays next Winter, may have the sight of
the proposals for a subscription at Mr. Shepheard's in

57

Broad Street. And any persons that are desirous of having a share in the performance thereof, upon application to Mr. Shepheard shall receive a satisfactory answer. N. B. — The subscription will be closed the last day of this month."

Eight months later another advertisement may be found in the *South Carolina Gazette*, which would seem to indicate that the "proposals" above referred to had borne fruit. For it is announced that:

" On Thursday, the 12th of February, will be opened the new theatre in Dock street, in which will be performed the comedy called the ' Recruiting Officer.'

" Tickets for the pitt and boxes will be delivered at Mr. Charles Shepheard's, on Thursday, the 5th of February. Boxes, 30s; pitt, 20s; and tickets for the gallery, 15s, which will be delivered at the theatre the day of playing.

" N. B. The doors will be opened all the afternoon. The Subscribers are desired to send to the stage door in the forenoon to bespeak places, otherwise it will be too late."

During this season plays were produced in Charleston at the rate of one a week; but the venture did not prosper, for all that, and the *Gazette* of the last week in May contains this epigram:

"ON THE SALE OF THE THEATRE

" How cruel Fortune, and how fickle too,
To crop the Method made for making you!
Changes tho' common, yet when great they prove,
Make men distrust the care of Mighty Jove;

The Romance of the American Theatre

Half made in thought (though not in fact) we find
You bought and sold, but left poor H. behind.
P. S. — Since so it is ne'er mind the silly trick,
The pair will please, when Pierrot makes you sick."

The wit and appositeness of this effusion is quite lost upon us of to-day. But its appearance in the *South Carolina Gazette* establishes beyond peradventure the fact that Charleston possessed a theatre nearly forty years earlier than has been generally believed. Charleston was a rapidly growing town at this time, and like all such, had a fine sense of the value of names. Hence what had been " the theatre in Dock street " is soon " the playhouse in Queen street." And here ere long a ball is being advertised as well as another production, " at the request of the Ancient and Honourable Society of Free and Accepted Masons," of the " Recruiting Officer," a piece which was much enjoyed by eighteenth-century audiences. The advertising columns of the *Gazette* contain two more allusions to this theatre — which probably stood on the lot of land later occupied by the rear portion of the old Planters' Hotel, within less than a hundred yards of the Huguenot and St. Philip's churches. The first notice, dated October 3, 1748, sets forth the virtues of a school " over against the Play House," and another, dated October 3, 1754, announces that a company of comedians from London will give the " Fair Penitent," tickets for which might be had of " Mr. John Remington and at the printer's."

" The Recruiting Officer," it will be recalled, was the play with which the New Theatre in New York opened

59

in 1732. Thus it was the earliest play known to have been acted in North America. That it was also acted in Williamsburg and in Charleston in 1736 entitles it to more than passing mention here. Written by George Farquhar, who with Wycherly, Congreve, and Vanbrugh ranks as a leading comic dramatist of the Restoration, its wit, sprightliness, and plot are all of a kind scarcely to be tolerated on any stage to-day. Yet, Leigh Hunt, a very competent critic, praised it highly for its characterization and for its charm of gaiety and good humour. New York had a chance to taste these qualities for itself in 1843 and again on February 8, 1885, the comedy being then revived by Mr. Augustin Daly and played as nearly as possible after the manner of its original production at Drury Lane in 1706, when Nance Oldfield acted the part of Sylvia. The eyes through which this New York revival was viewed are not so different from intelligently critical eyes of our own day that a reprint of a newspaper notice of the performance by one of the New York critics next day should be lacking in interest.

The Recruiting Officer

Captain Plume	Mr. Drew
Captain Brazen	Mr. Parkes
Justice Balance	Mr. Fisher
Sergeant Kite	Mr. Lewis
Mr. Worthy	Mr. Skinner
Bullock	Mr. Gilbert
Appletree	Mr. Bond
Pearman	Mr. Wilks

"PERDITA" ROBINSON
From the painting by Romney
See page 71

JOHN DREW AND ADA REHAN IN THE DALY REVIVAL OF "THE RECRUITING
OFFICER"
From the Theatre Collection, Harvard University

Balance's Steward.............Mr. Beekman
Mistress Melinda.............Miss Virginia Dreher
Rose.......................Miss May Fielding
Lucy.......................Miss May Irwin
Sylvia.....................Miss Ada Rehan

" 'I am called Captain, sir, by all the drawers and room-porters in London,' said Miss Ada Rehan at Daly's Theatre last night. And bravely she wore her red coat and sword, the martial twist in her cravat, the fierce knot in her periwig, the cane upon her button and the dice in her pocket. The audience was in ecstasies.

" It was a revival of ' The Recruiting Officer,' by George Farquhar. The manners of Queen Anne's day were reproduced on Mr. Daly's stage. Captain Plume and Sergeant Kite were enlisting the country lads and playing court to the country lassies. Justice Balance was keeping watch over the morals of his daughter Sylvia. Sprightly Mistress Melinda was intriguing for the hand of young Worthy. Brazen was bragging of his service in Flanders against the French and in Hungary against the Turks. The atmosphere was charged with love, and the stage resounded with the tap of the drum.

" The audience was in a curious and observant mood. The doings on the stage were of a wholly unfamiliar kind. The language sounded strangely fantastic to modern ears. Ladies held their breath at the bygone sentiment of the play. Men met in groups between the acts and wondered what was the secret of its original success. Its secret was tolerably simple. It was written at the time of Marlborough's earlier victories. Blenheim had just been won. A military fervor possessed the country. Rustics went marching round the fields with ribbons in their caps. The recruiting officer was seen in every town. The popular song of the hour was:

" ' Over the hill and over the main
To Flanders, Portugal and Spain;
The Queen commands and we'll obey;
Over the hills and far away.'

" Moreover, there was a steady flow of indecency
in the comedy. The town had been growing dull. Congreve had retired into the intimacy of the Duchess of
Marlborough. Wycherly was writing feeble poems under
the tutorship of that rising young man, Alexander Pope.
Vanbrugh was giving his attention to architecture.
Jeremy Collier and his moral tractate had exorcised the
merry devils off the stage and the pit mourned their
departure. So ' The Recruiting Officer,' with its broad
jests, was particularly welcome. Captain Plume, with his
amorous devices, became the ideal of the army, and
pretty Rose, with her chickens, furnished laughter for
the mess-room and the coffee-houses.

" Human nature has not much changed. Mr. Daly's
audience last night was as fashionable an audience as
could be gathered in the city. Yet the few suggestive
lines which he has left in the piece excited the loudest
laugh. Americans are not so squeamish with these old
plays. They know that the comedies of the Restoration
were not models of propriety. They know that George
Farquhar, the rollicking Irish captain, was not a preacher
of morality. And if the piece hung fire at times, if it
seemed a trifle heavy and monotonous, it was because
the spectators had been credited with a prudery which
they did not seem to possess.

" The company was a little out of its element. Mr.
Drew, in particular, should have been livelier and airier,
conducting his love affairs with as light a touch as
Charles Mathews might have conducted them in other
days, or Mr. Wallack to-day. Mr. Fisher, too, pressed

with too heavy a hand on such niceties of character as have been discovered in Justice Balance; and Mr. James Lewis, though discreet and refined in his humor, extracted none of the exuberant fun from Sergeant Kite with which critics of the past have supposed that unscrupulous personage to overflow. Mr. Skinner was a dignified young lover and Mr. Parkes amused as Brazen. But the honors of the evening rested with Miss Virginia Dreher, who looked radiantly beautiful in a web of lace and gold, and with Miss Ada Rehan, who had the bold step, the rakish toss and the impudent air of your true military gallant. She was not Peg Woffington, perhaps, but she was a charming woman in disguise and the town will be curious to see her."

Why early playgoers in the South liked this comedy will be easily understood. Captain Plume was, for many years, a part particularly favoured by dashing young actors endowed with handsome face, a fine person, and ingratiating manners. Farquhar had pictured himself while writing this character, and Wilks, his near friend, and the most distinguished actor of the time on the English stage, first gave it life. It is probable that many of the young Southerners who frequented the playhouses of Virginia and South Carolina were " just from London," like the Mr. Effingham of Cooke's novel, and so had radiant memories of the play as given over there.

The comedies of Farquhar and his contemporaries were produced considerably more often, in the South of this period, than the plays of Shakespeare. In the list of plays brought out at the Charleston Theatre in 1773-1774, the name of Shakespeare appears only ten times in a season of fifty-nine nights, while from a similar list, published in the *Maryland Gazette* at the close of David Douglass's Annapolis season of 1760, Shakespeare is seen to have been played only four out of twenty-eight nights. Seilhamer prints in full both the lists to which reference is here made, and which are of distinct interest, in that they supply the most complete records extant of these theatrical seasons before the Revolution. The fact that two editors in two different Southern States saw fit to give as much space to things theatrical as these two lists take up in their columns, shows conclusively that the attitude of the South towards the theatre was much more enlightened at this time than that of other sections.

Nearly everything that then held the stage was produced at least once during this Charleston season of 1773-1774. Nine of Shakespeare's masterpieces were given — including " Julius Caesar," for the first time in America; [1] eight of Garrick's productions, several of Bickerstaff's operas, Goldsmith's "She Stoops to Conquer," and the most successful works of Congreve, Dryden, Vanbrugh, Farquhar, Colley Cibber, Whitehead, Otway, and Addison. Theatrical happenings in Charleston at this period looked so important as news, too, that we find *Rivington's New York Gazette*, the best newspaper of the time, in the modern sense, noticing the opening of the Charleston Theatre! A correspondent appears, indeed, to have been present on this interesting occasion, for Hallam's acting is highly praised, the reviewer then

[1] April 20, 1774.

64

going on to remark: " The house is elegantly finished and supposed for the size to be the most commodious on the continent. The scenes, which are new and well designed, the dresses, the music, and what had a very pleasant effect, the disposition of the lights, all contributed to the satisfaction of the audience, who expressed the highest approbation of their entertainment."

Even at the end of the season the Charlestonians were delighted with their play-going privileges — which does not always happen. In the *South Carolina Gazette* of May 30, 1774, may be found the following:

" CLOSE OF THE CHARLESTON SEASON

" On Friday last the theatre which opened here the 22d of December was closed. Warmly countenanced and supported by the public, the manager and his company were excited to the most strenuous efforts to render their entertainments worthy of so respectable a patronage. . . . The exertions of the American Company have been uncommon and justly entitles them to those marks of public favor that have for so many years stampt a merit in their performances. The choice of plays hath been allowed to be very judicious, the directors having selected from the most approved English poets such pieces as possess in the highest degree the *utile dulce*, and while they entertain, improve the mind by conveying the most useful lessons of industry and virtue. The company have separated until the winter when the New York Theatre will be opened. Mr. Hallam being embarked for England to engage some recruits for that service. The year after, they will perform at Philadelphia and in the winter following we may expect them here with a theatrical force hitherto unknown in America."

Unhappily, this alluring promise was not fulfilled. For the Continental Congress, on October 24, 1774, passed a resolution recommending the suspension of all public amusements. Information of this resolution was conveyed to Manager Douglass in a letter from no less person than Peyton Randolph, the President of the Congress. So, willy nilly, Douglass played no more just then before lovers of the drama in the South.

Before we leave this period, however, we must go back a bit to take notice of a brief season during which the American company played at Annapolis in 1770. " Cymbeline " was one of the plays then produced, and the Miss Hallam, who in 1752 had made her " first appearance on any stage " at Williamsburg as Jessica, was now an Imogen of such charm as to elicit this very enthusiastic praise from " Y. Z." in the *Maryland Gazette*.

" MISS HALLAM AS IMOGEN. — To the Printer: — As I make it a matter of conscience to do justice to merit to the utmost of my abilities in whatever walk of life I chance to discover it, I shall take the liberty of publishing through the channel of your paper the observations which the representation at the Theatre on Thursday night drew from me.

" I shall not at present expatiate on the merits of the whole performance but confine myself principally to one object. The actors are indubitably entitled to a very considerable portion of praise. But, by your leave, gentlemen (to speak in the language of Hamlet) ' Here's metal more attractive.' On finding that the part of Imogen was to be played by Miss Hallam I instantly formed to myself, from my predilection for her, the most sanguine hope of entertainment. But how was I rav-

66

ished on experiment! She exceeded my utmost idea! Such delicacy of manner! Such classical strictness of expression! The music of her tongue — the *vox liquida*, how melting! Notwithstanding the injuries it received from the horrid ruggedness of the roof and the untoward construction of the whole house, methought I heard once more the warbling of Cibber [1] in my ear. How true and thorough her knowledge of the part she personated! Her whole form and dimensions how happily convertible and universally adapted to the variety of her part.

"A friend of mine, who was present, was so deeply impressed by the witching grace and justness with which the actress filled the whole character, that immediately on going home, he threw out, warm from the heart as well as the brain, the verses I enclose.

"The house, however, was thin from want of acquaintance with the general as well as the particular merits of the performers. The characteristical propriety of Mrs. Douglass cannot but be too striking to pass unnoticed. The fine genius of that young creature, Miss Storer, unquestionably affords the most pleasing prospect of an accomplished actress. The discerning part of an audience must cheerfully pay the tribute of applause due to the solid sense which is conspicuous in Mrs. Harman,[2] as well as to her perspicuity and strength of memory. The sums lavished on a late set whose merits were not of the transcendent kind, in whatever point of light they are viewed, are still fresh in our memories. And should these their successors, whose deportment, decency and unremitting study to please have ever been confessedly marked, meet with discounte-

---

[1] The allusion here is to Mrs. Theophilus Cibber, Colley Cibber's daughter-in-law, a very gifted London actress.
[2] This lady was Colley Cibber's granddaughter, it will be recalled.

67

nance, methinks such a conduct would not reflect the highest honor either on our taste or spirit.

" The merit of Mr. Douglass' company is notoriously, in the opinion of every man of sense in America, whose opportunities give him a title to judge — take them all in all — superior to that of any company in England, except those of the metropolis. The dresses are remarkably elegant; the dispatch of the business of the theatre uncommonly quick; and the stillness and good order preserved behind the scenes are proofs of the greatest attention and respect paid to the audience."

The poem of this correspondent's impressionable friend I will spare my readers; it is twelve stanzas long and invokes, one by one, all the goddesses whose names were ever found in any rhapsody of its class. One reference that it contains, however, — to " self-tutored Peale," — is of interest because the suggestion made that Charles Wilson Peale paint Miss Hallam in the part of Imogen was in due time improved.

Peale had been born in a town near Annapolis, and had won his way to the dignity of a portrait-painter through the various trades of saddler, silversmith, watchmaker, carver, and constructor of artificial teeth. In the winter of 1770-1771 he studied painting in Boston under Copley, and the probability is that he painted Miss Hallam as Imogen during the summer and autumn of the latter year. A poem highly commending his picture was printed in the hospitable pages of the *Maryland Gazette* on November 7, 1771. Whether the poet was over-kind to his efforts we cannot say; for absolutely no trace of the portrait can be found to-day.

The Romance of the American Theatre

Allusion is found in "Y. Z.'s" review of Miss Hallam to the "untoward construction" of the house in which this performance had been given. The time had now come, in truth, for a real theatre in Annapolis. Let us hear of the project as a contemporary writer, William Eddis, surveyor of customs, set it forth:

"Annapolis, June 18, 1771. . . . When I bade farewell to England I little expected that my passion for the drama could have been gratified in any tolerable degree at a distance so remote from the great mart of genius; and I brought with me strong prepossessions in behalf of favorite performers whose merits were fully established by the universal sanction of intelligent judges. My pleasure and my surprise were therefore excited in proportion, on finding performers in this country equal at least to those who sustain the best of the first characters in your most celebrated provincial theatres. Our Governor, from a strong conviction that the stage, under proper regulations, may be rendered of general utility and made subservient to the great interests of religion and virtue, patronizes the American Company; and, as their present place of exhibition is on a small scale and inconveniently situated, a subscription by his example has rapidly been completed to erect a new theatre on a commodious if not elegant plan. The manager is to deliver tickets for two seasons for the amount of the respective subscriptions, and it is imagined that the money which will be received at the doors from non-subscribers will enable him to conduct the business without difficulty, and when the limited number of performances is completed the entire property is to be vested in him. The building is already in a state of forwardness and the day of opening is anxiously expected."

This theatre, constructed of brick, with a seating capacity of about six hundred persons, was erected in West Street, Annapolis, on ground leased from St. Anne's Parish. And so greatly did it overtop in elegance the old church of the place, that there soon appeared, in the columns of the *Maryland Gazette*, a rhymed address from the church to the inhabitants of Maryland's ancient capital complaining that

> " Here in Annapolis alone
> God has the meanest house in town,"

and praying that the institution devoted to " peace on earth, good will to men " be housed at least as well as that given over to Shakespeare!

The opening bill here (September 9, 1771) was the " Roman Father " by Whitehead, the cast for which was as follows:

Roman Father	Mr. Hallam
Tullus Hostilius	Mr. Douglass
Publius	Mr. Goodman
Valerius	Mr. Wall
First Citizen	Mr. Morris
Second Citizen	Mr. Wools
Third Citizen	Mr. Parker
Fourth Citizen	Mr. Roberts
Soldier	Mr. Tomlinson
Valeria	Mrs. Henry
Horatio	Miss Hallam

Williamsburg in Virginia, Charleston in South Carolina, and Annapolis in Maryland were the only Southern cities which, before the Revolution, welcomed players. After the Revolution, however, Savannah, Richmond, and Baltimore also figured early in theatrical history. Savannah's theatre, or to quote Seilhamer, "what was called a theatre," opened August 24, 1785, with Addison's "Cato" and Garrick's farce, "Catherine and Petruchio," for the bill. The two leading actors, Kidd and Godwin, were dancing-masters as well as Thespians. But, instead of being able to ride these two horses successfully, they found themselves unable to ride either — in Savannah. Nor do we hear anything more of theatricals here until 1796; and even then the company was a summer one and made no very favourable impression on the town.

The first theatre in Baltimore was built in 1781 and was situated in East Baltimore Street, near the Presbyterian church. The first season here began January 15, 1782, and continued with considerable regularity until the June 15 following. The manager and leading man was Mr. Wall, an actor who for many years had been a member of the old American company. With the exception of him and his wife, however, all the names on the company's list were new to American theatre-goers.

One of these names is Mrs. Robinson, whom Seilhamer, with far more trustfulness than he displays anywhere else in his three huge volumes, conjectures to be the Mrs. Robinson famous in Court scandal and in the London stage gossip of the day as "Perdita." If a man who was solemnly writing a history of the theatre could suggest this identity, a woman, who is gaily discussing the

71

The Romance of the American Theatre

theatre's romance, may dwell slightly on it. That the
Mrs. Robinson of the Baltimore Theatre was an exceptionally gifted actress, just as " Perdita " was; that the
years during which she played in a province far from
London were precisely the years when " Perdita's "
whereabouts were most uncertain; and that, at just
about the time when Colonel Tarleton (who surrendered
with Cornwallis at Yorktown) returned to London and
set up housekeeping with " Perdita," Mrs. Robinson
disappeared from the bills of the Baltimore Theatre,
all lend plausibility, it cannot be denied, to Seilhamer's
hypothesis. Further, the unusual duration (sixteen years)
of " Perdita's " relation with her colonel might be
accounted for by the fact that the two had met in distant America when both were very sad at heart as a
result of the world's buffets and scorns.

The one fact which, to my mind, militates against this
theory is that the name on the playbills of Baltimore was
" Perdita's " own. I do not agree with Seilhamer that
" it never would have occurred " to the theatre-goers of
Baltimore to connect the Mrs. Robinson, whom they
admired at their theatre, with the notorious Mrs. Robinson who so short a time before had basked in the favour
of Drury Lane audiences. Baltimore was not so far
away from London as that — nor its playgoers so un-
intelligent.

One interesting event in this season of 1782 at Baltimore was the first production in America of Brooke's
tragedy " Gustavus Vasa," which, though ready to be
brought out at Drury Lane as early as 1739, had not yet

72

been given there — or anywhere else in London — because of the spirit of liberty which breathes through it. The play, when produced in this country, was inscribed to Washington as the deliverer of his country, and in the epilogue which accompanied its presentation at Baltimore, American independence was distinctly recognized. The last line of this epilogue unconsciously advocated " votes for women; " it pointed out that logically the man

> " Who bleeds for freedom will extend his plan;
> Will keep the generous principle in view,
> And wish the ladies independence, too."

The following season this company divided its time between Baltimore and Annapolis, where it went for the week of races which at that period attracted large numbers of the Maryland gentry. Among the names on the bills of the company we now find Mr. and Mrs. Dennis Ryan, of whom we shall hear more anon. A file of the playbills of this season is in the possession of the New York Historical Society, and for some time the receipts of each night, both in Baltimore and in Annapolis, may there be found. As an indication of the drawing power of the Baltimore Company of Comedians at the two Maryland cities in 1782, these figures are very interesting. The largest amount noted for Baltimore is £127 10 8 for October 18, when " Romeo and Juliet " was there produced, with the " Wrangling Lovers " as an afterpiece. The smallest amount taken in was £54 11 3, on October 1, when Miller's tragedy of " Mahomet the Impostor " was given. The best night at Annapolis, from the box-office standpoint, netted just about the same amount as the best night at Baltimore; but the play was not now Shakespearian. The Annapolis house was smallest when Farquhar's " Beaux' Stratagem," with the " Wrangling Lovers " as an afterpiece, was given. This was on November 6, and the amount taken in was £62 2 6. These seem like " paying " houses, but there must have been mismanagement somewhere, for the theatre closed abruptly in midwinter, and when it opened again on February 11 with Dennis Ryan in control, subscribers were informed that old tickets would not be received for the new series of performances. Evidently Baltimore playgoers did not resent this, however, for " to enable Mr. Ryan to accomplish the purposes of his undertaking," a number of Baltimore amateurs came to his support, and a successful season of four months ensued, with the usual Annapolis interlude.

Possibly some of the stage-struck gentlemen accompanied Mr. Ryan when he went to New York in the summer, there to conduct from June 19 to August 16 (1783) that series of performances made profitable by the continued presence in the town of a large number of British officers. Seilhamer calls this " a lost chapter in dramatic history," and such it indeed seems. Most of the pieces given had been previously played by Ryan's company at Baltimore, but " Macbeth," which he now put on, was new to the present band of players, as was " Oroonoko," a piece which languished from this date until the elder Booth revived it at the Bowery Theatre in

New York in 1832, himself assuming the title part. One of the "ladies" of Mr. Ryan's company in New York was Mrs. Fitzgerald, who, when she returned to England with the troops, after the manner of her kind, took with her a considerable sum of money which the manager — evidently in the hope of retaining her services — had advanced to her for salary. The advertisement in which this loss on Ryan's part was announced is full of interest by reason of the insight it gives us into the customs of the times.

"Theatre, New York, Oct. 17.
"Whereas a certain Eleanor Massey Fitzgerald has defrauded the subscriber of the sum of forty-six pounds, sixteen shillings, by entering into articles of indenture and immediately absconding — A Reward of Twenty Pounds will be paid to any person who can inform the Subscriber where she is harbored so that she may be brought to justice, previous to the 30th of this month.
"DENNIS RYAN."

Both the actress and the money were gone for good, however, and Ryan had to make the best of such talent and capital as still remained to him, when he again turned his face towards Baltimore for what was to be his last season there. Just one occurrence of this season is of sufficient interest to claim our attention, the first production in America, on February 3, 1784, of "The School for Scandal." This masterpiece of English comedy was first produced at Drury Lane, May 8, 1777; but it was not then published, and even Seilhamer, who knows so much, cannot tell us how Ryan secured a copy. By the

75

time the old American company gave the play in New York, December 12, 1785, there was no difficulty about play-books, however, for "Hallam's partner, Henry, was in possession of an authentic copy given him by the author, through his personal relations with the Sheridan family."[1] This edition was printed by Hugh Gaine in 1786, and so was available for use when the old American company opened in Baltimore with the comedy on August 17 of that year, and inaugurated their season at Richmond, on October 10, with the same piece.

The most interesting effort of the period towards the revival of the drama in the South was that made in Charleston this same winter by the Mr. Godwin whom we noted at Savannah as a dancing-master with managerial aspirations. Godwin's season lasted from September until the close of March, but inasmuch as he made, at its start, the fatal mistake of exhibiting his playhouse *gratis*, he failed to realize largely from the box-office. Douglass had built a theatre in Charleston before the Revolution, it will be recalled; consequently we must rank as the second theatre in Charleston the place thus paragraphed in the *New York Independent Journal* of August 5, 1786:

" HARMONY HALL. — We hear from Charleston, S. C., that a principal merchant of that city and a Mr. Godwin, comedian, has leased a lot of land for five years and have erected a building called Harmony Hall, for the purpose of music meetings, dancing and theatrical

[1] " History of the American Theatre," vol. II, page 185.

amusements. It is situated in a spacious garden in the suburbs of the city. The boxes are 22 in number with a key to each box. The pit is very large and the theatrum and orchestra elegant and commodious. It was opened with a grand concert of music *gratis* for the satisfaction of the principal inhabitants who wished to see it previous to the first night's exhibition. The above building cost £500 sterling. Salaries from two to five guineas per week, and a benefit every nine months is offered to good performers."

The subsequent history of Harmony Hall is not without interest. In the summer of 1794 it was occupied by the Placide Troupe and called the French theatre. A rendering of the *Marseillaise,* in which the audience joined, was now a feature of this house. Charleston had a large French population at this time, by reason of the fact that it had offered an asylum to the St. Domingo refugees driven out of their island by the horrible massacres of 1792. The mother of Joseph Jefferson, it is interesting to note, was one of these refugees. Towards the close of 1794, the name City Theatre was given to Harmony Hall, and a company, of which Mr. Solee appears to have been the manager, took possession. Here, on February 14, 1795, " Louis XVI" was given its first American production.

Another Charleston production of distinct interest was " The Apotheosis of Franklin," given on April 22, 1796. The advertisements declare that " nothing like this spectacle was ever before performed on this continent," and for once an advertisement spoke truly. Because it indicates how short a distance America had progressed

77

by the end of the eighteenth century, towards imposing scenic production, let us examine the " Apotheosis."

The first scene represented the sculptor, Houdon, at work on the tomb of Franklin. Although only a modest slab covers the grave of Benjamin and Deborah Franklin at Fifth and Arch Streets in Philadelphia, there were here two ambitious statues. One represented the United States holding the American eagle in the right hand and an appropriately inscribed shield and buckler in the left; the other depicted Prudence — that virtue being the Franklin attribute most in the public eye a century ago.

The second act was in three scenes. The first scene represented a gloomy cavern, through which were seen the river Styx and the banks of the Stygian lake. Charon here appears in his boat ready to convey Franklin to the Elysian Fields. But Elysium once reached, Franklin himself becomes an actor. For he must be led aloft by the Goddess of Fame, who will proclaim his virtues, and he must be conducted to the abodes of Peace by Philosophy, there to be introduced by Diogenes to all the learned and wise who inhabit this region. The last scene represented the Temple of Memory and was adorned with statues and busts of all the deceased philosophers and poets who had preceded Franklin to the Land of Shades. As the curtain fell, the statue of Philadelphia's Sage was placed on a vacant pedestal facing that of Sir Isaac Newton.

Yet to this performance, in honour of him who had struggled so hard for American liberty, no " person of

78

colour " was admitted! All Mr. Solee's advertisements contained an announcement of this discrimination, to which it was added that this ruling was " by regulation of the Common Council."

Before leaving our discussion of the theatre in the South I want to quote, by permission, from Eola Willis' just published work "The Charleston Stage in the XVIII Century," a review of that performance of the "Recruiting Officer" given in Charleston at the request of the Ancient and Honorable Society of Free and Accepted Masons, and referred to on page 59 preceding. In this volume has been established by scholarly and exhaustive research Charleston's claim to the honor of having fathered *the first article in an American newspaper which is in the nature of dramatic criticism.* The date is May 28, 1737, the place the South Carolina *Gazette*, and the notice as follows:

"Charles-Town, May 28
On Thursday Night last 'The Recruiting Officer' was acted for the Entertainment of the ancient and honorable Society of Free and Accepted Masons, who came to the Play-house about 7 o'clock in the usual Manner, and made a very decent and solemn Appearance; It was a fuller house on this Occasion than ever had been known in this Place before. A proper Prologue and Epilogue were spoke, and the entered Apprentices and Masters's Songs sung upon the stage, which were joined in Chorus by the Masons in the Pit, to the Satisfaction and Entertainment of the whole audience. After the Play the Masons return'd to the Lodge at Mr. Shepheard's in the same order observed in coming to the Play-House."

CHAPTER III

LOVERS of liberty no less than lovers of the theatre should give devout thanks that the British officers who served in America during our Revolution were exceedingly fond of " stage performances." For America owes much to the military Thespians in New York, Philadelphia, and Boston. On the one hand their absorption " in play-acting " increased the non-preparedness which made it possible for the Yankees to win; and on the other hand, by giving good plays in a creditable manner, these officers notably advanced the progress of the stage as an American institution.

Boston was the only city of any importance which, down to the outbreak of the Revolution, had persistently refused hospitality to plays and players. It is but little more than a legend that a dramatic performance was given in a coffee-house in State Street in Boston, in the latter part of the year 1750. The historians of the period fail to give most of the essential details of the affair, the names of those who promoted or took part in it, and other material incidents. The simple facts recorded are that it was Thomas Otway's old tragedy of the " Orphan " that was acted or attempted, the performers, with two

PLAYBILL FOR NEW YORK PERFORMANCE IN 1750 OF OTWAY'S "ORPHAN"
From the Theatre Collection, Harvard University

WILLIAM DUNLAP, FIRST AMERICAN MAN OF LETTERS TO MAKE PLAY-WRITING
A PROFESSION
From the Theatre Collection, Harvard University

exceptions, being local amateurs. The exceptions noted were English professionals, very likely from William Hallam's company, but recently arrived from England. The desire to witness this performance appears to have been extraordinary. That there was an unruly and almost riotous mob at the doors, and that a serious disturbance occurred, is recorded. This latter disturbance aroused the authorities, and the matter was brought to the attention of the General Court, with a petition to prohibit further trouble from a similar cause. That august body immediately enacted as follows:

" For preventing and avoiding the many and great mischiefs which arise from public stage plays, interludes and other theatrical entertainments, which not only occasion great and unnecessary expense, and discourage industry and frugality, but likewise tend generally to increase immorality, impiety and contempt of religion —
" Be it enacted by the Lieut. Governor, Council and House of Representatives that from and after the publication of this act, no person or persons whosoever shall or may for hire or gain, or for any valuable consideration, let or suffer to be used and improved any house, room or place whatsoever for acting or carrying on any stage plays, interludes or other theatrical entertainments, on pain of forfeiting and paying for each and every day or time such house, room or place shall be let, used or improved, contrary to this act, twenty pounds.
" Sect. II — And be it further enacted that if at any time or times whatsoever from and after the publication of this act, any person or persons shall be present as an actor or spectator of any stage play, interlude or theatri-

cal entertainment in any house, room or place where a greater number of persons than twenty shall be assembled together, every such person shall forfeit and pay for every time he or they shall be present as aforesaid, five pounds. The forfeiting and penalties aforesaid to be one-half to His Majesty for the use of the government, and the other half to him or them that shall inform or sue for the same, and the aforesaid forfeitures and penalties may likewise be recovered by presentment of the grand jury, in which case the whole of the forfeitures shall go to His Majesty for the use of the government."

This law of the Commonwealth, with the public sentiment largely in its favour, of course rendered stage plays prohibitive. There is little doubt that it was the presence of this law on the statute books which gave the final fillip to the theatricals instituted in Boston by General Burgoyne's officers late in 1775.

Faneuil Hall was the theatre used for these exhibitions, and announcements of the plays to be performed were made by hand-bills. Mrs. Centlivre's comedy, " The Busybody," Rowe's " Tamerlane," and Aaron Hill's tragedy of " Zara " were among the attractions offered, the drawing power of the latter being considerably increased by the fact that Burgoyne himself wrote a prologue for it. An interesting contemporary allusion to this entertainment is found in a letter sent by Burgoyne's brother-in-law, Thomas Stanley, the second son of Lord Derby, to Hugh Elliott: " We acted the tragedy of ' Zara ' two nights before I left Boston," he wrote, " for the benefit of the widows and children. The Prologue was spoken by Lord Rawdon, a very fine fellow and a good soldier, I wish you knew him. We took above £100 at the door. I hear a great many people blame us for acting, and think we might have found something better to do, but General Howe follows the example of the King of Prussia, who, when Prince Ferdinand wrote him a long letter, mentioning all the difficulties and distresses of the army, sent back the following concise answer: *De la gaieté, encore de la gaieté, et toujours de la gaieté.* The female parts were filled by young ladies, though some of the Boston ladies were so prudish as to say this was improper."

The performances at Faneuil Hall playhouse began at six o'clock, and the entrance fee was one dollar for the pit and a quarter of a dollar for the gallery. For some reason, either because the play was immensely popular, or because the currency gave trouble, those in charge were obliged to announce after a few evenings: " The managers will have the house strictly surveyed and give out tickets for the number it will contain. The most positive orders are given not to take money at the door, and it is hoped gentlemen of the army will not use their influence over the sergeants who are door-keepers to induce them to disobey that order, as it is meant entirely to promote the ease and convenience of the public by not crowding the theatre."

The most notable piece presented at Faneuil Hall was the local farce, " The Blockade of Boston," the authorship of which is generally credited to Burgoyne. Whether the General wrote this piece or not, he was the ruling spirit in its presentation. He was himself an amateur actor of no mean ability and had already written his first play, "The Maid of the Oaks," before coming to America. This play was originally acted, in 1774, at the Burgoyne home, The Oaks, on the occasion of a marriage fête in honour of Burgoyne's brother-in-law, Lord Stanley. Garrick was so taken with the piece, when he read it, that he brought it out at Drury Lane in 1775, with Mrs. Abington in the chief rôle. So, if Burgoyne did *not* write "The Blockade of Boston," it was not because he lacked ability to write a good play.

Whether this was a good play, we have no means of knowing. It has come down to us in history, not by reason of its dramatic excellence, but because of certain "business" not originally planned. It was booked to be given for the first time on any stage at Faneuil Hall on the evening of January 8, 1776. The comedy of "The Busybody" had already been acted, and the orchestra was playing an introduction for the farce, when the actors behind the scenes heard an exaggerated report of a raid made upon Charlestown by a small party of Americans. Washington, represented by an uncouth figure, awkward in gait, wearing a large wig and rusty sword, had no sooner come on to speak his opening lines in the play, than a British sergeant suddenly appeared on the stage and exclaimed: "The Yankees are attacking our works on Bunker's Hill." At first this was thought part of the farce; but when Howe, who was present, called out sharply, "Officers, to your alarm posts!" the audience quickly dispersed.

Timothy Newell, in his diary, says there was "much fainting, fright and confusion." And well there might have been, with the officers jumping over the orchestra at great expense to the fiddles, the actors rushing wildly about in their eagerness to get rid of their make-up and costume, and the ladies alternately fainting and screaming. They had to revive themselves, however, and get home as best they could, those poor ladies! For some time it was the chief delight of the patriot dames to relate how maids and matrons of the Faneuil Hall audience were obliged to pick their way home through the dark Boston streets unattended by any of their usual escorts.

The Tory sheet published by Madam Draper all through the siege of Boston, after reporting the interruption of the "Blockade's" first performance, adds: "As soon as those parts which are vacant by some gentlemen being ordered to Charlestown can be filled, that farce will be performed, with the tragedy of 'Tamerlane.'" The diary of John Rowe records that the play actually came off on January 22, 1776.

It has been said that desire to offend the prejudices of Puritan New England was a strong motive in the acting of the Boston Thespians. That hand-bills of the entertainments were sent regularly to Washington, Hancock, and other leading spirits among the Provincials bears this out. In the performances which soon followed at New York, however, the diversion of the soldiery was the main object. The moving spirits in the first New York season of the military Thespians were some of

85

the same officers who had taken part in the performances at Boston, including the young Captain Stanley whose letter has been quoted. He it was who wrote the Prologue for the re-opening of the John Street Theatre on January 25, 1777.

The bill on this first night of a series of seasons which lasted until 1783 was Fielding's burlesque, " Tom Thumb," a piece very well adapted to the initial effort of a company of amateurs, a company, which, at this time, was probably quite without actresses. The players were so fortunate as to have a zealous friend in the person of Hugh Gaine, who printed the *Mercury* at the sign of the Bible and the Crown in Hanover Square; and on this account we have a contemporary criticism of their New York début:

" On Saturday evening last the little Theatre in John street in this city was opened with the celebrated burlesque entertainment, ' Tom Thumb,' written by the late Mr. Fielding to ridicule the pathos of several dramatic pieces that at his time, to the disgrace of the British stage, had engrossed both the London Theatres. The characters were performed by gentlemen of the Army and Navy; the spirit with which this favorite was supported prove their taste and strong conception of humor. Saturday's performance convinces us that a good education and knowledge of polite life are essentially necessary to form a good actor. The Play was introduced by a Prologue written by Captain Stanley; we have great pleasure in applauding this first effort of his infant muse as replete with true genius. The scenes painted by Captain De Lancey had great merit and would not disgrace a theatre tho' under the management of a Garrick. The House was crowded with company and the Ladies made a brilliant appearance."

There is very little said here about the acting, it will be observed. Very likely the notice was written in anticipation of the event — inasmuch as it appeared on Monday, and the performance was on a Saturday evening. This was a very long time, it must be remembered, before the days when newspaper enterprise puts into the hands of " fans," as they scramble for their cars after a ball game, a categorical description of all the plays made on the diamond that very afternoon by the favourites for whom they have just been shouting themselves hoarse.

That the difficulties under which these military Thespians acted were many and varied goes without saying. For one thing, they had almost no play-books. In the *Royal Gazette* of December 22, 1779, appears the following notice: " The managers of the theatre, understanding that a gentleman purchased a set of Mr. Garrick's works from Robertson, printer, will be much obliged to that gentleman if he will resign the purchase over to the theatre for the benefit of charity, or lend them the particular volume that contains the comedy of ' Catherine and Petruchio.' " As this farce was soon afterwards produced, it would appear that the fortunate possessor of Garrick's works obligingly complied with this odd request.

The " charity " here referred to was something of a blind. At first, to be sure, the widows and orphans were actually paid a good deal of the money taken in at the door. But, later, there was a regular salary list for the actors and actresses. Dunlap says that fourteen performers got a dollar a day, even this modest sum being welcome to the officers by reason of the high price of necessaries in New York. "Circumstanced as these brave men are," declared one of the English journals, " such an exertion of their talents to increase their incomes deserves the greatest encouragement." Thus charity became a business, and the actors soon learned, as every amateur who " goes on " professionally learns, that there is a vast difference between what your friends say of your theatrical ability and what the professional critic says. A certain Lieutenant Spencer who acted in New York at this time and afterwards played " Richard III " at Bath, elicited this comment: " The *débutant* of last night has long been known as an excellent player — at billiards."

Major André of pathetic memory was one of the New York Thespians for a time, though he is more intimately associated with the performances given at Philadelphia during the winter of 1777–1778. In the Southwark Theatre, which Hallam had formerly occupied, Howe's Thespians began to offer plays very soon after their occupation of the Quaker City. In the diary of Robert Morton, then in his seventeenth year, may be found an allusion to the use of this building as a hospital, when the wounded soldiers were brought in, after the battle of Germantown. But, as the winter wore on, and this emergency use of the playhouse ceased, preparations were begun to inaugurate a series of dramas. In the *Pennsylvania Ledger* of December 24, 1777, appeared an advertisement for a person at the playhouse who could write a legible hand, and at the same time notice was given that those who had formerly been employed at the theatre might again obtain work there.

André was the moving spirit of all that subsequently went on here. For, though he was no carpet knight, he had rare facility in the arts — and he was young, gay, and charming. In an earlier book of mine [1] I have described at considerable length his relations at this time with pretty Peggy Shippen, who became the wife of the traitor, Benedict Arnold. So, alluring as that subject is, I will here proceed at once from André the man to André the artist. His talent in this way was by no means inconsiderable. Charles Durang, who wrote the " History of the Philadelphia Stage," remembered well one set of scenes that André painted at this time.

" It was a landscape," he records, " presenting a distant *champagne* country and a winding rivulet, extending from the front of the picture to the extreme distance. In the foreground and centre was a gentle cascade — the water exquisitely executed — overshadowed by a group of majestic forest trees. The perspective was excellently preserved; the foliage, verdure and general colouring artistically toned and glazed. It was a drop scene and André's name was inscribed on the back of it in large black letters. It was preserved in

[1] " Romantic Days in the Early Republic," Little, Brown, & Co., Boston.

the theatre until 1821, when it perished with the rest of the scenery in that old temple of the drama."

So successful were the plays projected and staged by André at the Southwark, that after the return of the Continental Congress to Philadelphia an attempt was made by some regular players to open a season there. But their efforts were promptly frowned down. " Frequenting playhouses and theatrical entertainments has a fatal tendency," the gentlemen in Congress asserted, " to divert the minds of the people from a due attention to the means necessary for the defense of the country and the preservation of their liberties." It was therefore resolved: " That any person holding an office under the United States who shall act, promote, attend, or encourage such plays, shall be deemed unworthy to hold such office and shall be accordingly dismissed." There is a story that on the very day this resolution was enacted, Lafayette asked Henry Laurens, who was then President of Congress, to go with him to the play. When Laurens told him what Congress had done, Lafayette said simply: " Then I shall not go to the play."

The States generally, however, failed to adopt the recommendations which Congress would have crammed down their throats, interdicting every form of amusement, and for nearly two years before the final departure of the British, plays were being regularly given at Baltimore, Annapolis, and New York. Of Ryan's season in New York during the winter of 1782–1783, we heard in the course of the Southern chapter.

The next New York combination worthy of extended

notice was the Hallam and Henry company, which from 1785 to 1792 flourished at John Street. It was in 1787, under the auspices of this management, that there here occurred the most notable performance America had yet seen, the initial production of Royall Tyler's admirable comedy, " The Contrast." This piece has little or no plot and scarcely any action, either. Nevertheless, the work is interesting to read — even after all this lapse of time — and must have been very interesting to see when produced at the old John Street Theatre, with Wignell [1] playing the rôle which has served, ever since, as the model of stage Jonathans.

Royall Tyler, the author of this piece, was born at Boston, Massachusetts, July 18, 1758, and belonged to a wealthy and influential New England family. He received his early education at the Boston Latin School and was duly graduated from Harvard. During the Revolutionary War, and afterwards in Shays's Rebellion, he acted as *aide-de-camp* with the rank of major on the staff of General Benjamin Lincoln. It was in connection with this latter office that he was sent to New York by Governor Bowdoin; Shays had crossed the border line

[1] Thomas Wignell was the son of a member of Garrick's company and first came to America at the outbreak of the Revolutionary War. He was connected with the John Street Theatre from 1785 to 1791. In 1794 he opened the Chestnut Street Theatre, Philadelphia, then the finest building of its kind in America. Mrs. Merry, whom he married only a few weeks before his death, in 1803, had, as Miss Brunton, been well known and much liked on the stage in England. In 1792 she married Robert Merry, a poet, and his means failing, they came together to America. Her first appearance here was in Philadelphia, in 1796, as Juliet. Merry died in 1798. After Wignell's death she married Warren, father of Boston's William Warren, who outlived her.

The Romance of the American Theatre

from Massachusetts into New York State, and his capture was ardently desired.

So Tyler, who had never before been outside New England, found himself in New York. At once his attention turned to the theatre, which was altogether new to him, and soon its fascinations were proving so potent that he became a constant visitor both behind and before the scenes. The performers speedily grew to be his friends — especially Wignell — who early had an opportunity to examine the manuscript of " The Contrast."

The theme of the play is the contrast between the meretricious standards of the fashionable world and the simple straightforward ideals of your true and self-respecting American. Hence, of course, its title. When the curtain rises, two *débutantes* of the period are discussing the latest style in skirts — mingling therewith a good deal of gossip — in quite the manner that a group of frivolous women assembling for a matinée " bridge " might talk of these same topics to-day. In the second scene there are some interesting Ibsenesque reflections about the relations between men and women, which almost persuade us that Maria, though she has perhaps been reading over-much about Sir Charles Grandison, is really a type of the awakening woman-soul.

Of course, the entire work is over-sentimental. But it is very much less offensive in this way than many another literary product of its time. And if Colonel Manly is a prig, his sister, Charlotte, is a very clever

92

young person.   Witness her characterization of the
colonel as one whose " conversation is like a rich, old-
fashioned brocade — it will stand alone; every sentence
is a sentiment."   That there is a great deal of wit and
humour in the piece we have seen from Jonathan's
description of the playhouse quoted in our first chapter.
The comedy is of its time, too, and could have been
written by none other than an American.   Jonathan,
snubbed for philandering with Jenny, who has just gone
off " in a swinging passion," declares thoughtfully
that if that is the way city ladies act, he will continue
to prefer his Tabitha with her twenty acres of rock, her
Bible, a cow, and " a little peaceable bundling."   The
one other bit of comic action in the comedy — aside
from this attempt of Jonathan's to kiss Jenny — is in
the last scene of the play's last act, where Colonel
Manly, upon whom Maria has decided to bestow her
overflowing heart, crosses swords with Dimple, the man
to whom this fair one's troth had been plighted before
he had taken a trip abroad to acquire the vices then
fashionable in England.   The original cast of this piece
seems of sufficient interest to be here reprinted:

Colonel Manly . . . . Mr. Henry
Dimple . . . . Mr. Hallam
Van Rough . . . . Mr. Morris
Jessamy . . . . Mr. Harper
Jonathan . . . . Mr. Wignell
Charlotte . . . . Mrs. Morris
Maria . . . . Mrs. Harper
Letitia . . . . Mrs. Kenna
Jenny . . . . Miss Tuke

After its New York season, " The Contrast " was successfully given in Philadelphia, in Baltimore — and in Boston for the benefit of the fire sufferers. Nor was it quickly forgotten. When Dunlap returned to New York, after his three years' sojourn in London, it was still the talk of the town, and he was glad to make the drawing of the duel scene which is herewith reproduced.[1]

The success of " The Contrast " is of vast importance to us in that it was perhaps the most powerful single influence in bringing about a complete revolution of sentiment with respect to the drama. Where the most reputable and law-abiding of the people had hitherto kept away from all theatrical amusements, they now experienced a decided change of heart towards plays and playhouses. Dramas by American authors followed each other in rapid succession. And soon even Washington found himself often at the theatre. In 1784 he had attended a performance of " Gustavus Vasa " played by the students of Washington College, Maryland, in his honour. But the first references that I have been able to find of his attendance at professional performances are contained in the diary he kept during the sessions of the Federal Convention. During the season when the ingenious Hallam was offering at the Southwark Theatre, Philadelphia, not a play, but a " Spectaculum Vitae," Washington was in the audience on July 10, July 14, and July 21.

On the evening after Washington's inauguration at

[1] From the engraving given as frontispiece to the reprint of the comedy, put out by the Dunlap Society of New York in 1887.

SCENE FROM "THE CONTRAST"
From a drawing by Dunlap

ROYALL TYLER, AUTHOR OF "THE CONTRAST", AND THOMAS WIGNELL, WHO TOOK THE PART OF JONATHAN IN THE PLAY, AND SO BECAME THE MODEL FOR ALL STAGE JONATHANS SINCE

From the Theatre Collection, Harvard University

New York, the little house in John Street was alight
with transparencies, one of which represented Fame as an
angel descending from heaven to crown Washington with
the emblems of immortality. And in this same house
the President was soon being celebrated in " Darby's
Return." Washington himself was in the audience on
the night of the first production of this work, in which
occur many passages that make a direct reference to
the President.

The piece is from the pen of Dunlap. Darby, a poor
soldier, returns to Ireland and recounts the adventures
through which he has passed in Europe and the United
States, and the various sights he has seen. In his " History "[1] the dramatist modestly speaks of the work as a
" trifle; " but he dwells with pardonable pride on the
pleasure which Washington appeared to take in the
piece.

" The eyes of the audience were frequently bent upon
his countenance," he says, " and to watch the emotions
produced by any particular passage upon him was the
simultaneous employment of all. When Wignell, as
Darby, recounted what had befallen him in New York, at
the adoption of the Federal Constitution, and the inauguration of the President, the interest expressed by the
audience in the looks and the changes of countenance of
this great man became intense. He smiled at these
lines alluding to the change in the government —

" ' There too I saw some mighty pretty shows;
A revolution, without blood or blows,

[1] " History of the American Theatre."

95

For, as I understood, the cunning elves,
The people, all revolted from themselves.'

" But at these lines —

" ' A man who fought to free the land from wo,
Like me, had left his farm, a soldiering to go.
But, having gained his point, he had, like me,
Returned his own potato ground to see.
But there he could not rest. With one accord
He's called to be a kind of — not a lord —
I don't know what, he's not a great man sure,
For poor men love him just as he were poor.'

the president looked serious; and when Kathleen asked

" ' How looked he, Darby? Was he short or tall? '

his countenance showed embarrassment, from the expectation of one of those eulogiums which he had been
obliged to hear on many public occasions, and which
must doubtless have been a severe trial to his feelings;
but Darby's answer that he had not seen him, because
he had mistaken a man ' all lace and glitter, botherum
and shine ' for him until all the show had passed, relieved
the hero from apprehension of further personality, and
so he indulged in that which was with him extremely
rare, a hearty laugh."

William Dunlap, whose production was thus enjoyed
by the Father of His Country, was the first American
man of letters who made play-writing a profession; he
wrote or adapted as many as sixty-three dramatic pieces.
He also drew and sketched somewhat — he had enjoyed

the privilege of art instruction in England under Benjamin West — and he furthermore turned out a number of biographies, including one of George Frederick Cooke. Of this production, Lord Byron wrote: "Such a book! I believe, since 'Drunken Barnaby's Journal,' nothing like it has drenched the press. All green-room and tap-room, drams and the drama. Brandy, whiskeypunch, and, latterly, toddy overflow every page. Two things are rather marvelous; first, that a man should live so long drunk, and next that he should have found a sober biographer." Seilhamer says that Cooke's love for the bottle is exaggerated in Dunlap's memoir, and though this seems to me impossible, I do feel that since Cooke, when sober, was a very great actor, his biographer might have given us more about his playing and less about his potations. Dunlap's "History of the American Theatre" was written when the author was quite an old man; it would seem generous to attribute to this fact the book's various inaccuracies. It should, moreover, be remembered that it is a much simpler thing to come along now and throw stones [1] at Dunlap than it was, nearly a hundred years ago, to get together the highly interesting data he presents concerning the early theatre in America.

The fact that Dunlap's father was a Loyalist had a good deal to do with the great love for the theatre which young William early exhibited. For, though the lad was born at Perth Amboy, New Jersey (February 10, 1766),

[1] Seilhamer, though he does not scruple to quote Dunlap when it serves his purpose to do so, never mentions *the man* without a sneer.

97

his family removed to New York during the occupation of that city by the British. Thus the boy was able to see most of the plays put on by the military Thespians there. When the war closed, he went to England to study drawing, but inasmuch as a missile thrown by a boyhood playmate had deprived him of the use of his right eye, he was considerably hampered as an artist, and so spent a large part of his time in London at the theatre. When he returned to America to find Royall Tyler's play enjoying a great success, he determined to become a dramatist. And he did. His first comedy was called "The Modest Soldier; or, Love in New York;" his second, "The Father, or American Shandyism." The one which we have seen Washington enjoying was his third.

Dunlap soon became a manager as well as a playwright, and he was thus on the inside of many of the theatrical enterprises of his day. More than any other American of his generation, indeed, he was in a position to note the development of the stage in this country — and to record those temperamental clashes behind the scenes which have so much to do with the making of theatrical history. A good deal of what he wrote in his "History" is of no interest to us to-day; and not a little of what he has painstakingly recorded at great length is exceedingly trivial. Here and there, however, we find in his pages things which are very interesting for the light they throw upon the customs of the times. Such is the debit and credit account of a performance of "Othello," given by Douglass in New York in 1761:

	s.	£	s.	d.
Box tickets sold at the door, 116 @	8	46	8	
Pit " " " 146	5	36	10	
Gallery " " 90	3	13	10	
Cash received at the doors		36	12	6
		£133	00	6

CHARGES

	£	s.	d.
To candles, 26 lb. of spermaceti at 3s. 6d. } " 14 lb. tallow 1s. }	£5	5	
To music, Messrs. Harrison & Van Dienval at 36s.	3	12	
To the front door-keeper, 16s., stage door-keeper, 8s.	1	4	
To the assistants, 13s., bill sticker, 4s.		17	
To the men's dresser, 4s., stage keeper, 32s., drummer, 4s.	2		
To wine in the second act, 2s. 6d.		2	6
To Hugh Gaine, for two sets of bills, advertisements, and commissions	5	10	
	£18	10	6

Balance £114 10s.

It is also to Dunlap that we owe that story about Henry's coach. " Henry was the only actor in America who kept a carriage. It was in the form of a coach, but very small, just sufficient to carry himself and wife to the theatre; it was drawn by one horse and driven by a black boy. Aware of the jealousy toward players, and that it would be said he *kept a coach*, he had caused to be painted on the doors, in the manner of those coats of arms which the aristocracy of Europe display, *two crutches* in heraldic fashion, with the motto, ' This or these.' "

In this little box the actor, who was lame, was wont to be transported, with his wife (dressed for the character she was to play) by his side, to the theatre in John Street, from his two-story brick house, painted yellow, on Fulton Street, between Nassau and Broadway, — the same house in which Hodgkinson, who succeeded Henry as Hallam's partner, lived later. In Hodgkinson's day a gate opened from the back of this house directly opposite Theatre Alley.

John Hodgkinson was an interesting person. Bernard speaks of him as " the provincial Garrick," and there seems little doubt that he was a man of considerable talent. His family name was Meadowcroft, and his father had kept a public house at Manchester, where John was potboy. The father dying, John's mother married again, and John was bound as an apprentice. He sang in the choir of one of the Manchester churches, and at the same time taught himself to play the violin well. He was also the leading spirit in a little band of amateur actors who gave their performances in a cellar. Thus he was fairly well fitted to take an obscure part on the stage, when, at the age of fifteen, he ran away from Manchester to Bath. After staying in Bath for some time, Hodgkinson, as he now called himself, got an engagement with a circuit manager who covered the Worcester, Derby, Nottingham, Wolverhampton, Retford, and Stamford theatres. Later he was taken on for the northern circuit. Here he worked hard and lived hard. " His professional success and his gallantries, running parallel with each other like the two wheels of a gig, left their mark on every road he travelled," is the way his biographer puts it. His first *affaire* of which there is record occurred at Chester, where Miss Chapman, an American girl long resident in England, who had run away from her husband, placed herself under his protection; and when Hodgkinson left the Newcastle company in 1789, he took with him a woman who had borne the Newcastle manager four children, which she now deserted. It was for the purpose of sloughing off this person that, towards the end of 1791, he wrote Hallam and Henry asking them if they had a " first line " vacant, but intimating that if he came to America, a place must also be made for a lady whom he would bring with him. This lady, Miss Brett, known in America as Mrs. Hodgkinson, was the daughter of a celebrated singer connected with Covent Garden and the Haymarket theatres. She herself had already attained some distinction in England as a singer. In appearance she was petite and girlish, with blue eyes and flaxen hair. The Lothario with whom she eloped was a huge creature — six feet, ten inches in height, if we may trust Dunlap, yet too fleshy to appear tall. With a broad nose, a round face, and gray eyes of unequal sizes, we may well believe that nature had done much towards making Hodgkinson a comical figure. There are those who say he had agreeable manners. But Dunlap is not among them; he has very little praise for the man, though he concedes that, as an actor, Hodgkinson had his points. " His ignorance of all beyond theatrical limits was profound," writes the historian. "He did not know who was the author of 'High Life Below Stairs' at the time he played the principal character in the piece. And at a time when he was the delight of the town, having made out a bill for poetical recitations, he was sportively asked by Judge Cozine: 'Who is that *anon* you have got in the bill among the poets?' and to the judge's astonishment, Hodgkinson answered in serious earnest and with an air of one showing his reading: 'Oh, sir, he is one of our first poets.'"

The American début of the Hodgkinsons was made in Philadelphia on September 26, 1792, at the Southwark Theatre, which in anticipation of the competition it foresaw from the new theatre then approaching completion on Chestnut Street, now put up strong bills and declared itself not really inaccessible. "Access to the old American Theatre in Southwark," said Dunlap's *Advertiser* naïvely, on the morning of the day that the new company was to make its bow to the public, "is becoming every day more and more easy. From the progress of pavements in that part of the town, riding and walking to it will soon in no season be disagreeable or difficult." Inasmuch as the Southwark's patrons had for more than a quarter of a century been finding that theatre inaccessible, it was not likely that just at the moment when a new and centrally located building was being prepared for their entertainment, they would be thus easily persuaded to think the old house convenient.

None the less, there was a good audience present on

the opening night, when Hodgkinson told the audience, in poetry of his own contriving:

" Across the vast Atlantic we have steered
To view that liberty so much revered;
To view the genuine sons of freedom's cause,
The favor'd land governed by reason's laws."

And Washington was there on November 14; hence we have this account in the *Federal Gazette* of the new-comer's affecting acting:

" When Mr. Hodgkinson, as Lord Aimworth, exhibited nobleness of mind in his generosity to the humble miller and his daughter, Patty; when he found her blessed with all the qualities that captivate and endear life, and knew that she was capable of adorning a higher sphere; when he had an interview with her upon the subject in which was painted the amiableness of an honorable passion; and, after his connection, when he bestowed his benefactions on the relatives, etc., of the old miller, the great and good Washington manifested his approbation of this interesting part of the opera by the tribute of a tear. Nor was his approbation withheld in the afterpiece when Mrs. Hodgkinson as Priscilla Tomboy, and Mr. Prigmore as Young Cockney, played truly up to nature. The humorous scenes unfolded in this piece, being acted to the life, received the approving smiles of our President."

Washington was more at home in the Southwark, indeed, than in any theatre with which his name is associated. For it chanced that, just about the time that the seat of government was changed from New York to Philadelphia, the players he had enjoyed in the former city shifted their background, also. Immediately the east stage-box of the Philadelphia house was fitted up expressly for the President's accommodation. The seats were cushioned — a rare attention in those days — the interior was gracefully festooned with red drapery, and over the front of the box was placed the United States coat of arms. Great ceremony attended the reception of the President here. A soldier was generally posted at each stage door; four soldiers were placed in the gallery; a military guard attended and a master of ceremonies in a full suit of black, with his hair elaborately powdered in the fashion of the time and holding two wax candles in silver candlesticks, was accustomed to receive Washington at the box door and conduct him and his party to their seats. The newspapers now took notice of the President's contemplated visits to the theatre. The *Federal Gazette*, for instance, announced, on January 4, 1791, that on the following evening Washington would attend the performance of " The School for Scandal," and " The Poor Soldier," and, on the sixth, the paper printed a criticism of the acting in both pieces, highly praising the principals and the production.

For a less stilted, and therefore more entertaining account of this particular evening, let us, however, turn to the sprightly letters of Abigail Adams, who, on January 8, 1791, wrote to her daughter: " I have been to one play, and here again we have been treated with much politeness. The actors came and informed us that a box was prepared for us. The Vice-President thanked

them for their civility, and told them he would attend
whenever the President did. And last Wednesday we
were all there. The house is equal to most of the theatres
we meet with out of France. It is very neatly and prettily
fitted up; the actors did their best; ' The School for
Scandal ' was the play. I missed the divine Farren, but,
on the whole it was very well performed."

Mrs. Adams, it will be recalled, was in London with
her husband when the latter was our first Minister at
the Court of St. James, and so had had opportunity to
attend the performances of the best players of the day.
The " divine Farren " here alluded to was Elizabeth
Farren, afterwards the Countess of Derby, who, about
1782, succeeded Mrs. Abingdon in comedy leads at the
Drury Lane. As a fine lady no less than as an actress,
the Farren was a great success. She had a house at the
West End, kept a carriage, and was courted by the nobility of both sexes. But though she always " played to
a single box," she did not otherwise fail in her duty to
the public, even though for many years she occupied the
difficult position of a countess-elect. Lady Teazle was
one of the Farren's most successful parts, and it is probable that Mrs. Adams had often seen her in it. It is
even possible that she was of the audience on that occasion when the Earl of Derby was unexpectedly ushered
into Joseph Surface's library! Fanny Kemble relates the
story thus:

" Mrs. Fitzhugh one day told me a comical incident
of the stage life of her friend, the fascinating Miss Farren. The devotion of the Earl of Derby to her — which

preceded for a long time the death of Lady Derby, from
whom he was separated, and his marriage to Miss Farren — made him a frequent visitor behind the scenes
on the nights of her performances. One evening, in the
famous scene in Joseph Surface's library in ' The School
for Scandal,' when Lady Teazle is imprisoned behind the
screen, Miss Farren, fatigued with standing, and chilled
with the dreadful draughts of the stage, had sent for an
arm-chair and her furs, and when the critical moment
arrived, and the screen was overturned, she was revealed
in her sable muff and tippet, entirely absorbed in an
eager conversation with Lord Derby, who was leaning
over the back of her chair."

One of the interesting productions with which the
huge and all-conquering Hodgkinson was connected,
first in New York and afterwards in Boston, was a kind
of opera called " Tammany, or The Indian Chief,"
and written by Mrs. Anne Julia Hatton, a sister of Mrs.
Siddons. Mrs. Hatton attempted the London stage in
1793, but not making any such success as was expected of
a Kemble, she sailed for New York, there to become the
bard of the American Democracy. She succeeded in
interesting the powerful Tammany Society in her opera,
and their wish that the piece should be produced amount-
ing to a command in New York, elaborate preparations
were made for bringing it out. A feature of the production was the gorgeous new set of scenes painted for it
by Charles Ciceri. Very tantalizingly Dunlap devotes
two pages in his " History " to the biography of this
scene-painter, about whom we care nothing, and does
not even outline the plot of this opera, which would be of

considerable interest to us as the first production from
a woman's pen ever staged in America.

The fact, however, that New York [1] was now making
occasional "productions," *plus* the further fact that
Philadelphia was about to open a second and very commodious theatre, added to the still more arresting fact
that even Boston (in 1792) had declared "stage plays"
to be essential to its happiness, would seem to prove
that the theatre had at last become an established
American institution.

The site selected for the initial Boston experiment in
the way of theatres was in what is now Hawley Street,
but which was then known as Board Alley, — because
originally only a short cut from State Street to Trinity
Church, on Summer Street — a region, at this time, of
mud and livery stables. It was probably one of these
stables that was fashioned into a theatre. Here, at any
rate, a stage was erected, and thus the "New Exhibition
Room" became an accomplished fact. Its first performance was on August 1, 1792, its manager being Mr.
Joseph Harper, who will be recalled as one of the men
associated with Hallam and Henry. The bill for the
opening of this first Boston playhouse is full of
colour:

[1] The Park Theatre, which dates from 1798, had much the look of
theatres of our own time. To be sure it had a pit, occupied only by men
and boys and equipped with board benches innocent of cushions. But
it was fitted with boxes, which quite resembled in aspect those of to-
day, a second tier, and a third tier. In the second tier of this early Park
Theatre there was a restaurant. The third tier — set apart, as in
most theatres of the period, for the dissolute of both sexes — was
equipped with a bar. In the space between the pit and the boxes, gentlemen of the audience promenaded between the acts.

NEW EXHIBITION ROOM

Board Alley

Feats of Activity

This evening, the 10th of August, will be exhibited dancing on
the Tight Rope by Monsieurs Placide and Martin.
Mons. Placide will dance a Hornpipe on a Tight
Rope, play a Violin in various attitudes, and
jump over a cane backwards and forwards.

INTRODUCTORY ADDRESS

By Mr. Harper

SINGING

By Mr. Wools

Various feats of tumbling by Mons. Placide and Martin, who
will make somersetts backwards over a table, chair etc.
Mons. Martin will exhibit several feats on a Slack Rope.
In the course of the Evening's Entertainment will be delivered

THE GALLERY OF PORTRAITS

or

THE WORLD AS IT GOES

By Mr. Harper

The whole to conclude with a Dancing Ballet called The Bird
Catcher with the Minuet de la Cour and the Gavot.

The steps leading up to these "feats of activity" in Board Alley are full of interest. On June 5, 1790, Hallam and Henry, who had already established play-houses in Philadelphia, New York, and Providence, presented to the Massachusetts Legislature a petition praying for leave " to open a theatre in Boston under proper regulations." The petition was not considered.

Two years later, however, an important contribution towards the establishing of such a theatre was made by John Gardiner, who, in a speech which he delivered in the House of Representatives on the expediency of re-pealing the law against theatrical exhibitions, gave evi-dence of deep learning as well as of a fine spirit of tol-eration. As this speech, when printed, makes nearly thirty thousand words, it must have consumed several hours in its delivery. The honourable Legislators could not have failed, as they listened, to learn a great deal about the history of the drama.

" I have lately dedicated a small portion of my early morning hours from other public business to investigate this subject," confessed Mr. Gardiner naïvely at the outset of his speech, " inasmuch as the drama and theat-rical exhibitions have been hitherto unknown in this country, and their history, nature and tendency little understood." Whereupon he proceeds to argue that " a theatre will be of very general and great emolumen-tary advantage to the town of Boston," because work-men must be employed to build it, and printers retained to get out its playbills after it has been built. Moreover, he points out: " Strangers who visit us complain much of the want of public places of resort for innocent and rational amusement; as in the summer and the fall months, our only public places of resort for amusement (the Concert and Assemblies) are dead and unknown among us. . . . Did the town of Boston possess a well regulated theatre, these strangers would, most probably, spend double the periods of time they generally pass in this town, to the great advantage of stable-keepers, the keepers of lodging houses, . . . the hairdresser, the shoemaker, the milliner " and many others. For a man, Mr. Gardiner had a wonderfully keen appreciation of the relation between plays and plumes.

That the ancient drama " took its rise in religion," that St. Paul quoted liberally from Greek poets and Greek writers of comedy, and that " the Song of Moses is a sacred dramatic performance " were other arresting ideas set forth in the early part of this speech. Following which, it was argued that the *manners* of the Bostonians needed the improvement that must inevitably follow carefully regulated dramatic entertainments! For, of course, it was decent drama only that this good citizen wanted, and to ensure such, he suggested the appointment of " five or more censors who should be annually chosen in town meeting from among the worthy fraternity of tradesmen, the respectable body of merchants, the learned sons of the law, and even from among the venerable, enlightened, and truly respectable ministers of the gospel in this great town."

Mr. Gardiner's arguments were opposed by Samuel Adams and Harrison Gray Otis. None the less, a theatre was soon possible to Boston, thanks to the speech from which we have been quoting, an effort which has been called " the most scholastic argument in defence of the stage ever written by an American." Not that the obnoxious law was repealed! With characteristic Puritan stubbornness, the Massachusetts Solons of that day steadily refused to remove the prohibition from the statute books. But Gardiner's speech had so influenced public opinion [1] that, during the summer of 1792, a few gentlemen determined to erect a theatre in Boston, in order to prove that a playhouse *need not be* the highly objectionable resort its detractors doggedly declared it.

As a devout Bostonian, I should have much preferred to record that our first theatre opened with an appreciative presentation of Shakespeare. But facts are stubborn things. I am, however, so fond as to believe that the gentlemen behind the theatre project would have preferred Shakespeare for an opening bill to the aforementioned " feats; " the reason for that curiously nondescript playbill was that they were feeling their way with the law. For almost two months " somersetts backward " and their ilk continued to be the pabulum here offered. And then, by way of transition to actual theatrical performances, came the disguised drama which we have met in other cities. " Othello," " Romeo and Juliet,"

[1] This John Gardiner, though the son of Sylvester Gardiner of Boston, had spent many of the impressionable years of his life in England — which accounts for his liberal attitude towards the theatre. His son, John Sylvester Gardiner, rector of Trinity, was " for many years the best and most influential Episcopal minister of Boston." He, too, loved the playhouse, as George Frederick Cooke discovered during his visit to Boston.

and " Hamlet " were among the Shakespeare plays thus masked and mangled in Boston. Considerable ingenuity was exercised, also, in remodelling Garrick's farce " Lethe " into a satirical lecture called " Lethe, or Æsop in the Shades," "pronounced" by Mr. Watts and Mr. and Mrs. Solomon. Otway's " Venice Preserved " was announced as a moral lecture in five parts, " in which the dreadful effect of conspiracy will be exemplified."

Growing a bit more bold, the management advertised that on October 5 " the pernicious effect of libertinism exemplified in ' the Tragical History of George Barnwell or the London Merchant ' " would be presented — still as a moral lecture, though delivered by Messrs. Harper, Morris, Watts, Murray, Solomon, Redfield, Miss Smith, Mrs. Solomon, and Mrs. Gray. Never before spoke a lecturer through so many mouths! Of course, the enemies of the theatre were not so stupid as to miss the fact that this time a real play with a good-sized cast was being presented at Board Alley. The aid of the law must be invoked to suppress such an outrage! The first attempt to do this failed, and performances continued to be given at intervals of two or three days. On November 9, Garrick's version of " The Taming of the Shrew," under the name of " Catherine and Petruchio," was presented; on the thirtieth " Hamlet " was given, with Charles Stuart Powell in the title character; and on December 3, the same actor assumed the leading rôle in " Richard III."

Then the blow fell. During a performance of " The Rivals," on December 5, Harper was arrested by Sheriff

Allen, at the end of the first act, for violating the law against theatrical presentations. The audience, which was largely composed of young men, was disposed to resent this treatment of their favourite and proceeded to tear down the seal of the United States from the proscenium arch and to cut into pieces the portrait of Governor Hancock, whose hand was seen to be behind the arrest. Only when Harper was admitted to bail would his over-strenuous friends desist from rioting and disperse to their several homes. The following day they were all loweringly on hand at a hearing given to the actor in Faneuil Hall. Perhaps it was their presence which secured for him a dismissal on the technical ground of illegality in the warrant of arrest. The fact that Harrison Gray Otis, who had hitherto opposed the theatre, was now on the side of play-acting, doubtless had its effect, also. But Hancock's opposition did not slacken in the slightest, and in a subsequent session of the Legislature, he alluded to the theatrical row as " an open assault upon the laws and government of the Commonwealth." That the people were determined to have theatrical performances, could not have failed to make itself clear even to him, however. And here again " The Contrast " came in to render its service of pacification. For that piece by a native Bostonian of irreproachable character was now given in the New Exhibition Room, — the last performance of any note to be there offered.

The experiment had been a success! The improvised theatre had served its purpose, and in the spring of 1793 it was taken down, and a movement initiated for the promotion of a playhouse on a larger scale. Subscribers to the project were found among the best people without any difficulty whatever — this in spite of the opposition of Samuel Adams, who in 1794 succeeded Hancock as governor and who, though he felt himself in ordinary matters to be simply an executive officer, stood out stubbornly as long as he lived against the popular desire for theatrical entertainments.

The new theatre was located at the corner of Federal and Franklin Streets, and with its opening on February 3, 1794, the dramatic history of Boston may be said properly to have begun. It was called the Boston Theatre (later the Federal Street Theatre) and was under the management of Charles Stuart Powell and Baker. It had been erected from plans furnished by Charles Bulfinch, then a young man, and a contemporary thus describes it:

" It was one hundred and forty feet long, sixty-two feet wide, forty feet high; a lofty and spacious edifice built of brick, with stone facings, iron posts and pillars. The entrances to the different parts of the house were distinct. In the front there was a projecting arcade which enabled carriages to land company under cover. After alighting at the main entrance, they passed through an elegant saloon to the staircases leading to the back of the boxes. The pit and gallery had separate entrances on the sides.

" The interior was circular in form, the ceiling composed of elliptical arches resting on Corinthian pillars. There were two rows of boxes, the second suspended by invisible means. The stage opening was thirty-one feet wide, ornamented on either side by two columns,

THE FEDERAL STREET THEATRE, BOSTON

See page 114

THE HAYMARKET THEATRE, BOSTON

See page 116

between which was a stage door opening on a projecting
iron balcony. Above the columns a cornice and a balustrade were carried over the stage openings; above
these was painted a flow of crimson drapery and the
arms of the United States and the commonwealth blended
with emblems tragic and comic. A ribbon depending
from the arms bore the motto, ' All the world's a
stage.'

" The boxes were hung with crimson silk, and their
balustrade gilded; the walls were tinted azure, and the
columns and fronts of the boxes straw and lilac. At the
end of the building was a noble and elegant dancing
pavilion, richly ornamented with Corinthian columns
and pilasters. There were also spacious card and tea
rooms and kitchens with the proper conveniences."

Great state was observed in performances here.
The " guests " were met by a bewigged and bepowdered
master of ceremonies and escorted to their boxes. Thence,
however, they could see the stage but dimly at best in
the feeble light of candles or by means of the more
objectionable, because smoky, illumination of whale-oil
lamps. Moreover, they might freeze in winter, for all
the effective heating apparatus provided. Very likely
it was to keep warm that the gallery gods threw things.
At any rate, the orchestra was obliged to insert a card in
the newspaper requesting the audience to be more restrained in the matter of pelting the musicians with
apple cores and oranges. The music, by the way, was
of high standard, Reinagh of Philadelphia being director.
In short, though Boston had come on slowly, it was now
conceded to possess the finest theatre in the country.

None the less, the new venture was a constantly losing one at first, and at the end of the second season Powell retired in disgust and bankruptcy. He chose to consider himself a much injured person, too, from the fact that the managers of the Boston, who were Federalists, were, as he believed, using their playhouse to offend their political opponents, the Jacobins. His grievance seemed so real to him that he was able to make it real to his friends, and they promptly set about erecting a new playhouse for him near the site of the present Tremont Theatre. This was called The Haymarket; it was opened to the public December 26, 1796, the bill offered being " The Belle's Stratagem."

Though very plain on the outside, the new house was capacious and elegant within, and if Boston had been large enough at this time to support two theatres, The Haymarket might have had a long and a prosperous career. As it was, however, the neck-and-neck race which Powell proceeded to run with the Federal Street house, at a rate of expense which was simply ruinous, soon swamped the younger venture, which lacked the financial backing of its rival.[1] At the end of a few seasons The Haymarket was abandoned, and in 1803 the building was razed.

[1] Even the destruction of the Federal Street Theatre by fire (February 2, 1798) did not seriously hamper its success. For the structure was promptly rebuilt, and it re-opened October 29, 1798, continuing as a theatre until 1835, when it was converted into a lecture room under the name of the " Odeon." It re-opened as a theatre, under its old name, in 1846. In April, 1852, it was sold and disappears from theatrical annals.

The Romance of the American Theatre

I think it has now been incontrovertibly established, that even in Boston the theatre had risen to the dignity of an " American institution," by the dawn of the nineteenth century.

CHAPTER IV

THE CURIOUS ADVENTURES OF CERTAIN EARLY ENGLISH STARS

AMERICAN managers who have written books about the stage are all agreed upon at least one point: that the downfall of profitable and artistically successful stock companies is directly traceable to the introduction of the " star " system. The employment of eminent actors for a limited period on large terms began, we are told, with the famous Mrs. Oldfield, and was next known in Garrick's and Macklin's cases. Its progress thus early however, was slow and was confined to actors of transcendent merit. In America Mrs. Henry was the first star of which we know, and in her case the distinction seems to have been due to the fact that her husband was a manager. Then followed Fennell (in 1796) for a short time, and in 1803 Cooper made a try at this experiment, succeeding so well that he was never again content to be a stock actor.

The attractiveness of these last-named tragedians created no jealous feeling among the regular performers, however, for it was recognized that there must be Hamlets and Richards and Othellos each season for a short time in every city. Nor was the unhappiness very acute when a man of Cooke's power or Kean's undeniable ability came over here to draw large houses and to take home big profits; the theatre was still the gainer, even if its manager only *shared* in the ample receipts. But by the time that a great number of stars of comparatively minor magnitude had come to America — and gone back with their profits — the managers had lost so much money that they could not even mention the starring system without bitterness. And the supporting actors were not always pleasant.[1]

None the less, since it is to the stars who have from time to time burst upon our vision that American theatregoers owe many of their most delightful hours,[2] we shall follow in this book the adventures of many of these interesting artists. Which luminaries to omit will be a puzzling question later on, but at the beginning of our chapter there is no such difficulty.

First among the stars, chronologically, as well as in interest, comes George Frederick Cooke, who was born in the city of Westminster, April 17, 1756, made his pro-

[1] One story connected with Macready's American experiences illustrates the exceeding difficulty actors from abroad sometimes had with native Americans who resented being cast for minor parts. Macready was rehearsing Hamlet with a man, who, in playing Guildenstern, continually (as bad actors are apt to do) pressed too near him. Remonstrances had no effect, and at length the offender came so very close that Macready, thoroughly exasperated, demanded: " What, sir, you would not *shake hands* with Hamlet, would you? " " I don't know," was the surly reply, " I do with my own President! "

[2] It is a fact worthy to be noted that visiting stars, such as Cooke, Kean, and Kemble, could then find over here companies of mixed English and American nationalities, fully able to support them in all the plays of their extended repertoires at all the then-existent American centres: New York, Boston, Philadelphia, New Orleans, Savannah, Baltimore, St. Louis, and Cincinnati.

fessional début with a company of strolling players at
Brentford in 1776, appeared, for one night only, at the
Haymarket Theatre, London, in the spring of 1778, and
then for a long period supported Mrs. Siddons, Mrs.
Jordan, and J. P. Kemble, contributing the while to
the development of those tragic powers which were later
to astound his auditors. On October 31, 1800, in the
forty-fifth year of his age, he first took the position he
deserved in his profession, appearing at Covent Garden
as Richard III, and leaping at once to the top round of the
ladder. During this first year of his success the desire to
eclipse " Black Jack " Kemble, the rival of all his waking
dreams, seems to have availed to keep Cooke fairly
sober, but for the next ten years — the period between
his first great success and his visit to America — his
life was punctuated with debauches which often caused
him to be hissed from the stage.

For Cooke's performance of Richard III there can
be found nothing but the highest and most enthusiastic
comment among the writers who were his contemporaries.
Crabb Robinson says that " Nature assisted him greatly
in the performance of this part, his features being strongly
marked and his voice harsh. There is besides a sort of
humour in his acting which appeared very appropriate."
Leigh Hunt pronounced Cooke " the Machiavel of
the modern stage," and Macready thought him so
peculiarly fitted to render the crooked-back tyrant that
" remembrance of him served to detract from my confidence in assuming the part." Unlike most actors who
have played Richard, Cooke never wore a hump nor

made the tyrant's legs of unequal size. This, notwithstanding the fact that these personal points are strongly marked in the text. Instead, he made Richard a "marvellous proper man," as may be seen by Sully's portrait herewith reproduced.

That the Shylock of this actor was also a very great piece of acting we have ample testimony. Lord William Pitt Lennox,[1] a devout worshipper of dramatic genius, has described for us a certain occasion in Chichester, when Cooke, though suffering considerably from his tendency to drink, played Shylock marvellously.

" Nothing," he writes, " could exceed the enthusiasm of the audience when Cooke appeared as Shylock. After a time he commenced — ' Three thousand ducats — well. For three months — well. Antonio shall be bound — well.' . . . I have seen the ' supernatural ' John

---

[1] Lord William Pitt Lennox is of interest to Americans who value theatrical gossip from the fact that he married for his first wife Mary Ann Paton, an early "queen of song." Mary Ann is said to have composed songs for publication at the tender age of five. Whether this be true or not, it is a fact that at eight she was appearing in public as a singer under the patronage of the nobility. When twenty, she joined the Haymarket company, making her début August 3, 1822, in the difficult rôle of Susanna in "The Marriage of Figaro." She was then very beautiful and had a compass from A to D or E. Not long after this Lord Lennox took her to wife; but since his fortune did not allow him to withdraw his lady from public life, difficulties ensued, and a divorce through the Scotch courts was arranged. That same year (1831) Lady Lennox married Joseph Woods, a tenor singer, with whom she subsequently made three visits to the United States, all of which were eminently successful so far, at any rate, as she was concerned. Their first appearance in America was at the Park Theatre, New York, September 9, 1833, as the Prince and Cinderella in the opera of that name. In 1843 Mrs. Woods entered a convent for a time, but she emerged to take up her operatic duties again, and when she died in 1863, she and her husband were living happily together near Manchester, England. During the height of Mrs. Woods's success, Lord Lennox often called on her behind the scenes, according to the testimony of George Vandenhoff.

Philip Kemble in ' Coriolanus,' the chivalrous Charles
as ' Faulconbridge,' the majestic Siddons as ' Con-
stance,' the classical Young as ' Brutus,' the impassioned
Kean as ' Richard the Third,' the plaintive O'Neil as
' Juliet,' the dignified Somerville as ' Hermione,' the
accomplished Macready as ' Macbeth,' the talented
Charles Kean as ' Hamlet,' the pathetic Ellen Tree as
' Desdemona,' Rachel in ' Les Horaces,' Fechter in ' La
Dame aux Camelias,' Salvini as ' Othello,' — and though
one and all in their respective characters have evinced
the finest conception, the most admirable portraiture
of the noblest creations of the Bard of Avon, they have
not erased from my mind the effect produced by George
Frederick Cooke in the delineation of ' the Jew that
Shakespeare drew.'

" But when, in the fourth act, Shylock, with balance
in hand, was gloating over his Christian victim, and
preparing to take the pound of flesh, an event occurred
that nearly paralyzed the audience. In whetting his
knife to cut the forfeiture from the bankrupt's breast,
the blade slipped and nearly severed the actor's thumb;
in a second the stage was deluged with blood. A cry
for surgical aid was raised by those who witnessed the
accident from the side boxes and front row of the pit,
and soon the curtain dropped, the manager coming
forward to request the indulgence of the audience until
the medical practitioner could decide whether Mr.
Cooke would be enabled to go through the remainder of
the performance. This appeal to the British public
produced the desired effect, and during the necessary
delay the majority consoled themselves by refreshing
the inward man with all the delicacies the house could
furnish — adulterated porter, mixed ale, flavourless gin-
ger-beer, sour cider, stale cakes, unripe apples, and acrid
plums."

After a few minutes of watchful anxiety, the manager came forward, Lennox goes on to say, and relieved the minds of the audience by reading a bulletin to the effect that *tetanus* need by no means be feared, and the performance would soon be resumed.

The manner in which Cooke was persuaded to come to America is quite an interesting tale. It was long said that he was kidnapped while drunk and brought over here! Certain it is that Cooper offered him twenty-five guineas a week for ten months, to play at New York, Boston, Philadelphia, and Baltimore, with a benefit at each place and twenty-five cents a mile for travelling expenses between the above-mentioned cities. His passage over the Atlantic was also assured outside of his profits. Cooke was glad to accept this offer but had to be spirited away by Cooper in one of his rare sober spells, lest the eccentric tragedian change his mind about making the trip. Moreover, though Cooper did not know it Cooke was engaged to Manager Henry Harris of London for the very time he was contracting to appear in America. The London papers condemned both actors severely for their business arrangement, but agreed that " to visit America was punishment sufficient for any crime. ' They are both transported, and let justice be satisfied.'"[1]

Cooke's own sober impressions of America are to be found in the following letter which he sent back to his friend Incledon:

[1] " Memoirs of Life of George Frederick Cooke," by William Dunlap: New York, 1813.

"Boston, New England (North America)
"Jan. 14, 1811.
"DEAR SIR: —

"This is the first letter I have written to Europe, from which my departure was only the result of a few hours' deliberation. On the 4th of October last, I sailed from Liverpool, and arrived at New-York on the 16th of November. The latter part of the voyage very tempestuous and many vessels lost. I was received by Mr. Price, one of the managers, in a very friendly and hospitable manner, and at whose house I remained while I continued in that city. On Wednesday, the 21st of November, I made my first appearance before an American audience, and was received by a splendid and crowded assemblage in a most flattering manner.[1] I acted seventeen nights to some of the greatest houses ever known in the New World. My own night exceeded four hundred guineas.

"On the 29th of December, in company with Mr. Price, I sailed in one of the best passage boats I ever saw, for Newport, Rhode Island, which we reached, after a most pleasant trip, in 22 hours; and after a short stay, left it in a commodious carriage for this town. We slept on Sunday at Taunton, and arrived here on Monday. My first appearance on Thursday following in the *new* play of Richard, which was repeated the next night. This was also my first play in New-York, where they had it three times, and so will the good people here. The house filled as at New-York, and my reception equally flattering. New-York is the handsomest and largest house. We return to that city on Saturday, the 29th, and about the 10th of March journey on to Philadelphia, from thence to Baltimore, where my engage-

[1] For this performance of Richard III at the Park Theatre, the receipts were $1155.

124

ment ends; but I shall return to New-York, to embark for Liverpool. My time was passed at the last mentioned city in a most agreeable manner, as almost every day, not of business, we had parties at Mr. Price's, or at the houses of some of the principal inhabitants. We are going on the same way here, with this exception, we are lodged at the Exchange Coffee-house, one of the largest and most extraordinary buildings I ever saw, and of consequence I miss and regret the kind, polite attention of Mrs. P. at whose house I imagined myself in my own, and feel highly gratified at the near prospect of returning to it. Mr. Bernard is one of the managers here; but I believe retires from it at the conclusion of the season. Theatricals are conducted at both theatres in a very respectable manner, and the companies superior to what I expected to meet — I may add, much so.

" G. F. COOKE."

The *couleur de rose* descriptions here embalmed were very annoying to Cooke when, in due time, an American paper copied from the London sheet, to which Incledon had promptly given this letter, the English actor's *early* impressions of the New World; by this time, Cooke was finding the restraints incident to being a guest of the Prices most annoying to one of his habits. For the " frequent entertainments " to which his letter refers were still being kept up. One, a tea-party at the paternal home of John Howard Payne, author of " Home, Sweet Home," Dunlap describes as follows:

" When Master Payne arrived with a coach to convey him to the tea-party, Cooke was charged much higher with wine than with wit. He was, however, dressed, and as he thought prepared, and it would not do on his companion's part to suggest anything to the contrary. . . . They arrived, and Cooke . . . was introduced into a large circle of gentlemen, distinguished for learning, or wit, or taste; and ladies equally distinguished for those acquirements and endowments most valued in their sex. A part of the property of the tragedian, which had been seized by the custom-house officials under the non-importation law, had not yet been released, owing to some delay from necessary form, and this was a constant subject of irritation to him, particularly that they should withhold from him the celebrated cups presented to him by the Liverpool managers; and now his introductory speech among his expecting circle was addressed to one of the gentlemen with whom he was acquainted, and was an exclamation without any prefatory matter of ' they have stolen my cups.'

" The astonishment of such an assembly may be imagined. . . . His cups triumphed over every image subsequently presented to his imagination. ' Madam, they have stopped my cups. . . . And my Shakespeare — they had better keep that: they need his instruction and may improve by him — if they know how to read him.'

" Seeing a print of Kemble in Rolla, he addressed it: ' Ah, John, are you there! ' then, turning to Master Payne, he in his half whispering manner added: ' I don't want to die in this country — John Kemble will laugh.'

" Among the company was an old and tried revolutionary officer — a true patriot of '76. Hearing Cooke rail against the country and the government, he at first began to explain and then to defend; but soon finding what his antagonist's situation was, he ceased opposition. Cooke continued his insolence, and finding that he was unnoticed, and even what he said in the shape of query unattended to, he went on: ' That's right, you are prudent — the government may hear of it — walls have ears.'

" Tea was repeatedly presented to him, which he refused. The little black girl with her *server* next offered him cake — this he rejected with some asperity. Fruit was offered to him and he told the girl that he was ' sick of seeing her face.' Soon after, she brought him wine. ' Why, you little black angel,' says Cooke, taking the wine, ' you look like the devil, but you bear a passport that would carry you unquestioned into paradise.'"

No wonder the company "separated early."

Many and noted were Cooke's little pleasantries of this kind while in society. In Baltimore a gentleman in whose home he was being entertained chanced to observe that his family were among the first settlers of Maryland. " Have you carefully preserved the family jewels? " inquired Cooke blandly. " Why, what do you mean? " questioned his host. " The chains and handcuffs! " was the visitor's reply.

It was at Baltimore, too, on being informed that Mr. Madison, the President of the United States, purposed to come from Washington to see him act, he declared violently: " If he does, I'll be damned if I play before him. What? I! George Frederick Cooke! who have acted before the Majesty of Britain, play before your Yankee president! No!—I'll go forward to the audience, and I'll say, ' Ladies and gentlemen — the king of the Yankee doodles has come to see me act. Me, me, George

Frederick Cooke! who have stood before my royal master, George the Third, and received his imperial approbation! And shall I expect myself to play before one of his rebellious subjects, who arrogates kingly state in defiance of his master? No, it is degrading enough to play before rebels, but I will not go on for the amusement of a king of rebels, the contemptible king of the Yankee doodles! ' ''

That Cooke consented to marry a daughter of the " Yankee doodles " seems only less remarkable than that he was sober long enough to go through a wedding ceremony. His biographer says that Mrs. Bahn, to whom he was united in New York on June 20, 1811, " proved to be a faithful help-mate and affectionate nurse to the day of his death." [1] The period of her service was only a little over a year, for he died at Bixby's Hotel, New York, September 26, 1812, aged fifty-seven years and five months.

His remains were buried in a vault beneath St. Paul's Church, where they rested nine years. In 1821, however, Edmund Kean, who was then acting over here, caused them to be disinterred and laid in a grave in the church-

---

[1] Mrs. Cooke, after her husband's death, kept a boarding-house which was much liked by theatrical and artistic people. Joe Cowell, who first came to New York in 1821, tells of a dinner he enjoyed there the Sunday after his arrival, as the guest of Edmund Simpson, one of the managers of the Park Theatre. " Simpson had only been married a short time, and, like myself and others, was waiting till the first of May to go into housekeeping; but he gave a very handsome dinner, on Sunday, at his boarding-house, kept by the widow of George Frederick Cooke, where I met Price's two brothers, William and Edward Noah, Jarvis, the celebrated painter, and most eccentric character, and a large party of gentlemen."

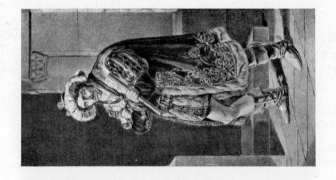

EDMUND KEAN
See page 133

THREE GREAT RICHARDS
JUNIUS BRUTUS BOOTH
See page 165

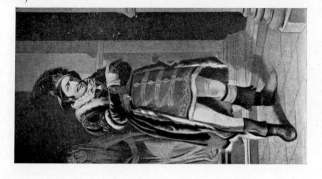

GEORGE FREDERICK COOKE
See page 120

EDMUND KEAN AS OTHELLO
After a drawing from life by John William Gear
See page 132

yard over which he erected the tomb [1] which has since
been repaired, first by Charles Kean, and later (in 1874)
by E. A. Sothern. At the time of this disinterment,
Kean carried off the toe-bone of Cooke, and Dr.
Francis, for phrenological purposes, took possession
of the great tragedian's skull. Once, several years
afterwards, this very skull was used at the Park Theatre
in a performance of "Hamlet," having been lent to
the management, in an emergency, by Cooke's old
friend, Francis.

Of Edmund Kean, who first came to our shores in
1820, Coleridge once felicitously remarked that "seeing
Kean act was like reading Shakespeare by flashes of
lightning" — so brilliant and so startling were the sudden illuminations, and so murky the dull intervals.
George Henry Lewes ranked Kean with Rachel only,
"who was as a woman what he was as a man," and declared him incomparably the greatest actor he had ever
seen, although admitting that he had "many and serious
defects." An artist, however, should be judged not by
his faults, but by his excellencies, and a man who was filled
with such passionate energy when on the stage that he
could throw Lord Byron into a fit (as happened once
when the poet had been witnessing Kean's rendering

[1] Kean was very proud of this service which he was able to render
Cooke, and once, after his own return from America, he requested a
guest at a supper-party he was giving, to make an epitaph for the stone.
Of course he expected something which would couple his name, in
complimentary fashion, with that of the great Cooke. What he got,
however, was this — according to George Vandenhoff, who preserves the
story:

"Beneath this stone lies Cooke interr'd;
And *with* him, — Shakespeare's Dick The Third!"

of the part of Sir Giles Overreach) certainly possessed powers of no ordinary kind.

It has been said that Kean owed nothing to his parents but his birth; and this is almost literally true, for the woman who was supposed to be his mother gave him scarcely any care at all, and for such sporadic " bringing up " as fell to his lot he was indebted to a Miss Tidswell, an actress connected with Drury Lane, who called herself his aunt. The date of the lad's birth is usually given as 1787, and it is known that when a mere baby he appeared on the stage of old Drury as Cupid. What scant schooling he received was at a small day establishment in Soho; but from this he ran away, as, indeed, he continued all his life to do from whatever of restraint or duty chanced to fall to his lot. The precarious life of a strolling actor was his throughout boyhood and youth, the name under which he played at this period being that of his reputed mother, Miss Carey. His twenty-first birthday, however, found him married — to an actress with whom for the next few years he underwent almost unbelievable hardships. Once husband and wife tramped over a hundred and fifty miles from one town where they had been playing to another town where they had succeeded in securing a fairly promising engagement. It was during this period of terrible privation that the actor's two sons were born, one of whom, Howard, died in infancy as a result of want and exposure. Edmund Kean knew thoroughly at this period the pangs of grinding poverty. Yet he felt within himself those great powers which were soon to be acclaimed by the world, and he never once lost his determination to climb to the very top of his profession.

Kean has himself written vividly the story of his early experiences in England. On a certain night in the year 1814 he was playing at Dorchester and " when the curtain drew up," he says, " I saw a wretched house: a few persons in the pit and gallery and three persons in the boxes. In the stage box, however, there was a gentleman who appeared to understand acting — he was very attentive to the performance. Seeing this, I was determined to play my best. The strange man did not applaud but his looks told me that he was pleased." Later in the evening this " strange gentleman," who proved to be the manager of the Drury Lane Theatre, asked Kean to breakfast with him the following day, — and a London offer followed duly.

At first London was cold to this miserable, half-starved actor from the provinces, but before the end of Kean's Shylock, that first night, his auditors perceived that a very great actor was there before them. " The pit rose at me," was his own oft-quoted description of his triumph.

" A man who asserts his claim to suffer as one of a race of sufferers " was this Shylock. Kean understood being " spat upon." A writer in *Blackwood's Magazine* seems to appreciate this.

" Edmund Kean," he says, "was an extraordinary actor and an extraordinary man. Without any advantages of education, and perhaps with all the disadvantages that could beset a birth and youth of poverty and desertion — for he seems never to have known who his father was, and even his mother's identity was doubtful — he yet struggled through difficulties that might have destroyed a mind of less energy, until he achieved triumphant success. With no recommendation of person — a low and meagre figure, a Jewish physiognomy, a stifled and husky voice — he seemed to be excluded by nature from all chance of personating tragedy; yet at his first step on the London stage he was acknowledged to be the founder of a new school, to give new meaning to some of the highest characters of Shakespeare; to refresh the feelings and change the worship of those who had for a quarter of a century bowed down to the supremacy of the Kembles; and finally to pour a new and most welcome flood of wealth into the long-exhausted treasury of the theatre."

For while the Kemble school was acknowledged to be magnificent and majestic, Kean was declared a school by himself, a school whose spirit was vividness, poignancy, and intensity. Fanny Kemble once very touchingly paid tribute to the unique powers of this man who eclipsed her father.

" Kean is gone and with him are gone *Othello, Shylock*, and *Richard*. I have lived among those whose theatrical creed would not permit them to acknowledge him as a great actor; but they must be bigoted, indeed, who would deny that he was a great genius — a man of most original and striking powers, careless of art, perhaps because he did not need it, but possessing those rare gifts of nature without which art is a dead body. Who that ever heard will ever forget the beauty, the unutterable tenderness of his reply to Desdemona's entreaties for Cassio, ' Let him come when he will; I can deny thee nothing; ' the deep despondency of his ' Oh, now farewell; ' the miserable anguish of his ' Oh, Desdemona, away, *away!* ' Who that ever saw will ever forget the fascination of his dying eyes in Richard when, deprived of his sword, the wondrous power of his look seemed yet to avert the unlifted arm of Richmond. If he was irregular and unartistlike in his performance, so is Niagara, compared with the waterworks of Versailles."

In the course of his first season at Drury Lane, Kean played sixty-eight nights to audiences of unprecedented size. His own share of the profits was upward of twenty thousand pounds. Such an immediate reward had never before fallen to the lot of an actor. Nor did his recompense come in the form of money only. Mrs. Garrick took a very great interest in him and endeavoured to coach him so that he might play his rôles after the manner of " dear David; " he was enormously praised by the critics, and many of the nobility sent him splendid presents. One distinguished personage even gave him a white elephant — in the form of a lion! Kean passed a large part of his time at this period attempting to educate this lion to accommodate himself to conditions in Lady Ryecroft's house in Clarges Street, which the actor had rented when prosperity dawned.

Kean's tour through America, where he opened at the Anthony Street Theatre, New York, November 29, 1820, as Richard III, was one continued march of triumph — until his quarrel with the people of Boston late in May, 1821. Upon a previous visit to the New England city, where he opened February 12, 1821, as Richard III, he was received by a huge and highly enthusiastic audience. His acting was the all-engrossing topic of fashionable discussion, and he became the lion of the day. Great pressure was brought to bear upon him to prolong his engagement, which had been for a strictly limited number of performances, but inasmuch as he was booked elsewhere, he had to leave, though regretfully, what he styled in his curtain speech on the last night as " the Literary Emporium of the New World." When he next found it convenient to tuck a few Boston performances into his schedule, it was approaching June, and many Boston folk were out of town. The manager of the theatre told him this and tried to dissuade him from coming, but Kean replied that he could draw at any time, and it seemed that he was right, for on the first night of this second visit, " King Lear " being the offering, a very fair house was out. On the second night the audience was slim, however; and on the third, when he was billed as Richard III, he could count only twenty people in front upon looking through the curtain at seven o'clock. Whereupon he refused to prepare for the performance and left in a rage for his hotel.

Scarcely had he gone when the boxes filled up, and a messenger was dispatched to bring him back. But he declined to come, and the manager was obliged to explain that his star's refusal to appear was for want of patronage. Of course those present were not pleased, and the newspapers had a great deal to say, next day,

134

about the scornful way the tragedian had treated his public. Accounts of the affair spread to New York, and Kean feared a riot.[1] So he published in the *New York National Advocate* a letter in which he endeavoured to justify himself at the expense of Boston audiences. " My advisers never intimated to me," he caustically observed, " that the theatres were only visited during certain months of the year; that when curiosity had subsided, dramatic talent was not in estimation." For this fling he had to pay dearly, as we shall see, when he next attempted — during his second visit to America — to win the favour of a Boston audience.

A discriminating critic somewhere speaks of the quality of Kean's voice, when on the stage, as " the music of a broken heart — the cry of a despairing soul." Such seems, indeed, to have been true of this great actor. He was his own worst enemy — and he knew it. Soon he became so careless of consequences that even the public that had long loved him and borne patiently with his faults, forsook him. Which brings us to the immediate cause of Kean's second visit to America (in 1825): the disgrace into which he had fallen in England on account of his relations with the wife of a London alderman named Cox. Her reputation was not immaculate and her husband appears to have remained blind a singularly

[1] These disagreements between Kean and his audiences in " the States " did not help him at all, rather curiously, with his public at home. A London critic observed, after his return, that " Kean's squabbles with American managers have been as much protruded upon the public as if they afforded grounds for another American war." Another critic caustically commented on the evident conviction of Kean that he had been " the special representative of Shakespeare in America."

long time — so far as Kean was concerned — before suing the actor for the alienation of his wife's affections. He won his suit, however, and immediately after the trial, the fickle public began to greet with hisses in the theatre this man whose work they had long acclaimed. The fact that Kean gave them scorn for scorn naturally did not help matters. At Edinburgh they hooted him from the stage, and in London, on one occasion, he was grudgingly allowed to say his lines after making this remarkable speech to his turbulent auditors: " If you expect from me a vindication of my private conduct, I fear I shall be unable to furnish one to your satisfaction. I stand before you as the representative of Shakespeare's heroes. The errors I have committed have been scanned by a public tribunal. In that investigation, feelings of delicacy prevented the disclosure of circumstances which might have changed the complexion of the case. This proceeded from feelings for others, not for myself. It appears that I stand before you, ladies and gentlemen, a professional victim. I apprehend that this is not done by your verdict. If it is done by a hostile press I shall endeavour to withstand it — if it is your verdict, I shall bow to your decision, remember with gratitude your former favours, and leave you."

The opposition continuing — and an invitation to make a second visit to America opportunely intervening — Kean decided to carry out his threat and leave. His wife had separated herself from him and was living on an allowance of £200 a year; Charles, who was still in Eton, but had already — to his father's immense disgust — begun to display signs of stage talent, sided with his mother. The boy was now cut off without a penny, and the mother's stipend was also withheld! Thus, Charles Kean, at sixteen, found himself forced to go on the stage to help support his mother. Barry Cornwall, who visited the elder Kean on the eve of this second trip to America, records that the actor " had all the air of desperation about him, and that his mind seemed shattered." He was, in truth, on the very edge, now, of insanity.

As might have been expected, this tour added nothing to Kean's American reputation. In Boston, where his previous slighting of his audience had been neither forgotten nor forgiven, he was received with hisses and with a fusilade of missiles both hard and soft. This, too, after he had apologized for his previous conduct as follows:

" To the editor, Sir, I take the liberty of informing the citizens of Boston (through the medium of your journal) of my arrival in confidence that liberality and forbearance will gain the ascendency over prejudice and cruelty. That I have suffered for my errors, my loss of fame and fortune is too melancholy an illustration. Acting from the impulse of irritation, I certainly was disrespectful to the Boston public; calm deliberation convinces me I was wrong. The first step towards the throne of mercy is confession — the hope we are taught, forgiveness. Man must not expect more than those attributes which we offer to God.

" EDMUND KEAN.

" Exchange Coffee House.
" Dec. 21, 1825."

Though Kean was not received in every city as he was in Boston, he was very glad to return to England after two seasons of America — and he never came over here again. He died, May 15, 1833, after having shown his forgiveness of his son by being willing to act with him, and having been reconciled to his wife by means of the following pathetic letter, written when death was very near:

> " Thursday.
>
> " MY DEAR MARY, Let us no longer be fools. Come home. Forget and forgive. If I have erred it was my head, not my heart, and most severely have I suffered for it. My future life shall be employed in contributing to your happiness; and you, I trust, will return that feeling, by a total obliteration of the past.
>
> " Your wild,
> " But really affectionate husband,
> " EDMUND KEAN.
>
> " Theatre Royal,
> " Richmond."

Kean passionately desired to be the last of his name to be mentioned in the annals of the stage. It was, therefore, a really terrible blow to him when he first learned that his son was resolved to go on the stage. Actual evidence that the important step was about to be taken reached him at Glasgow in the form of a playbill announcing the opening of the winter season at old Drury on Monday, October 1, 1827, and further declaiming that " Mr. Charles Kean, son of the celebrated tragedian, Edmund Kean, would then make his first appearance on any stage as Young Norval." The father was so overcome by this intelligence as to be quite unable to play for a time. When he recovered, he sent for his secretary and instructed him to go up to London at once, to secure a front seat in the pit for the night, " and never take your eyes off Charles while he is on the stage. Watch every movement, look and gesture, scan him well — and as soon as the performance is over, take the first conveyance you can find, and come back here and let me know the result. I shall take no other account of it but yours, and I shall sleep but little until you return."

The special messenger in due time came back with the report that, although young Kean had not been hissed at, he was " no great success."

Charles Kean, himself, thoroughly understood that he had not shed any glory on the illustrious name of Kean by this first performance of his, and, as soon as he could manage it, he set out to try his fortunes and enlarge his stage experience in the New World. Thus he made his first bow to the American public at the Park Theatre, New York, September 1, 1830, as Richard III, and for nearly two years and a half continued to play over here. But he had returned to London, as has been said, in time to appear with his father at Covent Garden (March 25, 1833), the elder Kean then playing Othello, the younger Iago, and Miss Ellen Tree, whom Charles later made his wife, acting the part of Desdemona. For eight or nine years after his father's death, Charles Kean worked hard and conscientiously at his profession, constantly gaining in power and popularity in his own country as well as in America. Four times in all he was over here in the course of his life, and always he was much liked. His wife, too, was popular here as well as in London. After her first American tour, which began in December, 1836, and lasted three years, she carried home twelve thousand pounds in cash. It was her sister Maria who, as Clari in Payne's opera of the same name, made "Home, Sweet Home" a great popular success.

Ellen Tree's own " sweet home," after her marriage, was in the house on Gerrard Street, Soho, which had formerly belonged to Edmund Burke, and here she and her husband gave frequent parties that were attended by many persons of distinction. The admiration Kean excited among the ladies of fashion was, however, a source of great disquietude to Mrs. Kean, and she was wont, during her frequent fits of jealousy, to absent herself from home — go into the country. " At least this was her idea," says Lord William Pitt Lennox, who preserves this bit of gossip, but the limit of her journey was Bayswater, then a medley of suburban cottages and market-gardens, long since obliterated by the brick and mortar of Tyburnia. The manager of the theatre in which both had engagements was well aware of their quarrels and separations, and on one occasion, by way of remedy, cast both of them for the two principal characters in ' The Jealous Wife.' They played the parts with spirit and for that time were reconciled." These two were very much in love with each other and so remained as long as they both lived. For, though Macready once contemptuously dubbed Charles Kean " the son of his father," he was really a great deal more than that as well as something less. In moral worth, Charles Kean was blameless, upright and honourable, infinitely his father's superior. And as manager of the Princess's Theatre in Oxford Street, a post which he assumed in 1850, he did the stage a great service by mounting Shakespeare in a nearly perfect manner. His company here was a very strong one, too, particularly so far as pretty women was concerned, — Ellen Terry, Agnes Robertson, and Carlotta Leclerq being among those who in their youth profited by Charles Kean's instruction.

Unhappily, this younger Kean had a bronchial trouble of long standing which marred his pronunciation and made him an easy prey of the wits. *Punch*, dwelling upon his inherent difficulties with his m's and his n's, once paid tribute to the " antiquarian researches by which he had made Shylock a vegetarian! " It is undeniable that Charles Kean, in this part, again and again said:

" You take my house when you do take the prop
That doth sustain my house; you take my life
When you do take the *beans* whereby I live."

CHAPTER V

THE ENTERTAINING OBSERVATIONS OF THE FIRST CHARLES MATHEWS

CHARLES MATHEWS, SR., who came to New York for the first time in 1822, was frightened nearly out of his wits, Dr. John W. Francis [1] tells us, by discovering that he had arrived just as the city was in the grip of one of its periodic attacks of yellow fever. There had been a great deal of joking in England over Mathews's determination to see what an American trip could do in the way of recouping his recent financial losses, and the comedian's friends had entertained themselves by quoting to him Doctor Johnson's opinion on the subject of the country across the sea: " Is not America worth seeing? " " Yes, sir," replied Johnson, " but not worth going to see." None the less, Mathews decided to make the trip, and, as we read his letters home, we are very glad that he had the courage of his desires. No more lively descriptions of certain phases of life here may anywhere be found. From Hoboken, New Jersey, he sent back his first letter to his wife (on September 6, 1822), in which he announced his safe arrival " after a most delightful passage of thirty-five days."

[1] In his " Old New York."

New York was in no mood for him just then, however, — nor he for it; so Baltimore was quickly sought, the visitor being kept in ignorance that that place, too, was undergoing the scourge. Here, none the less, Mathews made his début on the American stage, Monday, September 23, 1822, the vehicle chosen being his " Trip to Paris."

His success was immediate. When he gave his song, " London now is out of Town," to the music of the American national air, he received instant proof that he had " made a hit."

" They roared and screeched," he wrote his wife, " as if they had never heard anything comical before; and I don't think they have been glutted in that way. I discovered the never-to-be-mistaken token of pocket handkerchiefs crammed into the mouths of many of the pitt-ites. I had only to hold up my crooked finger when I wanted them to laugh, and they obeyed my call. I was most agreeably surprised, indeed, at finding them an audience of infinitely more intelligence and quickness than I had expected. Bartley had shrugged his shoulders at the idea of their taking the jokes. One of the London papers said I should be lost here; . . . but the neatest and best points were never better appreciated, even in London; and I am quite certain, from the effects, that the French language is generally much more understood here than in England."

None the less, there were a good many people in Baltimore at this time who would not go to the theatre, as Mathews soon found out. Consequently, it was arranged that when he made his return trip to the city, he should take the Assembly Rooms; "for there are persons who will not go into a theatre but would not object to a room, I am told." He bore away a very large sum for those days, from Baltimore. "My benefit," he wrote home, "produced one thousand dollars — a greater house by one hundred dollars than Cooke or Kean had. This has satisfied me of the actual enthusiasm of the Americans towards me."

Washington was the next city visited, "where the greatest house ever known before was $380. I had $550 and crowds went away. I played a second night and, under peculiar disadvantages, got $350; a very small theatre. My next (letter) will give you an account of a splash, for of New York I am most sanguine."

It was, indeed, a "splash!" Mathews's manager, Price, had the good sense to see that New York must be broken gently to the peculiar humour of this "star," and so insisted that he appear first in "the regular drama." Thus, it was as Goldfinch, in "The Road to Ruin," that England's greatest comedian first dawned upon a New York audience. Let us follow his own sprightly account of the occasion.

"Nothing could be more brilliant and decisive than my success. I opened to the greatest stock house ever known, — much greater than that of Cooke or Kean. Nearly 1800 dollars! My reception was more than rapturous; I never recollect anything more joyous in my life. They infused me with fun; I was in tip-top spirits and the songs were hailed with shouts. The *Tonson*

A "FIRST NIGHT" AT THE SECOND PARK THEATRE, NEW YORK, IN 1822.
THE ELDER CHARLES MATHEWS IS SHOWN ON THE STAGE
From a water-color drawing made by John Searle for William Bayard, Esq., in the posses-
sion of the New York Historical Society

See page 144

EXTERIOR OF THE PARK THEATRE, NEW YORK

From a drawing by C. Burton

[the rôle he assumed in the afterpiece] was equal in effect to the most successful of my former personations; and at the dropping of the curtain, huzzas cheered my efforts. The whole tone of my future proceedings will be taken from this night, for New York is the London of America."

An actor's benefit was then the test of his popularity, and that Mathews drew heavily when that occasion came around proved him unmistakably a success — more especially since the night was a very unpropitious one. To his wife the next day he wrote:

"I shall always think last night the greatest compliment ever paid me. The torrents of rain which fell during the whole day (and we in England don't know what rain is) would have totally destroyed the house in any town in which I have ever been. I had to wait for a hackney coach until the time I ought to have been on the stage; but walking was out of the question as nothing short of drowning appeared inevitable. It was thought by all that it would injure the house very materially as scarcely any private carriages are kept here. When I went in, to my great surprise as well as delight, Price said, ' Well, Sir, here they are. Your house is full. This is the greatest compliment ever paid to an actor in New York. I don't believe there is any other man that would have had such a house as this on such a night.' There were 1800 dollars, which is nearly as much as the house will hold. The rain must have done some injury else it would have overflowed instead of being full; and I believe that is all the difference. No enthusiasm ever was greater. . . . I look upon the remainder of my work as a settled point. All other towns will take their tone from this, as in England from London; and the curiosity to see me is such that Cooper and Phillips, the only stars excepting Booth, say that they fail because the people are hoarding up their dollars to see me. I send you a copy of a few lines in the newspaper of Wednesday. ' A very handsome compliment has been paid to Mathews such as cannot soon be forgotten by him. We learn that a party of gentlemen have chartered the steam-boat, *The Fly*, to bring them down from Albany (two hundred miles) to his benefit to-morrow evening; thus making a journey for one evening.' Another unsought puff which has caught my eye is this: ' The proprietors of the Brooklyn boat inform the public, that the steam-vessels *Fulton* and *Active*, will on the occasion of Mr. Mathews' benefit, start from Brooklyn at half-past five, and remain to carry the passengers back after the play.' These boats never cross the ferry after five on other occasions. Does this not look well? "

The social attentions Mathews received were likewise very gratifying to him. In London he had frequently dined informally with the king and was, of course, sought after in all the leading professional and artistic circles. Yet he informs his wife that " in point of compliments paid to an actor of reputation they are here far beyond our own country. Letters of recommendation are unnecessary. Generals, commodores (admirals here), judges, barristers, and merchants, have left their cards for me. Judge Irving, a brother of Washington

Irving, called, and introduced himself. Had I time and inclination I might get into a round of visiting in the very highest society, which is much more desirable and infinitely more polished than the English in general are willing to believe."

One attention, bestowed upon him in New York, which Mathews did not particularly enjoy — though with characteristic humour he made the best of it both personally and professionally — was that of the Rev. Paschal N. Strong, a preacher of the Dutch Reformed Church, who in a sermon called " The Pestilence — A Punishment For Public Sins " asserted that the coming of this actor was the cause of the yellow fever scourge! By a most amusing anachronism, as Mathews pointed out, this pious person made the drawing of crowds together in November one of the causes of a pestilence which began in July. Let us, however, read the clergyman's own words. No better commentary could be found on the attitude of a certain section of New York society of that day towards the theatre and all for which it stood.

" Must we not conclude that the spirit of dissipation is deeply rooted among us, when we find at this very time (when our inhabitants are called more solemnly than ever they were before to consider their ways and humble themselves before God), the *theatre*, — that school of Satan! — that nursery for Hell! is overflowing night after night with our citizens, to witness the mimicries of an actor whom God Almighty has sent here at this very time in his wrath, as a man better qualified by all accounts than any other in the world to dissipate every serious reflection, and harden men in folly and sin? If such be our spirit as a community have we not deserved God's chastisements? Can we not find in this thirst after dissipation a fruitful cause of our late calamity? "

Of course a wit like Mathews could not let this kind of thing pass by unimproved! The reverend gentleman promptly received a pleasant letter announcing that the actor intended to make him a prominent feature of his next English entertainment, and thanking him heartily for all that he had done for this visitor in the way of free advertisement! Here is the letter:

"New York, 1823.

" Sir, —

" Ingratitude being in my estimation a crime most heinous and most hateful, I cannot quit the shores of America without expressing my grateful sense of services which you have gratuitously rendered.

" Other professors in ' that school of Satan, that nursery for Hell!' as you most appropriately style the theatre, have been *ex necessitate*, content to have their merits promulgated through the medium of the public papers; but mine you have graciously vouchsafed to blazon from the pulpit.

" You have, as appears in your recently published sermon, declared me to be (what humility tells me I only am in your partial and prejudiced estimation) ' an actor whom God Almighty sent here as a man better qualified than any other in the world to dissipate every serious reflection.'

" What man! what woman! what child! could resist

148

the effects of such a description, coming from such a quarter? particularly as you at the same time assured the laughter-loving inhabitants of this city that the punishment incident to such a ' thirst after dissipation ' had been already inflicted by ' their late calamity,' the pestilence ' voracious in its thirst of prey! ' and you might have added thirsty in its hunger for drink. No wonder that the theatre has since been crowded, the manager enriched, and the most sanguine expectations of him whom you have, perhaps improperly, elevated to the rank of the avenging angel, so beautifully described by Addison, completely realized! For each and all of these results accept, reverend sir, my cordial and grateful thanks. Nor deem me too avaricious of your favours if I venture to solicit more. As you have expressly averred, in the sermon before me, that ' God burnt the theatre of New York, to rebuke the devotees of pleasure there resident,' permit me, your humble avenging angel, to inquire, by whom and for what purpose the cathedrals at Rouen and Venice were recently destroyed by fire, and in a manner which more especially implicated the hand of Providence? But, beware, most reverend sir, I conjure you, lest your doctrines of special dispensations furnish arguments and arms to the scoffer and atheist.

" One other request and I have done. You appear to be too well acquainted with my peculiarities and propensities not to be aware that, when I travel abroad, I am always anxious to collect something original and funny wherewith to entertain my friends and patrons ' AT HOME.' Now, sir, so little do the American people, in general, differ from their parent stock, whom it is my object to amuse, that I have as yet scarcely procured anything in which these qualities are united, except your aforesaid sermon; you will, therefore, infinitely oblige me if you will, on Sunday next, preach another on the subject of my angelic attributes, in which case you may rely on my being a most attentive auditor. I hope to have the opportunity of studying the peculiarities of your style and action. The gracefulness of Christian charity, humility and universal benevolence, which doubtless beam in your expressive countenance, will enable me to produce a picture of prodigious effect, of which all who know the original will acknowledge the likeness to be *strong!*

"I have, sir, the honour to be, most gratefully your obliged, angelic, yellow-fever producing friend,

"C. MATHEWS."

Boston was the next city which Mathews took by storm. He made the journey from New York by way of Providence, taking the water route, because told it would be "most pleasant and convenient." It proved to be neither, the time consumed being from nine o'clock Thursday morning until late Monday evening! Thus he had to disappoint the audience which awaited him in Boston on Monday. Mathews's quaint way of putting the situation is: "I could not possibly arrive until Tuesday though Phillips had cold beef ready for me and waited dinner on Sunday." He did reach his destination in time to enjoy a Christmas-day dinner in real English style, however, as the guest of the British Consul, and to his great delight, his Tuesday audience proved most cordial.

"They huzzaed when the curtain fell," he gleefully wrote Mrs. Mathews, "and the theatre was crammed. No money is taken here at the doors; and, as in Paris, tickets are issued only for the number the theatre will hold. On great occasions (of which only four have occurred, Cooke, Phillips, Kean, and myself) people speculate in buying up tickets. It is mobbing work to purchase them. So that the elbowing and overflowing symptoms are displayed of a morning instead of an evening. People who dislike this ceremony as much as I, employ porters, brawny fellows, chairmen, who frequently remain there all night. When they have purchased a number of tickets at a dollar each, they will sell them to the highest bidder; and four or six dollars are sometimes given. Last night is a proof that this theatre is not great enough for great occasions, as a repeated performance refilled the house and fellows took their station at twelve o'clock on Thursday night, and remained till the box-door opened to-day. Nothing can be more rapturous than my reception; and having made my hit here, the thing is established beyond reach of alarm or suspicion. The Bostonians have given themselves a name as critics, and it is said by themselves that this is more like an English town than any in America, — more literary people, better polished; and larger cities look up much to their opinion. Kean, in one of his speeches from the stage, called it a literary emporium. I shall stay here nearly a month longer and then back to New York. I can hardly hold my pen as I write — it is so cold. *You* have never seen ice, nor felt frost. My water-jug was frozen this morning. The ice was so thick that I could not break it with one of the legs of a chair. I am, thank God, so well that I bear it better than the natives — decidedly."

This winter of 1822–1823 must have been one of the " old-fashioned " ones, towards which our grandparents yearn. For Mathews can talk of little else than the cold and the sleighs, which were a novelty to him.

" Because of the bells on the horses," he declares, " this town is one continued scene of what they call merriment. But as neither small or large bells can convey such a sentiment to me, I have no other idea but a disagreeable ringing in my ears. If the poor horses are annoyed as I am I pity them." Nor could they inveigle the comedian to join in the sport, his invariable reply being that *sleighing* and *killing* were synonymous terms with him.

One letter to Mrs. Mathews is dated " Boston alias Frozen Regions, January 12, 1823 " and begins: " If you can hold a pen, dare to go from one room to another, or to open your mouth without fear of your words being frozen up — if you can exert any of your energies, then pity me as I envy you in such a case. This is the most trying climate that I ever imagined. In short, all you have read of Russia will apply to it. . . . I can only make myself happy by anticipating a thaw, and death to their mad frolics in their sleighs. They whisk along at the rate of about twelve miles an hour, and in open carriages like the half of a boat. So fond are they of the sport, that it is common for parties to go out at night ten or fifteen miles to adjacent villages, dance there and then return in these open sleighs. Funny people! "

Mathews's powers of imitation were so extraordinary that even his friends enjoyed seeing themselves as he reproduced them. There is no reflection upon his courtesy, therefore, to be made as a result of the following amusing story told to his wife in one of his letters from America.

" There is a physician here of the name of Chapman, to whom I had a letter from Washington Irving. I saw him in September last and had him instantly, and indulged in imitating him. When I went through in October I gave this imitation at a party here where everybody knew him. The thing was droll and a gentleman present not only laughed then but, when he went home, he laughed again at the recollection so immoderately that his wife really thought he had a hysteric fit. In perfect alarm she sent the servant off for their physician. He was from home and the servant, thinking his master dying, did not stop till he found a doctor. Just as the patient was recovering from the effects of his counterfeit doctor, in came the real Dr. Chapman; and when the patient heard the sound of his voice, he was off again, and was actually very near being bled while in his second fit. — A fact! "

One of Mathews's best witticisms about our climate was when he declared it " fit only for butterflies in summer and for wolves and bears in winter." Alongside of this we may place the following description of the circumstances under which he once wrote home, while stopping at a hotel in New York: " I am writing in a tub of hot water, with two black servants attending, each in a vapour bath, with their arms extended through flannel apertures, wiping my nose with hot

153

flannels, to prevent the breath freezing. By the time you receive this, a young summer (for there is no spring here) will compel me to abandon my cloth-coat."

One extraordinary incident of Mathews's first American tour was his performance in New York, on a wager, of the part of Othello. Strange to say, the attempt was received with great applause and had to be several times repeated. One of the critics of the time wrote: " It will hardly be credited that Mr. Mathews succeeded completely in this arduous character. We could not conceive that an actor, whose *forte* has been till now considered all comic, could so far divest himself of his humourous peculiarities, as to convey to his audience a very chaste, correct, pleasing, and even affecting picture of the unhappy Moor." Mathews possessed, however, too nice a sense of his own peculiar powers to allow himself to be tempted often out of his own special line of work. And though he was persuaded to do his Othello for a single night in Liverpool, after his return home, he did not repeat the experiment. The critics said that he was " brilliant in some passages, chaste and judicious in all." But they added that they preferred him in one of his " At Home's." And, since Mathews preferred himself that way, we do not find him again venturing into tragedy on the stage.

Something approaching tragedy for him intruded itself, however, into his personal life, about this time, in that his financial embarrassments were so great that he felt obliged to place on public exhibition his theatrical portrait gallery, which had been his pet hobby for years

This collection contained four hundred pictures, which, while not all of the first rank artistically, formed a unique illustration of the most brilliant period of England's histrionic history.

With the hope of still further retrieving his losses, Mathews made a second journey to America in 1834. This time his wife accompanied him; so that it is through her letters to their son that we now learn of his adventures — and follow the painful story of a very sick man, endeavouring to be as gay and sprightly, when before his audiences, as if he had never known an hour of suffering. On arriving in New York, he was distressed to learn that a strong public sentiment had developed against him since his last visit, owing, he was informed, to the fact that he had " ridiculed America " in one of his sketches. He met the accusation by giving the censured sketch entire and compelling his auditors to testify at its close that they could find nothing to object to in it.

Again he encountered an exceptionally cold winter, and this time his sufferings were real, not pretended, as on the former visit.

In Boston, where the comedian enjoyed a very good season, he and his wife made their headquarters at the Tremont House and received a great deal of social attention, one new acquaintance whom Mathews especially enjoyed being Doctor Wainwright. As the customs of the country did not then " allow a churchman to visit the theatre, Mr. Mathews took great pleasure," his wife writes, " in entertaining the Doctor in private whenever they met." The last church service poor Mathews ever attended was when he went to hear Doctor Wainwright preach, just before leaving Boston. "The doctor's sermon turned on a very affecting subject," records Mrs. Mathews, " on the probability that a reunion with those we most loved on earth would form a portion of the joys of the blessed hereafter. My husband wept continuously throughout the sermon, although he seemed unusually tranquil and happy the rest of the day." In New York Mathews appeared in public for the very last time. The bill for the occasion is interesting.

FAREWELL APPEARANCE OF MR. MATHEWS AT NEW YORK

This evening, February 11th, 1835, will be performed the comedy of

MARRIED LIFE

Mr. Samuel Coddle..............Mr. Mathews
Mr. Lionel Lynx................Mr. Mason
Mrs. Lionel Lynx...............Mrs. Chapman
Mrs. Samuel Coddle.............Mrs. Wheatley

In the course of the evening, Mr. Mathews will sing the Comic Songs of

The Humours of a Country Fair, and Street Melodies (a medley), including, Welsh, French, Scotch, Irish, African, Italian, Swiss and English airs with embellishments.

After which, an entertainment by Mr. Mathews, called

THE LONE HOUSE

Andrew Steward, Butler and Leader.....Mr. Mathews
Bechamel, a French valet..............Mr. Mathews
Frizwaffer, a German cook.............Mr. Mathews
Cutbush, a gardener..................Mr. Mathews
Captain Grapnell, a naval officer.......Mr. Mathews

Doors open at a quarter before six o'clock; performance commences at a quarter before seven.

From this evening Mathews grew continually worse, so that his journey back to England was one long chapter of horrors. He had literally come home to die, and he passed away June 28, 1835 — on his fifty-ninth birthday. Thus went out a talent so great and so unique that Macaulay said of it: " Mathews was certainly the greatest actor that I ever saw — I can hardly believe Garrick to have had more of the general mimetic genius than he. . . . I laughed my sides sore whenever I saw him." Perhaps the best summing up of this genial comedian's peculiar gift may be found, however, in the Sunday edition of the *London Times*, following his decease.

" As a companion he was delightful, as a friend sincere, as a husband and father exemplary, and, as an actor, he had no competitor, and will, we fear, never have a successor. . . . He was on the stage what Hogarth was on the canvas — a moral satirist: he did not imitate, he conceived and created characters, each one of which was recognized as a specimen of a class. Noth-

157

ing could exceed the correctness of his ear; he spoke all
the dialects of Ireland, Scotland and Wales with a fidel-
ity perfectly miraculous. He could discriminate between the pronunciation of the different writings of
Yorkshire, and speak French with the Parisian accent,
— the *patois* of the South or the guttural tone of the
Flemish. His powers in this way had no limit. His
knowledge of human character was no less remarkable.
Though his performances professed to be representations
of manners and peculiarities, they really abounded in
the fine analysations of character. Mathews did not
occupy the highest place in the drama; but he was
indisputably, and by the united suffrage of France,
England and America, the first in his peculiar walk. . . .
For seventeen years he, by his single exertions, delighted
all England — ' alone he did it! ' "

CHAPTER VI

TWO GREAT ENGLISH TRAGEDIANS WHOM WE WELCOMED GLADLY

About the time that the elder Charles Mathews first came to make us merry, William Augustus Conway, another English actor, also visited our shores. When Conway was making preparations to depart, the London press commented as follows: " On Friday Conway performed the part of Macbeth. He is about, we understand, to migrate to America, where we hope he will receive better encouragement than he has obtained here. He has certainly been hardly dealt with by the critics; they have taken a pleasure in exposing and heightening all his defects and in passing over the many traces of genius and judgment which are to be found in all his performances. Conway is not equal to the weighty part of Macbeth, but with the exception of Kemble, Kean and Young, he is as good as any other performer of the part. Conway wants study and discipline and a better carriage of his person. He is not wanting in natural feeling or in the leading requisites of his art."

Yet Conway's " carriage of his person " had not been

so inelegant that the " matinee girls " of his day failed in admiration of him. A susceptible " duke's daughter " was generally known to be quite beside herself for love of this Apollo (he was six feet, two inches in height), and he had won, also, the ardent love of Mrs. Piozzi, — who had been the Mrs. Thrale of Johnson's circle. This lady was seventy-three at the time of her infatuation for the actor and he was young enough to have been her grandson. But she is said to have proposed marriage to him, none the less, and repeatedly, in letters which may still be read, she tried to draw him to her side. In September, 1819, she wrote:

" Three Sundays have now elapsed since James brought me dearest Mr. Conway's promise to write me the very next, and, were it not for the newspaper which came on the 24th August — sending me to rest comfortable, though sick enough and under the influence of laudanum — I should relapse into my former stage of agonizing apprehension on your account; but that little darling autograph round the paper was written so steady, and so completely in the old way, whenever I look at it my spirits revive, and hope (true pulse of life) ceases to intermit, for a while at least, and bids me be assured we shall soon meet again. I really was very ill three or four days; but the jury of matrons, who sat on my complaints, acquitted the apricots which I accused, and said they (all but two) proved an alibi. Some of the servants, who were ill too, found out we had, in Bessy's absence, got some mildewed tea that lay in a damp closet at the last lodging. We are now removed to a palace, a Weston palazzino where we propose receiving Mr. Conway."

WILLIAM AUGUSTUS CONWAY
See page 159

THOMAS ABTHORPE COOPER
See page 163

There are many other letters in similar strain; for this extraordinary old lady continued her amorous correspondence with the handsome actor up to the very month of her death in the spring of 1821.

" We ourselves heard the late Charles Mathews say," asseverates a writer in the *New Monthly Magazine* for 1861 (very likely William Harrison Ainsworth, the editor of this publication) " — and no one who knew Mathews will question his veracity — that Conway had himself shown him Mrs. Piozzi's offer of marriage and asked his (Mathews') opinion and advice. Mathews told him at once that he could not honourably take advantage of it. ' That,' said Conway, ' is what I myself felt; but in a matter so important to one so poor as I am, I also felt that my own decision should be confirmed by the opinion of a friend. I now know what to do.' This, we repeat, we heard from Mathews himself, at the time the circumstance occurred, and we therefore believe it."

Conway's conduct towards Mrs. Piozzi appears to have been honourable in the extreme, however. Though he was in pecuniary straits at the time of her death, he returned to her estate a check for £500 which the aged lady had sent him a few days before she passed away, and among his effects, sold in New York after his own sad end, was a copy of Young's " Night Thoughts," on which was written " Presented to me by my dearly attached friend, the celebrated Mrs. Piozzi."

That Conway was grossly ill-used by many of the English critics, there can be no doubt. Hazlitt wrote very cruelly of him in the 1818 edition of his " View of the English Stage," declaring, among other things, that his " motion was as unwieldly as that of a young elephant." This criticism ends with the significant words: " Query, why does he not marry? " In justice to Hazlitt it should be said that this passage was omitted from the later editions of his book, and that he made a public apology for having written it.

The career of this much-abused actor was full of colour and movement. Born in London (in 1789), he was sent as a boy to the Barbadoes, where he grew up to young manhood under the guidance of a clergy-man-tutor. He returned to England at the age of eighteen, witnessed a play for the first time — at Bath, where he afterwards was cultivated so eagerly by Mrs. Piozzi — and was immediately seized with an ardent desire to go on the stage. Macready offered him an opening in Dublin, where he played with the beautiful Miss O'Neil — for whom he conceived a violent but unavailing passion. Through Charles Mathews he was given an opportunity to appear at Covent Garden, and he there played several parts of importance between 1813 and 1816. Then he disappeared from the London stage for several years, though he may be found in the bill of the Haymarket during the summer of 1821. After that he withdrew definitely from the view of English play-goers as a result of the malignant attacks to which reference has already been made; and, at the close of 1823, he started for America.

His début in New York, on January 12, 1824, in the

part of Hamlet, yielded him sixteen hundred dollars, and the critics of the New World, unlike those of London, accorded his performance enthusiastic praise. So pronounced, indeed, was his success, that Thomas A. Cooper, then a great favourite of the New Yorkers, made an arrangement to play with him, and for a number of performances the Park Theatre was crowded nightly as a result of this partnership.

Then, quite suddenly, Conway withdrew to Newport, Rhode Island, for the purpose, it was said, of preparing himself to take holy orders. The news that Macready was about to come to New York had proved too much for him. For nothing could shake his " fixed idea " that Macready was visiting the country for the express purpose of crushing him. Moreover, the American papers, not to be outdone in cruelty by those of London, about this time began to impugn the motives behind his religious zeal and to question, salaciously, the relations which had existed between him and Mrs. Piozzi. As a result of all this, Conway became morbidly dejected. In the course of a voyage from New York to Charleston, in the winter of 1828, it was noted how melancholy he was and that, although the weather was very raw, he wore only summer clothing. On January 24, when the passengers were going down to dinner, he told the captain " he should never want dinner more," and presently flung himself overboard. His body was not recovered. The love letters of Mrs. Piozzi, found among his effects, were sold in New York and afterwards published in London. They pitifully demonstrate that Dr. Johnson was quite right when he warned his friend that she should not give too free vent to her emotions.[1]

Junius Brutus Booth, father of the great Edwin, — and of the unhappy maniac who shot Abraham Lincoln under a mistaken sense that he was thus serving the highest good of his country, — we had made welcome just a few years before; and well we might, for the elder Booth was one of the most interesting characters stage history in America has ever known.

Born at St. Pancras, London, May 1, 1796, the son of Richard Booth, a cultivated lawyer, he was destined by his father for a brilliant legal career. It chanced, however, that this father was a strong believer in personal liberty, as was instanced by an attempt that he made to serve in our Revolutionary War and by the fact that all visitors to his house were obliged to render obeisance to a portrait of George Washington which hung on the wall of his drawing-room. So, when he learned that his son did not care to follow the profession he had chosen for him — preferring instead to go upon the stage — he did not long attempt to thwart the lad's preference. Young Booth's first appearance was at Deptford, in December, 1813, after which, for several months, he played on the Continent as a member of a strolling English company.

[1] Leslie Stephens doubts the authenticity of these letters, but other commentators declare them quite in Mrs. Piozzi's style. The fact is that beauty was one of this lively lady's tastes; and Conway was exceedingly good-looking. Moreover, though she was well along in years, her spirits were still young. On the evening of her eightieth birthday she gave a concert ball and supper at Bath, to nearly seven hundred people, she herself leading off the first dance!

Yet so potent is ambition, when linked with great talent, that early in 1817 he was acting Richard III at Covent Garden and making such a profound impression that he immediately came to be regarded as the rival of the great Kean! The " Keanites " and the " Booth-ites " struggled together in London for some time, each claque endeavouring to maintain the supremacy of its chosen idol. Meanwhile Kean and Booth played counter-parts together and profited greatly by the excitement which their adherents had fanned into flame.

Four years elapsed between this London season and Booth's sailing for America, in the spring of 1821. They were years of continuously brilliant success; it was by no means because he could not find appreciative audiences in England and on the Continent that Junius Brutus Booth came to the New World.

The city in which he first acted over here was Richmond, and the part he first assumed that of his favourite, Richard III. His triumph was immediate and tremendous, the critics pronouncing him the equal if not the superior of both Cooke and Kean.

An engagement at the Park Theatre in New York was promptly offered him, and there he opened, October 5, 1821, as Richard III. Here there was the wildest enthusiasm over his performance, one of the reviews predicting that " with the aid of close study and practice, this astonishing young man [he was still under twenty-five] would become the first actor of the age."

At Booth's first benefit in New York, the house was crammed, and he had twelve hundred dollars to bear away with him. This appears to have been the nucleus of the sum with which he purchased his farm, the Bel Air, in Baltimore, to which he became greatly attached and with which so many stories about him are connected.

The spring of 1822 found him playing in Boston for the first time, after which he made a round of all the leading cities of the country. Two visits to England, engagements at Rotterdam, Amsterdam, and Brussels, periods of service at New Orleans, Baltimore, and New York — interspersed with various professional tours and with weeks, too, of forced retirement — now followed.

There is, however, no intention to sketch Booth's career here, either in sequence or in detail; the space at our disposal can be much more profitably employed by quoting, from a very rare brochure,[1] which has fallen into my hands, some of the anecdotes told of this extraordinary man and of his compelling genius.

Once he was the guest at the " Hermitage," near Nashville, Tennessee, of General Jackson and his wife, and entertained them by reading aloud portions of the Scriptures and of " Paradise Lost." For this actor knew and greatly loved literature. To a visitor who was condoling with him on the loneliness of his farm he replied: " I am never without company. I am surrounded by congenial spirits. I converse and hold counsel with the great and good of all ages. Look — there are Shelley, and Byron, and Wordsworth; here are ' rare Ben Jonson,' Beaumont and Fletcher, and Shakespeare and

[1] " The Actor, or a Peep Behind the Curtain: " New York, 1846.

Milton; with them time never wearies, and the eloquent teachings that fall from their leaves are counsellors and guides. *These* are my companions," concluded Booth, triumphantly pointing to his library and to his old arm-chair, " and I am never less alone, than when alone."

Booth's devotion to this farm and to the agricultural occupations with which he busied himself there became almost a monomania. He not only superintended the management of the place but " drove his team afield," like any other practical farmer. A novel sight it must have been to see the great tragedian disposing of his turnips and cabbages in market — and not infrequently giving them away when no purchaser could be found. One Saturday evening when he was due to play Richard in Baltimore, neither threats nor solicitation could induce him to go to the theatre until he had made a satisfactory disposition of his vegetables. The consequence was that, in order to secure his actor, the manager had first to hunt up a purchaser for the wares of the amateur farmer.

One of Booth's eccentricities, if so we may regard it, was a firm belief that it was a positive sin to destroy and even more wicked to consume anything that had life. For a period of three years he lived entirely upon vegetable food, even oysters being, in the quaint language of his chronicler, " sacred from his appetite." At this time occurred the incident of the passenger pigeons, a long and graphic account of which may be found in the *Atlantic Monthly* files for 1861. A young clergyman in a Western city received, one evening, a note from Booth,

who was then playing in the town, asking that a place of
interment be given in the churchyard to his " friends."
The minister, mistaking the word "friends" for "friend,"
and thinking the actor wished to bury some dear comrade,
called on Booth at his hotel, to offer help and sympathy.

" Was the death of your friend sudden? " he asked
sympathetically.

" Very," was Booth's brief reply.

" Was he a relative? "

" Distant," came the non-committal answer. And
then the actor, as if desiring to change the subject, asked
his caller if he would like to hear him give " The Ancient
Mariner." In delight the clergyman said that he would,
indeed; and soon Booth was reading that weird poem
as only he knew how to read. When he had ended, he
began to argue about the sin of eating animal food, turning over the pages of the Bible to find texts to support
his opinions. Then he invited the minister into the next
room to " look at the remains."

What met their eyes was no human corpse, however,
but a number of dead passenger pigeons spread out on a
large sheet. These Booth took up tenderly in his arms,
explaining, as he did so, that they had been shot in mere
wantonness. The young divine was much impressed by
the words of his host, but, inasmuch as he could not accede to the request that these dead pigeons be accorded
full burial rites, the two soon parted, Booth now looking
very black and malevolent. The cloud which often ob-
scured his mind had again descended.

Once, in the very high tide of his early successes, this

erratic genius wished to retire from the stage and accept the position of a lighthouse keeper, with a salary of $300 a year! On another occasion, after a drunken bout with his friend, Tom Flynn, he thought himself to be Othello, and hurled his companion to the floor with such force that the other, knowing his opponent to be beside himself, felt forced to defend his life by hitting Booth over the face with a poker — a punishment that broke the actor's nose and so spoiled at once his beauty and his voice.

Edwin Booth has written very delicately and beautifully of his father in an endeavour to explain away "much that was imputed to vices of the blood." Great minds to madness closely are allied, he pleads. " Thus Hamlet's mind, at the very edge of frenzy, seeks its relief in ribaldry. For like reasons would my father open, so to speak, the safety-valve of levity in some of his most impassioned moments. At the very instant of intense emotion, when the spectators were enthralled by his magnetic influence, the tragedian's overwrought brain would take refuge from its own threatening storm beneath the jester's hood, and, while turned from the audience, he would whisper some silliness or ' make a face.' . . . My close acquaintance with so fantastic a temperament as was my father's so accustomed me to that in him which appeared strange to others that much of Hamlet's ' mystery ' seems to me no more than idiosyncrasy. It likewise taught me charity for those whose evil or imperfect genius sways them to the mood of what it likes or loathes."

Junius Brutus Booth never spoke of things theatrical

when at home and was decidedly opposed to having any of his children go on the stage. Not that he considered this calling unworthy, but that he was only too conscious of the enormous drain it makes upon the nervous system. For, more than most actors, he consciously threw himself, before the play as well as during the performance, into its peculiar atmosphere. Thus, if " Othello " was billed for the evening, he would wear a crescent pin on his breast all that day. When Shylock was to be his part, he was a Jew in anticipation and would converse by the hour, if in Baltimore, with a learned Israelite among his acquaintance there, quoting portions of the Talmud the while. For Booth knew Hebrew well enough to be able to play Shylock in that language, Arabic sufficiently to talk with travelling jugglers in their own tongue, and was sufficiently a master of French stage traditions to render acceptably the Orestes in Racine's " Andromaque " before a French audience at New Orleans.

Even George Frederick Cooke, whose Richard III is said to have excelled all others, was not better in the death scene of this play than was Booth, if we may trust the critics. " His eyes, naturally large and piercing," wrote H. D. Stone, " appeared to greatly increase in size and fairly to gleam with fire, while large drops of perspiration oozed from his forehead and coursed down his cheeks."

The most interesting criticism that I have found on Booth's acting is from the pen of Walt Whitman,[1] whom

[1] See *Boston Herald*, August 16, 1885.

most of us know much better as a poet than as a commentator on the drama:

" I happened to see him [Booth] in one of the most marvellous pieces of acting ever known. I can (from my good seat in the pit pretty well front) see again Booth's quiet entrance from the side as, with head bent, he slowly walks down the stage to the footlights with that peculiar and abstracted gesture, musingly kicking his sword which he holds off from him by its sash. Though fifty years have passed since then, I can hear the clank and feel the perfect hush of perhaps three thousand people waiting. (I never saw an actor who could make more of the said hush or wait, and hold the audience in an indescribable, half-delicious, half-irritating suspense.) . . . Especially was the dream scene very impressive. A shudder went through every nervous system in the audience; it certainly did through mine.

" Without question Booth was royal heir and legitimate representative of the Garrick-Kemble-Siddons dramatic traditions; but he vitalized and gave an unnameable *race* to those traditions with his own electric idiosyncrasy. The words, fire, energy, *abandon* found in him unprecedented meanings. I never heard a speaker or actor who could give such a sting to hauteur or the taunt. I never heard from any other the charm of unswervingly perfect vocalization without trenching at all on mere melody, the province of music."

Booth's last appearance on the stage was on November 19, 1852, at the St. Charles Theatre, New Orleans. The Creoles had always loved him and borne patiently with his lapses; on this occasion he made them very happy with a brilliant performance. Then he set out for

171

Cincinnati on a Mississippi steamer and died while on his way, with no member of his dearly-loved family to close his brilliant eyes. When Rufus Choate heard that he had passed away, he exclaimed, in deep sorrow, " Then there are no more actors! "

Yet at that very hour, in a distant Western city, the parts that Junius Brutus Booth had played with such astonishing power were being done — and well done, too — by the son whom he had named Edwin, after America's greatest native tragedian, and who was destined to become the most glorious Hamlet the world has ever seen.

CHAPTER VII

EDWIN FORREST, the first American tragedian native to our soil, belongs peculiarly to the nineteenth century. For the century was only six years old when he was born; and he did not die until December 12, 1872. The history of his life is thus almost synchronous with the history of the American stage during this period. Because of which, as well as because Forrest was an intensely interesting personality, his career of necessity looms large in any work dealing with the American drama. Moreover, Forrest was intensely American in his sympathies, his prejudices, his training, and his enthusiasms. He may, also, be said to have been typically American in the way in which he carved out a new field of activity for himself.

Forrest stands forth as the very first American star who shone with transcendent brilliancy. For James Fennell and Thomas Abthorpe Cooper, both of whom had " starred " before him, were not native Americans, though they are usually so regarded. Nor did they possess powers in any way comparable with his.

John Bernard has amiably characterized Fennell, in his " Retrospections of America," as " one of the most extraordinary specimens of a class it had been my fate

173

so frequently to meet, and my humble endeavor to immortalize — the eccentric. Eccentricity is a sort of orderly disorder; or, if that sounds too Irish, a peculiar arrangement by which the greatest contradictions are placed in juxtaposition, as though kitchen utensils were ranged round a drawing-room. Most dazzling schemes for acquiring wealth and fame were, in Fennell's case, the drawing-room furniture; while the kitchen implements were those dramatic talents by which he cut his loaf and cooked his dinner. He was a projector of the most genuine 'South Sea Bubble' species. . . . That arrant jade, Fancy, was ever luring him into debt and disgrace, while his sober spouse, Judgment, would lead him back to the stage and a subsistence."

Frequently, however, Fennell's blithesome resourcefulness served him in very good stead, even while pursuing his workaday life on the stage. As for instance, on that occasion when he was playing Macbeth in a summer company whose property man had become so enamoured of Shakespeare that he frequently forgot the duties of his office. On this particular evening the " blood " was missing; but a well-directed blow, aimed by Fennell at the property man's nose, effectively remedied this deficiency, and Macbeth's hands and dagger were as gory, when he returned from killing Duncan, as even the youngest pit-ite could desire.

Fennell was born in London in 1766, received a good education, and studied for the bar. In 1787 he resolved to be an actor, and made his début at the Edinburgh Theatre. At about this time he began, too, to write for the press, issuing a magazine called the *Theatrical Guard-*

ian. After spending some time in Paris, Fennell came to the United States and in 1793 made his first appearance in Philadelphia with immediate success. He became the idol of the town, and but for his extravagant habits and erratic disposition, might have accumulated a great deal of money. At this period he was a rival of Thomas Abthorpe Cooper, and in 1808 the two favourites played a joint engagement at the leading theatres of several cities. Once Fennell alone played thirteen weeks in Philadelphia to receipts which aggregated thirteen thousand dollars. This is said to have been " the greatest instance of patronage ever given to the American drama."

Yet he was soon attempting to earn a modest livelihood by conducting an academy in Charlestown, Massachusetts. And then, having by good luck come into a considerable amount of money, he established some salt works near New London, Connecticut. This led to his financial ruin. He died in Philadelphia on June 14, 1816, in extreme poverty.

When his fortunes were at their lowest ebb, Fennell wrote his " Apology," in which may be found many picturesque bits about the actor-life of the time, though the book as a whole is extremely tedious. We here learn, for instance, that Fennell once played the Moor of Venice at Edinburgh dressed in " a coat, waistcoat and lower garment of white cloth cut in the old-fashioned style; the coat and waistcoat loaded, or rather ornamented with broad silver lace; to which was superadded a black wig with long hair, and to which was suspended

175

a ramillies of about three feet in length. This, with the addition of a pair of white silk stockings and dancing pumps, made up the equipment."

Cooper's starring experience dates from 1803. He had observed that Fennell received in six or eight nights a larger remuneration than was paid to him for three months of regular service, and that, too, for work which appeared to be far less laborious than the drudgery of a stock actor. So he determined to make the big adventure.

Born in England in 1776, the son of a physician who left him fatherless at the age of eleven, Cooper was be-friended by William Godwin, a distant relative, and was thus brought early into intimate contact with the girl who became Mrs. Shelley. At sixteen he tried to go on the stage, applying for " any kind of a post " to Stephen Kemble, who gave him a chance. He was promptly hissed at Edinburgh, but persisted nevertheless, and soon displayed so much promise that in 1796 he received an offer from Wignell, then manager of the Philadelphia Theatre.

The distinguished Mrs. Merry and her husband, John Bernard, and William Warren were among young Cooper's fellow-passengers in the trip across the At-lantic. He arrived in New York, October 18, 1796, played a preliminary season at Baltimore, and then made his début at the Chestnut Street Theatre, Phila-delphia (December 9, 1796) in the character of Mac-beth. On February 28, 1798, he first appeared as Ham-let at the recently completed Park Theatre, in New

York, with which his subsequent fortunes were a good deal identified. The difference between the " then " and the " now " in the matter of salaries will be seen when it is said that Cooper at this time received only $25 a week for playing leads; in 1799 he began to draw $32, and by 1801 he was receiving $38, though all the while a great favourite with box, pit, and gallery. Mrs. Merry drew $100 a week for playing parts opposite to him. Cooper thought he could do better than this and proceeded to prove it. In 1803 he went to London, and on June 10 of that year played Othello at Drury Lane, to the Iago of George Frederick Cooke and the Cassio of Charles Kemble.

His reputation thus enlarged, he returned to New York where, playing three times a week at the Park, he averaged $750 nightly. When it is realized that the city's entire population at this time was not over seventy-five thousand, it will be seen that Cooper was indeed a great success as an actor. He was a capable manager, also. In 1808 he became associated with Stephen Price, a well-known man of fashion in New York, who afterwards became the lessee of the Drury Lane, London, and together they brought out many successes.

In 1815 he left Price to be sole manager of the Park and began his career of travelling star. For years he made his journeys in a large gig, expressly constructed for the uncertain roads of that era, which he drove tandem. Thus, in his prime, he played no less than one hundred and seventy-six leading characters in sixty-four different theatres, driving himself, the while, some twenty thousand miles.

A very picturesque career, this, but of course not typically American — as was Forrest's.

Edwin Forrest started as a poor lad with no position or influences which could account in any way for his exceedingly remarkable and very early success; and he fought his way up the ladder, rung by rung, as if he were saying to himself every hour of the day: "There's plenty of room at the top." That his father was Scotch and his mother German only served to make his Americanism more pronounced.

The story of this boy's early life reminds one, in its simplicity and its self-conscious idealism, of Benjamin Franklin's life as set down in the matchless "Autobiography." For here again there was a frugal father, a devout, God-fearing mother, and several other children besides *a youngest son, who would get on*. Because this son gave more striking signs of talent than any of his fellow fledglings in the crowded home nest, the parents were ambitious to make a parson out of him. At first his natural tendencies encouraged this idea, for after attending service in the old Episcopal church, he would hurry home, make a pulpit of a stuffed semicircular chair with a pillow placed on the top of its back for a cushion, mount into it, and preach from memory to his admiring sisters, who formed the "congregation," long passages from the sermon which had lodged themselves in his retentive memory. But — and this detail would have been a very significant one to a mother trained, as many modern mothers are, to note the implications of a youngster's tastes in play — the *costume* was a very important accessory to the preaching of this parson. He would never open his mouth until he had spectacles across his nose and a pair of tongs hung around his neck to represent the stole worn by the divine he was enacting.

The premature death of the boy's father necessitated early self-support on the part of the young Thespian, however, and he was successively a printer's devil, an errand boy in a cooper-shop, and an under-clerk in a ship-chandlery of his native Philadelphia. But his chief amusement continued to be " playing theatre," and his one diversion later was passing enchanted evenings in the Old Southwark where, while his love of the play was satisfied by witnessing the " acted drama," his patriotic passion was fed by gazing at the box midway in the first tier, which was known as the Washington box from the fact that it had often been occupied by the President and his family during the days when Philadelphia was the nation's capital.

It was in this theatre, then under the management of Charles Porter, that Forrest, as a lad of eleven, made his first appearance on any stage. The part assigned him was that of a girl, and, boy-like, he devoted great care to the make-up of his upper person, stuffing out his dress, adjusting his ringlets, and fastening very securely upon his head the turban his sister had made for the occasion. But his huge boy's boots were quite forgotten, and when they showed forth under his short petticoats,

179

he was hissed in no uncertain fashion. The manager said he had disgraced the theatre, and no amount of coaxing would secure him another chance. So Forrest characteristically took matters into his own hands, got himself up as a harlequin, dashed before the footlights while the manager was busy running down the curtain, and delivered himself of some verses which contained a facetious reference to his late ungainly heels and, by dint of agile hand-springs and flip-flaps, wrung from the astonished audience burst on burst of applause.

As a reward for this exploit, he was now given a chance to show what he really had in him, and on November 17, 1820, he made his first appearance at the Walnut Street Theatre in the character of Young Norval. Though he was only fourteen at the time, he acquitted himself so well that William Duane, then one of the ablest and most experienced editors in the country, wrote an appreciative notice of his work, pointing out that the " sentiment of the character had obtained such full possession of the youth as to take away every consideration of an audience or a drama, and to give, as it were, the natural speaking of the shepherd boy, suddenly revealed by instinct to be the son of Douglas." The lad's self-possession, beautiful voice, and careful articulation were also mentioned with praise. For this lad had not been wasting his scant leisure hours, and the results of his study and elocution practice showed in his performance. His biographer tells an interesting story to show how young Edwin carefully followed up every

suggestion looking to advancement in his chosen profession.

One evening, as he was standing in front of one of the
Philadelphia theatres, his attention was fixed on the
two mythological figures inscribed Thalia and Mel-
pomene which stood in niches on either side. " Who
are Thallea and Melpomeen? " he inquired of an elder
comrade. " Oh, I don't know; a couple of Grecian
queens, I guess," was the reply. But a gentleman, over-
hearing, stepped forward and explained that the ladies
were respectively the Muse of Comedy and the Muse of
Tragedy and added that at any bookstore might be
had a copy of Walker's Classical Pronouncing Dictionary, to which such questions could be referred
with the certainty of a correct answer. Edwin bought
the volume at once and profited by it, too. Profited
so much that, when the theatre was torn down, some
years later, he was able to buy the two statues with
the intention of having them set up in his own private
theatre.

Naturally, a lad thus ambitious of stage success attained it. After his successful début, he followed up
every possible opening and suggestion until, at the age
of sixteen, he secured an engagement with Collins and
Jones to play leading juvenile parts in their theatres
in Pittsburgh, Cincinnati, and Lexington. The salary
was eight dollars a week, and the places in which they
played were so wretched that in Pittsburgh the audiences
were forced to shelter themselves under umbrellas
from the leaks of the roof, as Forrest sustained the part

of Young Norval. When the company had closed its season at Lexington, early in 1823, they all set off on a cross-country " trek " for Cincinnati, the women packed away in covered wagons with the theatrical paraphernalia, the men on horseback. The journey occupied the better part of two weeks, for it was not until March 6, 1823, that they opened in the old Columbia Street Theatre of Cincinnati in " The Soldier's Daughter," Forrest, who lacked three days of being seventeen, assuming the part of Malfort. At this time he was so poor that when his dog, by way of morning diversion, gnawed into shreds one of his only pair of boots, he had to get around the dilemma by pretending to have a sore foot, thus making it possible for him to appear in public wearing a shabby old slipper.

The impression made by the youth's character upon all who met him at this time may be understood from the fact that an excellent boarding-place was secured for him in Cincinnati through the personal intervention of General Harrison, who was subsequently President of the United States. The General feared that if young Forrest boarded with the other players he would form bad habits, and he wished to guard him from this, as he considered him a young man of extraordinary ability, destined to excel in his profession. Forrest was then a very beautiful youth, with deep brown eyes, a complexion of marble clearness, and a graceful though sinewy form.

Forrest's first real opportunity of any importance came when James H. Caldwell, the New Orleans manager, offered him (in 1824) an engagement at eighteen dollars a week as an actor in his stock company. Here many experiences of varying value were his. For the most voluptuous, passionate, and reckless social life of any city in the United States was that of New Orleans at this time. And this handsome young actor, whom everybody welcomed gladly, was impressionable and eager to drink deep of every cup which should contribute to his understanding of life. Caldwell at first introduced his *protegé* to all his friends and gave him good parts; then, growing jealous of him, he forced him, who was tingling with youth, to play continually the rôles of old men. Very wisely, Forrest, instead of resenting this openly, made it his business to study the peculiarities of age in feature, gait, and voice. At this time, too, during a vacation period, he lived for a time with the Indians, and made that study of the red man's character which was afterwards to prove of such inestimable value to him. Another opportunity which came to Forrest, while at New Orleans, was that afforded by the chance to play with the celebrated and ill-starred Conway. " Othello " was one of the pieces put on, and as Conway depicted the noble Moor in all his jealousy, love, madness, vengeance, desperation, and remorse, Forrest watched, lynx-eyed, and lost not one detail. He was wont to date from the witnessing of these performances one of the epochs in the development of his own dramatic power. Also epochal was the attraction he now felt for Miss Jane Placide, first actress in the New Orleans company, and then a very sweet and

183

beautiful girl of twenty. It was because of a quarrel that he had with Caldwell concerning this lady that Forrest left New Orleans, having first challenged and " posted " his former manager.

There was no difficulty now about securing an engagement, however, and we find him, in the fall of 1825, member of a stock company at the Albany Theatre, ready to meet and profit by the second great experience of his professional life. This was acting Iago to the Othello of Edmund Kean. Kean was making his second visit to America, and he was now much broken by his bad habits from his best estate. Still his genius lingered fascinatingly, and he delivered his climacteric points with all his wonted power. Forrest knew this, and he was most anxious to " play up " to the great man. Accordingly he called on him at his hotel, on the forenoon of the day they were to act together, for the purpose of securing any directions the master might have to give him. He was graciously received, but the only directions bestowed by the star were to keep in front of him and not wander in attention any of the time that Iago and Othello were on the stage together.

That night, however, the young American actor gave a new idea to the great Kean. For having studied his part for a considerable period, Forrest had come to the conclusion that Iago, instead of being the sullen and sombre villain he was usually represented, *to have deceived Othello*, must needs have been very fascinating, seemingly sincere, and full of surface good humour. So in delivering the important lines:

184

"Look to your wife; observe her well with Cassio;
Wear your eye thus, not jealous, — nor secure,"

Forrest was frank and hail-fellow-well-met in all save
the last two words. But there, suddenly, as if his deep
knowledge of good and evil had, without his volition,
thrust itself, as it were, to the surface, he almost hissed
the words "nor secure," thus conveying a horrible
suggestion of malevolence which electrified the house
and caused Kean to say to him excitedly, after the performance: "In the name of God, boy, where did you
get that?" Forrest, trying hard to conceal his triumph,
replied calmly: "It is something of my own." "Well,"
said the great man with conviction, "everybody who
speaks the part hereafter must do it just so." Nor was
this idle praise. At a public dinner given to Kean in
Philadelphia, soon after this, he said that he had met one
actor in this country, a young man named Edwin Forrest, who gave proofs of a decided genius for his profession, and who would, as he believed, rise to great eminence.

Already that coveted opportunity, a New York engagement, was assured to Forrest by his good work in
Albany. For Prosper M. Wetmore, one of the proprietors of the nearly completed Bowery Theatre, having
heard of his acting, had journeyed up to Albany to see
the work for himself, and was so much pleased that an
offer to play leading parts during the first season, at a
salary of twenty-eight dollars a week, was promptly
made to the young man. Meanwhile, however, there

was the summer to be got through without money; for the Albany venture had not been a financial success, and Forrest, among others, was dismissed unpaid. Yet he managed somehow to transport himself to New York. While staying there, utterly without funds, it chanced that, by doing a kindness to an actor with a large family, — playing Othello for his benefit at the Park, — he convinced even his future manager that he was a wonder. That individual graciously lent him money to pay his debts and take his wardrobe out of pawn. Whereupon, Forrest got a chance to play in the South during the summer, and so was able to carry four hundred dollars home to his mother, at the end of what had promised to be a wholly unprofitable holiday period.

When the Bowery finally opened, in the fall of 1826, Forrest as Othello at once made such an impression that the stockholders sent him their personal congratulations and raised his salary from twenty-eight to forty dollars a week. From this success may be traced the first absolute hold made by Forrest upon the attention of cultivated auditors and intelligent critics; for the Bowery, it must be recalled, was then a very different theatre from what it afterwards became, when the newsboys took forcible possession of it, and the fire-laddies in its neighbourhood were the arbiters of public taste. The following year he was re-engaged there for eighty nights at a salary of two hundred dollars a night. At least sixteen thousand dollars assured, that season, for this actor who had just passed his twenty-first birthday!

Early in February, 1827, Forrest played for the first time in Boston at the old Federal Street Theatre. The character he assumed was Damon; Pythias was in the audience. For James Oakes " of the old Salt Store, 49 Long Wharf," who was destined to be Forrest's most intimate friend throughout his whole life, was one of those "in front" that night. After the performance, he went around to the actor's dressing-room and took the first steps in the relation which was to mean so much to them both. Oakes was at this time a little less than twenty and had a passion for the drama equal to Forrest's own. He at once constituted himself Forrest's unsalaried press-agent, and it is not too much to say that a great deal of the extraordinary reputation this actor soon built up was due to the unwearied nursing of his growing fame to which Oakes devoted himself as a diversion and labour of love.

In the course of a rather large reading of biography, I have never encountered any relation between men so tender and so beautiful as this friendship of forty years. They wrote to each other constantly, Forrest and Oakes; they were together for holidays whenever possible, and they told each other everything. "From top to bottom, inside and out and all through, I am, dear Forrest, forever yours," Oakes writes. And Forrest replies: " I have never met a man whose heart beat with a nobler humanity than yours. I am proud to be your friend and have you for mine. God bless you and keep us always worthy of one another." Oakes once said that the friendship between him and Forrest was more like devotion of a man to the woman he loves than the relation usually subsisting between men. And this is borne out by Alger's [1] sketch. " Every summer for the last thirty years of his life Forrest made it a rule," he says, " to spend a week or a fortnight with Oakes, when they either loitered about lovely Boston or went into the country or to the seaside and gave themselves up to leisurely enjoyment. . . . These visits were regularly repaid. Whenever they met, after a long separation, as soon as they were alone together, they threw their arms around each other in fond embrace with mutual kisses, after the manner of lovers in our land, or of friends in more tropical and demonstrative climes. Streets in land owned by Forrest were frequently named after Oakes, the room opposite his own in one of his houses was called Oakes's Chamber, and in his Broad Street mansion in Philadelphia there was a portrait of Oakes in the entry, a portrait of Oakes in the dining-room, a portrait of Oakes in the picture gallery, a portrait of Oakes in the library, and a general seeming presence of Oakes all over the house. Early one summer day, while visiting there, Oakes might have been seen, wrapped in a silk morning-gown of George Frederick Cooke, with a wig of John Philip Kemble on his head and the sword of Edmund Kean by his side, tackled between the thills of a heavy stone roller, rolling the garden walks to earn his breakfast. Forrest was behind him urging him forward."

From the hour these two met, Forrest took no step either of professional or personal importance without

[1] " Life of Forrest," William R. Alger: J. B. Lippincott and Co.

first consulting Oakes. It is probable, therefore, that the Bostonian had a share in the plan executed by Forrest early in his career with a view to securing some strictly American plays for our stage. The project resulted in heavy money losses to its promoter, but it secured for the American stage " The Gladiator," " Jack Cade," and " Metamora," all of which contained parts played by Forrest with great success. But not, be it understood, without decided opposition on the part of the dramatic critics, who were committed to English plays and to the English school of acting. Bryant, Halleck, Leggett, and many other distinguished New York journalists of the period were Forrest's devoted friends; but there were other editorial personages who were determined to " write down " this zealous advocate of American plays, whose robustious style was being widely imitated by men utterly without his genius. In certain circles it became the fashion to ridicule Forrest and all that he did.

Yet he continued to draw huge houses and to make a tremendous amount of money. So much money that he felt himself entitled, after five years of constant labour, to a two years' absence in Europe. Before he sailed, a farewell banquet was tendered him at the City Hotel by the leading men of New York, and a medal struck in honour of the occasion. Then, freighted with the good wishes of all who knew him well, he sailed for his well-earned period of travel, study, and recreation.

From Paris, especially, he sent home glowing descriptions of the things he saw and the theatres he attended.

" I have been to the Louvre, the Tuileries, Place Vendome, and St. Cloud," he wrote, — " here, there and everywhere — and I have not yet seen a twentieth part of the objects which claim a stranger's attention. One cannot go into the streets for a moment, indeed, but something new attracts his curiosity; and it seems to me that my senses, which I have heretofore considered adequate to the usual purposes of life, ought now to be enlarged and quickened for the full enjoyment of the objects which surround me. I have, of course, visited some of the theatres, of which there are upwards of twenty now open. I went to the *Theâtre Port St. Martin* the other night to see Mademoiselle Georges, now, on the French stage, the Queen of tragedy. I saw her perform the part of Lucrece Borgia, in Victor Hugo's drama of that name. Her personation was truly beautiful, — nay, that is too cold a word; it was grand, and even terrible. Though a woman more than fifty years old, never can I forget the dignity of her manner, the flexible and expressive character of her yet fine face, and the rich, full, stirring and well-modulated tones of her voice. How different is her and nature's style from the sickly abortions of the present English school of acting, lately introduced upon the American stage. In Mademoiselle Georges you see no servile imitations of a bad model; but you behold that sort of excellence which makes you forget you are in a theatre, — that perfection of art by which art is wholly concealed, — the lofty and the thrilling, the subdued and the graceful, harmoniously mingling, the spirit being caught from living nature. I had been led to believe that, in France, the highest order of living excellence had died with Talma. It is not so. I consider Mademoiselle Georges the very incarnation of the tragic muse."

Forrest had always deeply reverenced Talma, and in no act performed during his stay in Paris did he take more satisfaction than in quietly placing a laurel crown on the obscure grave of France's greatest actor. One other allied experience of his, while in Paris, must be recorded. He had been persuaded by a manager to attend the début of a youthful *protegé* of whom much was hoped and, after witnessing the performance, the American was urged to give an opinion of the aspirant's powers. "He will never rise beyond a respectable mediocrity," Forrest at once declared. "It is a perfectly hopeless case. There are no deeps of latent passion in him. But that Jewish-looking girl, that little bag of bones with the marble face and the flaming eyes, — there is demoniacal power in *her*. If she lives and does not burn out too soon, she will become something wonderful." The "little bag of bones" was the then unknown Rachel.

While he was in Paris news came to Forrest of the death of the actress over whom he had quarrelled with Caldwell. One finds the following entry in his diary at the time: "And so Jane Placide is dead. The theatrical people of New Orleans, then, have lost much. She imparted a grace and force and dignity to her rôle which few actresses have been able so admirably to combine. She excelled in a profession in the arduous sphere of which even to succeed requires uncommon gifts, both mental and physical. Her disposition was as lovely as her person. Heaven lodge and rest her fair soul."

Forrest returned to America in September, 1836; but he stayed only long enough to say good-by. For he had determined to accept the very flattering offers which had been made to him to play a series of engagements in the principal British theatres, and sailed almost immediately to fulfil this contract. The desire to see him again on the stage in Philadelphia and in New York was so general and so eagerly urged, however, that he played six nights in each city before sailing. The crowd and excitement at the opening night of the Philadelphia engagement was almost unprecedented, all the passages to the house being blocked with applicants for admission two hours before the rising of the curtain. In New York, at the Park, it was the same story. Box tickets were sold at auction for twenty-five dollars each, and the tragedian's personal profit for the six performances amounted to three thousand dollars. The critics generally pronounced his acting deepened and improved by his months of rest and travel, and the plaudits of his auditors showed that, to their minds, his work was well-nigh perfect. They, no less than he, recalled with emotion, too, the night some ten years before when, poor and almost unknown, he had played Othello in that very house for the benefit of a distressed brother-actor.

In Drury Lane Theatre, on October 17, 1836, Forrest made his first professional appearance in England. The rôle he had chosen was Spartacus, and the immense audience, which crowded the theatre from dome to pit, received his acting with marked approbation. But for the play they felt little enthusiasm, and when he at-

DRURY LANE THEATRE, LONDON, IN WHICH EDWIN FORREST FIRST ACTED IN ENGLAND

WILLIAM C. MACREADY AS SHYLOCK

tempted to include the author of " The Gladiator "
in their approving verdict, there were protests and repeated cries that he let himself be seen in Shakespeare.
He was quick to take the hint. The bill on twenty-four
out of the thirty-two nights he played here was Shakespeare, — Macbeth seven times, King Lear eight, and
Othello nine.

" This approbation of my Shakespeare parts gives
me peculiar pleasure," he wrote his friend Leggett, " as
it refutes the opinions very confidently expressed by a
certain *clique* at home that I would fail in those characters before a London audience. But it is not only from
my reception within the walls of the theatre that I have
reason to be pleased with my English friends. I have
received many grateful kindnesses in their hospitable
homes, and in their intellectual fireside-circles have
drunk both instruction and delight. I suppose you saw
in the newspapers that a dinner was given to me by the
Garrick Club. Serjeant Talfourd presided, and made a
very happy and complimentary speech, to which I replied. Charles Kemble and Mr. Macready were there.
The latter gentleman has behaved in the handsomest
manner to me. Before I arrived in England he had
spoken of me in the most flattering terms, and on my
arrival, he embraced the earliest opportunity to call
upon me, since which time he has extended to me many
delicate courtesies and attentions, all showing the native
kindness of his heart, and his great refinement and good
breeding."

This passage should be remembered when we come to
the historic feud between Forrest and Macready.

One of the " intellectual fireside-circles " to which

Forrest resorted with particular delight, while in London, was that of John Sinclair, the distinguished English vocalist. The attraction was Catherine Norton Sinclair, the lovely daughter of the house. Miss Sinclair had a fine mind, as well as a beautiful person, and that she fully returned the profound passion which Forrest, from their first meeting, felt for her, there seems no doubt. For, more than thirty years afterwards, when the man was lying cold in death, this woman, for whom he had suffered so much, said brokenly: " The first time I saw him — I recall it now as clearly as though it were but yesterday, — the impression he made was so instantaneous and so strong, that I remember I whispered to myself, while a thrill ran through me, ' This is the handsomest man on whom my eyes have ever fallen.' "

He was the " handsomest man on whom her eyes had ever fallen," she the " first woman he had ever desired to marry; " to their conjugal life, and not to their courtship days, was to be applicable Shakespeare's saying,

" The course of true love never did run smooth."

For no obstacles whatever presented themselves to their union, and on one of the fairest days in June, 1837, they were married in St. Paul's Cathedral, London, setting out, very soon afterwards, for the husband's home beyond the seas. In Philadelphia, where the tragedian opened at the old Chestnut Street Theatre, that fall, his wife made a deep and lasting impression, by reason of her native delicacy of mind and the refinement of her manners, on the friends to whom he presented her. It is hard to believe that such a woman as she then seemed and as many of the letters which she has left behind represent her could have been guilty of the low *amours* of which Forrest later accused her. But that he was honest in his conviction that she had sinned against her marriage vows we must believe. And that, whether guilty of adultery or not, she had so misconducted herself as to spoil his adoring ideal of her is also a fact. Thus, after ten short years of heaven, there succeeded many long and dreary years of what must have been hell for them both. For besides the pain of separation, mutual misunderstanding, and corroding distrust, there was the horror of publicity, — inasmuch as " in an evil hour for himself, in an evil hour for his art and for the struggling drama in America, Edwin Forrest threw open the doors of his home to the scrutiny of the world and appealed to the courts to remove the skeleton which was hidden in his closet." [1] Of that more anon.

The year after Forrest returned from his successful season in England, he presented for the first time in America Sir Edward Bulwer Lytton's " Lady of Lyons " and astonished his friends, no less than his enemies, by the brilliant success he made of his part; that Forrest was really a great actor was never more clear than when he assumed with satisfaction to even the most carping of critics the highly romantic rôle of Claude Melnotte. Another interesting incident of these years, during which his domestic life was still one of perfect felicity, was the visit paid by the actor to ex-President Jackson, then

[1] Sketch of Forrest by Lawrence Barrett.

living in retirement at the Hermitage, Tennessee. One of the topics these two ardent Democrats [1] discussed together was the proposed annexation of Texas. Forrest never forgot the way in which the stooped and faltering sage was quickened at once into the passionate prophet by the ardour of his belief in this measure. It was upon the memory of this experience, which proved the electric capacity of feeble old age to be suddenly charged and to emit lightnings and thunders, that Forrest modelled the great explosions of his Richelieu.

And now we come to the beginnings of the famous feud with Macready. That the Englishman bestowed upon Forrest, during the latter's first professional engagement in London, attentions for which the American was duly grateful, we have already seen. On the surface, indeed, the two were almost friends. Yet there could be no real sympathy between an ardent democrat, who devotedly loved the profession of the player, and a snob who had all his life felt the deepest aversion to this career. In 1843 Macready came to the United States for the first time, played a successful series of engagements, and was well received everywhere. The two or three weeks that he was acting in New York he made his headquarters at the home of the Forrests, and the American tragedian, with exceedingly fine feeling, refused urgent invitations from several managers to appear in rival houses at the time of Macready's visit to other cities. Notwithstanding all this, however, Mac-

---

[1] Four years previously Forrest had been offered the Democratic nomination for Congress.

ready went back to England full of a corroding jealousy of Forrest. The press, by constantly comparing the two actors, had succeeded in making both of them self-conscious, and though Forrest probably had as little to do with unkind notices of Macready as Macready had directly to do with the harsh criticism which greeted Forrest, when the American next visited London, a bitter professional jealousy had been aroused between them.

Then Forrest did a really outrageous thing to Macready when the latter was playing Hamlet in Edinburgh. While the Englishman was careering across the stage, flourishing his handkerchief above his head and acting his conception of the mad prince as he spoke the lines:

" They are coming to the play; I must be idle.
Get you to a place,"

Forrest gave vent to a deep and prolonged hiss as a sign of his profound disapproval of this " business." The right of a spectator to express his condemnation of a player by hissing was then unquestioned, and had Forrest not been a brother-actor in notoriously unfriendly relations with Macready, nothing would have been thought of the matter. Forrest was always wont to maintain that it was simply *as a spectator* that he hissed Mr. Macready, vigorously asserting, in a letter to the *London Times*, that " there are two legitimate modes of evincing approbation and disapprobation in the theatre, — one expressive of approval by the clapping of hands, and the other by hisses to make dissent; and as well-timed and hearty applause is the just meed of the actor who deserves well, so also is hissing a salutary and wholesome corrective of abuses of the stage; and it was against one of these abuses that my dissent was expressed. . . . The truth is Mr. Macready thought fit to introduce a fancy dance into his performance of ' Hamlet ' which I thought, and still think, a desecration of the scene. . . . That a man may manifest his pleasure or displeasure after the recognized mode, according to the best of his judgment, actuated by proper motives and for justifiable ends is a right which until now I have never once heard questioned; and I contend that right extends equally to an actor *in his capacity as a spectator*, as to any other man." The charge of professional jealousy Forrest contemptuously dismissed; but he could not have failed, in his most sincere moments, deeply to regret that he had not been restrained, that unhappy night at Edinburgh, by feelings of professional courtesy.

At this time in Britain and later in New York, however, it seems to have been a case of the pot calling the kettle black. For although Forrest steadfastly refused to have anything to do with an organized opposition to Macready, when the Englishman made his second visit to America, he did not disdain to enter into a war of words with his rival, thus fanning to a flame a fire already fierce. The English articles *pro* and *con* had all been copied in America, it must be recalled, and had naturally lost nothing by the process. So, when Macready began his closing engagement in New York, in May, 1849, the elements of a storm were at hand. For the Bowery boys loved Forrest scarcely less than they loved a fight. What ensued belongs to Macready's story rather than to Forrest's; and the entire episode is so disgraceful to the American stage that it would have been passed over in silence did it not represent, historically, the climax of that hysterical devotion, on the part of the public, to the private interests of stage idols which is now almost extinct.

Another flagrant illustration of this sort of thing was to mark the career of America's leading tragedian. We refer to the public demonstrations which he permitted, not to say encouraged, after he had taken into court the unhappiness of his home. It has often been remarked that where his passions were concerned, good taste, as a guiding principle, made little appeal to Forrest. A man of finer sensibilities, who had for ten years enjoyed the love of a wife whom he tenderly cherished and passionately adored, would have suffered in silence whatever buffets and scorns might come to him on the woman's account. But with Forrest, as with Othello, jealousy once excited could not be downed or nobly borne.

Alger [1] describes categorically the cause of the initial seed of jealousy planted in the spring of 1848, while Forrest was fulfilling a professional engagement in Cincinnati, his wife being then with him. He also gives in full the famous " Consuelo " letter, afterwards sent, it was alleged, to Mrs. Forrest by the man who, some months earlier, had given the husband cause for suspicion. To one of Forrest's " ample experience of the

[1] In his " Life of Forrest."

199

world this letter seemed to leave no doubt of an utter lapse from the marriage vow on the part of its recipient," he says in his hero's defence. But this conclusion does not appear at all inevitable to a dispassionate reader of the missive. And that it did not *at first* appear inevitable to Forrest, we must believe, inasmuch as he at once wrote an oath of innocence couched in the most stringent and solemn terms, which he was apparently satisfied by seeing his wife sign. But jealousy,

> " . . . the green-eyed monster which doth mock
>   The meat it feeds on,"

now had a bitterly-resentful husband in its clutches, and after the actor had brooded in silence for a whole year over what he felt to be his wife's broken faith, he confessed to a near friend what was troubling him, exclaiming passionately, when his listener attempted to defend Mrs. Forrest by praising her physical and spiritual beauty: " She now looks ugly to me; her face is black and hideous." Yet in the interim he had been writing his wife letters full of tenderness and devotion!

A violent and final rupture came on a day when Mrs. Forrest exclaimed: " It is a lie," to some cutting remarks made by the actor concerning her sister. Restraining himself with difficulty, Forrest said painfully: " If a man had said that to me he should die. I cannot live with a woman who says it." And he did not. From that moment separation was inevitable. They mutually decided, however, that the cause of their parting should not be made known. Before leaving the house, she asked him to give her a copy of the works of Shakespeare as a memento of him. "He did so, writing in it 'Mrs. Edwin Forrest, from Edwin Forrest,' a sad alteration from the inscription uniformly made in the books he had before presented to her, — ' From her lover and husband, Edwin Forrest.' He then accompanied her in a carriage to the house of her generous friends, Parke and Fanny Godwin."

Parke Godwin was the close associate in journalism of Charles A. Dana and of William Cullen Bryant, whose daughter he had married. The fact that he and his friends sided with Mrs. Forrest undoubtedly did much, at the very beginning of the estrangement, to create a favourable impression in the lady's behalf. On March 1, 1849, Forrest procured a legal separation from his wife, allowing her fifteen hundred dollars per annum. It was agreed that they should live apart on this basis, each being silent as to the cause of their trouble. For a time they kept to this and corresponded at intervals, the wife in one letter asserting her conviction that "some day your own naturally noble and just mind will do me justice, and you will believe in the affection which, for twelve years, has never swerved from you. I cannot, nor would I, subscribe myself other than yours now and ever, Catherine N. Forrest." Yet she finally declared that she would consent to a divorce if this would promote his peace of mind. And he, at last, admitted that it was his wish so to put a final termination to a state of things which was wearing out his life.

The next step in this wretched business was the filing

by Forrest of an application for divorce in Philadelphia. This was instantly followed by a similar application on the part of Mrs. Forrest in New York. The ensuing trial, with its incrimination of adultery and its recrimination of the same offence, began in December, 1851, and lasted for six weeks. Those who care for the details of the matter may find them *ad nauseam* in the papers of the time. For the evidence and arguments were reproduced in the press with a minuteness never before known in America, and the public appeared to enjoy itself hugely as it listened or read.[1] " Many of the most respectable citizens stood waiting, eager to rush in at the first opening of the doors," records the *New York Herald's* representative the morning after the case began to be tried. And he then describes as follows the appearance on the first day of the trial of the two people chiefly concerned. " Mrs. Forrest was habited in black, wore a black silk bonnet lined with a white cap and had a black lace veil covering her face. . . . Mr. Forrest wore his usual dress, namely a black frock coat with velvet facings, collar *a la* Byron and a considerable display of snowy linen."

Unless there was a great deal of perjury on the part of the various witnesses called, husband and wife were about equally guilty of the offence with which each charged the other. But Mrs. Forrest almost at once won the sympathy of the public by her chaste and gentle bearing; and her husband quite as soon lost whatever advantage he may have had to start with by his bluntness and

[1] Several editions of the entire evidence were published in book form, too.

violence. The verdict was in the woman's favour, Forrest being condemned to pay the court costs and three thousand dollars a year alimony.[1] Five times he appealed, only to be baffled and overthrown at the end; and it was not until 1868, after eighteen years of the hardest kind of fighting, that he finally abandoned further resistance and paid over the full award, — sixty-four thousand dollars. Of this sum all but a pittance of five thousand dollars had already been eaten up by the expenses incident to the trial.

The bad taste which we have previously noted in Forrest now again came to the front. He did not disdain to use for purposes of advertisement this tragedy in his domestic life. When he reappeared at the Broadway Theatre, a fortnight after the close of the trial, he permitted a sign, " This is the people's verdict " to be hung across the crowded house and in his speech at the close of the performance there were repeated references to his " cause, not my cause alone, but yours, the cause of every man in this community, the cause of every human being, the cause of every honest wife, the cause of every virtuous woman, the cause of everyone who cherishes a home and the pure spirit which should abide there." At the close of this engagement, which had been throughout one of unprecedented houses, Forrest declared that such a demonstration vindicated him more than a thousand verdicts, " for it springs from those who make and unmake judges."

[1] Mrs. Forrest was given permission to marry again, he being denied that privilege.

Not only in New York but wherever he played, during the years that succeeded the first verdict against him, the publicity which had been given to this squalid divorce suit served as a means of drawing large crowds to the theatre. From Portland and Boston to Cincinnati and St. Louis, from Buffalo and Detroit to Charleston and New Orleans, the effect was the same. A manager had only to announce Forrest's name to cause throngs to flock to see him play. Wild applause always greeted him on his entrance, and after the final curtain had been rung down, he was frequently serenaded at his hotel. Of course, he was accumulating a great deal of money all this time. In 1851 he changed his residence from New York to Philadelphia, taking his three sisters to live with him. To these good women he was ever tenderly devoted. And he outlived them all.

The first intimation of failing strength came to him in 1865, while playing Damon at the Holiday Street Theatre in Baltimore. To his horror he found, when he finished his part, that he had suffered a partial paralysis of the sciatic nerve. Gone for ever now was the sturdy gait and the proud tread of the herculean actor. The following year, none the less, he went to San Francisco, in response to very flattering offers, making his début in the Opera House there as Richelieu before an immense audience. The first ticket sold for this performance brought five hundred dollars. For thirty-five nights he played to an aggregate of over sixty thousand persons and was paid twenty thousand dollars in gold.

As late as the season of 1871–1872, when he was in his

sixty-sixth year, he travelled over seven thousand miles and acted in fifty-two different places between October 1 and April 4. His receipts were over thirty-nine thousand dollars, derived from Philadelphia, Columbus, Cincinnati, New Orleans, Galveston, Houston, Nashville, Omaha, Kansas City, St. Louis, Chicago, Pittsburg, Cleveland, Buffalo, Detroit, Rochester, Syracuse, Utica, Troy, Albany, New York, and Boston. At Kansas City excursionists were brought by railroad from a distance of a hundred and fifty miles at three dollars each the round trip.

That he was still playing superbly may be gathered from the following account of his work in Lear made by a distinguished author in a private letter after seeing him play at the Globe Theatre, Boston. " I saw Lear himself and never can I forget him, the poor disowned wandering king, whose every look and tone went to the heart. . . . I could not suppress my tears in the last scene. . . . The whole picture will stay in my memory so long as soul and body hang together." Which reminds me of Forrest's reply to J. B. McCullough of the *St. Louis Democrat*, when, towards the end of the older man's life, that gentleman remarked to him: " I never saw you play Lear as well as you did to-night." " *Play* Lear," retorted the veteran, rising laboriously from his chair to his full and imposing height, " *Play* Lear! What do you mean, sir? I *play* Hamlet, Richard, Shylock, Virginius, if you please, but by God, sir, I *am* Lear." Nor was this wholly imaginative. His hearthstone was deserted, and it seemed to him as if all the world was ungrateful and that in his old age he stood alone, unkinged.

Forrest was a lover of beautiful things and of rare old books. Gabriel Harrison describes a Thanksgiving Day spent at the Broad Street residence, towards the close of the great tragedian's life, in which the old folio edition of Shakespeare, 1623, was taken out of its case and exhibited with the greatest possible tenderness and pride. Other rare things of the stage that had belonged to Garrick and similarly famous actors were also shown. " Then he conducted his guest to the basement of his house, and exhibited a perfect little theatre, containing scenery, footlights, and room enough to seat at least two hundred people. 'Here,' he said, 'I have had little children perform a whole play which I have rehearsed with them to my great pleasure.' This remark," Harrison comments, " was a proof of his tender heart; it showed that half a century of buffets with the hard world had not chilled the impulses of youth."

Forrest had all his life dearly loved children and been very tender with them. One cannot help feeling that, if his son had lived, the estrangement between him and his wife would somehow have been averted. There is a beautiful story about one occasion when, as a young man acting at the Old National Theatre in Boston, he hurried from the playhouse, Metamora's paint only imperfectly removed from his cheeks, to nurse the sick baby of a woman staying at the same hotel. The child had been ailing for many days, and its mother was quite worn out from caring for it. But Forrest paced up and down the room all night long, soothing it, and when the doctor came the next day, he said that the vitality which the

EDWIN FORREST AS KING LEAR

EDWIN FORREST

See page 173

infant drew from the man's strong breast, against which it had finally slept, had been the means of saving its life.

His own life's span was drawing to a close. A shattering illness in the spring of 1872 compelled him to retire definitively from the stage, and though he gave some public readings after that, he made no great success of it. After reading " Othello," on Saturday afternoon, December 7, 1872, in Tremont Temple, Boston,[1] he was glad to journey back to his Philadelphia home as quickly as he could. And there, on the morning of December 12, his servant found him dead in his bed. He had slipped away quietly and painlessly in the night. His will provided a retreat for aged actors, which was opened in 1876. Of it Wilson Barrett has said that it is " like a gentleman's country seat, and the old actors and actresses his honoured guests." There are seldom more than a dozen women and men here resident at a time, the idea being that these guests of Edwin Forrest's bounty shall have every comfort and be allowed every privilege possible. Each year Forrest's guests appropriately celebrate his birthday by giving a play.

Mrs. Forrest, or Mrs. Catherine Norton Sinclair, as we must now perforce call her, survived her husband

---

[1] The *Boston Journal* of December 9, 1872, gave about five lines of fine print to Forrest on this occasion: " The audience included much of the genius and culture of our community, although the attendance was not, numerically speaking, all it should have been." The impassioned scenes from " Othello " were delivered, the critic added, " with the marked dramatic power for which Mr. Forrest is distinguished."

nearly twenty years. Soon after the trial she determined to go on the stage and played a season at Brougham's Lyceum (later Wallack's), opening on February 2, 1852, in "School For Scandal." After that she played "Lady of Lyons," "Much Ado About Nothing," "Love's Sacrifice," and "The Patrician's Daughter." George Vandenhoff, a prominent English actor who now supported her, trained her for her parts, and he has categorically described, in his interesting volume, "An Actor's Note-Book," the terms of their alliance. He was an utter stranger to this lady, he declares, until "some time in 1851," when he was invited — even urged — to "coach" her for the stage. At first he was reluctant to do this because he believed that it was too late in life for her to take such a step; but upon her representation that she would probably have to earn her living in this way, he consented to help her prepare three or four parts. Since she had no money with which to pay her teacher, it was agreed that in consideration of his instructions and of his performing with her, he was to have an equal share of such profits as "her temporary and factitious attraction would secure." (Vandenhoff had been trained for the law.)

It was by Vandenhoff's advice, we are told, that the lady played Lady Teazle the night of her New York début. He regarded this as the one part in which she could give a fairly artistic performance. These details are of interest from the fact that Vandenhoff was considerably criticized at the time in the belief that he had "put money in his purse by taking advantage of Mrs.

Sinclair's necessities." From his statement of their financial relations, it would appear, however, that not for some years did he even " come out even " on the deal.

During the Sinclair-Vandenhoff engagement at the National Theatre, Boston, in the spring of 1852, the theatre was destroyed by fire, the dramatic stock company losing most of its belongings. The old Boston Theatre, on Federal Street, was available, however, and there Mrs. Sinclair was enabled to complete her Boston time. She left New York for England on June 16, 1852. She appeared at the Museum, Albany, New York, in January, and at the Varieties Theatre, New Orleans, Louisiana, in March, 1853. She later toured California and Australia, supported by Henry Sedley, another excellent actor, who had married Anne Sinclair, her sister. Finally Mrs. Sinclair became the proprietress of a theatre in San Francisco, and is said to have realized two hundred and fifty thousand dollars therefrom. Her last professional appearance on any stage was on December 18, 1859, when she played in New York for charity. She died, June 9, 1891, at the New York residence of her nephew, William Sedley.

CHAPTER VIII

A PLAYER WHO INSPIRED A SONG AND ANOTHER WHO COMPOSED ONE

GABRIEL HARRISON, whose " Memoir of Forrest " — written from his own personal knowledge of the man and actor — has several times been quoted, at this point may very well introduce us to the woman player of the nineteenth century whom he regards as alone worthy to stand alongside Forrest. Of the many players he had seen — and he names the elder Vandenhoff, the elder Wallack, Charles Kemble, Charles Kean, Hamblin, Joseph Jefferson, Davenport, Edwin Booth, Charles Dillon, McCullough, Barrett, Irving, Hackett, Matilda Heron, Fanny Kemble, Charlotte Cushman, Rachel, Ristori, Clara Morris, Mary Anderson, and Mrs. Duff, only the last-named player, he asserts, was anything like equal to Forrest in elocution, grandeur, electrical force, and detail of finish. " Like some new star of great purity and light, this lady," he declares, " quietly came among the dramatic luminaries, and as quietly and mysteriously disappeared. That her genius was not early and fully recognized and ranked with the celebrated Sarah Siddons is the most mysterious thing belonging to the history of the stage. It is with me impossible to conceive anything nearer to dramatic perfection in voice, elocution, facial expression, gesture, and graceful movement than was possessed by this accomplished and beautiful woman. Her face, delicate and refined in all its outlines, her rather large gray eyes full of soul and intelligence, her figure of medium height with fine proportions, — every personal trait excited the most refined admiration alike on and off the stage."

Inasmuch as Mrs. Duff's last appearance as an actress was seventy-five years ago, naturally there can be found no living witness to the wonderful power of her work. But John Gilbert, who is well remembered as a person quite competent to acclaim great acting, often asserted that " she was, without exception, the most exquisite tragic actress he ever saw." The elder Booth called her " the best actress in the world; " by the elder Kean she was rebuked for attracting from him his proper share of the night's applause; Forrest declared her the most desirable leading woman with whom he had ever been associated; and Horace Greeley gave it in print as his deep conviction that " her Lady Macbeth has never since been equalled."

Joseph N. Ireland, who has written a delightful little biography of Mrs. Duff, attributes her failure to attain imperishable fame to the fact that she rose to distinction and popularity in Boston and Philadelphia before being introduced to the stage of the Metropolis. New York, a century ago, insisted upon discovering its own favourites.

"Like London," Ireland judicially observes, "New York can sometimes be jealous of her sister cities, and does not like to be called upon to worship the idol of another and a smaller place; and, therefore, though critical judgment pronounced Mrs. Duff worthy of the highest praise, the public — with honourable exceptions — finding that she bore no foreign endorsement, looked upon her simply as the favourite of a provincial town, and did not greet her advent with that generous and enthusiastic welcome she so well deserved. The few who saw her were charmed with her personations, but fashion could not be induced to interest itself in her behalf, or to crowd the house when her name was first announced. She was heartily applauded but not numerously followed; and, although she finally won her way to every heart, she never became an attraction powerful enough to secure a permanent engagement in New York's leading theatre."

Since nearly all this woman's remarkable professional life was passed in America, we have every right to claim her as an American actress, but by birth she was English, having first seen the light in London in 1794. At the age of fifteen she and her two younger sisters became attached to the Dublin Theatre in the capacity of dancers; all three were singularly sweet and charming girls, and on an occasion when the gentleman amateurs of Kilkenny, following the fashion of the time, engaged the ladies from the Dublin Theatre to assist them in their annual benefit performance for the poor of their city, Moore, the Irish poet, met and fell passionately in love with Mary Dyke. But since she did not return this affection, he transferred his attentions to Elizabeth Dyke,

the second sister, whom he soon after married. It was
Mary Dyke's rejection of the poet's suit which gave rise
to the celebrated song,

> " Mary, I believed thee true,
>   And I was blessed in thus believing;
> But now I mourn that e'er I knew
>   A girl so fair and so deceiving, —
>   Fare thee well.
>
>   .   .   .   .
>
> " Fare thee well. I'll think of thee;
>   Thou leav'st me many a bitter token;
> For see, distracting woman, see,
>   My peace is gone, my heart is broken. —
>   Fare thee well."

Whether Mary Dyke really was as " deceiving " to
Moore as he here poetically asserts we shall never know.
But inasmuch as he was a man of the world who had
already attained the age of thirty when he first met this
child of fifteen, and inasmuch as he comforted himself by
marrying the younger sister quite promptly, we may
assume that his heart was not " broken," save in a
metaphorical and poetic sense. It is a fact, however, that
on the single occasion (in 1828) when this sister returned
from America for a professional engagement in England,
Mrs. Moore did not come near her but sent word from the
fashionable watering-place where she was then staying
that it would not be convenient for them to meet.

Yet Mary Dyke's only offence against Moore had been
that of clinging, in spite of the poet's blandishments, to

the man for whom she had already formed an attachment — John R. Duff, a young actor then connected with the Dublin Theatre. He and Moore had been classmates in Trinity College. Duff has been described as an Apollo in person and as a Crichton in accomplishments. He had been intended for the bar, but the fascination of the stage overcame him, and since he showed great promise, he was recommended by Cooper to Messrs. Powell and Dickson of the theatre in Boston, by whom he was immediately engaged. Before sailing for America, he married Mary Dyke, then still less than sixteen.

Thus, when she made her début in Boston, December 31, 1810, as Juliet, Mrs. Duff was really at an age and in a situation to appreciate keenly the emotions and anxieties of Capulet's daughter. At this time, however, she made no such success in the part as she afterwards attained. Her next appearance was on January 3, 1811, when she acted Lady Anne in " Richard III " to no less a tragedian than George Frederick Cooke. She also supported Mr. Cooke during his later engagements; and on February 10, 1812, she played Ophelia to the Hamlet of John Howard Payne, who was then in the height of his popularity.

Beginning with the fall of 1812, the Duffs were for five years in the company of Messrs. Warren and Wood of the Philadelphia and Baltimore theatres. But the husband was still the drawing power, Mrs. Duff being only a pretty *ingenue*. By 1817, however, when she was again in Boston — where her husband had become associated

MRS. DUFF, WHOSE ACTING HORACE GREELEY GREATLY ADMIRED. HER REJEC-
TION OF THE HAND OF THOMAS MOORE INSPIRED A FAMOUS IRISH LOVE SONG
From the Theatre Collection, Harvard University

JOHN HOWARD PAYNE
After a daguerreotype by Brady
See page 221

with Powell and Dickson in the management of the
Federal Street Theatre, — her work in " Macbeth "
attracted the favourable attention of the critics, and
when she played Juliet, in February, 1818, to the Romeo
of Cooper, she was greeted as one who had " arrived."
In October, 1820, Boston theatre-goers were talking of
little else than her impersonation of the heroine in
" Jane Shore," and when, on the thirteenth of this same
month, she gave her impassioned representation of
Hermione in " The Distrest Mother " — taken from
Racine's " Andromaque " — she fairly electrified her
auditors. Throwing aside all tameness and restraint,
she now showed fully the fire and passion that had long
been slumbering in her soul. For, while her genius had
been developing, life had pressed her hard. She was
never free from the care of a young and growing family
(ten children in all were born to her during her professional career) and it was very likely for this reason that
she was able to give such a presentation of a mother's
love and tenderness as has never been equalled on our
stage.

When Mrs. Duff was rehearsing Hermione for the
Orestes of Edmund Kean, the visiting star requested her
to play with less force and intensity or her acting would
throw him into the background. She said she must play
her best; and she did, with the result that the audience
insisted, that night, upon giving to her fully half of the
applause. Kean himself was so impressed by her power
that he declared her the superior of any actress on the
British stage, — an opinion that he frequently reiterated.

The *Boston Gazette*, in reviewing this performance, said:
" The eye of fancy almost beheld the sacred shade of
Racine descending from above to proclaim her for his
own resuscitated Hermione." And it added: " Those who
have seen Mrs. Duff's Ophelia will remember it through
life. Certain it is she has the power, and we have felt
it, to consecrate sorrow, dignify emotion and kindle the
imagination as well as to awaken the sympathies."
When the elder Booth played Hamlet to Mrs. Duff's
Ophelia, May 20, 1822, he was so astounded by her acting
that he declared her above all competition, either in
Europe or America. In Philadelphia as well as in Boston
the receipts immediately doubled when she was supporting Booth.

But though the critics were unanimous in high praise
of her powers, the New York dilettanti insisted upon
regarding it as a piece of presumption that a stock
actress from the Boston and Philadelphia theatres should
have dared to present herself as a star on the Metropolitan stage. In consequence many of them avoided the
theatre during her stay, — so many that Price and Simpson did not have the courage to engage her for a long
season at the Park and so force their patrons to become
acquainted with her extraordinary gifts. A year or
two later, while playing at the then new Bowery Theatre,
Mrs. Duff was able so to divert the Park's patronage
that the managers must have deeply regretted their
previous lack of enterprise. Mr. Duff was with his
wife during her Bowery engagement; but that he had
by no means kept pace with her phenomenally rapid

advancement is very clear from the notices. Conway and Forrest were far more nearly on a par with her now. She was being called " the Mrs. Siddons of the American stage " — and a London engagement for her was being arranged.

Because of the prejudice then supposed to exist in London against everything American, this actress was announced as " From the Theatre Royal, Dublin " when, on March 3, 1828, she appeared at Drury Lane in the tragedy of " Isabella," with Macready playing Biron. The comments of the London press were very various. One paper spoke of her as " a respectable but not a remarkable performer," while another declared " her eye the finest since the time of Mrs. Siddons " and prophesied " it will be the fault of the management if Mrs. Duff does not do great things for the Drury Lane Theatre. There is no actress in her line now on the London stage with so much intellectual energy." The *Gazette*, on the other hand, declared " her fright was so excessive as to prevent the possibility of forming a decided opinion as to her merits." And this was very likely true. To appear in a strange theatre (enormous in size and designated by Mrs. Siddons herself as " the wilderness ") before an unfamiliar audience and in another land proved so much of an ordeal that the actress positively suffered, as she afterwards confessed, from stage fright.

This first London appearance made her ill. And soon after her second appearance (on April 14), she and her husband suddenly set sail for home. Stephen Price, then manager of the Drury Lane, would not grant her the salary Mr. Duff thought she ought to have, it would seem; so for the two nights she had played in London she received — nothing.

In America, however, her success was unabated; even New York tardily came to appreciate her. When Horace Greeley saw her at the Richmond Hill Theatre, February, 1832, as Lady Macbeth, he wrote most enthusiastically of her talents, and later he kept lamenting in print her prolonged absence from the New York stage, saying that it was a disgrace to the dramatic taste of the city that she was not called for in terms too decided to be misunderstood. Mrs. Duff, in fact, seems to have been the only actress who ever made a lasting impression upon the famous editor. In " Recollections of a Busy Life " may be found the following passage: " At Richmond Hill I saw her personate Lady Macbeth better than it has since been done in this city, though she played for thirty dollars per week and others have since received ten times that amount for a single night. I doubt that any woman has since played in our city — and I am thinking of Fanny Kemble — who was the superior of Mrs. Duff in a wide range of tragic characters."

No less than one hundred and thirty-eight characters were personated by Mrs. Duff during a period of nine months. Where is the actress now who could carry such a burden? And she played for a wretchedly small reward, too. Moreover, her husband had died in 1831, and she had to carry alone, as best she could, the burden of her large family. No wonder the poor lady became temporarily insane from so much work and worry. But after a period she recovered her health, played in various cities outside New York very acceptably, as before, and in the autumn of 1835 was engaged to give a season at the new little Franklin Theatre, Chatham Square.

This was the climax of her fame. Every night the house was filled to overflowing with those who, if perhaps not the most fashionable of the city's theatregoers, were certainly the most intelligent. " All were spellbound as of old. Her soul-subduing voice still melted the hearts of the sternest listeners, and caused the tears of sympathy to moisten many a man's unwilling cheek. Sorrow, sickness and disappointment had not quelled the fire of genius . . . and in every varying emotion of the soul Mrs. Duff was still the pathetic, powerful, brilliant and impassioned actress whose magnetic quality aroused the enthusiasm of her audiences and sustained their interest in her characters unflagging to the end." [1]

Then, quite suddenly, she married again, the man of her choice being Joel G. Seaver of New Orleans. This marriage appears to have been consummated, on the lady's part, for the sake of escaping the pecuniary difficulties which threatened to overwhelm her; but Mr. Seaver — or Sevier, as he found it to his advantage to call himself when practising law in New Orleans — apparently made his wife happy in retirement, for only occasionally, and then for charitable purposes, did she again tread the boards.

[1] " Mrs. Duff," by J. N. Ireland, p. 126.

Born and educated a Roman Catholic, she now became a most devout and zealous communicant of the Methodist communion and strove in every possible way to forget and disassociate herself from her former stage connection. Once, to be sure, her old friend, James Rees of Philadelphia, sought her out in her comfortable home and succeeded in arousing her to pride in her dramatic achievements. But only momentarily. " 'Tis past now," she said; " that was my worldly life; the present, and I hope the future, my heavenly life."

Yet there were still stormy days to be endured before this good woman attained " Heaven, her home." In 1854, Mr. Seaver's political opinions having rendered him unpopular in New Orleans, they quietly left that city, ostensibly for Texas. And then for twenty years old friends of Mrs. Seaver could get no trace whatever of her — nor be assured of her decease. Finally, it was discovered that she had been living in New York all the time, at the home of her youngest daughter, Madame Reillieux.

Brilliant company often assembled here and talked of plays and players, little dreaming that the quiet old lady in the gray silk gown and cambric cap, whom they sometimes met for a few minutes, was the former fascinating actress whose remarkable gift for tragedy had been highly praised by all the leading players of the day. Madame Reillieux was the last surviving daughter and as she died before her mother, no notification was sent to the many old friends of the famous actress, when she herself passed away September 5, 1857, in the sixty-

third year of her age. Even the place of her burial was
unknown until 1874, when it was discovered that she
lies interred with this beloved daughter in a single name-
less grave in Greenwood. A humble stone, bearing the
simple inscription, MOTHER AND GRANDMOTHER,
is all that marks the final resting-place of this greatest
and grandest actress of her day.

Another player of extraordinary ability, who died
in obscurity after a life full of disappointment, was John
Howard Payne. More untrue things have probably
been written of Payne than of any other American, —
either with or without a stage background. Yet there
is one very interesting episode in his career about which
the public at large knows nothing — his hopeless love
for the widow of Shelley, who at this time was herself
enamoured, it would appear, with the whimsical and
fascinating Washington Irving.

Payne was born in New York, June 9, 1791, — not in
Boston, as was stated on the inscription which for many
years stood over his temporary grave in Tunis. In
Boston he received his early schooling, however, and, by
seeing in the shop windows pictures of the celebrated
Master Betty, became fired with ambition to enter upon
a stage career. Payne's father was a schoolmaster and
for a time was settled at East Hampton, Long Island,
where he married John Howard's mother. Thus the
lad, though city-bred, had authentic early associations
with a " lowly cottage " and with " birds singing gaily
that came at his will," from the fact that his holidays

were spent at his grandparents' home. The years of disastrous and more or less disillusionizing stage experiences which intervened did not succeed in effacing the sweet childhood memories through which he has earned immortality.

A fatally precocious youth, possessed of very remarkable beauty, Payne early attracted to his side plenty of influential friends, who smoothed for him the path to an early and successful début. Thus he was only seventeen, and looked much younger, when he made his first bow to the public as an actor at the Park Theatre, New York, February 24, 1809. Dunlap, who was present, says that " the applause was very great. Boy-actors were then a novelty, and we have seen none since that equalled Master Payne." Very extravagant things were said of the young actor, a special New York correspondent sending to a leading Boston paper the dictum that " in force of genius and taste in *belles lettres* there are few actors on any stage that can claim competition with this one." The public seemed of similar opinion, for notwithstanding a heavy snow-storm, the very large sum, for those days, of fourteen hundred dollars was taken in at the Park when he played Romeo, in the course of this first engagement, to the Juliet of Mrs. Darley.

In Boston, that spring, he was enormously applauded for his work as Young Norval in Holmes's " Douglas " and for his impersonation of the Prince in " Hamlet." Similar triumphs greeted him in Providence, Philadelphia, Baltimore, and Charleston; as well as again in New York, when he played with George Frederick

Cooke. Then he went to England, where in 1813 he secured an engagement at Drury Lane through the good offices of Benjamin West. The press notices were very complimentary, too complimentary, perhaps, for the young man's best good. Having been superlatively praised for effects which he achieved without much preliminary effort, he did not work continuously, as a successful actor must. And when the wonder of his precocity had worn off, he was discovered to be really not much of an actor after all.

Moreover, he had now become interested in dramatic writing as a result of a friendship formed with Talma in Paris, and as this opened a new field of labour to him, his connection with the stage became thenceforth that of a poet rather than a player, though he did act occasionally in the provinces and later, for his own benefit, in America. The plays which Payne either wrote or translated or adapted number more than sixty. Yet it is because of a song in his opera, " Clari, the Maid of Milan," that we remember him to-day. This song has had a more universal circulation than any other song written before or since. Upwards of one hundred thousand copies were issued by its publisher in London in less than one year after its publication, the profit yielded *to him* being over two thousand guineas; Payne got two hundred and fifty pounds for a batch of plays of which " Clari," in which the song occurs, was one.

Yet Payne was never forced to " starve in a garret," as has been picturesquely represented. The varied and interesting life of a playwright-critic and man about town was being enjoyed by him at the very period when he is supposed to have been sunk in gloom and penury. This the letters to Mrs. Shelley clearly show. This interesting correspondence [1] began late in 1824, Mrs. Shelley being then not quite twenty-eight years old, while Payne was six years older — one year older than Shelley would have been had he lived. Through Payne Mrs. Shelley had already met Irving in Paris, where the two Americans had been acting as partners — with an equal share in the profits — in the adaptation of French plays to the London theatres. Irving, however, had then gone to Spain. After Payne had been back in London for some time, all the lady's letters to the author of " Home Sweet Home " were sent by him to Irving, with a note saying that he (Payne) had discovered that Mrs. Shelley had been cultivating him " only as a source of introduction " to Irving. Poor Payne, in this long letter to Irving, admits that though he loves in vain, he loves sincerely the fascinating widow of Shelley!

When Payne returned to America, early in the summer of 1832, a benefit was offered him " in the name of his native city, New York; " on this occasion, ladies of fashion sat in the pit (ordinarily devoted exclusively to the use of men in those days) and paid five dollars for the privilege. The price of every part of the house, indeed, was raised to five dollars, excepting the gallery, which was fixed at one dollar, the then usual box-price. When it is added that the house was filled from pit to dome, it

[1] " The Romance of Mary W. Shelley, John Howard Payne and Washington Irving," Bibliophile Society, Boston, 1907.

ELLEN TREE (MRS. CHARLES KEAN), WHOSE SISTER, MARIA, POPULARIZED
"HOME, SWEET HOME"

THE MOTHER OF EDGAR ALLAN POE

MRS. JOHN DREW, SENIOR, AS MRS. MALAPROP

See page 328

will not seem so strange that the receipts for the night were over seven thousand dollars. For this " great dramatic festival " at the Park, Forrest, Charles and Fanny Kemble, George Barrett, Cooper, and J. W. Wallack, among others, volunteered.

The failure of the Boston benefit of the following spring to equal anything like New York's record in receipts was very likely due in large measure to the fact that a pretty poor bill was offered for the very high prices charged.[1] In New Orleans, where Payne was given a benefit in 1835 at the Camp Street Theatre (Tyrone Power being one of the actors of the occasion), the receipts were $1006.50.

This New Orleans benefit marks Payne's last association with the drama in America. He subsequently served his country as an intermediary in claim settlements with the Indians, and from 1843 to 1845 and again from 1851 until his death, April 9, 1852, as consul at Tunis. Nearly thirty years after his death his remains were carried from Tunis to America, through the friendly offices of W. W. Corcoran, and on a bright day of March, 1883, were deposited in Oak Hill Cemetery, Washington, as the assembled company sang together the immortal lines of " Home Sweet Home."

[1] R. B. Forbes, in *The Critic* for December, 1882, describes this Boston fiasco as follows: " The eventful night came. In the second row appeared the committee and their families and friends *en grand tenue*, modestly giving up the dress circle to ' the sovereign people,' who were expected by thousands. In the lower part of the house appeared about two hundred editors, critics and boys eating peanuts. Finally, the curtain rose and four short plays were enacted, almost in pantomime, as no sane man could be expected to say much before so much light and so few persons. . . . This benefit was forever after known as the Festival of Pain.''

CHAPTER IX

FORREST'S ENEMY, MACREADY, AND SOME STARS WHO
CAME AFTER HIM

THE Macready whose coming to America poor Conway
had so dreaded opened at the Park Theatre, New York,
as Virginius, October 2, 1826, played his great characters
with much success in Boston, Philadelphia, and several
other cities, and received for his efforts the tidy sum of
two hundred and fifty dollars a night. William Charles
Macready was an actor who knew his commercial value
and seldom failed to get it. Forrest's violent disagreement with Macready and the riots which sprang therefrom are an old story to readers of theatrical memoirs,
but it must be re-told here for the sake of record and com-
pleteness. The significant thing about the whole episode
seems to be that though Forrest was thoroughly wrong
in the matter, he, rather than Macready, gets our sympathy; there was something so outrageously smug and
self-satisfied about this snobbish Englishman who de-
spised his profession!

Moreover, everything *except* the approval of American
audiences had gone Macready's way! The son of a
celebrated county manager, he had had a very good
education; and when a decline in the family fortunes

made it advisable for him to go on the stage, success there came quickly. At twenty-three he was playing good parts at Covent Garden for a salary of eighteen pounds a week, and the Hazlitt who lampooned poor Conway was praising him highly. Opportunity to travel in France and Italy and to see the noted actors of both countries was then his; after which he made an advantageous marriage and set out to conquer America.

America duly conquered, Macready returned to England and was soon making an artistic, if not pecuniary, success of an English company which (in 1828) he took over to Paris. Then he became manager of the Covent Garden Theatre and proceeded to produce many of the original plays with which his fame is identified. When he made his second visit to America, in 1843, he was manager of Drury Lane Theatre. This time he stayed with us over a year, and while in New York was the guest of the Forrests.

Macready's third and last American engagement began in September, 1848. His career was now, at any rate, to be marked by thunder-clouds, as he very soon discovered. For the idol of the American " People," Edwin Forrest, had not been given a fair hearing in London, and Philadelphia, the city of Forrest's birth, promptly let Macready know that he was held responsible for this. When he performed " Macbeth " he had to do it almost in dumb show, amidst occasional showers of nuts and rotten eggs; but he played through the part and at the end addressed the audience, pledging his

sacred word of honour that he had never shown any
hostility to " an American actor." This called forth a
public letter from Forrest, in which he confessed boast-
fully to having hissed Macready at Edinburgh but denied any part in the organized opposition which had been
shown the visitor; he added, with superfluous offensiveness, that *his* advice had been to let " the superannuated
driveller alone." In New York Macready was again the
victim of a conspiracy, one of his staff, Mr. John Ryder,
having been offered, as was later shown, a large bribe
to come forward and swear falsely that Macready had
conspired to render Forrest a failure in England. Of
course the offer was indignantly refused. All the better-
class opinion of New York was with the visiting star; but,
none the less, rowdyism prevailed.

A plan for hissing Macready from the stage, upon his
appearance in New York, had been submitted to Forrest. The latter refused, of course, to countenance the
conspiracy. But this did not prevent the theatre from
being crowded with the Englishman's enemies when, on
May 7, 1849, he began his engagement at the Astor
Place Opera House. The play was obliged to proceed
amid a tumult of yells and hisses, and at the end of the
third act the performance stopped, and the visiting
star returned to his hotel. His desire was to set sail
at once for England, but in response to the urgent wishes
of his friends he agreed to make one more attempt to
play, and on May 10 " Macbeth " was advertised.

Upon the opening of the doors that night, the theatre
filled almost instantly with people who were favourable

228

WILLIAM C. MACREADY

See page 226

MASTER JOSEPH BURKE
After a drawing by T. Wageman
See page 232

FANNY ELLSLER
From a drawing by W. K. Hewitt
See page 231

to the actor, nearly all the others being excluded; but Macready's enemies did not by any means go quietly home. Instead they filled the streets and waited for the most favourable moment to precipitate their attack. That moment soon came outside the theatre, as it had already come inside. Stones were hurled against windows of the building, smashing them to atoms, and at one time it seemed as if the destruction of the entire edifice was inevitable. Macready himself barely escaped with his life by being hurried out of the front door in disguise and helped to make his way through the crowd. Meanwhile the militia had been called out, and when orders to disperse had been greeted by the angry crowd with yells and hoots of derision, the soldiers were bidden to close their columns and fire. The result was that one hundred and thirty-four rioters were killed outright, and over a hundred wounded; while the remainder of the now-sobered mob dispersed into the darkness.

It is a pity that so disgraceful an occurrence must needs be chronicled at all, and I have purposely made my account as brief as possible. Those who desire to see the episode set forth categorically are referred to the pages of Macready's " Diary."

As an antidote to the stiffness of Macready, I may very well insert here a little sketch of Céleste, the first dancer to win lasting enthusiasm in America. The dancers, of which there were several at this period, were wont to come on after the main offering of the evening. Thus it was that Mlle. Céleste made her first appearance in America at the Bowery Theatre, following a performance of "School for Scandal," on June 27, 1827, in which Mrs. Charles Gilfert, the wife of the manager, had acted Lady Teazle. Céleste is said to have been born in Paris, August 6, 1814, where at a very early age she was placed in the *Conservatoire* as a pupil. While still a child, she appeared with Talma, the greatest of French tragedians; she still looked to be only a child when she made her début in New York. Her grace and beauty attracted universal admiration and won for her the hand of Mr. Elliott, an American gentleman, to whom she was married in 1828, and by whom she became the mother of an only daughter.

After dancing with success in the principal theatres of this country, she sailed from New Orleans for England, where she made many profitable appearances in the provinces, previous to coming out in London as Mathilde in "The French Spy." France, Italy, and Germany subsequently welcomed her in this rôle — as did also New York on November 17, 1834. Then began an American tour which lasted for three years, during which she is said to have netted two hundred thousand dollars. She came over here for a third visit in 1838, was with us again in 1840, once again in the fall of 1851,[1] and finally and rather unexpectedly, — for thirteen years had now elapsed since her last visit — in 1865. It was rumoured that her farewell American tour was made necessary

[1] She then played, while in Boston, at the old National Theatre, on Portland Street, and was billed, at her request, as may be seen from an autograph letter to the manager now preserved in the Boston Public Library, as "Directress of the Theatre Royal Adelphi, London."

by unfortunate investments which had seriously impaired her hitherto ample fortune.

In her prime, Céleste was a very beautiful creature, with a handsome face, eloquent dark eyes, and a face which was expressive beyond that of any actress of her time. Her every movement, too, was full of grace and charm.

"The power, pathos and effect of her pantomimic acting have never been approached," says Ireland, "while her assumptions of male attire and heroic character were marvellous exhibitions of daring ambition and successful achievement. Her success in America has been equalled among women only by Fanny Kemble and Jenny Lind,[1] and among the multitude she was undoubtedly the most popular of the *trio*. On her last appearance, her face indicated the ravages of time by an increased sharpness of feature, and her whole person seemed emaciated; but her powers as an actress were in no wise diminished."

If Céleste looked to be only a child, when she came to us first, Master Joseph Burke, generally known as "the celebrated Irish Roscius," actually *was* a child. He made his first appearance in America, October 22, 1830, at the Park Theatre, New York, as Young Norval. His success was of the most decided character, his nine nights of performance attracting, Ireland tells us:

[1] Fanny Ellsler, who in the forties of the last century made a tremendous success here as a dancer, does not properly come within the scope of this book. Nor does Jenny Lind, whom Barnum featured as "The Swedish Nightingale" in 1850. Both are, however, pictured and described in my "Romantic Days in Old Boston."

231

The Romance of the American Theatre

" Houses averaging twelve hundred dollars each. As
a prodigy, in both music and the drama, he has been
unapproached by any child who has trodden the American stage, though we are assured that he was inferior
to Clara Fisher at the same early age. His readings
were always discriminating and forcible. . . . His performance of Richard, Shylock, and Sir Giles was so
good that none sneered at the absurdity of a child
assuming such parts; while his comedy, especially in
Irish parts, was so full of native, genuine humour,
that he never failed to convulse his audience with
laughter."

Young Burke was the son of a Dublin physician of
good family, and *at the age of five* had appeared on the
boards of the Dublin Theatre Royal. His success at
this time was so great that all the leading theatres of
England were opened to him at once. Then he came to
America, where he was similarly the rage. But his
popularity waned in time, as it was bound to do, his last
successful theatrical appearance being at Wallack's
National in January, 1839. A period of thorough study
of the violin followed, after which he reappeared with
Jenny Lind.

Christopher Columbus Baldwin of Worcester has an
interesting reference in his " Diary " to the talents and
drawing power of Master Burke.

" He is now 12 years of age and is the most famous
actor on any American stage. He is about the common
size of a boy of 12 years, trim, well built, with light hair
and black eyes, and rather a pleasant looking lad. There

232

is nothing in his phrenology that indicates such talents as he undoubtedly possesses. He is very pleasant as an actor and has none of those indescribable faults which so many have, such as attempting to change their voice or countenance and worst of all their gait without concealing the great agony they are put into in doing it. I went to see him four nights successively. I became tired of him on the last night, and concluded him to be a boy after all. There were good houses each night."

Master Burke at this time played for two weeks in Boston in the following plays: " Speed the Plough," " Merchant of Venice," " Man and Wife," " Richard III," " Romeo and Juliet," " Hamlet," " Heir at Law," " Poor Gentleman," " Paul Pry," " John Bull," " Douglas," " West Indian." He was also leader of the orchestra and took as many as six parts in one farce.

For Charles and Fanny Kemble, when they came to our shores in 1832, New York had only the most rapturous of welcomes. Ireland records that " the sensation created by the appearance of Mr. and Miss Kemble had been equalled in kind only in the days of Cooke and Kean, and in duration and intensity was altogether unparalleled." One of Kemble's sisters, Mrs. Whitelock, had long been highly esteemed in the United States, and of his famous brother, John Philip Kemble and his superlatively gifted sister, Mrs. Siddons, New York theatre-goers had been hearing enthusiastic accounts for nearly half a century. Thus it was, in part at least, because of what they represented in the way of inherited stage tradition [1] that New York " rose " to the Kembles. Let us, therefore, trace briefly their history as a family.

Old Roger Kemble, the first of the line of which we need take notice, had been a stroller in early life and was later a struggling manager. Yet, though he was accorded little more distinction by his contemporaries than if he had been the proprietor of a Punch and Judy show, Roger Kemble was a gentleman in instinct and bearing, and the plays which he produced were usually those written by William Shakespeare. He had several children — all players — who became famous in the following order of greatness, Mrs. Siddons, John Philip, and Charles.

John Philip his father intended for the priesthood, and so he received a classical education. But the stage beckoned, and he responded with alacrity — the more so since his sister, Sarah, had already attained success on the boards. He made his first appearance in London, on September 30, 1783, as Hamlet, and though the critics would not admit that his performances were " equal in effect to those of Mrs. Siddons," he soon became the leading actor of his era, holding that distinction until, towards the end of his career, his supremacy was challenged by Edmund Kean. Hazlitt was only expressing

[1] Charles Kemble and his daughter were both deeply conscious that their acting gift was a family possession. Once, when they were playing in Baltimore, they came, in the course of a stroll about the town, to a print-shop in whose window was being exhibited an engraving of Reynolds's Mrs. Siddons as " The Tragic Muse," and Lawrence's picture of John Kemble in Hamlet. " We stopped before them," writes Fanny, " and my father looked with a great deal of emotion at these beautiful representations of his beautiful kindred in this other world."

FRANCES ANNE KEMBLE
From the painting by Thomas Sully, made in 1832, in the possession of the Boston Museum
of Fine Arts
See page 238

MRS. SIDDONS AS LADY MACBETH

After the painting by Harlow

See page 237

JOHN PHILIP KEMBLE

After the painting by Sir Thomas Lawrence

See page 234

the opinion of all playgoers of his time when he wrote: "We feel more respect for John Kemble in a plain coat than for the Lord Chancellor on the woolsack." Charles Lamb went so far as to declare that "it was difficult for a frequent playgoer to disencumber the idea of Hamlet from the person of John Kemble," and Matthew Arnold, after seeing many other Hamlets, asserted that, "in spite of his limitations, John Philip Kemble was the best Hamlet after all," Macready wanting "person," Charles Kean, "mind," Fechter "English," and Wilson Barrett "elocution." Kemble had a fine sense of his own greatness, too. Samuel Rogers declares that when the actor was living at Lausanne, towards the end of his life, he used to feel rather jealous of Mont Blanc; he disliked hearing people always asking: "How does Mont Blanc look this morning?"

The transcendently great member of the Kemble family was, however, John Philip's sister, who in 1773 married Henry Siddons, a well-meaning actor who was, also, a gentleman. Not long afterwards, Mrs. Siddons attracted the favourable attention of the gifted and powerful David Garrick, but at this stage of her career she did not make a success in London, inasmuch as she had not yet arrived at the maturity of her powers. There intervened, indeed, several seasons of laborious touring in the provinces, succeeded by four seasons at Bath at the modest sum of £3 weekly. Here her work so steadily grew in power that Sheridan made her an offer to come to Drury Lane and — to the great dismay of her Bath admirers — she determined to accept the invitation.

The simplicity of the times is illustrated by the fact that, after advertising that she would show to the Bath people " Three Reasons " why she must seek the larger field, she trotted out to the edge of the stage, at the end of her farewell performance, her three children, Henry, Sarah and Maria, and proceeded to declare in lines of her own composition:

> " These are the moles that bear me from your side,
> Where I was rooted — where I could have died.
> Stand forth, ye elves, and plead your mother's cause:
> Ye little magnets, whose soft influence draws
> Me from a point where every gentle breeze
> Wafted my bark to happiness and ease —
> Sends me adventurous on a larger main,
> In hopes that you may profit by my gain."

Mrs. Siddons never possessed the slightest sense of humour. Off the stage, as well as on — and in Sir Joshua Reynolds's great picture — she was " The Tragic Muse." So thoroughly a part of her profession was she that even her table-talk often flowed into blank verse!

From the time of her reappearance at Drury Lane (October 10, 1782) Mrs. Siddons was for thirty years at the head of her profession. A critic of our own time, Brander Matthews, declares that she was " probably the greatest actress the world has ever seen; " the critics of her time made the same assertion stripped of any qualifications whatever. She was not only Queen of Tragedy throughout this period, but Queen of London as well; good, stupid Charlotte created nothing like the

interest that " the Siddons " did. Her greatest part,
in the opinion of many, was Lady Macbeth, in which the
celebrated Mrs. Pritchard had made a great success.
Mrs. Pritchard, to be sure, had never read the play
through[1] and was wont to act the ambitious queen
decked out in hooped petticoat and powdered hair.
The Malcolm of the " Macbeth " in which Mrs.
Siddons was the queen and John Philip Kemble the
Thane of Cawdor was likely to be Charles Kemble,
eleventh child of Roger Kemble and of his wife. Like
his eldest brother, Charles received a good education,
the profession for which old Roger intended him being
that of the civil service. He received, and for a time
held, a post-office appointment. But soon he, too,
drifted to the stage, making, after his rough edges had
worn off, the most gifted and graceful of Romeo's and
a Charles Surface of such fascination as London had
never seen before. In 1803 he left Drury Lane and went
with the other members of his family to Covent Garden,
in which John Kemble had bought a share. And when
the great John retired he presented to Charles this
interest of his. Unfortunately, however, Charles Kemble
was nothing at all of a manager, and profits at the famous house began steadily to decline. After many years

[1] " Sir," said Dr. Johnson to Boswell, in explanation of the mechan-
ical manner in which Mrs. Pritchard played this character, " she had
never read the tragedy of ' Macbeth ' through. She had no more thought
of the play out of which her part was taken than a shoemaker thinks of
the skin out of which the piece of leather of which he is making a pair
of shoes is cut." Mrs. Pritchard herself admitted to a friend, who
supped with her one night after she had been acting Lady Macbeth,
that she had never perused the whole tragedy!

of hard work, he one day found himself on the verge of bankruptcy.

It was then that Fanny Kemble came to the front, her one and only object in going on the stage being to save her family from the ruin that threatened. For, in spite of her dramatic temperament and her very great gift as an actress, Frances Ann Kemble (born in London, November 27, 1809) always professed contempt for the profession of acting. That she had marked literary gifts one cannot read her charming books and deny. But she was a fine actress, also — even if she did not love the stage. In appearance she strongly resembled her beautiful aunt, though it was cleverly remarked that she " looked like Mrs. Siddons seen through the diminishing end of an opera-glass."

Though it was for the purpose of averting a family crisis that this charming young person had gone on the stage, once launched, she acquitted herself in a way that did no violence to the family reputation. The part chosen for her début (which was very successful) was that of Juliet, and her mother, an excellent actress, was the nurse. That night Charles Kemble presented his daughter with a lovely Geneva watch, which she promptly christened " Romeo " and tucked carefully under her pillow before going to sleep.

Juliet for a hundred and twenty nights at a salary of thirty guineas a week now followed; and several other parts, too, were acted in London with success before father and daughter set out, in the summer of 1832, to further mend their fortunes in America. Fanny made her

début at the Park Theatre in New York as Bianca in
" Fazio." " Her triumph here was complete," declares
Mr. Ireland; " as she was the acknowledged Queen of
Tragedy from Boston to New Orleans, without a rival
near her throne." The contemporary criticism is no less
enthusiastic. In the *New York Mirror* of September 22,
1832, I find:

" Miss Fanny Kemble did not disappoint expectation. Of higher praise she cannot be ambitious for never
was expectation raised to such a pitch. . . . It is exhila-
rating to behold, in a young country like ours, so true a
feeling for all that is most exquisite in art. We doubt if
London could give her a welcome more earnest, or applause more enlightened. Her person is petite, but our
stage is not so large as to make that objectionable. Her
acting is most easy and elegant, with more of the French
than the English manner in it; and perfectly original in
our eyes, accustomed as they are to something more
staid and homely. They say that Madame Vestris, in
England, is distinguished for having built her action
upon a similar school; but we are strangers to Vestris,
and were she all that her most earnest admirers picture,
she could not exceed, even if she equal, the grace and
deep power of Fanny Kemble."

Nor did Charles Kemble's work fail of praise. In
this same notice the critic tells a story about " a raw
countryman who bustled into the theatre," and standing
near his side, exclaimed, " wiping his brow with one
hand as he pointed to Kemble with the other, ' That's
the prince! ' Charles Kemble was every inch a king in
his appearance, the *beau ideal* of poets and romancers."

He could even carry his audience with him when he played Romeo to his daughter's Juliet, as he was forced to do early in his New York engagement!

The quiet power of the Kembles' acting was a good deal of a surprise to New Yorkers, and it was distinctly to their credit that they appreciated duly the fine artistry of these newcomers. Even Fanny had her doubts, at the very first, as to the degree of success they had made.

" I am not sure," she wrote Mrs. Jameson, " that our acting is not rather too quiet — tame, I suppose they would call it — for our present public. Ranting and raving in tragedy and shrieks of unmeaning laughter in comedy, are not, you know, precisely our style, and I am afraid our audience here may think us flat. . . . One gentleman observed to another, after seeing my father in ' Venice Preserved,' ' Lord bless you! it's nothing to Cooper's acting — nothing! Why, I've seen the perspiration roll down his face like water when he played Pierre! You didn't see Mr. Kemble put himself to half such pains! ' "

There is more about New York than about the theatre in these first letters sent back by Fanny to her friends on the other side. She gives devout thanks that " baths are a much cheaper and commoner luxury in the hotels here than with us; a great satisfaction to me, who hope in heaven, if I ever get there, to have plenty of water to wash in, and, of course, it will all be soft rain-water there." Again, she comments on the joy with which the " sons of the gentlemen who are volunteer engineers and firemen respond to the firecalls, tearing up and down the streets accompanied by red lights, speaking trumpets, and a rushing, roaring escort of running amateur extinguishers, who make nights hideous with their bawling and bellowing." Also, she notes with surprise the fact that " Dr. Wainwright, rector of the ' most fashionable ' church in New York, a very agreeable, good and clever man, expressed great delight at having an opportunity to meet us in private, as his congregation are so strait-laced that he can neither call upon us nor invite us to his house, much less set his foot in the theatre."

The Kembles first visited Philadelphia in the autumn of 1832 and were very cordially received. They found much to like in the place as well as in the people. " It has altogether a rather dull sober, mellow hue," wrote Fanny, " which is more agreeable than the glaring new-ness of New York. There are one or two fine public buildings, and the quantity of clean, cool-looking, white marble which they use both for their public edifices and for the door-steps of the private houses has a simple and sumptuous appearance which is pleasant." One very pretty incident she related of her Aunt Dall's going into a Quaker shop to make a purchase, and of the master saying to her: " And how doth Fanny? I was in hopes she might have wanted something; we should have great pleasure in attending upon her." So the next day " Fanny " went thither and bought herself " a lovely, sober-coloured gown."

Yet it was from the Philadelphia which had received her thus cordially that this child of a famous actor-

family sent home to a friend one of her most passionate
outbreaks against the stage:

" It is very well that our audiences should look at us as
mere puppets, for could they sometimes see the real
feelings of those for whose false miseries their sympathies are excited, I believe sufficiently in their humanity
to think they would kindly give us leave to go off and
go home. Ours is a very strange trade and I am sorry
to say that every day increases my distaste for it. . . .
I do not think that, during my father's life, I shall ever
leave the stage; it is very selfish to feel regret at this, I
know, but it sometimes seems to me rather dreary to
look along my future years, and think that they will be
devoted to labour that I dislike and despise."

It was also in Philadelphia that Fanny Kemble met
and married Pierce Butler, following which event she
retired from the stage for about ten years. Some of
these years she passed with her husband on his Georgia
plantation — growing all the while more and more
inclined to take the side of the Abolitionists as against
that of the slave-holders, of whom he was one. That
her sympathies had long been with the oppressed blacks
we have only to read her girlish letters to understand.

Fanny Kemble was still a care-free girl, however,
when, in the spring of 1833, she was the "star" of the
hour in Boston and, from her rooms in the Tremont
House, was able to witness the edifying spectacle of
crowds gathering at the theatre doors for hours before
the place was open.

The Romance of the American Theatre

"And then rushing in, to the imminent peril of life and limb, pushing and pommelling and belabouring one another like madmen. Some of the lower class purchasers, inspired by the thrifty desire for gain, said to be a New England characteristic, sell these tickets which they buy at the box-office price, at an enormous advance, and smear their clothes with treacle and sugar and other abominations, to secure, from the fear of their contact of all decently-clad competitors, freer access to the box-keeper. To prevent, if possible, these malpractices and to secure to ourselves and the managers of the theatre any such surplus profit as may honestly be come by, the proprietors have determined to put the boxes up to auction and sell the tickets to the highest bidders. It was rather barbarous of me, I think, upon reflection, to stand at the window while all this riot was going on, laughing at the fun; for not a wretch found his way in that did not come out rubbing his back or his elbow, or showing some grievous damage done to his garments. . . .

"The opposite window of my room looks out on a churchyard and a burial-ground; the reflections suggested by the contrast between the two prospects are not otherwise than edifying. . . . But Boston is one of the pleasantest towns imaginable. It is built upon three hills, which give it a singularly picturesque appearance, and I suppose suggested the name of Tremonte Street, and the Tremonte Hotel, which we inhabit. The houses are, many of them, of fine granite, and have an air of wealth and solidity unlike anything we have seen elsewhere in this country. Many of the streets are planted with trees, chiefly fine horse-chestnuts, which were in full leaf and blossom when we came away and which harmonize beautifully with the gray colour and solemn handsome style of the houses."

Fifteen years later Fanny Kemble was again in Boston
" professionally," this time to give some of the Shakespearian readings to which she now had turned her attention and in which she, as well as her audience, took
deep satisfaction. A journalist of the last century, reviewing [1] the contribution made by these readings to
the proper appreciation of Shakespeare in America, said
that Mrs. Kemble (for after her divorce from her husband, it was thus that she called herself) had been able
through this medium to do for Shakespeare what no
other living being of that time could have accomplished.

" In listening to her, we have the unexampled pleasure
of seeing one of Shakespeare's plays, with each part
superbly rendered. Yes, *seeing*, for do we not forget
the dais upon which she sits, the dark red screen behind
her, the table with its pile of books — do not these simple
surroundings dissolve and melt away into arching forests or palace halls at will? and does not each character
step before us in the costume of the day, whether it be
Cleopatra, dying amid long-forgotten Egyptian splen-
dours, or Titania with her robe of woven moonbeams, or
Bottom with ass's head? . . . Thus she is enabled to
do for Shakespeare what she could not have done had
she remained on the stage; she gives us each one of his
characters equally well played, a pleasure never yet enjoyed in the theatre.

" In ' Macbeth,' " continues the critic, " all the parts
of which she makes as distinct as she does deeply tragic,
Lady Macbeth is not more terrible than, in their way,
are the three witches. This whole scene which Shakespeare evidently did not mean to make grotesque but

[1] In *The Galaxy* for December, 1868.

244

terrible, is travestied on the stage, but in Mrs. Kemble's hands it is what it was meant to be, wild, weird, appalling."

Apropos of which may be quoted an amusing anecdote from the diary of the poet Longfellow, who always went to hear Mrs. Kemble when she was in Boston, and who on February 18, 1857, recorded: ". . . At Mrs. Kemble's reading of Macbeth at Tremont Temple. Just as she was giving the words of Banquo on first seeing the Witches —

> ' What are these
> So withered and so wild in their attire,'

three belated women came trailing down the aisle to a front seat directly in the range of her eye. The effect was indescribably ludicrous."

The book from which Mrs. Kemble was wont to read on these occasions was a huge one which had come down to her from her aunt, Mrs. Siddons. And, towards the latter part of her life, at least, she appeared in ordinary afternoon dress and on a perfectly bare platform. To create, thus unaided, the illusion of forests and palaces, with Rosalind or Titania or Lady Macbeth dominating them, was indeed to prove herself an artist.[1]

In 1838 came to us for the first time Charles James Mathews, who was a wit, even as his father had been. Witness his own description of his personal appearance:

[1] Coming of a family of " *real* artists," she used to say that she never felt herself deserving of that honourable name.

" Even when I was a baby, folks laughed the moment they saw me, and said, ' Bless the little dear! what a funny face it has! ' The ' off-side of my mouth, as a coachman would say, took such an affection for my ear, that it seemed to make a perpetual struggle to form a closer communication with it; and one eyebrow became fixed as a rusty weathercock, while the other popped up an inch, apparently, beyond its proper position." Mathews overflowed with delicious nonsense,[1] some of which Leigh Hunt appreciatively repeats.

Mathews early conceived an attachment for the famous Madame Vestris, who, because she had been on the stage for a quarter of a century before he made his tardy début at the age of thirty-six, was generally declared to be " old enough to be his mother." In point of fact, she was just three years his senior.

Madame Vestris had had an exciting career. At fourteen she was brought out by the famous ballet master, Armand Vestris, who afterward married her out of hand in France. It soon developed that he already had a wife, however, so she promptly left him and proceeded to construct a career of her own. By reason of her charming voice, her graceful figure, and her great intelligence she now made an enormous success in Italy and France as well as in London and, after playing for £200 a week at Drury Lane and Covent Garden jointly, decided to take a theatre of her own. Her production of " The Court Beauties " — the beauties in question being the

---

[1] One of his sayings was: " If there are no theatres in the hereafter, the hereafter must be a very dull affair."

rather well-known ladies at the Court of Charles II
(Nell Gwyn, the Duchess of Portsmouth, Castelmaine,
Lucy Waters, and La Belle Stuart) — was the sensation
of the day, so elaborately were all the details of scenery
and costume carried out.

To the gifted lady who had planned and financed all
this magnificent representation, an American tour was
proposed, in 1838, by Price, who had theatrical connections both in London and in New York. Though the
offer made was one of great pecuniary benefit, Madame
Vestris demurred, finally asking if her " pupil," Charles
James Mathews, might not be engaged also. " Well,"
answered Price, " if you go out together you must get
married."

" *Married!* " exclaimed the astonished pair in concert.

" Yes," replied the manager inexorably, " and the
ceremony must take place publicly here and be verified
by the London newspapers." Mrs. Baron Wilson, who
preserves this dialogue,[1] adds that " the widow turned
her smiling eyes upon the young actor, eyes whose power
no man could resist, and that soon a tear of real affection added itself to the smile." On July 18, 1838, therefore, Charles James Mathews married this Ninon de
l'Enclos of her day. Never did a marriage create a
greater sensation. Especially in the Olympic Company
comment on the alliance was piquant and prolonged.

Immediately after their marriage, the pair set out for
America to fulfil a contract to act for one year. They
were to be paid £20,000, but their stay was very short.

[1] In " Our Actresses."

For though Madame Vestris was carefully billed as "Mrs. Charles Mathews," New York theatre-goers, recalling her variegated past, remained cold to her. Elsewhere in America her audiences pronounced her *passée* and refused to allow her charming singing and vivacious acting to compensate for her indisputable decline in good looks and for her tarnished name. Yet Madame Vestris was a very clever person and was long very popular in London. As an actress she seems to have done the kind of thing our own Lotta [1] made very popular a quarter of a century later.

Though much less had been expected of Charles James Mathews than of his wife, Americans were disposed to be kind to him, because of his father, and he made a decided hit. Remembering this, he came over again the year following the Madame's death, in 1856. This time his success at the Broadway Theatre, New York, was very pronounced. He was so lucky, too, as to be able to take back to England as his wife Mrs. A. H. Davenport, who had been Miss Weston, and who made him, as he declares, " a prudent, economical, industrious little helpmate, who by her clear little head and good little heart, at length did for me what I had never been able to do for myself — kept my expenditure within my income." Twice again the younger Mathews was in New York:

[1] Lotta Mignon Crabtree, born in New York in 1847, was one of the brightest soubrettes that ever delighted a public. She has recently (1924) died in Boston, leaving to various societies devoted to the promotion of humane conditions for animals the great fortune she made while on the stage. Another famous actress who accumulated considerable wealth was Maggie Mitchell, who made a very great hit as Fanchon in an adaptation of George Sands' novel, "La Petite Fadette."

MADAME VESTRIS AS OLIVIA IN " JOHN OF PARIS "
See page 246

LOTTA AS THE MARCHIONESS

MAGGIE MITCHELL AS FANCHON

in April, 1871, at the end of his world-tour, and a year
later, after he had played all over the United States and
Canada, for a closing engagement at Wallack's. To the
very end of his career he retained in his work all the
lightness and brilliancy of a lad of twenty. E. A. Sothern
declared him " the founder of the present school of light
comedy."

CHAPTER X

EARLY NINETEENTH CENTURY AUDIENCES

TYRONE POWER,[1] who played over here during the years 1833, 1834, and 1835, in his delightful book, "Impressions of America," has given us several very illuminating glimpses of Americans as he saw them. At the outset of the book he distinctly disavows his intention of " boring his readers with a series of playbills, or a journal of his theatrical career." None the less, because he rightly feels that it would have been mere affectation to eschew the subject altogether, we do get bits of his adventures while touring the country, and particularly his impressions of the audiences he faced. He had been told that theatre-goers in New York had no taste whatever for Irish character, and as they had been accustomed to associate with representatives of the Emerald Isle a ruffian with a black eye and straw in his shoes, there

[1] Tyrone Power was born in Ireland November 22, 1797. In July, 1815, he made his début at Newport in the Isle of Wight as Alonzo in " Pizarro." In 1817 he married, and a year later, coming into possession of his wife's fortune, left the stage. Two years later he went on an exploring expedition in the vicinity of the Cape of Good Hope, but as this proved disastrous he returned to London, once more took to the stage, and after ten years of success in England and Ireland came to America for the first time. His last appearance on any stage was March 9, 1841, at the Park Theatre, New York, as Gerald Pepper and Morgan Rattler. He was lost on the steamship *President*, which sailed from New York for Liverpool, March 21, 1841.

250

would be absolutely no appreciation for a quiet and natural portrait of the well-disposed Irishman. Exactly the same warning, it is interesting to note, with which the delightful Irish Players, who were so much enjoyed here not many years ago, were at first met. Power, unafraid, determined to see for himself, and with no other engagement than one for twelve nights in New York, bravely crossed the Atlantic to test our taste. Of course he was full of anxiety on the night of his début (August 28, 1833), the more so since the day had been the hottest of a very hot season. Yet he was very well received when he made his bow at the Park. The house was exceedingly crowded — " from pit to roof rose tier on tier one dark unbroken mass " — and he made his first bow " amid greetings as hearty " as ever he had received in his life.

" I saw no coat off, no heels up, no legs over boxes," he records, evidently in allusion to the revolting description Mrs. Trollope [1] had given of the theatre manners encountered during her visit over here a few years earlier. These times had passed away; " a more English audience I would not desire to act before."

The Park Theatre, Power describes as " of the horseshoe form, with three tiers of boxes; is handsome, and in all respects as well appointed as any theatre out of London. The orchestra is at present excellent, and

[1] This lady, in her very entertaining book, " Domestic Manners of the Americans," accuses us of many shocking lapses from good breeding and self-restraint while in public. In one New York theatre she even observed a mother administering natural nutrition to her child between the acts!

under the direction of a very clever man — Penson, formerly leader at Dublin. The company I found for my purpose a very fair one, my pieces requiring little save correctness from most of those concerned, except where old men occur and all such parts found an excellent representative in an American actor called Placide. Descended of a long line of talented players, he possesses a natural talent I have rarely seen surpassed, together with a chastity and simplicity of style that would do credit to the best school of comedy. . . . There is a representative of old women here, too, a native, Mrs. Wheatley, an inartificial, charming actress, with a perfect conception of all she does."

In Philadelphia, Power appeared at both the Walnut Street and the Chestnut Street houses.

" The Walnut is a summer theatre and the least fashionable," he writes, " and here it was my fortune to make my début to the Philadelphians with good success: a French company occupied at the same time the Chestnut, where, after a seven nights' engagement at the other house, I succeeded them; the proprietors being the same at both. These houses are large, handsome buildings, marble-fronted, having ample and well-arranged vomitories; and are not stuck in some obscure alley, as most of our theatres are, but standing in the finest streets of the city, and every way easy of approach: within they are fitted up plainly but conveniently, and very cleanly and well kept. I prefer the Chestnut as smaller and having a pit — as I think all pits should be — nearly on a level with the front of the stage, instead of being sunk deep below, looking, when filled, like a huge dark pool, covered with upturned faces.

" A crowded audience, Philadelphia, presents as large

a proportion of pretty, attractive women as are anywhere to be seen; and the male part is singularly respectable and attentive.[i] . . . The unreserved laughter
in which they indulged I found abundant applause, and
in well-fitted houses the best assurance that they were
pleased. The company here was a very good one, and
the pieces as well gotten up as anywhere in the States."

Concerning Boston, Power is similarly enthusiastic,
though he finds it difficult to pause in his raptures over
the Tremont Hotel long enough to give us even a brief
description of the Tremont Theatre, just across the street.

" Immediately opposite the great hotel is the Tremont
Theatre, certainly the most elegant exterior in the
country, and with a very well-proportioned, but not well-
arranged *salle*, or audience part. I commenced here on
Monday the 30th of September, three days after the
closing at Philadelphia, to a well-filled house, composed,
however, chiefly of men. My welcome was cordial and
kind in the extreme; but the audience, although attentive, appeared exceedingly cold. On a first night I did
not heed this much, especially as report assured me they
were very well pleased; but throughout the week this
coldness appeared to me to increase rather than dimin-

[1] The testimony to be found in the " Diary " of Christopher Columbus
Baldwin of Worcester concerning the manners of the Park Theatre
audience during 1833 is, however, as follows: " There is small pleasure
in attending the theatre compared with attending it in Boston, and the
reason is found in the more perfect police regulations in the latter place.
The Boston Theatre is as quiet and orderly between the acts and scenes
as a company collected for religious worship. But in New York everything is in confusion. The boys are cracking nuts and throwing the
shells as in Shakesperian time, while orange peels, apples and vulgar
language are thrown from the gallery." Evidently the theatre conduct
of the day was different at different times — depending on the kind of
people attracted to the playhouse on each occasion.

ish, and so much was I affected by it, that, notwithstanding the house was very good, I, on the last day of my first engagement of six nights, declined positively to renew it, as was the custom in such cases, and as, in fact, the manager and myself had contemplated: on this night, however, the aspect of affairs brightened up amazingly; the house was crowded; a brilliant show of ladies graced the boxes; the performances were a repetition of two pieces which had been previously acted, and from first to last the mirth was electric; the good people appeared by common consent, to abandon themselves to the fun of the scene, and laughed *à gorge deployée*. At the fall of the curtain, after, in obedience to the call of the house, I had made my bow, the manager announced my re-engagement; and from this night forth I never drew a merrier or a pleasanter audience.

"It was quite in accordance with the character ascribed to the New Englanders," continues this very fair-minded observer, "that they should coolly and thoroughly examine and understand the novelty presented to their judgment, and that being satisfied and pleased, they should no longer set limits to the demonstration of their feelings. In matters of graver import they have always evinced the like deliberate judgment and apparent coldness of bearing; but beneath this prudential outward veil they have feelings capable of the highest degree of excitement and the most enduring enthusiasm. . . . Some of the kindest gentlest and the most hospitable friends I had were, as they say here, 'real Yankee, born and raised within sight of the Statehouse of Bosting.'"

During Power's second visit to New York, he went to look over the Opera House which had been built there very suddenly by subscription.

TYRONE POWER
After a drawing by D'Orsay
See page 250

THE FRENCH OPERA HOUSE, NEW ORLEANS, ERECTED IN 1860
See page 263

Copyright, Detroit Publishing Co.

The Romance of the American Theatre

" It is about the size of the Lyceum; arranged after the French fashion, having stalls, a *parterre*, and *balcon* below; and above, two circles of private boxes, the property of subscribers. Some of these are fitted up in a style of extravagance I never saw attempted elsewhere. There has been a sort of rivalry exercised on this head, and it has been pursued with that regardlessness of cost which distinguishes a trading community where their *amour propre* is in question. Silks, velvets, damask, and gilt furniture form the material within many; and, as the parties consult only their own taste, the colours of these are various as their proprietors' fancies. I do not find the *ensemble* bad, however; whilst the shape and mounting of the *salle* are both unexceptionable.

" This effort, however creditable to the good taste of the city, is premature, and must be doomed to more failures than one before it permanently succeeds. A refined taste for the best kind of music is not consequent upon the erection of an opera-house, nor is it a feeling to be created at will. Even in the metropolis of England, with a capital so disproportionate, and possessing such superior facilities for the attainment of novelty, did the continuance of this refined amusement depend solely upon the love of good music, it would quickly die, if not be forgotten. From time to time, a small but efficient and really good Italian troupe, will, without doubt, find liberal encouragement in the great northern cities, and also in New Orleans, provided they make a short stay in each; but, rapidly as events progress here, I will undertake to predict that a century must elapse before even New York can sustain a permanent operatic establishment." (Events, it is interesting to note, did, as a matter of fact, progress in this direction considerably more rapidly than Mr. Power thought possible.)

The theatre in Washington our visiting Irishman

found " a most miserable looking place, the worst I met with in the country, ill-situated and difficult of access; but it was filled nightly by a very delightful audience and nothing could be more pleasant than to witness the perfect *abandon* with which the gravest of the senate laughed over the diplomacy of the ' Irish Ambassador.' They found allusions and adopted sayings applicable to a crisis when party [1] feelings were carried to an extremity. The elaborate display of eloquence with which Sir Patrick seeks to *bother* the Spanish envoy was quoted as the very model of a speech for a non-committal orator, and recommended for the study of several gentlemen who were considered as aiming at this convenient position, very much to their amusement. The pieces were ill mounted, and the company unworthy the capital, with the exception of two very pretty and very clever native actresses, Mesdames Willis and Chapman. The latter I had the satisfaction of seeing soon transferred to New York, in which city she became a monstrous favourite, both in tragedy and comedy. . . . I acted in Washington seven nights on this occasion, and visited the city again in May, when I passed three or four weeks most agreeably. I had the pleasure, too, during this last visit, of seeing the plans for a theatre worthy the audience, and which, I trust, has by this time been happily erected as the greatest part of the fund needed was readily subscribed for."

Pittsburg, at the time of Power's visit, was without the many millionaires that now distinguish it; but it had the smoke from which they grew. Though the theatre of the place was not yet a year old, " the ornamental parts of the interior were already disfigured," we read.

[1] Andrew Jackson was President at this time.

256

" The smoke which fills the atmosphere day and night fully exonerates the people from the charge of being wilfully regardless of neatness in the arrangement of their dwellings. I found the manager of the theatre, Mr. Wemyss, at his post, and all things in tolerable order. At night the house, calculated to contain about one thousand persons, was filled; though how the people made their way home again I do not know; even the short distance I had to explore on the line of the principal street, I found beset with perils; loose pavements, scaffold-poles, rubbish, and building materials of all kinds blocked up the sidewalk in several places, which had to be avoided by instinct, for light there was none, natural or artificial."

One non-theatrical adventure of Mr. Power, while in Pittsburg, must here be quoted, because it shows the temper of the man. While walking in the woods outside the city, he came upon a little colony of charcoal-burners.

" From their colour they might have been Iroquois, or negroes; but the first reply I got to my hail rendered any inquiry as to the country unnecessary.

" 'Hola! my friend,' shouted I, at the top of my voice, as a tall, half-naked being stalked out of one of the huts, from which I was separated by a deep ravine; 'pray step this way for one moment.'

" The man did as I desired, without a word; a couple of attendant imps hanging on to the strings of his knees.

" ' I'm sorry to trouble you,' I added, as he drew within easy speaking-distance; ' but the fact is, I have lost my road, and fear to lose my dinner.'

" ' I' faith, thin, sir, if you'll tell me whereabouts you lost the road I'll find you the dinner, and go back and

257

look for the road while you're atein' it; with the blessing o' God, it will be the first road I seen since I've ben this side o' Pittsburg, to say the laste.'

"Maybe you've seen a fine aisy-goin' road betune Cork and Cove,' I replied, in the same accent.

"'Maybe I haven't,' grinned the pleased charcoal-burner, laughing from ear to ear. 'Och murder! You're the devil, sure! wasn't it the last ten miles I ever toed of Irish ground? Long life to you, sir! wait till I call the wife. Molly asthore, come out av id, for here's a witch of a gintleman here. Jem, you robber, go and bid your mammy stir herself and come here.'

"Away ran Jem and his brother, or rather flew. I laughed immoderately whilst my countryman, with the most puzzled air, exclaimed: 'Och murder! but it's the quarest thing alive. Sure you must have know'd us?'

"He was now joined by his wife and two or three others of the little family, who all appeared nearly of an age. Poor Molly, the Mistress, looked weak and haggard, and told me she 'had the shakes on her for the last six months.' She was affected to tears when her husband told her of my witchcraft, in knowing where they were from, and joined in begging that 'I'd come around and take a bite o' cake and a sup o' spirits and water, to keep me from feelin' faint till I got my dinner.'

"I requested, however, as my time was short, that one of the little ones might at once put me on the nearest track by which I would reach the bridge; so I left my friendly countryman and with a 'God send you safe home, sir!' he turned to his humble dwelling, to think with a full heart of that distant home my chance visit had recalled in all its freshness, and which although he may never look to revisit, no son of poor Ireland ever forgets."

The Romance of the American Theatre

In Albany Mr. Power encountered one of those curiously hostile crowds which, from time to time, during the nineteenth century, turned out to make life wretched for visiting actors.

" I had been advised," he says, " not to visit this city professionally, but being strongly solicited by the worthy manager, I decided to go. ' Mischief lay in my way, and I found it.' . . . The only disagreement I ever had with an audience, in fact, occurred here, and, roundly, thus it happened: On the evening when I was advertised to make my début to an Albany audience, I at my usual hour walked to the house, dressed, and was ready; but when, half an hour after the time of beginning, I went on the stage, there were not ten persons in the house. The stage-director and myself now held a consultation on the unpromising aspect of our affairs. He ascribed the unusually deserted condition of the *salle* to the sultry and threatening state of the atmosphere, which had deterred the neighbouring towns of Troy and Waterford from furnishing their quota, — those indeed being his chief dependencies. I was opposed, on policy, to throwing away our ammunition so unprofitably; and so after due deliberation, the manager agreed to state to the few persons in front, that ' with their permission ' the performances intended for this night would be postponed until the evening after the next following; as, in consequence of the exceeding smallness of the audience, it was feared to be the play would prove dull to them, as it must be irksome to the actors. Nothing could be received with better feelings on the part of the persons assembled; not a breath of disapprobation was heard. They instantly went away; but soon after I reached home, I found, by the report of one or two gentlemen who had since been at the theatre seeking admittance,

259

that a considerable excitement prevailed, and that at the public bars of the neighbourhood the affair was detailed in a way likely to produce unpleasant effects on my first appearance.

" The appointed night came, the house was filled with men and everything foreboded a violent outbreak; the manager appeared terrified out of his wits; but, as far as I can judge, behaved with infinite honesty. . . . It was now found that an actor or two needed in the piece were absent. These worthies, the chief agitators in this affair, were, in fact, in front of the house to assist in the expected assault upon a stranger and one of their own profession. On this being explained to the manager he said he was aware of it, and had threatened to discharge the individuals; but relying upon the affair terminating in my discomfiture, they did not fear being sustained by the same intelligence which they now directed against me.

" On my appearance the din was mighty and deafening; the volunteer champions of the public had come well prepared, and every invention for making the voice of humanity bestial was present and in full use. The boxes I observed to be occupied by well-dressed men, who generally either remained neutral, or by signs sought that I should be heard. This, however, was out of the question; and after long and patient abiding ' for patience is the badge of all our tribe,' I made my bow and retired, when the manager, who had on the night in question dismissed the house, made his bow, and after silence was obtained, begged that the audience would give me a hearing, assuring them on his own knowledge that I had not contemplated insulting them.

" I again came forward, and after some time, was permitted to say that I could in no way account for a simple matter of business being so misrepresented as to occasion this violent exhibition of their anger; ˙ that, before the audience in question was dismissed, its permission had been obtained; that, had I really contemplated insult, it is hardly probable I should wait two days to encounter the anger of those I had sought to offend. I further said that, on the common principle of what they professed, I was entitled to a hearing, since the sense of the majority was evidently with me; and that, if the disorder continued, I should, for the sake of that respectable majority, sincerely regret this, since the character of their city for justice and hospitality would be more impeached than my prospects be injured. After this the row was resumed with added fierceness: not a word of either play or farce was heard; but I persisted in going through with the performance, being determined not to dismiss a second time.

" The whole thing, I was afterwards assured, arose from stories most industriously circulated by one or two ill-conditioned actors, backed by inflammatory handbills and a scurrilous print. . . . Yet I have never been able to regret a momentary vexation which obtained for me many friends, and made known to me the sterling good feeling existing in Albany, of which I might otherwise have remained ignorant. . . . I concluded my engagement, which was only for four nights, and left the theatre with a promise to return."

Baltimore, Charleston, Savannah, and Columbus were in turn visited by the gifted Irishman, but he has little or nothing to say of his theatrical experiences in these places. In discussing New Orleans he is more communicative.

First he describes the American Theatre, which he found " a large, well-proportioned house, with three rows of boxes, a pit or *parquette*, as it is termed, sub-divided as in the French Theatre; each seat is numbered, and, being taken at the box-office, is secured to the purchaser for any part of the evening. The company was a very tolerable one; and in the person of a nephew of Mr. Farren's, I found an adjunct of much importance to me — an excellent old man.

" My next anxiety was about my audience, not its numbers, as I was assured every seat in the house was disposed of, and this as far as could be allowed for every night I might perform; but I felt solicitous with respect to its character and composition, of which I had received very discouraging reports. . . . On Tuesday I made my début; and never was man more agreeably surprised than myself when, after making my bow, I for the first time took a rapid survey of the aspect of the house: the *parquettes* and dress boxes were almost exclusively filled by ladies, *coiffées* with the taste which distinguishes French women in every country, and which becomes peculiarly striking here, where are to be seen the finest heads of dark hair in the world; many wore bonnets of the latest Parisian fashion, and all were more dressed than it is usual to be at theatres in America. This attention to costume on the part of the ladies, added to their occupying the pit, obliges the gentlemen to adopt a correspondent neatness; and hence it occurs that, when the New Orleans theatre is attended by the belles of the city, it presents decidedly the most elegant-looking auditory of this country. I found them in manner equal to their appearance; a greater degree of repose and gentility of demeanour I never remember to have noticed in any mixed assembly of any place. My first engagement was for twelve nights, four nights per week. On my return from Natchez I acted a like number more with equal patronage."

Of that famous institution, the French Opera House at New Orleans, Power has given us the following fascinating glimpse:

" I visited it several times and found it an exceedingly well-appointed, handsome place, with a company very superior to the American Theatre and having its pieces altogether better mounted. It is to this house the Creole families chiefly resort, as well, indeed, as the American ladies of the best class, most of whom are good French scholars; within this *salle* on any Sunday evening may be seen eyes as bright and forms as delicately proportioned as in *la belle France* itself.

" The building, whereof this theatre forms a part only, is a very extensive one, having as a part of its establishment a large ball-room, with supper rooms attached; and, in addition to this, a variety of hells, where gambling flourishes in full practice: from the *salon* where the wealthy Creole plays his five-hundred-dollar *coup*, to the obscure den where roulette does its work, with a pace slower but as sure, at the rate of half-dollar stakes. I have looked in on these places during the performances, and never without finding them full. Such establishments, ruinous and detestable under whatever guise and in whatsoever place they are permitted, become doubly dangerous when placed under the same roof and carried on in obvious connection with what should be at all times an innocent recreation, and which ought and might be one of a refined and moral tendency. The scenes of desperation and distress which gambling yearly gave rise to in this place amongst a people whose temperament is peculiarly excitable, coupled with a recent and terrible *exposé* have at length roused the legislature of Louisiana to release themselves from the stigma of owing any portion of their revenue

263

to a tax which legalized this worst species of robbery and assassination. This very session I had the gratification of seeing a bill brought into the House, and promptly carried through it, making gambling felony, and subjecting its followers to corresponding punishment. The French Theatre will henceforward, I hope forever, be freed from the disgrace which such an association necessarily reflected upon the drama and all concerned with it." [1]

At Natchez Mr. Power's first advertised performance had to be put off, for the extraordinary reason that the oil of the theatre's lamplighter had been so affected by frost that it refused to burn at short notice. The actor had chanced to encounter one of the rare cold spells which occasionally grip this town in February.

Two days later " the weather was a little milder so I took a gallop into the country, dined early and about six walked out of town to the theatre preparatory to making my bow. The way was without a single passenger, and not a creature lingered about the outer doors of the house; the interior I found in the possession of a single lamplighter who was leisurely setting about his duties; of him I inquired the hour of beginning, and learnt that it was usual to commence about seven or eight o'clock — a tolerable latitude; time was thus afforded me for a ramble, and out I sallied, taking the direction leading from the town. I had not proceeded far when I met several men riding together; a little further on another group, with a few ladies in company, passed leisurely by, all capitally mounted: others, I perceived, were fast approaching from the same direction. It now oc-

[1] " Impressions of America," vol. II, p. 175.

curred to me that these were the persons destined to form the country quota of my auditory; upon looking back, my impression was confirmed by seeing them all halting in front of the rural theatre, and fastening their horses to the neighbouring rails and trees.

" I now hastened back to take a survey of the scene, and a very curious one it was: a number of carriages were by this time arriving from the town, together with long lines of pedestrians. . . . The whole party having come up, and the horses being hitched in front of the building to their owners' satisfaction, all walked leisurely into the theatre, the men occupying the pit whilst in the boxes were several groups of pretty and well-dressed women. The demeanour of these border gallants was as orderly as could be desired; and their enjoyment, if one might judge from the heartiness of their laughter, exceeding.

" After the performance there was a general muster to horse; and away they rode in groups of from ten to twenty, as their way might lie together. These were the planters of the neighbouring country, many of whom came nightly to visit the theatre, and this from very considerable distances; forming such an audience as cannot be seen elsewhere in this hackney-coach age. Indeed, to look on so many fine horses, with their antique caparisons, piquetted about the theatre, recalled the palmy days of the Globe and Bear-garden."

CHAPTER XI

RACHEL AND FECHTER

It was in " Tripler Hall," which had been erected on the west side of Broadway for the New York début of Jenny Lind (but was not completed in season for this event), that Mlle. Rachel and her French company made their first New York appearance, September 3, 1855. The house had been renamed " The Metropolitan " for this occasion, and the bill announcement was as follows:

Rachel's Dramatic Company

I beg respectfully to inform the public of New York that

Mlle. Rachel's First Performance

will irrevocably take place on

Monday next, the 3rd of September

It will consist of Corneille's tragedy entitled

" Les Horaces "

Mlle. Rachel will appear as Camille

The performance will begin at 7.20 o'clock precisely, with Jules de Premeray's new comedy, in two acts, in which the three sisters of Mlle. Rachel will appear.

The Romance of the American Theatre

The second performance will take place Sept. 4, when Racine's tragedy

" Phèdre "

will be presented, with Mlle. Rachel as Phèdre.

The third performance on Thursday, Sept. 6, when

" Adrienne Lecouvreur "

will be presented, with Mlle. Rachel as Adrienne, and the fourth performance, on Friday, September 7, will consist of

" Marie Stuart,"

a tragedy by Lebrun, with Mlle. Rachel as Marie.

Prices of admission to Mlle. Rachel's performances:

Orchestra seats, Parquet and First Circle	$2	Parquet Circle Upper Circle	$3 $1

Raphael Félix, manager of the Rachel company.

" Rachel *achieved* last night," wrote the critic of the *New York Tribune* the day following that great tragedienne's first appearance. " When the enthusiasm which greeted her entrance had died away into silence, we thought we had never seen her look to such advantage, or wear such classic air. . . . When uttering her first words to Sabina what immediately struck us was the extraordinary expression of her mouth, always, as it were, threatening to break into some fierce burst of passion; but surrounded with an incomparable grace when the feelings she represents are of joyous character. The deep, sonorous voice, guttural almost by the strength of its intensity and vehemence, next rivets the attention. But the paramount power she wields is that from

267

the moment she enters on the stage we cannot let our eyes leave her for an instant. It is an indescribable fascination. We feel that every movement, every gesture, even her very breathing is replete with some thought which we fear to lose if she passes from us.

" The house was brilliantly attended," declares this reviewer in his concluding paragraph, "including most of the distinguished men of the country, and being, perhaps, the most severely classic before which Rachel has ever played. There was but one feeling: she surpassed expectation; and the enthusiasm of shout and flowers in which it found expression evidently convinced her that the American people know how to appreciate and reward true genius." [1]

Of her Phèdre the *Tribune* critic writes in similar strain, declaring that " from the moment of Rachel's coming on the stage a strange feeling of melancholy falls on the heart at witnessing the sufferings which rack and torture her, breaking out in terrible outline on every lineament of that beautiful face, which presents a picture of anguish such as Rubens would have hung over with ecstasy."

This same paper devotes nearly three columns, on September 10, to praise of Rachel's costumes and diamonds, declaring that the latter, valued at $245,000, " throw such a lustre over the stage, when she enters as Adrienne, that you can almost fancy you see one of the heroines, clad in precious stones who are pictured around the court of Solomon." The jewels worn on the

[1] For "Adrienne Lecouvreur" the crowd was " so dense that chairs were placed along the centre pathway."

actress's turban during the second act of Adrienne were
presented to her, we are then told, by " the pious and
good Queen Amelia, the widow of Louis Philippe. . . .
It speaks the noblest answer to lying canards which small
curs bark after Rachel, that she has retained through life
the love and regard of this model Queen, that Rachel
is one of the friends with whom the Queen in her exile
life corresponds, and that Rachel's last act, before leaving England, was to visit her fallen mistress, to whom in
her sorrow she pays even a deeper homage than in her
royal hour." All of which makes it fairly clear that the
New York Tribune, at any rate, had been quite captivated
by Rachel.

Colonel T. Allston Brown is considerably less sure
than was the *Tribune's* critic that the great French actress
made an unqualified success in New York. " Her voice,"
he declares in his exhaustive " History of the New York
Stage," " was no longer so full and round as when I had
seen her in Paris some years previously, and she appeared,
too, not to have fully recovered from the fatigue of her
sea voyage." That the high prices militated against the
visitor's success, this chronicler seems in no doubt;
and he declares the language another impediment. The
French colony in New York was a small one then, of
course, and not one American in twenty, probably, had
the slightest acquaintance with the French language.
Then, that the classics presented by Rachel necessitated
no change of scene throughout the piece, and that the
curtain failed to fall between the acts, was obviously very
puzzling to many of those present, according to this

reviewer. Nor did he find the actress *at all beautiful,* though he admits that " her worn, weary aspect and her sad mournful eyes, were not ill-suited to the tragic rôles she assumed." [1]

After the very first, Rachel tried to fill her house by a reduction of the high prices originally demanded. She even sang " La Marseillaise," at the end of each night's play, in order to please the middle-class play-goers, but this must have been a rather dreary business as she no longer possessed anything of a singing voice. A still further attempt to impress the people who did not speak French [2] or approve of theatre-going was by means of "readings,"which the distinguished tragedienne gave at the Broadway Tabernacle on her off nights.

From New York Rachel went to Boston, where she made her début, October 27, 1855, at the Boston Theatre. Her second — and last — New York season was played partly at the Academy of Music, where she alternated with Italian opera, and partly at Niblo's Theatre; the latter place was preferred by her management because it was a smaller house and easier to heat.

It was, however, at Philadelphia, not New York, that she experienced the chill which caused her death. Her brother and manager, it appears, had conceived the

[1] " History of the New York Stage," Vol. I, p. 430.
[2] Even the critics of that day were not altogether sure of their French classics, it would appear. At any rate we find the *Tribune's* representative expressing the hope (Monday, September 10, 1855) that " Messrs. Darcie and Corbyn will, for the future, bring out their excellent books of plays in fit time. ' Adrienne Lecouvreur ' was not brought out until half-past three on the evening before the play, and from not having had time to read it thoroughly, we committed an error in our synopsis of the last scene."

brilliant idea of saving money by *omitting* to heat the Walnut Street Theatre, which he had leased, and, on an extremely cold night, Rachel, with but a slight covering over her shoulders, sat in the wings at a table near the prompter, studying the book of the play in a temperature of about forty degrees. Next morning she awoke gasping with pneumonia. She recovered sufficiently to sail for Charleston, S. C., where she was able to give one performance of "Adrienne Lecouvreur," (December 17, 1855), but that proved to be her last appearance on any stage. Finding it useless to try to act, she returned to Europe, took up her residence at the Villa Sarden, Cannes, and there died, almost alone, January 5, 1858.

Of Rachel's last New York appearance— at Niblo's [1] — the *Tribune* wrote:

"New York has confirmed with a rare enthusiasm the flattering verdict which Paris, London, Berlin and St. Petersburg had already pronounced upon the genius of this great *tragédienne*. She has performed in this city twenty-nine times to houses which certainly on the average, taken at the very lowest, have yielded three thousand dollars each night. . . . This, we can say from a pretty accurate knowledge of Mlle. Rachel's receipts at the capitals of Europe, is far away the largest amount she has ever received for a similar number of nights' performances, confirming the fact which the experience of every really great artist who has visited this country attests, that in no other is genius so highly appreciated or magnificently rewarded. The visit of Rachel cannot but have a permanent literary, as well as artistic influence."

[1] On November 17, 1855.

It was estimated that some thirty thousand people, at least, in the city, would have read a tragedy of Corneille or Racine as a result of this actress's visit. And New York had previously been quite innocent of the French classics!

In a very sprightly and diverting volume made up of contributions sent to the *Figaro* by Léon Beauvallet, who was a member of Rachel's company, we get a number of " inside " glimpses into the ups and downs of this American adventure. The ship on which the company sailed from Liverpool was named the *Pacific*. The first hardship encountered was by reason of " the strange and unnatural marriages " between diverse food-stuffs — " rice mixed with rhubarb, cream with gooseberries," and the like. Rachel, finding herself " not sea-sick but very ill at ease," kept her cabin for the greater part of the voyage, refusing even to be diverted by the gift of a large box of American perfumery, presented to her in mid-ocean by an admirer on board.

For the captain's dinner, however, the great tragedienne graciously condescended to emerge and to take her seat in the place of supreme honour. In the course of this dinner, Rachel was toasted, we learn, by A. T. Stewart, " worth forty millions." But she would not make a speech — either in poor English or excellent French.

The hotel at which the gifted one put up on landing was the St. Nicholas on Broadway; and here, at midnight, she was aroused by a belated band come to serenade her. But the day following the tribe of Félix disposed itself in separate lodgings in various parts of the town. "This," says our lively chronicler, " did not fail to excite the inquisitiveness of all the New York tattlers," and there was profuse speculation on the subject. But the only explanation offered was that " the Félix family lived thus separately — because they lived separately; that was all."

M. Beauvallet was not much impressed by the appearance of the gentlemen at Rachel's début. He found them to be " dressed very simply and all a good deal troubled by the fact that they have ripped their gloves." The ladies, however, were all " in ball-dress," with " diamonds by the shovelful and flowers as if it rained flowers."

Then follows an amusing account of the obvious boredom of the New Yorkers while the piece preceding the tragedy was given, and a graphic picture of the way in which they all then " listened " to Corneille — turning over their pamphlet translations in concert, " as if a regiment in black uniform was executing a military order."

When Rachel appeared, she was greeted " by three or four salvos of applause — only. The Americans appeared to consider it a matter of course that the French tragedienne should leave her native land and risk her life to have the pleasure of repeating poetry in the country of Washington and Benjamin Franklin. . . . Tragedy, we all perceived that first night, is not to the American taste."

Meanwhile the sale of novelties upon which the name of the great tragedienne had been hastily imposed, went on merrily. A Broadway restaurant keeper offered pudding *à la Rachel;* a lady's shoemaker displayed gaiters *à la Rachel;* there were coiffeurs *à la Rachel*, and fruit dealers even produced from somewhere a melon *à la Raphael Félix.*

Raphael Félix was greatly in need of some such soothing flattery. For though at first he did a thriving business exchanging American dollars for little pieces of pasteboard at his office on Wall Street, by September 25, the eleventh night, he was very glad, M. Beauvallet assures us, to sell places at $1.50 each for a " Reading " by Mlle. Rachel at the Broadway Tabernacle. " But it is a horrible thing to recite tragic Alexandrines in a black dress, and especially to recite them in a sort of church! "

Boston suited M. Beauvallet — and it is to be hoped Mlle. Rachel also — much better than New York. The star made her headquarters, while in the modern Athens, at the Tremont House and played at the Boston Theatre.[1] An election was in progress at the time of her visit, and the actor journalist describes with true Gallic wit the " naïveté of the candidates who have their portraits painted in distemper, on huge transparencies, to captivate the voters." But the voting did not interfere with Rachel's houses nor with the " splendid toilettes " and " the long line of private carriages drawn up before the theatre in honour of the occasion."

---

[1] This playhouse, which still stands on Washington Street, was opened September 11, 1854. It was then the largest and most elegant theatre in the country. On gala occasions a dancing-floor could be fitted over the orchestra-chairs and the house used as a ball-room. It was so used when the Prince of Wales visited this country in 1860.

What did interfere with the receipts was (1) the resentment felt by the press because certain of its representatives had been given poor seats, and (2) the indignation of the public, because speculation in tickets was tolerated by the management. M. Raphael Félix and his associates were even inelegantly characterized as *sangsues d'Europe.*[1]

To her mother Rachel wrote the following letter descriptive of her satisfaction with America:

"New York, September 25, 1855.
" Dear and Tender Mother, —
" I received on my arrival in New York your letter, or rather your *letters,* by which I learn of the joy you experienced in getting mine written on board the *Pacific.* Well, you may continue to be joyful since I have not felt so well for fifteen years. I eat and sleep like a child; I play tragedy with Herculean force — and I am growing fat! ! !

" So do you take care, dear Mamma, that you keep yourself solidly enough on your two legs to support my kisses on my return for *I* shall be strong enough to overturn the station at Paris at that moment when I see you there on the platform with my children. Great Heavens, how far I am still from that moment, the eighth of March. But then, isn't it better to pass the time in a climate which suits me so well than to suffer at Paris as I have suffered, or to be sent at a moment's notice into the south by that worthy body of French physicians

[1] It was, besides, a " week of jubilee " in Boston, and the stockholders of the theatre, therefore, were resentful that their splendid house, which might have brought in seven or eight thousand dollars by the employment of the stock actors, netted them " only $500 a night or perhaps less." Rachel's receipts averaged over $3500 a night for her eight performances.

who, when they don't know how to cure sick people, send them ' out of this place ' to make them die elsewhere.

" It sha'n't be so with me; I am coming back to laugh in their faces and I hope to live as long as — my old aunts! All my love to you, dear Mother, and to my dear little ones." [1]

A month later, in a letter from Boston, she admits great weariness and confesses that, by reason of having taken cold in the train, she is coughing " like the consumptive which she is not." Her physicians meanwhile testified, as we find in the *Boston Advertiser* of October 31, 1855, that she was " affected with an irritation of the lungs too severe for her appearance." When she recovered sufficiently to play and — at her last Boston performance — to sing the Marseillaise, wrapped in the folds of the tri-colour flag, she excited " plaudit after plaudit from the packed house."

To turn from Rachel's lively letters to a sober recital of biographical facts is to get back to earth with a thud. Yet, of course, it must be written down here that Elisa Rachel Félix was the daughter of a Jewish pedler, who was wont to wander through Germany, France, and Switzerland, in the twenties of the last century, struggling constantly to sell enough of his wares to satisfy the hunger of his young and growing family. While the pedler's cart was halted at Munf in Switzerland, Mère Félix withdrew to the " Golden Sun " inn and there, on March 24, 1821, presented her husband with the

[1] *Rachel d'après sa correspondance:* Paris, 1882.

an insignificant appearance, and common speech. Do not ask her who Tancrède, Horace, Hermione are, or about the Trojan war, or Pyrrhus, or Helen. She knows nothing; but she has that which is better than knowledge. She has that sudden illumination which she throws about her; she grows ten inches taller on the stage; she raises her voice and extends her chest; her eyes brighten; she treads like a sovereign; her voice vibrates, instinct with the passion that agitates her."

Such praise soon crowded the theatre and made it possible for Père Félix to draw some sixty thousand francs a year because of his daughter's talents.[1]

No characterization that I have seen of Rachel's astonishing talent seems to me so striking as that of George Henry Lewes when he declared her " the panther of the stage."

" She moved and stood and glared and sprang," he says, " with a panther's terrible and undulating grace. There always seemed something not human about her. She seemed made of different clay from her fellows — beautiful but not lovable. Her range was very limited but her expression was perfect within that range. Scorn, triumph, rage, lust and merciless malignity she could represent in symbols of irresistible power; but she had little tenderness, no womanly caressing, softness, no gaiety, no heartiness. She was so graceful and so power-

[1] One American actress, Anna Cora Mowatt, who saw Rachel about this time, has recorded that there was something terrific, something overwhelming in all her characters. " From the moment she came upon the stage," she writes, " I was always under the influence of a spell. Her eyes had the power of a basilisk's upon me, and flashed with an intense brightness which no basilisk's could have rivalled. I never expect to see that acting equalled — to surpass it in impassioned force and grandeur, appears to me impossible."

MLLE. RACHEL
After the painting by Lehmann
See page 266

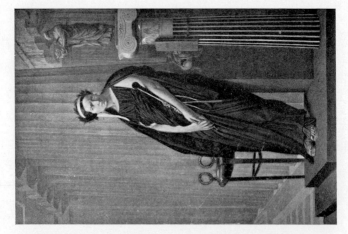

RACHEL AS PHÈDRE

FECHTER AS HAMLET

See page 282

ful that her air of dignity was incomparable; but, somehow, you always felt in her presence an indefinable suggestion of latent wickedness. The finest of her performances was Phèdre. Nothing I have ever seen surpassed this picture of a soul torn by the conflicts of incestuous passion and struggling conscience; the unutterable mournfulness of her look and tone as she recognized the guilt of her desires, yet felt herself so possessed by them that escape was impossible, are things never to be forgotten. Whoever saw Rachel play Phèdre may be pardoned if he doubt whether he will ever see such acting again."

Rachel did not undertake this, her greatest rôle, until 1843, when she was fresh from the experiences of being abandoned by Walewski, one of Napoleon's natural sons. Two years earlier she had made her great artistic and social career in London.[1] Of her then, Fanny Kemble, who knew acting when she saw it, has this to say:

" Everybody here is now raving about her. . . . Her appearance is very striking; she is of a very good height, too thin for beauty but not for dignity or grace; her want of chest and breadth, indeed, almost suggest a tendency to pulmonary disease, coupled with her pallor and her youth. . . . I was very much pleased with her quiet grace and dignity, the excellent *bon ton* of her

[1] At the time of this visit to London, Rachel still bore an unblemished reputation as a woman. Her admission into good society would not otherwise have been possible. " For our fine ladies," says Sir Theodore Martin, in this connection, " had not as yet been so completely educated out of the simplest rules of propriety as not to be startled by the announcement of an actress, ushered into their drawing-room as ' *Mlle. Sarah Bernhardt et son fils.*' "

manners. . . . She is completely the rage in London now; all the fine ladies and gentlemen crazy after her, the Queen throwing her roses on the stage out of her own bouquet, and viscountesses and marchionesses driving her about *à l'envie l'une de l'autre*, to show her all the lions of the town."

All these happyfying attentions from the English nobility — the most interesting of which was perhaps the call and complimentary note of the Duke of Wellington — did not, however, prevent this brilliant young creature from receiving a very rude shock just as she was about to return to France. "The name of the disease from which I have been four days in bed, is hemorrhage," she explained in a letter home. And we all know, if Rachel did not, that hemorrhage is generally the prelude of pulmonary consumption.

She did, indeed, "live on some days" — even some years, after this attack. But life was no more "beautiful" for her, and it was finally with real relief that she breathed her last early in 1858, in the France "whose language she had saved from destruction."

With Rachel in Paris had acted, as a youth, the next distinguished star to burst upon our vision — Charles Albert Fechter. "Magnetic glamour" John Coleman has concisely declared to be the most striking characteristic of this man. One almost catches the magnetism as one absorbs this pen picture of him: Fechter was "of middle height; figure more sturdy than elegant; features distinctly Hebraic, vivacious, expressive, powerful, changeful as the colour of a chameleon's skin;

olive-complexioned; piercing but penetrating eyes, now melting with the languor of love, now ablaze with the lurid light of hell; firm, well-cut mouth, which opened and shut like the jaws of a bull-dog; massive head with a thatch of dark brown hair; bull neck, splendidly poised, but a little too short. Such was Fechter when first I beheld him. He was then a man of forty but, had I not known it, I should have guessed him five and twenty at the outside. At first the voice seemed guttural, the French accent unendurable, but it was only at first. After a few moments the voice made music and I forgot all about the accent."

An Englishman by birth,[1] with a German name which he insisted upon pronouncing as if it were French, Charles Fechter (" Fayshtair " he wished it to be called) certainly had in him enough cross-strains to produce a temperamental character. The man's art, however, was pre-eminently French, and French, too, was in childhood his mother-tongue, though he taught himself to speak English fluently and with a generally correct accent. The lad's father intended him to be a sculptor, but the lure of the theatre early made its successful appeal, and by the time that Charles was twenty he was acting at the *Théâtre Français* with Rachel. But advancement did not here come as rapidly as he desired, so he set off to play for a season in Berlin. All the ways, works, and words of Germany, however, were

[1] He was born in London, October 23, 1824, but was sent to a French school as a child; and, by the time his school-days were over, his parents were living in Paris.

281

distasteful to him then and always, and he therefore proceeded (in 1847) to assail London. There, for four months, he acted at the St. James Theatre with such success that the Queen and Prince Consort were constantly among his auditors.

It was not until ten years later, though, and after he had made a very great success in Paris in the " Corsican Brothers " and as Armand Duval in Dumas's " Dame aux Camélias," that Fechter took London permanently by storm. Then, at the Princess's Theatre, he played Ruy Blas in English to overflowing houses, and having for four months studied the stern Anglo-Saxon tongue for sixteen hours out of the twenty-four, on March 20, 1861, essayed Hamlet.

No one had ever played Hamlet at all as Fechter played it, and in every drawing-room his conception of the part and the Saxon aspect he gave the Prince — with fair face and light flowing hair — proved the " open sesame " to conversation. For one hundred and fifty nights his interpretation of the tragedy held London.

Charles Dickens has said that " no innovation in art was ever accepted with so much favour by so many intellectual persons, pre-committed to and pre-occupied by another system as Fechter's Hamlet." *Blackwood's Magazine* (in 1861) declares this Hamlet the very best its critic had ever seen. Yet it would appear to have been Fechter's " magnetic glamour " rather than his understanding of Hamlet's character which swept his auditors off their feet. Henry Austin Clapp, a Boston critic of the nineteenth century, records that, one day, while talking with the actor about his interpretation of the Danish prince, and trying to make him understand why he (Clapp) had disagreed with his conception of the part, he discovered that Fechter *actually did not know the meaning* of some of the English words upon which his interpretation turned. This prince, Fechter insisted, did not procrastinate but pursued his task with vigour. " Do you not recall," he urged, " the words of Hamlet's mother in the Queen's closet: ' I come to *wet* thy almost blunted purpose? ' " It was thus made plain that Fechter had never distinguished " whet " from " wet " and that he had no notion of the force of " blunted." " His idea was that the Ghost's declared purpose was to ' *wet* ' *down* and so *reduce* the excessive flame of Hamlet's zeal." [1]

Hamlet, however, was only one of the many successes Fechter made in England at this time. Assuming the lesseeship of the Lyceum, he presented for very long runs, " The Duke's Motto," " Ruy Blas," " The Lady of Lyons," his own drama " Rouge et Noir " (founded on " Thirty Years of a Gambler's Life "), " Monte Cristo," and " Black and White," which he had written in colaboration with Wilkie Collins. None the less, there would seem to be some truth in Clapp's conjecture that, since Fechter definitely abandoned England for America, when he came over here in 1870, he must have felt that he had outworn the best of his favour in the British Isles.

Here, people promptly went mad over the man just

[1] "Reminiscences of a Dramatic Critic."

as they had done in London. To be sure, the critics, led by William Winter, disapproved, for the most part, of the way in which he acted " Hamlet," but the crowd, captivated by his "magnetic glamour," raved over his Ruy Blas and Claude Melnotte and would not keep away from the theatre even when " Hamlet " was the bill. Boston accepted the new star with the rapture it usually accords only to turbanned prophets of some new religion. Mr. Arthur Cheney made him general manager of his Globe Theatre; an admirable actress, Carlotta Leclerq, was engaged as his leading lady; to James W. Wallack were given the second leading parts, and for a short time it looked as though Boston was to enjoy a season of unprecedented dramatic interest. Unhappily, however, Fechter's " artistic temperament " utterly disqualified him for success as a manager, dissensions ensued, and on January 14, 1871, he appeared at the Globe for the last time. Subsequently for a number of years he played his old parts in many American cities, and once he even returned to England. But his vogue was over, and the death-blow was given to his "magnetic glamour," when, in 1876, he fell on the ice and broke his leg. After that he appeared publicly only on rare occasions, living, for the most part, in utter retirement on the farm which he had bought in July, 1873. Fechter had always said that his crowning ambition was " to keep a farm and carters."

Coleman relates [1] that an English actor, while playing in Philadelphia, was one day waited upon by " a some-

[1] " Players and Playwrights I Have Known," by John Coleman.

what obese agriculturist in a long coat of homespun and a broad brimmed hat. The visitor proved to be Fechter, who had come to seize and bear away his old friend to his farm of fifty-seven acres at Rockland Centre in Bucks county. The Englishman met with a hearty welcome. Dogs and guns and fishing-rods abounded, but the great actor's heart was far away. His spasmodic fits of gaiety were varied by intervals of sadness and silence. The mere mention of his meteoric career in England came back upon and stabbed him. . . . The world had been at his feet; he had been saturated with praise, surfeited with adulation; he had been idolized by women, envied by men; his friends and intimates had been the ' choice and master spirits of the age ' and now —

" ' After all,' growled he savagely, ' Charles V retired to die in a monastery; why shouldn't Charles Fechter die in a farmhouse? ' Then with a sudden transition to tearful tenderness, he continued: ' When you get back to England, if you see any one who cares for poor Charley — man or woman — give my love to 'em; and now, good-bye, old fellow.' "

Fechter died August 5, 1879. Not long afterward John McCullough erected to his memory, in the cemetery at Philadelphia, a monument surmounted by a bust of the gifted actor and crowned with a laurel wreath. On the base of the marble are inscribed these words:

" Genius has taken its flight to God."

CHAPTER XII

VISITING STARS OF A LATER DAY

THE impetus to Rachel's visit to America had been given by the tremendous success which Ristori, an Italian actress, had made in Paris. Adelaide Ristori was born in an obscure town of Italy, January 29, 1822, her parents being humble comedians. When only four years old she played children's parts, and at the age of twenty had attained distinction at Parma. Later she was successful at Leghorn, her talent at this period being in comedy, and her favourite plays the works of Goldoni. In 1847 she married Marquis Capranica del Grillo, and for about two years withdrew from the profession. During the siege of Rome she laboured as a sister of charity in the hospitals.

The year 1850 found her again on the stage, however, playing " Francesca di Rimini " and " Mary Stuart " in the Italian cities; and in 1855 she made a début in Paris, where she immediately scored a great success. Subsequently, she appeared in Spain, Holland, St. Petersburg, Berlin, and Constantinople. She visited America for the first time in 1866. Then she came again in 1874 and still again in 1884. It is sad to note that at the time of this last tour she had lost her ability to hold an audience.

From Ristori's own pen [1] we have a delightful account of these visits to America.

" In the beginning of September, 1866," she writes, " I visited, for the first time, the United States, where I remained until the 17th of May of the following year. Great was my impatience to reach that country and to be the first to carry my own language into the noble land of Washington, where, in the midst of a feverish devotion to industry and commerce, the arts and sciences still held a prominent place.

" I commenced at the Lyric Theatre in New York on the 20th of September with ' Medea.' I could not have wished for a warmer welcome than that which there greeted me. . . . Leaving New York, I was summoned to all the cities, large and small, of the States.

" . . . In North America there are invariably two weekly afternoon performances, Saturday and Wednesday. The passing stars appear on those days in a house wholly filled by the fair sex. Their applause is naturally less noisy and more modest, but the bravos are always given with much intelligence and at the right moment. The young girls came in such crowds to my performances that I was often obliged to order the removal of the wings to make room for them even on the stage. I tried to measure my play in such a manner that my neighbours should not lose a single movement."

In 1885 Ristori was again in the United States, and during this visit she had " the satisfaction of playing ' Macbeth ' with the renowned actor, Edwin Booth,

[1] "Adelaide Ristori: An Autobiography." Doubleday, Page & Co.

the Talma of the United States." This performance occurred at the Academy of Music in New York, on May 7. Ristori herself writes that " it was a most artistic event and the people came in eager crowds, filling that immense hall to its utmost capacity." Another interesting event of this New York visit was her acting of Schiller's " Mary Stuart " in English to the support of a German company.[1] The artist records with much satisfaction her experiences, at this time, with an " American compartment-car, equipped with a piano, a library, a china-closet, pictures and flowering plants." Here she and her company lived for the better part of five months " as in one's own home or on board a yacht."

Fanny Kemble has left us a vivid description of the way in which Ristori was rushed about in this car by her managers, during her last visit to America, and comments on the deterioration in the great Italian's acting which inevitably resulted.

" I went to see a morning performance of ' Elizabeta d'Ingleterra ' by her. Arriving at the theatre half an hour before the time announced for the performance, I found notices affixed to the entrances, stating that the beginning was unavoidably detained by Madame Ristori's non-arrival. The crowd of expectant spectators occupied their seats and bore this prolonged postponement with American — i. e. unrivalled — patience, good-temper and civility. We were encouraged by two or three pieces of information from some official personages, who, from the stage, assured us that the moment

---

[1] In Boston, at the Boston Theatre, she played in Italian while her support did their parts in English.

Madame Ristori arrived (she was coming by railroad from Baltimore) the play would begin. Then came a telegram, she was coming; then an announcement, she was come; and driving from the terminus straight to the theatre, tired and harassed herself with the delay, she dressed herself and appeared before her audience, went through a part of extraordinary length and difficulty and exertion — almost, indeed, a monologue — including the intolerable fatigue and hurry of four or five entire changes of costume, and as the curtain dropped, rushed off to disrobe and catch a train to New York, where she was to act the next morning, if not the evening of the same day. I had seen Madame Ristori in this part in England, and was shocked at the great difference in the merit of her performance. Every particle of careful elaboration and fine detail of workmanship was gone; the business of the piece was hurried through, with reference, of course, only to the time in which it could be achieved; and of Madame Ristori's once fine delineation of the character, which, when I first saw it, atoned for the little merit of the piece itself, nothing remained but the coarse clap-trap points in the several principal situations, made coarse and not nearly as striking even, by the absence of due preparation and working up to them, the careless rendering of everything else, and the slurring over the finer minutiae and more delicate indications of the whole character. It was a very sad spectacle to me." [1]

Shortly before Ristori made her last tour of America, Tommaso Salvini, who had enjoyed the advantage of early training in Ristori's company, came over here for the first time. This was in 1873.

[1] " Records of a Girlhood."

Salvini's father and mother were both players, but intended that this son should follow the law. As in the case of so many other youths who later became distinguished actors, however, fate and inherited instincts proved too strong for the boy, and the stage was the vocation ultimately chosen. Because of the rare talent he early displayed, Salvini enjoyed the tutelage, first, of the great Modena; then, as has been said, he became a member of Ristori's company. Before coming to America he was a star in his own right and had been accorded most enthusiastic praise in Spain, Portugal, and all over Italy.

For some years Salvini refrained from attempting the inevitable tour of the " States; " he knew so well that Italian was " Greek " to most theatre-goers of this country. Finally, however, his desire to make the journey became so keen that he yielded to the persuasions of an Italian theatrical speculator, with the result that he and his company first appeared at the Academy of Music, New York, on the evening of September 16, 1873, the play chosen being " Othello."

Many critics of unimpeachable authority have pronounced Salvini's impersonation of the Moor one of the greatest theatrical performances of our time; Edward Tuckerman Mason [1] thought so highly of it that he has written a whole book about it, a book in which every detail of the " stage business " is carefully described for the benefit of future generations. George Henry Lewes [2]

---

[1] " The Othello of Tommaso Salvini."
[2] " Actors and the Art of Acting."

ADELAIDE RISTORI AS MARY QUEEN OF SCOTS

TOMMASO SALVINI AS OTHELLO

declared that the enthusiasm produced at Drury Lane by Salvini's " Othello " was comparable only to that inspired by Kean and Rachel.

New York went wild with enthusiasm over this performance. The critic of the *Tribune*, on the day following Salvini's début, devotes nearly a column and a half of fine print to commendation:

" It was a brilliant occasion," we read, " and it was signalized by a noble achievement in dramatic art. Both were immensely enjoyed. The assemblage that greeted Salvini — largely composed of foreigners — was sensitive, enthusiastic, hearty, and prompt in spontaneous demonstration. American intellect, culture and taste were abundantly represented in the gallant throng and they were thoroughly fired with the prevalent ardour. So lively a flutter of preliminary curiosity succeeded by such strained suspense, such distressful sympathy and such a wild access of whole-hearted admiration it has seldom been our lot to witness.

" There is never an uncertainty of significance," continues this review, " in the response of the multitude when its heart is touched; and upon this memorable occasion its heart was not touched merely, but was shaken as with a mighty tempest of passion and of grief. No more intimate correspondence could exist between actor and auditor than that which was established between Salvini and the multitude that gave him welcome. It was that electric current whereby soul answers to soul. It was that touch of nature which makes the whole world kin. . . . If ever this tremendous tragedy of ' Othello ' was offered in a fitting spirit, it was offered last night in the Academy of Music. We do not allude to circumstances of scenery and stage-management.

These are good things, but they are not uncommon, and relatively, they are not important. Besides, these attributes of the representation were not conspicuously excellent. Edwin Booth's learnedly accurate, steadily poetic and brilliantly pictorial setting of this play remains the best, and by far the best, that this public has ever seen. But ' Othello ' on this occasion was acted with a vast and desperate earnestness of purpose, and such circumstances as are thus implied may well be accounted exceptional. . . . An atmosphere of terrible reality swathed the entire action and elevated the incidental pageant . . . and Shakespeare's vast, lurid, thrilling and agonizing delineation of the strife of great passions and the mortal conquest of evil over love, goodness, innocence and beauty was borne home to the inmost heart in the full stature of its sublimity, if not always in the full scope of its meaning."

The physical advantages and resources of Salvini for the part of Othello were extraordinary. Consequently his Moor " had the Oriental state and massive grandeur. There is a tiger latent in his blood. . . . He lived out the horrible agonies of Othello — in the scene of Iago's temptation of his faith — as we could wish to be spared from seeing any human creature do again. . . . There can be no sort of doubt that he has won a very great success." [1]

One very cheering thing about these foreign " stars " is that many of them were good enough to embalm in delightful books their early impressions of America. Salvini has told us in his " Autobiography " how very much he liked us, and why. The " liberty " which he

---

[1] *Tribune* review.

everywhere breathed intoxicated him, for he had taken an active part in the war of Italian independence, and Mazzini and Garibaldi were his friends. " I could fancy in New York," he tells us, " that I had come back to my life of a youth of twenty, and was treading the streets of republican Rome."

That he could not play Shakespeare in English was a source of great regret to him; but he felt — quite rightly — that his auditors understood him all the same, " or, to put it better, caught by intuition my ideas and my sentiments."

During his initial tour of America, Salvini gave one hundred and twenty-eight performances in the principal American cities. In 1881 he was over here again, brought this time by John Stetson of the Globe Theatre, Boston, who conceived the novel idea of presenting an Italian star who should be supported by an American company. At first Salvini was dumbfounded at the mere thought of such a combination, declaring, in dismay, that the cues would go hopelessly wrong. But upon being assured by Stetson's representatives that American actors were " mathematicians " and could memorize perfectly the last words of his speeches, he was persuaded to undertake the experiment — and there is no evidence that he ever regretted the decision. For, after a few rehearsals with his English-speaking colleagues, he came to understand the words of Shakespeare — if not the English language from which those words were taken.

Another Italian player of our own time whom Ameri-

293

cans have greatly enjoyed is Eleanora Duse, who was born in 1859 on the border of Piedmont and Lombardy, of a family which, like Salvini's, was of good actor stock. At the age of thirteen Duse was playing with her parents, undergoing hardships which soon impaired her health and stamped her face for all time with that strangely wearied look which makes it at once so sad and so fascinating.

Her first pronounced success came at Naples, then she was acclaimed at Milan, and in 1892 she found herself with an international reputation by reason of her performances at Vienna and in the principal cities of Europe.

Her American début was made in 1893 at the Fifth Avenue Theatre, New York, in the rôle of Camille. That year London saw her for the first time. Then she was married to Signor Checchi, but the union not proving a happy one, she came again (in 1902) to America. Now with especial aptness could she be described as " a lean figure, peculiarly attractive, though scarcely to be called beautiful; a melancholy face with a strangely sweet expression, no longer young, yet possessed of a pale, wistful charm; *la femme de trente ans*, who has lived and suffered, and who knows that life is full of suffering; a woman, without any aggressive self-confidence, yet queenly, gentle and subdued in manner." [1]

Nearly twenty years after she had definitely retired from the stage she was forced by the exigencies of post-

[1] " Six Modern Women: Psychological Sketches." By Laura Marholm Hansson.

ELEANORA DUSE
From the Theatre Collection, Harvard University

MODJESKA AS ROSALIND

war conditions to return in order to earn her living. She died (April 21, 1924) in a Pittsburg hotel. With her there passed what the critics have, almost universally, conceded to be the most famous, if not absolutely the greatest, performer on the stage known on either hemisphere to two generations of playgoers.

Modjeska, who, however, played in English and not, as did Duse, in her native tongue, was another foreign visitor whose career reads like the pages of fiction. But the legend that her father was a Polish prince, who cut her out of his will and affections because she chose the stage as a profession, has not even a grain of truth in it. The fact is that she was one of ten children born to a musician of Cracow, and there was great joy in the home circle when this daughter of the house began to help support the family by becoming an actress.

When " Hamlet " first dawned on Helena's horizon, the impression made upon her by the beauty of the poetry and by the wonderful characterization was overwhelming. " I worshipped at once," she said later, " the great master-work of that powerful man born and buried somewhere on the British Islands centuries ago. He became my master then and there and remained so throughout my theatrical career." The " Hamlet " she had seen was in German — and she dearly loved the works in that tongue of Goethe and Schiller, whom she had long studied; yet when the opportunity came to her, in 1863, to play German tragedy, she could not bear to do so. For this was just at the time of the Polish insurrection, and the street bands playing the Polish national airs made her feel as if her desertion of the Polish stage for the German at such a moment would be equivalent to becoming a traitor. The national stage was a passion with Modjeska, and nothing but her determination to play Shakespeare in English could ever have availed to shake her devotion to her native tongue. Even when Dumas *fils*, hearing such wonderful accounts of her performances, invited her, in 1867, to come to Paris and play Marguerite Gautier in his "Dame aux Camélias," she refused. Playing in the French language was as little to her taste as was the life commonly led by French actresses.

For, by instinct, Modjeska was an affectionate, home-loving woman, one who prized as among the highest joys of life the duties of a wife and mother. But she was also an artist to her finger-tips, and she believed that the gift of tragic interpretation was a thing she had no right to wrap in a napkin and lay aside. Very likely this feeling was intensified by the unhappiness of her first marriage. The man whose unpronounceable Polish patronymic became modified, for America, into Modjeska, was not the Count Bozenta (Charles Bozenta Chlapowski) with whom Americans associate her; she did not marry this young Polish patriot until 1868, and her only son, Ralph, was by her earlier husband.

On the day following her marriage to the gallant young Count (September 12, 1868) Modjeska went to Warsaw in response to an invitation to give a series of performances at the Imperial Theatre there, and as a result of the triumph then made, she was soon engaged for life as the leading lady of this theatre. For eight years she served — until her health broke down. Then she and her husband sailed for America at the head of a little body of Polish patriots, with the high purpose of founding a kind of Brook Farm in California. After visiting the Centennial Exhibition in Philadelphia, they set about this task, building a house and purchasing cattle, hens, and chickens, in the hope that the climate and natural law would do the rest. Sienkiewicz, the famous novelist, was one of their community. His attitude towards farming amusingly resembled that of Hawthorne when at Brook Farm; and like Hawthorne, he soon wearied of "playing chambermaid to a cow." Thus the husband and son of the gifted actress were soon doing all the rough outdoor work, while she herself was forced to cook, scrub, and make butter. Yet even by the exercise of the severest economy on the part of the colonists, they soon found they could not make a living out of the land, and Modjeska determined to act in English, which language she had not at that time learned.[1] The part she chose was "Adrienne Lecouvreur," so favorite a rôle with her that once, playing it, she failed to perceive that she

---

[1] Another foreign actress of distinction who, after coming to this country made America her permanent home, was Mme. Janauschek, first seen on our stage, October 9, 1867, at the Academy of Music, New York, as Medea. This rôle, and Brunnhilde, she played in German, not attempting to act in English until 1871. Born in Prague in 1830, Janauschek underwent great privations in her youth but she triumphed over all obstacles and from her first appearance at Frankfort in 1848 made a continuous success until her kind of tragic rôle went out of fashion and her vogue declined.

was carrying a shoe-horn in her hand in place of a fan.

The Fifth Avenue Theatre, then managed by Stephen Fiske, was the scene of Modjeska's early New York triumphs. But " Adrienne " did not draw there, owing to the fact that the mass of theatre-goers found its French name a drawback. A young girl amusingly explained to Madam Modjeska that one felt very stupid telling people about seeing a play if one could not be sure of pronouncing its name correctly. With " Camille " there was no such difficulty, and the title-part, as played by the new Polish actress, soon established her success beyond a peradventure. There had been several Camilles in New York before this time (1878) and Modjeska herself heard a great deal about the wonderful performances of Clara Morris and Matilda Heron. But her conception of the part was entirely different from theirs, owing chiefly to the fact that she had just read Arsène Houssaye's story of " Marie Duplessis," who had served for the model of Dumas's play and who, it is said, was so cultured and refined in appearance, and spoke of art with such good judgment that Franz Liszt, meeting her in the foyer of the theatre, took her for a princess. Modjeska followed up this suggestion with very good effect, representing Camille as reserved, gentle, intense in her love — an exception in every way to her kind.

Probably the most satisfying artistic experience of Modjeska's whole life was her engagement as co-star with Edwin Booth, the year before Booth's death. Lawrence Barrett had arranged this tour, which took them through many middle western towns as well as to large cities, and Otis Skinner was among the promising young people in the company.[1] The close companion-ship with Booth which Modjeska and her husband en-joyed during this tour meant a great deal to them both, and her account of the company's journeyings is full of appreciation of the great actor's beautiful character. Once, after a performance of "Merchant of Venice," they were all talking of trees and Booth said, rather shyly: "I think the trees have feelings. I do not know what religion I have, but I believe the trees love us when we treat them kindly. Why should we have such affec-tion for them if they do not reciprocate it in some unfelt and unseen way? I planted once a grove of trees on my grounds. I sold the place long ago, but I never go to New York or back without stepping upon the platform to look at them. They are as dear to me as children."

The World's Fair at Chicago cost Modjeska her right to return to Poland. For, having accepted an invitation to speak there on the day devoted to the Polish dele-gates, she impulsively gave full sway to her patriotic resentment against the Russian government and so, two years later, found herself *persona non grata* in Russia and Russian Poland. But this did not matter greatly, inasmuch as her husband and son had both become naturalized American citizens, and her home, when she was not playing, was now in California. From that

[1] It was at this time and in Indianapolis that Skinner "wore his natural legs without fleshings" while playing Macduff, thus causing a critic to declare that " a little less meat and a little more dressing would have been not only more artistic but more agreeable."

halcyon retreat she was persuaded, in April, 1905, to come to New York for a testimonial given her on the afternoon of May 2, 1905, at the Metropolitan Opera House before a brilliant audience. This occasion was her farewell to New York, and she thought it would also be her farewell to the American stage. But, yielding to the persuasions of friends, she indulged in one more tour, which lasted until April, 1907.

Two years later, in April, 1909, she passed quietly away at her home on Bay Island, East Newport, California, leaving many friends to mourn her loss and an admiring public to proclaim that, in her, the art of acting had had one of its loftiest exponents in our day.

Another exquisite actress of Shakespeare, who, if she had not died so young, would probably have taken rank above every other woman mentioned in this book, was Lilian Adelaide Neilson, who was born in Kent, England, in 1850, and made her first appearance at Margate in 1865 as Julia in the "Hunchback." Immediately afterwards she appeared at the Royalty Theatre, London, as Juliet. Leaving London in 1872, she made a tour of the United States, where she was a great favourite. Her other American visits were in 1875, 1877, and in 1879. She died in 1880, while on a visit to Paris. In explanation of her picture herewith reproduced, Austin Brereton wrote in his "Dramatic Notes:" "When Adelaide Neilson played Juliet, there was not much fuss made about the scenery or the dresses. She might have played it in a barn, but whoever saw her must remember always her tear-stained face as she stood in pure white satin before the nurse and reproached her for her insult to the memory of Romeo. That is a picture no years can destroy."

Sarah Bernhardt is, of course, almost of the present time. Yet, a book of this sort would be incomplete without referring to this world-artist, and giving a slight sketch of her fascinating and many-sided personality. Sarcey pictures for us the manner of her admission to the Paris Conservatoire. There was an examination to be passed and all that this little girl knew was the fable of the "Two Pigeons;" but she had no sooner recited the lines —

> " Deux pigeons s'aimaient d'amour tendre
> L'un d'eux, s'ennuyant au logis — "

than Auber summoned her to his side.

" Enough," he said. " Come here." And the little girl, who was pale and thin, but who had wonderfully intelligent eyes, did as she was told.

" Your name is Sarah? " he questioned.

" Yes, sir."

" You are a Jewess? "

" Yes, sir, by birth; but I have been baptized."

" She has been baptized," said Auber, turning to his colleagues. " It would have been a pity if such a pretty child had not. She has said her fable of the ' Two Pigeons ' very well. She must be admitted."

And admitted she thereupon was, — this convent-bred Jewess of thirteen years. Almost at once she began to show the genius that was in her and, by the time she was twenty-five, was drawing a salary of six thousand francs at the Comédie Français. Her talent was so undeniable and her success so immediate that there seems to have been absolutely no reason why she should have strained constantly after personal notoriety — as she is generally believed to have done. Her own version of the matter, however, is that the reporters would never let her alone. There may have been considerable truth in this; apparently, it was an uncomplimentary newspaper criticism which caused her to send in her resignation to the Comédie and set off, in 1879, for the conquest of London.

From London she embarked for her first visit to America and was led into New York — and thence all over the " States " — by the gentle hand of Manager Jarrett, who saw to it that Sarah of the golden voice obtained everything that she wanted in the way of publicity. Her account of the tactful manner in which Jarrett met the banal inquiries of the first relay of reporters is amusing. She had just replied to the stock inquiry, " Which is your favourite rôle? " with " That is no concern of yours! " and was about to answer in similar vein the question, "What do you eat as soon as you wake in the morning? " when Jarrett interposed and suavely assured the reporter that the first food consumed daily by his precious French star was oatmeal, and that later on she always indulged herself in mussels! [1]

None the less, the newspapers generally were very kind to Mme. Bernhardt during this initial visit to

[1] " Memories of My Life," Sarah Bernhardt.

302

America. The *New York Tribune,* on the morning after her début,[1] devoted two columns to a consideration of the event, its critic characterizing the distinguished French actress as " one of Nature's voices divinely ordained to interpret beauty."

" Madame Bernhardt," continues this reviewer, " is clearly a woman of genius, but we should not from this performance infer that it is a genius of the highest order. There was no hint of the great dominant brain of such a woman as Cushman or the awful power of imaginative exaltation that was the unrivalled excellence of Rachel. . . . Her power is, beyond all doubt, the magnetic force and fascination of a nature genially fired by emotion, and a nervous system sensitive to every passing wave of excitement, — but it is the genius of a woman who is strange rather than great, bizarre rather than glorious, portentous rather than overwhelming; and her art is the flute and not the organ. . . . To greet her last night there had come together one of the most splendid audiences ever gathered within the walls of a theatre. She has made a very brilliant beginning in America. She may not be a great woman; we do not think she is . . . but she is a wonderful person; she exerts a strange and thrilling power, she is accomplished in theatrical finesse; and within a certain field, which seems to be limited to sentimental realism, she is a great actress."

There is no question that the crowd enormously enjoyed Bernhardt, not only the crowd within the playhouse, but the crowd outside. All the approaches to

[1] Bernhardt's first appearance in America was at Booth's Theatre, November 9, 1880, the play given being " Adrienne Lecouvreur."

Booth's theatre were blocked with people hours before
the performance began that first night, as high as
twenty-five dollars being paid for a single seat; at the
box-office alone more than seven thousand dollars were
taken in. After the performance the immense throng
adjourned to the street outside the Albermarle Hotel,
where Gilmore's Band serenaded the actress in " Marseillaise " and " Star Spangled Banner." These attentions the wonderful Frenchwoman appeared to enjoy
quite as much as she had enjoyed the bouquets rained
on the stage at the close of her performance.

She appears to have similarly enjoyed being the
centre of the admiring throng that flocked to enjoy a
private view of her paintings and sculptures one afternoon during this engagement. On this occasion she was
described as:

" Dressed in white, with a cloud of lace hiding in its
soft folds the materials of her dress, and with long loose
gloves coming up to her shoulders and meeting the
short sleeves that she wore like, and yet unlike, the pictures of her that we see in the shops. She is not more
than common tall nor is she absurdly thin. She looks
much more like an American woman and a New Yorker
than a Frenchwoman, and not in the least like a Jew.
Her hair, worn in a frizzle over her low forehead, is
colourless and characterless, and her face takes on the
set expression of indiscriminate cordiality of greeting,
only to lose it every other minute and assume a sadly
wearied look. But her vivacity is wonderful and so,
also, is her self-possession. Every one who was introduced to her went away with the dazed conviction he
or she was the especial object of the lady's cordiality."

LILY LANGTRY, THE ENGLISH PROFESSIONAL BEAUTY, AND SARAH BERN-
HARDT. THIS PICTURE WAS MADE IN NEW YORK IN 1887
From the Theatre Collection, Harvard University

SIR HENRY IRVING

All of which convinces me that at receptions, as on the stage, Bernhardt played a part and played it well. I could not have described more accurately than do the sentences just quoted the way this lady looked to me and comported herself, *some twenty years later*, when I first met her at a reception given for her in Boston.

Henry Irving and Ellen Terry are so nearly of our own time that all lovers of the theatre remember them well; and most of my readers could probably tell me quite as well as I can tell them, that Irving made no less than eight professional tours of America,[1] at first accompanied by Miss Terry and at last alone. In 1907, Miss Terry came by herself for the first time, — acting in modern plays, — and she has since been over here on a lecture tour. Irving died October 13, 1905, almost immediately after the last curtain had fallen on his impersonation of Becket. Miss Terry is still with us in the flesh, as charming and as in love with life as ever, — though she is now seventy-seven.

Henry Irving was born at Keinton, a village near Glastonbury, Somersetshire, England, on February 6, 1838. His family name was Brodbribb, and in christening he received the names of John and Henry. When he went on the stage, in 1856, he assumed the name of Irving; but it was not until he had used it for several years, and made it eminent, that he obtained from Parliament the legal right so to call himself. On July 19, 1895, he received the honour of knighthood from Queen Victoria, an honour well deserved by reason of his il-

[1] In 1883, 1884, 1887, 1893, 1895, 1899, 1901, and 1903.

daughter who was afterwards to make the fortunes of the whole tribe of Félix. That the child was a potential gold-mine was not then realized. Not, indeed, until the family, still scarcely above the pauper line, had been living for some years in Paris — Rachel and her sister singing in the streets for bread — did Rachel's power become apparent. Then Choron, a music-master, took an interest in her and secured for her a place in a dramatic class. Here Mademoiselle Mars heard her, at the age of fifteen, recite with such fire the lines from Hermione in " Andromaque " that she interested herself to get the child into the *Comédie* — to play children's characters. But Rachel had no mind to undertake this line of work, and it was not until she had made 'something of a name for herself, at the *Gymnase Theatre*, that she began a lasting connection with the *Comédie*. Here, on June 12, 1838, she made her real début, the part being that of Camille in Corneille's tragedy " Les Horaces " — the very part in which she was to take America by storm seventeen years later.

It was Jules Janin, the great French critic, the future enemy of Fechter, who first called attention to Rachel's extraordinary talent, by proclaiming her:

" The most marvellous actress (although still only a child) that this generation has seen on the stage. . . . It is nothing short of marvellous, this uneducated child, without art, without preparation of any kind, thus becoming the interpreter of our grand old tragedies. She blows their ashes into a flame by her genius and energy; and remember, she is small, ugly, with a narrow chest,

lustrious services to the stage as well as because, in private life, he was possessed of the knightly virtues. His ashes appropriately rest near those of Garrick, in the Poets' Corner of Westminster Abbey. For, like Garrick, he was a great theatrical manager; like Garrick, too, he was a man of brilliant mind and tremendous energy, and if his achievements as an actor are not to be classed with Garrick's, this was not for any lack of idealism in him or because he did not work hard at his chosen calling.

Critics generally are agreed that, for a man who could "neither walk nor talk," Irving made a simply amazing success as an actor. This was very largely due to his tall, impressive figure and to his face — far and away the most fascinating face which has ever been seen on our stage. The high forehead, set off by strongly marked and exceedingly flexible eyebrows, the large, positive nose, the narrow, sensitive lips, the strong, thin jaw, the glowing and cavernous eyes — and, to crown all, the long and somewhat wavy, iron grey hair — combined to make a head which, even if empty, would have meant a fortune for an actor. Irving's head was by no means empty. The man was a most devout student of stage history, with a deep and highly intellectual interest in everything that bore even remotely upon his work. Hence his success, in spite of obvious disadvantages. Henry Irving was a man of one passion and that for his calling. No task was too arduous, no drill too exhausting, no expenditure, either of money or energy, too great, if so there might be attained better results for the piece in hand. Such absolute sincerity and single-mindedness must spell success in any career.

If you would understand and appreciate Henry Irving, read Ellen Terry.[1] I know of no other instance in literature where a woman, who has set out to write her own life, gives us instead a supremely illuminating picture of the work and aims of a professional partner, and that partner a man. Miss Terry frankly concedes that Irving was an egotist and that all his faults sprang from this fact. But, she insists, he was an egotist of a great type, never a mean egotist. " So much absorbed was he in his own achievements that he was unable or unwilling to appreciate the achievements of others. It would be easy to attribute this to jealousy but the easy explanation is not the true one. He simply would not give himself up to appreciation. . . . Perhaps it is not true, but, as I believe it to be true, I may as well state it: *It was never any pleasure to him to see the acting of other actors and actresses.* All the same, Salvini's Othello I know he thought magnificent, but he would not speak of it."

Their first American tour came in 1883, after the co-stars had achieved marked success in the Lyceum productions of Shakespeare.[2] The Star Theatre, New

---

[1] " The Story of My Life; " Ellen Terry. S. S. McClure Co.

[2] Charles Reade, who was early one of Ellen Terry's warm admirers and devoted friends, has left us in his " Journal " a very striking description of her personal appearance at this stage of her career: " Her eyes are pale, her nose rather long, her mouth nothing particular. Complexion a delicate brick-dust, hair rather like tow. Yet somehow she is *beautiful.* Her expression kills any pretty face you see beside her. Her figure is lean and bony, her hand masculine in size and form. Yet she is a pattern of fawn-like grace. Whether in movement or repose, grace pervades the hussy."

York, was the place, and " The Bells " the play in which the company opened.[1] Miss Terry was in the audience this first night, there being no good part for her in " The Bells." From her box she observed that the Americans *" wanted* to like them " — and studied with great interest the men and women who crowded the theatre to its doors. The way the women dressed did not commend itself to her, the combination of Indian shawls and diamond earrings not being at all to her taste. On her own first night she played Henrietta Maria to Irving's Charles I. " Twelfth Night " was, however, the great success of this first American tour, Irving's Malvolio offering the most adequate presentation of the character that America had ever seen.

Miss Terry had made her first great success as Olivia in a play fashioned by W. G. Wills from Goldsmith's " Vicar of Wakefield." An opportunity to play a similarly congenial part now came to her when Irving put on " Faust " and cast her for Margaret. Preparations for this production included a delightful tour of Germany, Irving, in his prodigal fashion, acting as host to a considerable number of people connected with the theatre, including Miss Terry and her daughter, " Edy " Craig. At Nuremberg he bought nearly all the properties used later in the play and stored his mind full of valuable impressions. " Faust " proved the greatest financial success of any of the Lyceum productions, for Mephistopheles provided Irving with a part exactly suited to his peculiar abilities, and Miss Terry as Mar-

[1] October 29, 1883.

garet was enchanting. She took domestic pride in the fact that she used a real spinning-wheel on the stage, and was able to make progress with her work right under the eyes of the audience.

When Irving put on "Macbeth," Sargent was so impressed with Ellen Terry's Queen that he begged permission to paint her. The resulting picture long hung in the Beefsteak Room at the Lyceum Theatre, but is now preserved in the Tate Gallery, London. Burne-Jones was another artist who was greatly impressed by the beauty of Ellen Terry in this part, declaring that she looked like a great Scandinavian queen, and that her presence, her voice and her movement made "a marvellously poetic harmony."

When Irving began to do "Dante" and "Becket," his long alliance with this gifted woman came naturally to an end, because there was no proper part for her in either of these plays. She then proceeded to act modern drama, both in this country and in England.[1]

[1] On Miss Terry's seventy-sixth birthday (February 27, 1924) the London *Times* declared her "our greatest actress even though no great part was ever written for her." Her distinction, it was then noted, was that she had always been "very woman, impulsive, instinctive, passionate, responsive to all the joy and beauty of life while keeping alive also to the great contribution which she might make to the theatre with which her entire life has been associated." On February 12, 1925, Miss Terry was invested at Buckingham Palace as Grand Dame of the Order of the British Empire, so crowning with the highest honors that could be conferred upon a woman a career which had done so much for the modern English stage. The dispatch noted that, after a few minutes' quiet chat with the King, Miss Terry was taken along by her attendants to the Queen's sitting room where Her Majesty recalled a visit paid to the Lyceum before she was married to see Dame Terry and Sir Henry Irving in "Charles I." The Queen herself helped the famous actress to get comfortably settled in her wheel-chair after the investiture and its succeeding interview.

CHAPTER XIII

EDWIN BOOTH: "HOPE OF THE LIVING DRAMA"

EDWIN BOOTH was born at his father's farm in Belair, Maryland, on the night of November 13, 1833, a night fittingly marked by a series of meteoric showers. He was named Edwin after Forrest, who had been his father's friend but was never his; without intending to do so, young Booth superseded the elder tragedian in the public esteem.

The relationship of these two Edwins to the American theatre, William Winter has stated in a few pregnant sentences. When the nineteenth century dawned, he shows us, Hodgkinson and Cooper were the principal tragic figures on the American stage; but by the middle of the century, Forrest was the reigning theatrical monarch. It was under Forrest that America, theatrically, attained for the first time a character of its own; then came Charlotte Cushman and E. L. Davenport to emphasize the fact that we were no longer a province of England.

Yet the art of acting was not spiritual and intellectual — as well as American — until Edwin Booth rose to eminence. He it was who gave to dramatic expression in this country sensitiveness, taste, and feeling.

The Romance of the American Theatre

Americans who regard the theatre as a force for great good in our life as a people cannot render too much honour, therefore, to Edwin Booth. For, as Augustin Daly said in his final tribute: "Booth was, certainly, the greatest tragic actor of his time, and beyond dispute, the noblest figure, as man and actor, our stage has known this century."

The most impressionable years of the lad Edwin's life were passed in the purlieus of the stage, where it was his singular office to act as mentor, dresser, companion, and guide to his highly gifted but exceedingly erratic father. This father seems never to have concerned himself much about his son's education, but he was steadily opposed to having Edwin on the stage, and when the decisive first step was taken, in a half-accidental manner, he gave it only negative countenance.

Young Booth played his first part at the Boston Museum on September 10, 1849, assuming the rôle of Tressel in "Richard III," for the sake of relieving an overworked prompter, to whom this character had been assigned. The elder Booth, hearing what was to happen, called his son before him and interrogated him as follows:

"Who was Tressel?"

"A messenger from the field of Tewksbury."

"What was his mission?"

"To bear the news of the defeat of the king's party."

"How did he make the journey?"

"On horseback."

"Where are your spurs?"

Edwin glanced quickly down and said he had not thought of them.

" Here, take mine."

The youth did as he was told and went out to perform his part. When he returned to the dressing-room, he found his father still there, with his feet upon the table, apparently engrossed in thought.

" Have you done well? " asked the elder Booth.

" I think so," replied Edwin.

" Give me my spurs," directed the parent laconically.[1]

The news that young Edwin Booth had made a success on the stage soon spread, and a number of managers requested that father and son should appear together. But to this suggestion the elder Booth would not listen; once, in refusing such an offer, he volunteered that Edwin was a good banjo player and could be announced for a solo between the acts, if so desired. Apparently he saw nothing humourous in this concession. None the less, the youth soon got his chance. The place this time was New York, Richard III was again the play, and on this occasion, also, he got a part by accident. His father was billed at the National as the crooked-backed tyrant, but, when the hour arrived to set out for the theatre, sullenly declared that he would not stir from his lodgings. Edwin's entreaties were utterly without effect. " Go act it yourself," said the impracticable parent, with the utmost calmness. At the theatre the much-tried youth explained that his father could not be persuaded to play that night and, in desperation,

Asia Booth Clarke: " The Elder and The Younger Booth."

JUNIUS BRUTUS BOOTH AND HIS YOUNG SON EDWIN
From the Theatre Collection, Harvard University

EDWIN BOOTH AS HAMLET

gave the message with which he had been charged. Eagerly the distracted manager seized upon the substitute, hurried him into the garments of the part, and without making any explanation to the audience, sent him on in his father's place. Naturally, the crowd which had turned out to see a famous tragedian in his most characteristic rôle were disappointed at the substitution of a stripling and showed it, but soon perceiving who was playing in old Booth's place, they became considerate and appreciative — and at the end of the play Edwin was called out amid hearty applause. Whether the elder Booth, who had meanwhile taken a place in the auditorium to witness the outcome of the experiment to which he had capriciously subjected his son, was more pleased or pained at this result, does not appear.

In California, where young Booth soon found himself and where the news of his father's sudden death was brought to him in 1852, all the vicissitudes of a pioneer actor in a new country were cheerfully undergone. Once the company came very near starving, and many of them had to trudge back to the nearest town through the deep snow. On another occasion Booth was obliged to travel from place to place on horseback, followed by wagons containing the stage properties and the other members of the company.

Junius Booth, Edwin's brother, was acting as stage manager of this little group of Thespians, and he had the enterprise to take a San Francisco hall and announce Edwin in a series of the great characters of the English

Romance of the American Theatre

drama. Most of these characters were familiar to the young actor from reading and from watching his father act; the kindness of the press in reviewing him in these rôles encouraged him to undertake a few parts which he had not seen so often and so did not know so well. One of these characters was Hamlet, not at all the Hamlet of his maturity, but still an interesting and a praiseworthy performance.

Then intervened an adventurous trip to the islands of the Pacific and to Australia, where he was supported by Laura Keene. Returning to San Francisco he was offered an engagement at the Metropolitan Theatre, recently opened there by Mrs. Catherine Sinclair, with James E. Murdoch as first star. Later, Booth and this lady formed a partnership to travel; for this he was never forgiven by Forrest.

Booth now turned eastward, playing first at the Front Street Theatre, Baltimore, and then setting out for a tour of the South. Washington, Richmond, Charleston, New Orleans, Mobile, and Memphis were among the capitals which received him cordially; and in Boston, where in April, 1857, he first played Sir Giles Overreach at the Howard Athenaeum, he demonstrated conclusively that he was to be a great actor — even as his father had been before him. Of course a New York success was now a foregone conclusion.

Lawrence Barrett was in the company when, on May 4, 1857, Booth, now *announced* as Duke of Gloster, made his bow at the Metropolitan Theatre. He describes the star of this occasion as " a slight, pale youth, with black, flowing hair, soft brown eyes full of tenderness and gentle timidity, and a manner mixed with shyness and quiet repose." It had been very distressing to Booth to find that he had been heralded in the papers and on the New York billboards as the "Hope of the Living Drama;" yet it was precisely this, in very truth, that he proved himself to be. For Forrest was just beginning to lose his grasp upon the sceptre which he had wielded so long, the elder Wallack was now playing his farewell engagements, and Davenport was spending his fine energies in parts not of the first rank. Thus there was a place ready and waiting for a man of strong and original power. Booth was recognized as that man.

Having now definitely "arrived," Booth could afford the luxury of a wife and the happiness of a home. On July 7, 1860, at the New York home of Rev. Samuel Osgood, D. D., he was married to Miss Mary Devlin, daughter of a Troy merchant. Mary Devlin was an exquisite creature who, though trained for the profession of music, had attained considerable success as an actress; she it was who played Juliet in New York to the Romeo of Charlotte Cushman on June 22, 1858. Shortly after her marriage to Booth, the two sailed for England, and she never again appeared on the stage.

The Booths remained in England until September, 1862, and at Fulham, London, their only daughter, Edwina (Mrs. Ignatius Grossman), was born. The object of Booth's English visit was to play his leading characters in London and the Provinces, and this he did

315

with considerable success; but owing to the outbreak of the Civil War, a lively dislike of " Yankees " was then prevalent in England, and this tended to hasten the actor's return to America. Moreover, Mrs. Booth's health was no longer good. Scarcely had her husband established her in their home at Dorchester, Massachusetts, and set out to fulfil his engagement at the Winter Garden Theatre, New York, when the gentle Mary he so deeply loved left him forever. The shock and sorrow of this sweet woman's death was a terrible experience for Booth; yet this very blow cured him for all time of the intermittent craze for drink which he had inherited from his erratic father. From the day his Mary died he was a changed man. Tobacco, however, he continued to use to excess, thus impairing his health.

With what nobleness of spirit Booth bore the great affliction which had come to him may be seen in a letter which he sent at this time to the Dr. Osgood who had married him, and which I am here permitted to print through the kindness of Mrs. Mabel Osgood Wright, daughter of that esteemed and lamented clergyman:

" Dorchester, March 7, 1863.

" REV. SAMUEL OSGOOD: —

" My dear Sir, — In acknowledgment of your kind letter of condolence and advice I can only offer you my poor thanks.

" I was not aware, until it was too late, that you were in Boston, or I should have begged of you, who blessed us in the wedding of our hopes, a prayer on that sad day when they all withered: need I tell you how sincerely I regretted your absence?

" Two little years have, indeed, taught me much. I have touched in that brief space the extremes of earthly joy and grief, a joy scarce understood till it was snatched from me; a grief far beyond my poor conception until He laid his rod upon me. A reality — sterner than ever I imagined — has torn from my eyes the rosy veil through which I looked upon the world.

" You have been pleased to mention my art and to express the hope that I may be spared to serve it long and faithfully; if it be His will I bow before it meekly, as I now bear the terrible affliction He has seen fit to lay upon me, but I cannot repress an inward hope that I may soon rejoin her who, next to God, was the object of my devotion.

" When I was happy my art was a source of infinite delight and pride to me, because she delighted in my success and encouraged me in all I did; I had then an incentive to work, to achieve something great. But my ambition is gone with her; it can give me no pleasure to paint a picture of my grief and hold it up as a show for applause again.

" My agony will be too intense to render properly those passions of woe, and sufferings which till now I thought required years of study and practise, but which, alas! I have too quickly — too deeply, learned.

" Her applause was all I valued — gaining it I felt there was something noble in my calling; her criticism was the most severe and just — feeling this I felt also there was something higher to be attained, but now I can only regard my profession as the means of providing for the poor little babe she has left with me; the beauty of my art is gone — it is hateful to me — it has become a trade.

" Pardon me for thus trespassing upon your patience, and think only of the grateful feelings your sympathy

317

has awakened in my heart, and of the firmness of my resolve to live for the dear innocent whose goodness shall be my guide to her so deeply loved and mourned.

"With sincerest wishes for your health and happiness, believe me,

"Your servant,

"Edwin Booth."

Booth gave up his Dorchester residence, took a house in New York, and contemplated retirement from public life; but his sorrow soon drove him to desire his art even more than he had desired it before, and he embarked on two theatrical enterprises of magnitude and importance. One of these was the purchase, with John S. Clarke, who had married his sister, Asia, of the Walnut Street Theatre in Philadelphia; the other was the leasing of the theatre on Broadway, opposite the end of Bond Street, whose name had recently been changed by Dion Boucicault from the Metropolitan to the Winter Garden. Booth's connection with this house covered the period from September, 1862, to March, 1867; his association with the Walnut Street Theatre was from the summer of 1863 till March, 1870, when he sold out his interest to Clarke.

In November, 1864, occurred at the Winter Garden the most notable production of "Hamlet" this country had ever seen. Scenically, this "Hamlet" was a triumph of poetic art; and the acting of the leading rôle was such as to make Edwin Booth the Hamlet *par excellence* of the American stage. For one hundred nights he held the stage in this part. Then the play

PLAYBILL OF "OUR AMERICAN COUSIN" ON THE NIGHT JOHN WILKES
BOOTH SHOT LINCOLN

This bill is extremely rare, in that it shows the patriotic verse hastily inserted by the printer when he received word from the management that Lincoln was to be in the audience that night. Another edition without the verse had previously been struck off.

From the Theatre Collection, Harvard University

JOHN WILKES BOOTH

was transferred to the Boston Theatre, where it drew large audiences and elicited the greatest possible enthusiasm.

During this visit to Boston there fell upon Booth the terrible sorrow and disgrace of his brother's mad act at Washington. On the fatal evening of April 14, 1865, our actor, having performed his rôles in " The Iron Chest " and " Don Caesar de Bazan," retired for the night at the home of his friend, Dr. Orlando Tompkins, in Franklin Square, where he was visiting. " On the following morning," writes the son of his host,[1] an old family servant, his coloured valet, greeted him with: ' Have you heard the news, Massa Edwin? President Lincoln done been shot and killed.' ' Great God,' said the horrified tragedian, ' who did that? ' ' Well,' replied the negro, ' they done say Massa John did it.' " Of course it was out of the question for Booth to play in Boston or anywhere else in America for some time after that. Several months passed before he was again seen on the stage; then he became identified for all time in the public mind with that Prince of Denmark who, like himself, had drunk the bitter water of affliction.

That Booth deeply admired Lincoln, — for whom, his sister tells us, he cast the first and only vote of his life, in the autumn of 1864, — made the knowledge that this foul deed had been wrought by his brother well-nigh intolerable. In the noble letter which he sent to the manager of the Boston Theatre, a reply to that gentle-

[1] In his " History of The Boston Theatre."

man's tactful communication conveying the sad news, Edwin Booth records his very deep sorrow because " a good man and a justly honoured and patriotic ruler, has fallen by the hand of an assassin. . . . Whatever calamity," he adds, " may befall me and mine, my country, one and indivisible, has my warmest devotion."

This tragedy so preyed upon Edwin Booth's mind that he never went to Washington again, and it was nearly a year before he could be persuaded to return to the stage. Finally, however, financial necessity, added to the urgent solicitation of his friends, availed to bring him back in " Hamlet " to the Winter Garden Theatre. As he made his entrance there, January 3, 1866, he was greeted by nine great cheers, while the assembled spectators rose to wave hats and handkerchiefs and to cover the stage with a shower of bouquets. Thus emphatically assured that the public was by no means holding him responsible, even remotely, for his brother's deed, Booth took up his professional career with renewed zest. A series of revivals, comparable only to Charles Kean's revivals of Shakespeare in London, succeeded one another. This series was delayed for a time by a fire which destroyed the Winter Garden, but it was taken up again when, on February 3, 1869, Booth's Theatre opened with a magnificent production of " Romeo and Juliet." Booth himself was, of course, the Romeo on this occasion; the Juliet was Miss Mary McVicker, step-daughter of J. H. McVicker, who was for many years a leader of theatrical management in

Chicago. This lady Booth made his wife on June 7, 1869, at Long Branch, New Jersey, where for a time they resided. Their married life extended over a period of twelve years, but was greatly clouded, at the end, by the wife's insanity.

The success of Booth's Theatre was immediate and enduring; throughout those years when it was under the control of its chief owner, the receipts were very large. The lavish way in which " Othello," " Winter's Tale," " Julius Caesar," " Merchant of Venice," " Much Ado About Nothing," and other great Shakesperian plays were here successively presented not unnaturally left but a small margin of profit, however, and since Booth was an unskilful financier, bankruptcy was inevitable at the end. But the noble plays which were here nobly put on none the less registered the highwater mark of dramatic achievement in this country. Booth felt very strongly that the stage might and should be made an instrument for great good, and it was in that spirit that he conducted his theatre. To a clergyman who once wrote to him, asking if he could not be admitted through a side door in order to witness, unobserved, these notable productions of Shakespeare, the actor-manager replied: " There is no door in my theatre through which God cannot see." And to the *Christian Union* (now the *Outlook*), which had requested from him an article on the moral aspects of the theatre, he replied: " If the management of theatres could be denied to speculators, and placed in the hands of actors who value their reputation and respect their calling,[1] the stage would at least afford healthy recreation, if not, indeed, a wholesome stimulus to the exercise of noble sentiments." That the theatre should be a mere "shop for gain" and "open to every huckster of immoral gimcracks" seemed to Booth a very terrible thing.

Booth's ideal of acting was as high as his idea of what a theatre should be. The players whom he assembled were artists of tried and proved ability. Edwin Adams, James W. Wallack, Jr., Mrs. Emma Waller, D. C. Anderson, James Stark, Mark Smith, Thomas J. Hind, Jr., Charles R. Thorne, Jr., Mary Wells, and Fanny Morant were among those who, for a considerable period, were enrolled in the company, while such better-remembered names as Maurice Barrymore, Charles Fisher, Louis Aldrich, Frank Mayo, Charles Barron, John Drew, Eben Plympton, and Otis Skinner were at times his associates in this venture. Charlotte Cushman Booth greatly admired and with John Gilbert, J. H. Hackett, John McCullough, Charles Kean, E. A. Sothern, John Brougham, James E. Murdoch, Edwin L. Davenport, W. J. Florence, and many other contemporary players his relations were most cordial. None of these, however, were in any sense his rivals. Not even Fechter, who was the sensation of several hours, or Lawrence

[1] Booth respected his calling so much that nothing could make him laugh on the stage. Once in Waterbury, Connecticut, when the baggage failed to arrive, he played the first three acts of "Hamlet" in ordinary street clothes, acting his own part with so much earnestness that the subordinates of the theatre, as well as his audience, became quite oblivious to the ludicrous appearance of the King and of the Ghost — the latter with a tin dipper on his head in lieu of a helmet.

322

Barrett, whom the great tragedian honoured as a co-star and loved as a friend, threatened at any time to eclipse Booth. The actor who did do this was Henry Irving, and nothing finer can be said of Edwin Booth than that, at this crisis, he gave Irving cordial welcome as a player and as a man.

Irving's attitude towards Booth had, from their first meeting, been one of eager coöperation. During the second visit of the American tragedian to London (in 1880), his English brother was most kind and friendly; it was at Irving's suggestion that there occurred at the Lyceum Theatre the notable revival of " Othello," in which Booth acted the Moor, Irving the Iago, Ellen Terry the Desdemona, and William Terriss the Cassio. This engagement was for three performances a week and was scheduled to last a month. The advance sale of tickets was more than four thousand dollars, and the artistic success of the venture correspondingly great.

It was, however, from his tour of Germany that Booth appears to have derived the greatest pride and joy afforded by his long life as a player. At the Residenz Theatre, in Berlin, where he opened on January 23, 1883, he appeared as Hamlet, King Lear, and Iago, while Hamburg, Bremen, Hanover, and Leipsic were other German cities at which he was enthusiastically received. Previous engagements had prevented him from acting at Coburg and at Weimar. His season ended on April 7, in the Stadt Theatre, Vienna, where vast crowds had attended his every performance. The trophies presented to Booth with true German effusion at each of these cities were among his most treasured possessions; they are now preserved with other relics at the Players' Club, New York.

The summer following this eventful winter was passed by the actor at his home in Newport. He never went abroad again. On November 5, 1883, he resumed acting at the Globe Theatre, Boston, and soon after this established in that city the quaint and beautiful home at 29 Chestnut Street (now the residence of Mrs. Robert Farley Clark), from which his daughter Edwina was married to Ignatius R. Grossmann on May 16, 1885. With Madame Ristori he acted in " Macbeth " at the Academy of Music, New York, on May 7, 1885; with Salvini, a year later, he played Hamlet and Othello in the same place. In 1887 the Booth-Barrett combination was formed; in 1889 he was with Modjeska; and on April 4, 1891, his active professional career closed — with the character of Hamlet — at the Academy of Music, Brooklyn. His health at this time was not good, but he had no thought that this would be his last appearance on any stage; in responding to the loud and prolonged cheers that greeted him on this occasion, he told his auditors that he hoped soon for an improvement in health, and that he trusted he might then serve them better.

A letter which he sent to his friend, Aldrich, in the following fall, and which I am here permitted to reproduce through the kindness of Mrs. Aldrich, was full of his old-time sweetness and humour. It has to do with a beautiful bedstead on which Booth had slept for many years and which he presented to the Aldriches when he

EDWIN BOOTH

THE " ROYAL COUCH OF DENMARK "

broke up his Boston home. This " royal couch of Denmark," as they came to call it, now dominates one of the guest rooms at the Aldrich home on Mt. Vernon Street, Boston.

The letter is dated November 17, 1891, and was written from the Players' Club, which Booth had founded in Gramercy Park, and where, in the third-floor rooms reserved for his use, he passed the final years of his life.

" Dear Tom," it begins, " Bless thee! Thy wink was timely wunk and made me merry! Sweet be thy slumbers in thy royal bed, for I s'pose you'll try at least a nap in it — but be careful how you tumble out of it; remember my adventure with your four poster in your room of state one dark night, long ago, when dear old Tripp howled to greet me, — and now he's canine-ized. . . . Hope you'll soon be here to have a chat through our pipes. I'm still pretty much of a weakling but in better condition than I've been for many months. . . . Shall be glad to see Tal [Aldrich's son, Talbot]. Love to all. Am anxiously waiting news from Florence. He was lately chosen for Barrett's place on the board of directors. Adieux! Yours forever,

" EDWIN."

William Winter, who has written a tender and beautiful " Life " of Booth, and who was his dear friend, says that it was their intention to write together in the Players' Club, with the aid of its library, a history of the theatre in America. Owing to various circumstances the plan miscarried. But what a book that would have been!

The sweet patience which had always been a marked

quality of Booth's character did not fail him when sickness and suffering fell to his lot. He died on July 8, 1893, full, as he had lived, of happy belief in a world beyond the grave. He was laid at rest, beside the wife of his youth, in Mount Auburn Cemetery. Thomas Bailey Aldrich, the poet, — who, with Charles P. Daly, Horace Howard Furness, Joseph Jefferson, A. M. Palmer, William Bispham, and Eastman Johnson, acted as pallbearer — wrote to Winter that when Booth's coffin was lowered into the grave " the sun went down." It has not since come up. No American actor since Booth has been able to move and stir audiences as his Hamlet stirred them. Perhaps the reason lies in that closeness of association between Edwin Booth and Hamlet the Dane, of which Henry Austin Clapp has spoken in his " Reminiscences," — an association " which will abide as long as the man and his art and life are remembered. For in largeness and sweetness, in rare delicacy and sensibility, Booth was nobly human to the core, after the pattern of the most human of all the creations of the poet. Like the melancholy prince, he was required to drink the bitter water of affliction, and to hold his peace when his heart was almost breaking; and, in its extraordinary depth and reserve, his soul, even as Hamlet's and Milton's

" ' Was like a star, and dwelt apart.' "

CHAPTER XIV

WHAT Booth was to tragedy in this country Joseph Jefferson was to comedy. Like Booth, he came of a well-known actor-family; like Booth, he had the highest respect for his art; and — again like Booth — he was a scholar and a gentleman. Jefferson has very pleasantly told his life story in his delightful " Autobiography," a book which no lover of the stage should fail to read. Yet since it would be absurd to write at all of the American theatre without giving some sketch of its most gifted comedian, it behooves me here to record that Rip Van Winkle Jefferson began his active life on the " boards " at the age of four, by being dumped from a paper bag carried by Thomas D. Rice, who was impersonating an eccentric and agile negro and who sang this couplet:

> " Ladies and gentlemen, I'd have yer for to know,
>   I'se got a little darkey here, to jump Jim Crow."

Whereupon both the man and the diminutive lad, who was dressed exactly like him, danced the dance and sang the song that are remembered to this day.

From this beginning, Jefferson served his apprentice-

327

ship as an actor through a boyhood and youth passed in roving west and south with his father, playing the while in all sorts of barns and cabins until, by the time he was twenty, he knew enough about the stage to be acceptable in Chanfrau's Company at the National Theatre, New York. A bright young English girl, then playing at the National, consented, on May 19, 1850, to become Mrs. Joseph Jefferson, and that fall husband and wife acted together at the Olympic. The next year Jefferson was transferred to Niblo's Garden in the same list with Lester Wallack, Mrs. John Drew, and Charles Wheatleigh. Then he became stage manager for Henry C. Jarrett, who owned the Baltimore Museum, where both Henry and Thomas Placide, J. W. Wallack, A. H. Davenport, and Mary Devlin were acting. Later he became manager for John T. Ford in Richmond, Virginia, made a tour of the Southern States and was engaged by W. E. Burton to act for a time in the Arch Street Theatre at Philadelphia.

It must have seemed good to young Jefferson to be back in the Quaker City even temporarily, for there he had been born, February 20, 1829, and there his father and grandfather had delighted audiences before him. For the Joseph Jefferson that most of us know was the fourth generation of a famous family of actors. His great-grandfather had gone on the stage under Garrick's patronage, or at least with his help and advice. His grandfather, an able and even brilliant actor, had also made for himself a notable name.

After the Philadelphia engagement, Jefferson went

to Europe for a season of recreation and study, joining
Laura Keene's company on his return in November, 1856.
In 1857 he played Dr. Pangloss, and the next year he
shared with E. A. Sothern the glory of " Our American
Cousin," playing Asa Trenchard with scarcely less success than attended Sothern's Lord Dundreary. Then
he went to the Winter Garden, of which William Stuart
and Dion Boucicault were at this time managers, and
while there played Caleb Plummer and wrote the version of " Oliver Twist " in which J. W. Wallack, Jr.,
made Fagin famous. Matilda Heron was the Nancy
Sikes of this production.

Early the next year Jefferson's wife died, and to ease
his loneliness he took to wandering, California, Australia,
South America, and England being in turn visited.
Meeting Dion Boucicault in London, at the end of
these wander-years, he confided to him his desire for
a new play and his faith that an acceptable piece could
be made of Irving's story of Rip Van Winkle, with the
result that Boucicault at once began work on the version
which Jefferson was soon to make famous. There had
been several dramatizations of this story before, and Jefferson himself had acted in one of them, but the possibilities of the subject had just been freshly called to his mind,
he tells us, by coming on an allusion to his father's
acting, as he lay lazily reading in the loft of an old barn
one summer day of 1859. The book before him was " The
Life and Letters of Washington Irving," and this is the
passage that caught his eye: " September 30, 1858. Mr.
Irving came in town to remain a few days. In the evening

went to Laura Keene's Theatre to see young Jefferson as Goldfinch in Holcroft's comedy of 'The Road To Ruin.' Thought Jefferson, the father, one of the best actors he had ever seen; and the son reminded him, in look, gesture, size and 'make,' of the father. Had never seen the father as Goldfinch, but was delighted with the son."

Apparently this passage kindled anew Jefferson's enthusiasm for Irving's work. "He was anxious to appear in London," wrote Boucicault later, "and all his pieces had been played there. The managers would not give him an appearance unless he could offer them a new play. He had played a piece called 'Rip Van Winkle,' but when he submitted this for their perusal they rejected it. Still, he was so desirous of playing Rip that I took down Washington Irving's story and read it over. It was hopelessly undramatic.

"'Joe,' I said, 'this old sot is not a pleasant figure. He lacks romance. I daresay you make a fine sketch of the old beast, but there is no interest in him. He may be picturesque, but he is not dramatic. I would prefer to start him in a play as a young scamp, thoughtless, gay, just a curly-headed, good-humoured fellow such as all the village girls would love and the children and dogs would run after.' Jefferson threw up his hands in despair. It was totally opposed to his artistic preconception. But I insisted and he reluctantly conceded. Well, I wrote the play as he plays it now. It was not much of a literary production, and it was with some apology that it was handed to him. He read it, and when he met me I said: 'It is a poor thing, Joe.' 'Well,' he replied, 'it is good enough for me.' It was produced. Three or four weeks afterward he called on me, and his first words were: ' You were right about making Rip a young man. Now I could not conceive and play him in any other shape.' " [1]

The thing was, indeed, almost perfect, and when given its initial performance at the London Adelphi, on the evening of September 4, 1865, scored a great success, as it deserved to do. For the part, as interpreted by Jefferson, had the irresistible charm of poetry. Moreover, it is perhaps the most profoundly moral piece which has ever drawn large and promiscuous audiences to a theatre. A minister once wrote of the play: " No sermon, except that of Christ when He stood with the adulterous woman, ever illustrated the power of love to conquer evil, and to win the wanderer as that little part (of Rip) does, so perfectly embodied by this genius which God has given us, to show in the drama the power of love over the sins of the race." In similar strain William Winter has testified to the wonderful, lasting impression produced by Jefferson's acting of this part: " Not Edwin Booth's Hamlet, nor Ristori's Queen Elizabeth . . . nor Adelaide Neilson's Juliet, nor Salvini's Othello," he once wrote, " has so towered in popularity or so dominated contemporary thought upon the influence of the stage."

Henceforth Jefferson was permitted to play little else than Rip. In 1867 he married Sarah Isabel Warren,

[1] In " Famous Actor Families of America," by Montrose J. Moses. T. Y. Crowell Co. New York.

a distant relative, and his private life was again a happy one. He continued to play almost till the time of his death, in 1905. The service that he has done to the American theatre by elevating the social and intellectual standing of the actor could not easily be estimated. A former President of the United States was his familiar friend and playmate in the evening of his days, and the two leading universities of this country were proud to make him a Master of Arts. Moreover, at the time of his death, he was president of "The Players" — which again links his name as it should be linked with that of Edwin Booth.

Sothern has been mentioned as one of the early partners of Jefferson's great success. His career, also, is full of interest.[1] He had been intended by his father for the profession of medicine, but by reason of a student's joke (I believe he painted *green* a corpse upon which he had been told to practise dissection) was expelled from the Medical School. After trying business without any great success, he wandered into the profession of an actor. This work he found congenial, even if it brought him only a very scanty income, and it was with the utmost joy, therefore, that he accepted an offer to sail for Boston and

[1] Edward Hugh Sothern (born in New Orleans, December 6, 1859) is the son of Edward Askew Sothern; he first appeared in small parts with his father at Abbey's Park Theatre, New York, in 1879. He was leading comedian in the company of John McCullough and has had much experience in many kinds of parts. Latterly he has played Shakespeare with Julia Marlowe, whom he married August 17, 1911. (Virginia Harned, also an actress, was his first wife.) Julia Marlowe was born in England in 1870, but came to America when only five years old and has been connected with the stage here from her twelfth year. Her metropolitan début was made as Parthenia in "Ingomar."

JOSEPH JEFFERSON AS RIP VAN WINKLE
See page 327

E. A. SOTHERN AS LORD DUNDREARY

MATILDA HERON

act at the National Theatre. His début occurred on November 1, 1852, in the character of Dr. Pangloss. Mrs. J. R. Vincent was then a member of the National's company, and she promptly befriended the young actor and his gently-born girl-wife. Sothern had not recovered from his tendency to practical joking, however, and he made his new friend quite miserable for a time with " spiritual manifestations." From the National the young Englishman went to the Howard and then, discovering, as he naïvely remarked, " that Boston was not exactly the field for success," he went to New York and got an engagement with Mr. Barnum to play twice a day for twenty dollars a week at his Museum in the Herald building. Some years later, after a varied career, he stumbled into fame and fortune as Lord Dundreary in " Our American Cousin," at Laura Keene's Theatre in New York.

One part which Sothern played successfully, a part very far from that with which his posthumous fame is identified, was that of Armand to the Camille of Matilda Heron.

Miss Heron introduced to America perhaps the best known English version of Dumas's piece; it is said that her share of the profits from this venture were no less than one hundred thousand dollars. Yet she died very poor after a career full, on its professional side, of triumphs, and on its domestic side, of troubled romance.

Born in Londonderry, Ireland, December 1, 1830, of humble farmer folk, Matilda Heron was barely twelve when brought by her parents to America, and sent to school near the Walnut Street Theatre in Philadelphia. She early became enamoured of the theatre and its people; her first stage appearance was at the Walnut Street, February 17, 1851, as Bianca in Milman's tragedy of " Fazio." The year following she played Juliet in Washington to the Romeo of Charlotte Cushman. Here her success was so great that Thomas S. Hamblin of the Bowery Theatre, New York, engaged her to be his leading lady. Philadelphia, Boston, and San Francisco in turn received her, the latter city with enthusiasm which knew no bounds. " Miss Heron has been so lauded by the press, since her arrival in California," declared one of her critics, " that we should be almost obliged to invent a new dictionary from which to search for words to express our high estimate of her talent." The eligible young men of the city, too, were all at the actress's feet.

Upon one of them, Henry Herbert Byrne, a brilliant lawyer, she bestowed her hand in marriage. The ceremony was performed secretly, June 10, 1854, in St. Patrick's Church, San Francisco, and for five days they were together. Then, according to a previous arrangement, the bride set off to take her departure from the stage, in the East; her husband was to join her after he had completed some important business undertakings. He did so, but remained with her but a single day. Why they parted has never been known, for the wife is said to have spoken of Byrne, in her later days, as " the first love of her life; " and there is every evidence

334

that to him, also, their separation spelled tragedy. He died in 1872, leaving to a friend his considerable fortune.

Meanwhile Miss Heron became more and more famous; and contracted, too, another unhappy marriage. This union, however, endured a dozen years, and from it sprang one daughter, Bijou, upon whom the mother lavished all the pent-up affection of a richly emotional nature. Miss Heron died in New York, May 7, 1877.

The Camille of Matilda Heron was not the first or the best America had known. But it became the most popular by reason of its amazing, almost revolting naturalness. She had seen Mme. Doche in the part in Paris, had perceived at once its enormous " drawing " possibilities, and within a month had translated it, mastered the business of the rôle, and sailed for home ready to play it. She did play it first in October, 1855; but it was not until 1857 that she gave it in New York and won a great metropolitan success. No harrowing thought, no disgusting detail was lacking in the character as she gave it. Yet this very offensiveness added to its power. William Winter,[1] as well as scores of other critics, had only the highest praise for her work in this rôle. " She had a wildness of emotion, a force of brain, a vitality in embodiment and many indefinable magnetic qualities, that combined," he declares, " to make her exceptional among human creatures. . . . She appeared in other parts but Camille was the part she always acted best. It afforded the agonized and agonizing situation which

[1] *New York Tribune*, March 12, 1877.

alone could serve for the utterance of her tempestuous nature."

Another emotional actress who made a pronounced success of Camille — though she is more intimately associated in our memory with the big Sardou rôles — was Fanny Davenport. The Davenports are very closely bound up, indeed, with dramatic history in America during the latter half of the nineteenth century. E. L. Davenport, Fanny's father, was Boston-born (November 15, 1815) and had enjoyed an early acquaintance with Forrest and with George H. Barrett, then a member of the old Tremont Theatre Company; Barrett, indeed, secured for the youth an opening at Providence to support the elder Booth and so started him on his theatrical career. Making a success in this initial rôle, Davenport got an opportunity to play at Newport in Douglas Jerrold's " Black-eyed Susan," and this led to his being engaged as a member of the stock company at the Tremont Theatre, Boston. For two seasons he had valuable utility experience at this house, going thence to the Walnut Street Theatre, Philadelphia, where he stayed for three years. A brief engagement at the old Bowery Theatre, New York, — playing Titus to the Brutus of Thomas Hamblin, — now intervened, after which Davenport began his long career as a star. The connection with Mrs. Anna Cora Mowatt, which soon followed, was a very fortunate thing for them both, these two excellent players drawing large houses wherever they appeared, whether in America or in England. Because Macready had become attracted to his work, Davenport remained in England for seven years. Then, in August, 1854, he and his wife (formerly Fanny Vining, daughter of a London comedian) sailed for home, opening at the Broadway Theatre in New York on September 11, in " Othello." Everywhere Davenport was warmly greeted, and when he reached Boston, in the course of his starring tour (on January 1, 1855), to play Hamlet, a banner bearing the words: " Welcome home, E. L. Davenport," was flung across the street. During the years immediately following he played a great deal with Miss Cushman, and in the summer of 1858 was a member of the stock company at the Boston Theatre. On August 29, 1859, he obtained control of the Howard Athenaeum.

There had been good companies before at this famous old theatre, — Joseph Jefferson was a member of the 1853–1854 group of players, — but the men and women whom Davenport assembled were altogether unusual in their high average of ability; they included Mrs. Farren, Mr. and Mrs. W. J. Florence, Matilda Heron, Julia Dean Hayne, Mr. and Mrs. J. W. Wallack, Jr., John Brougham, Edwin Booth. John McCullough, Lawrence Barrett, and W. J. LeMoyne were other well-known actors occasionally connected with the Howard during Davenport's régime of over two years. The relations of the company to their manager were delightful. For all admired and respected Davenport and when he put up a notice: " Boys, don't smoke, and if you love your manager, turn down the gas," they were glad to accede to both requests.

At the Davenports' home there were no less than nine little people, and it was, therefore, rather a convenience than otherwise that some of the children had usually to be seated at a little side table, set apart for the naughty. Once, when Fanny was occupying this board all alone, Booth, who was usually there for Sunday dinner, came in, and perceiving her shame and mortification, took his chair from the place reserved for him at the big table and set it close beside the little girl's. Then he quietly ate his meal with her.

To a friend Fanny Davenport once wrote that her first appearance on any stage was at the Howard Athenaeum, Boston, July 4, 1858, when her father and mother and the whole company sang " The Star-Spangled Banner."

" I stood beside my mother," she said, " and held the American flag, and I remember receiving the praise of the one dearest to me in all the world, for trying to wave the flag when the line ' the star-spangled banner in triumph shall wave ' was sung. I was then in my seventh year and, being too small to move the flag alone, my father helped me. I wore a white frock, open-work stockings, low slippers and a red, white and blue sash.

" My first appearance in a play was at the same theatre in one of W. J. Florence's burlesques. Sothern had just played an engagement and I came on dressed like Dundreary, and did the sneeze and the hop, with a line from ' Our American Cousin.' From the first year he took the theatre my father put my name in the list of the company because it pleased me and made me think that I was on the stage. I think he allowed me

FANNY DAVENPORT

See page 338

E. L. DAVENPORT, THE ELDER

See page 336

CHARLOTTE CUSHMAN

MARY ANDERSON

to appear once after the first two seasons; then I was
sent to school and did not play a part until I was thirteen
years old."

How many parts Fanny Davenport played after that
and how extraordinarily well she played them there is
no need to say here. Her first adult rôle was in the combination her father formed with J. W. Wallack, Jr.; after
this she played soubrette parts in Louisville, and then
she passed to the Arch Street Theatre in Philadelphia,
where, under the management of Mrs. John Drew, and
while appearing in dramas, farces, and operas, she attracted (1869) the notice of Augustin Daly and was invited to enter service at his New York Theatre on
Twenty-fourth Street, near Broadway. Her subsequent
repertoire was of appalling length and scope. Yet it is
of her Sardou period, as has been said, that most of us
think, when the name of Fanny Davenport is mentioned
— such power and passion, such a wealth of artistic
temperament did she display in these rôles. She died
at her summer home in South Duxbury, September 26,
1898.

No less famous a manager than Davenport was
" Baron " James H. Hackett, father of the James Hackett
now on the stage. Hackett was a man of cultivation
and fine tastes, and he had, in addition, a considerable
turn for business. But he had been a successful amateur
as a youth, and so, whenever his speculative ventures
went badly, his fancy turned with loving thought to the
stage as a career. In April, 1827, he enjoyed a brief —
very brief — season at the Covent Garden Theatre,

London; his first real success came when he played Falstaff to Kean's Hotspur in New York, in 1832. He remains to this day the best Falstaff the American stage has ever known. Subsequently he tried to play serious Shakesperian rôles, and if scholarship alone were necessary to this end, he would have succeeded. He and President John Quincy Adams once had an interesting correspondence concerning the character of Hamlet, and Hackett finally played the part. But not to his own satisfaction. He had come almost to agree with Adams, indeed, that Shakespeare at his best was too subtle to be presented adequately on the stage. Those who are interested in this theory should look up Hackett's "Notes and Comments on Shakespeare."

The only woman player native to our soil to whom the adjective "great" can fitly be applied was Charlotte Cushman, — according to the dictum of Henry Austin Clapp, William Winter, and various other critics who were her contemporaries. Beauty, certainly, had nothing to do with this actress's success. Gaunt of figure and homely of feature, she was so conspicuously lacking in the personal gifts that usually go to make up a stage heroine that she frequently had the greatest possible difficulty in persuading managers to give her even an audience.

George Vandenhoff tells a story which strikingly illustrates this, a story the more convincing from the fact that it was related to him by the manager chiefly concerned, Maddox of the Princess's Theatre, London. Charlotte had applied to Maddox for an engagement.

She had brought with her letters from many people likely to have weight in theatrical circles, — and she had already proved, in America, that she could act. But her personal appearance was so far from prepossessing that the little Hebrew was as obdurate as Shylock in declining her proffered services. Repulsed, though not conquered, she rose to depart; but, as she reached the door, she turned and exclaimed: " I know I have enemies in this country; but — (and here she cast herself on her knees, raising her clenched hand aloft) so help me — ! I'll defeat them! " She uttered these words with the energy of Lady Macbeth and with the prophetic spirit of Meg Merrilies — and of course made an impression. Immediately Maddox promised her an appearance, and afterwards gave her an engagement in his theatre. Thus it came about that she was playing the Queen to Forrest's Macbeth on that occasion when the American tragedian fancied himself the victim of Macready's jealousy and persecution.

Lady Macbeth was the part in which Miss Cushman made her first great success, in 1837, when she was only twenty-one years old; this was, also, the rôle in which she took her farewell of the stage at the Globe Theatre, Boston, May 15, 1875. It was one of her greatest achievements. Clapp has said [1] that he never knew a voice so saturated with anguish as Miss Cushman's, when pronouncing Lady Macbeth's soliloquy near the opening of the second scene of the play's third act, especially the four lines:

[1] " Reminiscences of A Dramatic Critic."

... " Naught's had, all's spent,
When our desire is got without content:
 'Tis safer to be that which we destroy
Than by destruction dwell in doubtful joy."

Miss Cushman had seen Cooper and Mrs. Powell act, and from these players, who maintained the tradition of the stately Kembles, she had insensibly acquired something of the majestic Kemble style. This grand manner served her particularly well in her Queen Katharine of " Henry VIII " — a rôle which is generally accounted her crowning achievement. All the commentators dwell with tremendous enthusiasm on her work in this piece — especially towards the end of the play, when speaking Katharine's last command that she " be used with honour " after her death, and, " although unqueened, be interred yet like a queen and a daughter of a king."

It is as Meg Merrilies, however, in the stage version of " Guy Mannering," that Miss Cushman is best remembered. Her first opportunity to do this part came when she had been on the stage only four years and arose from an emergency caused by the illness of the actress who had been cast for the rôle. She was told, a few hours before the overture, that she might *read* the lines. She was determined to act the part instead; and act it she did — superbly. What concentration, what trained powers of mind and body this presupposes — to have memorized in one afternoon over forty speeches, at the same time inventing the business, preparing the

342

make-up, and vitalizing the conception of a character like Meg Merrilies! The strange and witchlike creature that resulted was a very wonderful figure, and the same might be said of Miss Cushman's Nancy Sykes. Lawrence Barrett, who played Fagin to her Nancy, has declared her death scene in this play superlatively thrilling. " Her management of her voice as she called for Bill and begged him to kiss her, sounded," he said, " as if she *spoke through blood*."

Rather curiously, Miss Cushman, though an essentially womanly woman, was fond of playing male rôles. Marguerite Merington attributes this taste partly to Charlotte's generous desire to bring forward her beautiful sister Susan; she declares it possible, however, that Miss Cushman's active nature rebelled against the encumbrance, physical and psychic, of petticoats in the exercise of art, " as in the case of Rosa Bonheur. Indeed, placing the portraits of these two famous women side by side," says Miss Merington,[1] " one notes many points of resemblance in the square outline that marked each face, the strong yet mobile features, the clear, direct gaze, and a certain manliness in the general effect, that nevertheless does not gainsay a lovable femininity."

Vandenhoff, who was often the Mercutio when Miss Cushman played Romeo, strongly resented her assumption of this rôle. " There should be a law against such perversions," he insists. " Romeo requires a *man*, to feel his passion and to express his despair. A woman, in

[1] In the *Theatre Magazine*.

343

attempting it, unsexes herself to no purpose, except to destroy all interest in the play, and all sympathy for the ill-fated lovers." Claude Melnotte, Cardinal Wolsey, and Hamlet were other prominent male parts which Miss Cushman played. Lawrence Hutton pronounced her Wolsey a most remarkable performance and praised highly, too, the earnest and truthful manner in which she played Claude.

In view of the three or four-hundred-dollar-a-week salaries now frequently paid to leading ladies — costumes being supplied — it is interesting to learn that for many years Miss Cushman received only a modest twenty-five dollars a week, upon which she had to dress her rôles besides supporting herself and her family. It is not strange, therefore, that later, when her material reward became greater, she sometimes showed herself to be a little grasping. William Winter relates that when arrangements were being made for her farewell performance at Booth's Theatre, she was much more interested in the amount of extra salary she was to receive for that night, than in the elaborate exercises planned for the occasion. And I have it on unimpeachable authority that she disposed of the bronze statues presented to her on the occasion of her farewell performance at the Globe Theatre, Boston, for money, arguing that as she already possessed similar ones, the money was much better worth having. All of which is, perhaps, only another way of saying that Charlotte Cushman was blessed with a generous share of New England thrift. To read these anecdotes of her is to recall, indeed, David Garrick's protecting care for candle-ends. Like Garrick, however, she could give lavishly to worthy causes — she contributed more than eight thousand dollars to the Sanitary Commission — and, also like Garrick, she did much, by the dignity of her private life, to elevate the tone of the acting profession.

Another American woman who has done this is Miss Mary Anderson, perhaps the most celebrated of all our native-born actresses, and a player whose natural endowments Miss Cushman at once recognized. Her advice to the girl was to begin " at the top," where, as Daniel Webster said, there is always plenty of room. This counsel Mary Anderson devoutly followed. At the age of sixteen she made her début in Louisville in the part of Juliet and, the verdict being in her favour,[1] the manager gave her a regular engagement. Thus from January, 1876, until the season preceding her marriage and retirement to private life, she played with increasing popularity throughout the chief cities of the United States. In 1883 she appeared at the Lyceum in London and acted as Parthenia in " Ingomar " with success in England and Ireland. Her last professional performance was at Washington, in the spring of 1889; the last part that she acted was Hermione.

This was in the famous revival of the " Winter's Tale," one of the few great productions of which I am able to speak from first-hand knowledge. To be sure, I was only a girl of sixteen when I saw Miss Anderson in this piece,

---

[1] John McCullough was especially enthusiastic over her work and said so.

and as I was not a precocious child I was much more impressed by her serene and radiant beauty than by the power of her acting. Yet I do recall very clearly the overflowing joyousness of her Perdita and I also remember well the gracious loveliness of her Hermione. For of course I was not affronted, as the Shakesperian critics [1] claimed to be, by the doubling of the parts nor by the expurgating of the text to suit the changed and chastened taste of the nineteenth century.

Since her marriage to Mr. Antonio de Navarro, June 17, 1890, this gifted actress has only occasionally appeared in public, and then for the benefit of the charities of London. Just before the War, however, she came to New York to assist in staging "The Garden of Allah," thus delighting, once more, by her presence, the hearts of her many American friends.

Lawrence Barrett and John McCullough were two other gifted players contemporary with Booth; I am thus coupling them for the reason that they were partners, for several years, in the important matter of managing the California Theatre in San Francisco. Moreover, there were several points of resemblance in their careers. Both were of Irish origin, both worked their way up from the very bottom, and both succeeded, by dint of unceasing study and strenuous effort, in attaining high positions on the American stage.

---

[1] The critics insisted that " confusion " must needs result from this doubling and that in spite of the fact that the only actually necessary changes in the play were the omission of four lines of Perdita's part and the introduction of a harmless dummy for about three minutes before the curtain fell.

Barrett was born at Patterson, New Jersey, April 4, 1838, and passed at Detroit, Michigan, a cramped and sordid childhood. He managed somehow, while still only a boy and very meagrely educated, to obtain a humble post in a theatre and here he became possessed of a single but very precious book, Doctor Johnson's Dictionary. By the light of the candle-ends, which had been thrown away in the dressing-room of the theatre, he studied his treasure of a dictionary at odd hours and so improved himself that in the season of 1853 he was cast for a small part in " The French Spy." Acquitting himself creditably of this he was given opportunity to play other minor characters. Then he obtained an engagement at Pittsburg and for two years acted in a stock company there, supporting various visiting stars, among them Julia Dean of alluring memory.

New York first knew Barrett in 1856; very soon after this he supported many of the leading players of the day. Boston, Philadelphia and Washington then enjoyed his work as a resident actor until he joined Edwin Booth's company at the Winter Garden for the season of 1863–1864. Three years later he made his first professional visit to England. Subsequently for some time he was associated with John McCullough as a San Francisco manager, then, in 1870, he made the success of his career by giving us the best Cassius America has ever known.

Barrett's second professional visit to England was made in 1884, when he acted at the London Lyceum as Yorick and as Cardinal Richelieu. Returning to Amer-

347

ica, he became Edwin Booth's manager and acting partner. On March 20, 1891, he died suddenly at the old Windsor Hotel, New York, and was buried at Cohasset, where he had long had a home, " buried so near the ocean," says William Winter, who was his close friend, " that its waves almost break over his grave, and its mournful music is his perpetual dirge."

In the library of this Cohasset home Barrett had passed many of the happiest hours of his life, reading Roman history and the classics, of which he was particularly fond, and chatting with his beloved friend, Edwin Booth, who always spent part of the summer with him, about their coming seasons or their plans for the Players' Club. Many of my readers may have seen a charming picture of these two great actors in this library, Booth meditatively smoking a long-stemmed pipe, while Barrett busied himself writing at a broad desk near by. In the background books are everywhere — the Macaulay, De Quincey, Carlyle, and Walter Scott, that Barrett so dearly loved. And the Browning, too, whose " Blot in the Scutcheon " he succeeded in making so convincing as a play, that the English poet wrote to him: " Had Macready been a Barrett, I should have been a dramatist." The last year of Barrett's life he was in communication with another poet, Lord Tennyson, who was rewriting " Thomas a Becket " for his production. Irving ultimately produced this play, as is well remembered.

Barrett's last appearance on the stage was made at the Broadway Theatre, New York, as De Mauprat, in " Richelieu." Booth was acting the Cardinal and, at

LAWRENCE BARRETT

ELLEN TERRY AS MARGUERITE

the end of the third act, while lying on a bed simulating death, he was horrified to hear Barrett whisper, as he bent over him: " I cannot go on." Real death was now staring the younger man in the face. Another player had to take Barrett's place, and the day following he passed away.

McCullough, his old comrade, had already been dead six years — after retirement for two years because of mental collapse. Born near Londonderry, Ireland, November 14, 1832, of a family so poor that this son could not write (though he could read a little) when he first came to America at the age of fifteen, John McCullough, like Barrett, had raised himself by sheer force of will-power to educated self-respect and to a position of authority on the American stage. The first play he ever saw was Shiel's tragedy of the " Apostate " at the old Arch Street Theatre, Philadelphia; from that moment, he was unremitting in his study of books of every kind. One of the works that he read was " Chambers Encyclopedia of English Literature," a volume which he absorbed entire in a month, becoming so familiar with its contents that he could discourse volubly, years afterwards, on the career of any writer therein treated. His memory was always extraordinary. To it he owed his first opportunity to play a good part. For it chanced that, while he was yet a youth and of only slight stage experience, Davenport, who had been cast at the Howard Athenaeum for the rôle of Robert Landry in the " Dead Heart," fell ill, and his place had to be supplied at short notice. McCullough was told at noon that he would be

349

expected to read the part that night. He took the lines home, studied them all that afternoon in his little hall bedroom, and that night went on letter perfect in one of the longest parts of modern romantic drama.

Forrest, who had learned of McCullough's perseverence and promise, early extended a helping hand to the youth, and for many seasons McCullough travelled through the country playing seconds to the more famous trage- dian. Then, following Forrest's advice, he stayed for a number of years in San Francisco, conducting the for- tunes of the California Theatre. Financial difficulties compelled him to abandon this enterprise, however, about 1874 (Barrett had withdrawn five years earlier), so that we must think of him as a star in the last ten years of his life. In 1881 he presented " Virginius " and " Othello " with great success at the Drury Lane Theatre, London, but soon after this his health began to decline, and his last appearance on any stage was at McVicker's Theatre, Chicago, September 29, 1884. The final scenes of his life were unspeakably sad.

There was nothing sad, however, about the man when he was in good health. He was very fond of practical jokes and lost no opportunity to divert himself in this way. Winter tells a story about a sea voyage which Mc- Cullough and Forrest once made together during which the older tragedian was acutely seasick most of the time. Finally there came a calm spell, and as the day was Sunday preparations were made for morning worship. McCullough had caught a glimpse of the clergyman in- vited to preach that day, and in a spirit of pleasantry he told Forrest that he was handsome, a very good reader, and exceedingly eloquent. Forrest, feeling better, and welcoming a diversion, thought he would go down to the saloon and attend the service. McCullough mischievously saw to it that Forrest should have a seat well up front and quite near the elderly and depressing parson, who, as he knew, possessed a nasal voice particularly offensive to sensitive ears. As the discourse proceeded, the wind began to blow again. Forrest being in a conspicuous place, could not well withdraw, and suffered a good deal. But not enough to please McCullough, it would appear, for after the service had ended, he told the minister that his friend had greatly enjoyed his sermon and would be glad to see him in his cabin. The clergyman, flattered, went below at once, only to be greeted by Forrest with a volley of reproaches and the accusation that he had offended the Almighty with his confounded blathering.

"I am very sorry, sir," the poor minister retorted with what dignity he could muster, "to hear you speak thus of my Lord and Master."

"Your Lord and Master!" roared Forrest, between groans of agony, "your Lord and Master never went to sea but once, and then He got out and walked ashore; I wish to Heaven I could!"[1]

Another player of Irish blood who has added to the glories of the American stage is Ada Rehan. Miss Rehan was born in Limerick, Ireland, April 22, 1860, but she

[1] For this anecdote I am indebted to William Winter's book, "Other Days," published by Moffat, Yard & Co. New York.

came to this country in early childhood and made her stage début, when only fourteen, at Newark, New Jersey. Philadelphia, Baltimore, Albany, and Louisville, then in turn claimed her as a member of their local stock companies, her work all the while growing in brilliancy and breadth until in 1879 Augustin Daly engaged her to play important rôles in his splendid company in New York. Here she stayed until Daly's death in 1899, playing such Shakesperian characters as Rosalind, Katharine, Viola, Beatrice, and Portia and greatly distinguishing herself, also, in the part of Lady Teazle and in other leading rôles of the famous old comedies. How well she bore off Nance Oldfield's famous part of Sylvia in the revival of Farquhar's " Recruiting Officer," which Daly put on in 1885, we have seen in an earlier chapter. Perhaps Miss Rehan's most rollicking success was, however, obtained as Katharine in Shakespeare's " Taming of the Shrew." She and Otis Skinner made a very great triumph in this piece when they starred together in it some fifteen or twenty years ago.

It was through Augustin Daly that Clara Morris, also, came into her own. Miss Morris was Canadian by birth, but passed most of her long life in this country and early went to school to stock companies of the West. Thus she developed into an actress of such power that Augustin Daly was glad to engage her, in 1870, for parts in his famous New York Company. But it was chance that enabled her immediately to play a leading part for him. " Man and Wife " was on the eve of production when Miss Morris joined the company, and the lady who usually enacted the sentimental heroine had decided that she did not like her part. The actress who would ordinarily have taken her place had gone out of town for a holiday without leaving her address. Thus Miss Morris received a character which enabled her to leap, at one bound, into metropolitan prominence.

The gift of tears, which was soon discovered to be hers, proved a great asset in the kind of rôles which now fell to her lot. She possessed, too, decided originality in treatment of her parts. When she found that she was to play Cora in " L'Article 47 " she made a study of insanity, both in asylums and medical books, with the result that on the play's first night (April 2, 1872) she impersonated the madwoman in such realistic fashion that the blood of the most hardened theatre-goers turned cold in their veins.

When Miss Morris played the heroine of " Alixe " at the old Fifth Avenue Theatre, January 21, 1873, William Winter declared her acting " one of the best pieces of nature interpreted by art " that he had ever seen. In this part, as she played it, could be seen, he added, that very rare thing on the stage, " an adequate and superb revelation of woman's passionate love."

After the destruction of the Fifth Avenue Theatre by fire, on New Year's Eve, 1873, Mr. Daly's Company played for a time at the Broadway Theatre, and here Miss Morris made a powerful impression in " Madelein Morel," her part being the congenial one of a repentant Magdalen who has turned nun, but who, at a thrilling crisis, calls down the wrath of Heaven upon her false lover. It was now evident that the company's leading lady had grown to the proportions of a star, and henceforth, until her retirement from the stage, Miss Morris was seen in this capacity in all the principal theatres of America. A gifted writer, as well as a powerful actress, she succeeded in shedding a great deal of light upon real life behind the scenes as well as upon the technique of her profession. "When I am on the stage," she once said, "there are three separate currents of thought in my mind; one, in which I am keenly alive to Clara Morris, to all the details of the play, to the other actors and how they act and to the audience; another, concerned with the play and the character I represent; and finally, there is the thought that really gives me stimulus for acting."

To Clara Morris in this country, as to Ellen Terry in England, poets have been wont to write verses. We may very well close our chapter with these lines of Edmund Clarence Stedman which have been addressed to her:

> " Touched by the fervour of her art,
>   No flaws to-night discover!
> Her judge shall be the people's heart,
>   This western world her lover.
> The secret given to her alone
>   No frigid schoolman taught her: —
> Once more returning, dearer grown,
>   We greet thee, Passion's daughter! "

CHAPTER XV

AMERICA'S OWN "LIVELY ART" AND WHAT IT HAS MEANT TO OUR STAGE

THE suggestion for the title of this chapter has come to me from that highly original volume [1] in which Gilbert Seldes ingeniously defends the claim to recognition as modern art of slapstick in the films, as interpreted by Charlie Chaplin, of the "popular song," as manufactured by George M. Cohan, of the comic strip, of burlesque, of circus clowns, of acrobats and of ragtime. Ragtime for us in America began in the minstrel show. Minstrelsy must be closely related, therefore, to these other afore-mentioned lively arts. And so far as being "native" is concerned, Negro minstrelsy undoubtedly "leads all the rest."

Lawrence Hutton declares that Negro minstrelsy is "the only branch of the theatrical art, if properly it can claim to be an art at all, which has had its origin in this country. While the melodies it has inspired are certainly our only approach to national music." [2]

It is interesting to note that no less distinguished an

---

[1] "The Seven Lively Arts." Harper and Brothers, 1924.
[2] "Curiosities of the American Stage," page 91. Harper and Brothers.

355

actor than Edwin Forrest was the first person to make use on our stage of natural Negro character for dramatic purposes. This was when Forrest was under the management of Sol Smith and in the course of a summer engagement which he was playing in Louisville, Kentucky, in the summer of 1823. On this epoch-making night in the history of the American stage we learn that Forrest "acted the dandy in the first piece, a Negro in the second and Sancho Panza in the concluding pantomime, all for the sum of $2.00."[1] It was not until 1828, however, that there was seen for the first time on our boards the new and peculiarly American form of entertainment known as minstrelsy which had its origin in the singing and dancing of the slaves on the plantations of the wealthy Southerners.

A Southern gentleman desiring amusement for his guests was wont to call in those among his slaves who could sing and dance, and when he sent out invitations for a party it was often the slaves who played the dance music. Authorities differ as to the exact date when white actors began to realize that there was money to be made by imitating the black man when thus employed. The first announcement that I have been able to discover of the impersonation of the singing Negro on the stage is found in Russell's *Boston Gazette* of Monday, December 30, 1799, in the same issue in which there is a page devoted to the great virtues of George Washington, who

[1] "Theatrical Management in the West and South for Thirty Years; interspersed with Anecdotal sketches; Autobiographically given by Sol Smith, retired actor." Harper and Brothers, 1868.

had died at Mt. Vernon the December 14th preceding. In this advertisement we find it stated that at the end of act second of the presentation of the tragedy "Oronooko," "The Song of the Negro Boy" will be sung. A footnote adds that "the theatre will be hung with mourning."

There is no indication here that the bill that night was to be at all affected by the passing of the Father of his Country. Apparently the fact that the inhabitants had, that morning, on call of the Selectmen of Boston, met in Faneuil Hall " to consult on measures of paying suitable respect to the memory of the disceased Gen. Washington" left them free to enjoy tragedy, pantomime and Negro song in the evening.[1]

I am indebted to the research of the late Charles T. White for the lead which has enabled me to find this advertisement and to quote it accurately. It is particularly interesting that White should have been able to establish so early a date for the Negro on the stage because he himself was part and parcel of Negro minstrelsy and was instrumental in introducing to the stage Daniel

[1] It should in fairness be said, however, that the theatre had already been closed for some days. We read in the *Gazette* of Thursday, December 26: "On the moment of the announcement of Gen. Washington's death, the doors of the Boston theatre were closed. This tribute of respect to the greatest man that ever existed reflects much credit upon Mr. Barrett who, being among the first admirers of such transcendent worth, disinterestedly sacrificed his personal emolument and was followed by the whole company who also cheerfully consented to give up their advantages." Moreover, those who so desired could honor Washington the next evening by attending the reopening of Mr. Bowen's Temple of Fame, where thrifty advantage had been taken of the great man's decease by headlining "an excellent figure of General Washington expressive of the late melancholy event."

The Romance of the American Theatre

Webster O'Brien,[1] better known as Dan Bryant, probably the most famous minstrel of them all.

The first band of Negro minstrels, according to Mr. White (who was himself born in 1821 and began his stage life by playing the accordion), was organized in the boarding house of a Mrs. Brooks in Catherine Street, New York City, late in the winter of 1842, and consisted of "Dan" Emmett,[2] "Frank" Brower, "Billy" Whitlock, and "Dick" Pelham, familiar names for minstrels being the custom in this branch of the profession. This group, still according to Mr. White, made their first appearance in public for Pelham's benefit at the Chatham in New York, February 17, 1843; later they visited many other cities and even went to Europe. In this company, all were "end men" and all "interlocutors." They all sang songs, played instruments, danced "jigs" and did the "essence of Old Virginia" and the "Lucy Long Walk Around." White started a company of his own which he called "The Kitchen Minstrels" and for many years was prominently before the public as manager and performer in connection with "The Virginia Serenaders" and a number of other minstrel companies which

[1] Born in Troy in 1833. Made his first appearance in New York at the age of twelve as a dancer at the Vauxhall Garden. After a period of great popularity as a minstrel he for a time gave up burnt cork and traveled as a "white" star about this country and England; but he returned to minstrelsy in 1868 and played the darky until he died in 1875.

[2] The name of Dan Emmett will survive when that of all the other Virginia Minstrels has utterly disappeared, save from such books as this one. For Dan Emmett composed the war song of the Confederate army, "Dixie." Emmett wrote this piece, not in the heat of patriotism, however, but quite in cold blood, and used it as a marching song for Bryant's Minstrels, its first rendering being in Mechanics Hall on lower Broadway, September 12, 1859.

358

bore alluring names. Barney Williams was one of the "brothers" in "The Ethiopian Operatic Brothers," and played the tambourine at the end of the line.

To the Christy Minstrels, who for many years advertised themselves as "Organized in 1842," a date which would, of course, give them precedence of Charley White's group — just as it was meant to do — is, however, generally conceded whatever distinction attaches to the claim of being "the first to harmonize and originate the present style of Negro minstrelsy." [1]

The leader and founder of Christy's Minstrels was Edwin P. Christy, and the company began its metropolitan career at the hall of the Mechanics Society, 472 Broadway, near Grant Street, early in 1846, there remaining until the summer of 1854, when Edwin P. Christy retired from business and was succeeded by George Harrington, who took the stage name of George Christy.

It was Christy to whom we owe the minstrel show in the form we now know it, in that it was he who originated the idea of seating the men in a semicircle on the stage with the interlocutor or middleman in the center making the announcements. Before the days of Christy the songs of the minstrels were reminiscences of the songs heard when the Negro was at work on the river steamboat, in the sugar fields or at the camp ground, — songs

[1] Daniel Emmet explains that by this is undoubtedly meant the singing in concert and the introduction of various acts which were universally followed by other bands on both sides of the Atlantic and led, in England, to the habit of bestowing on all Ethiopian entertainers the generic name of "Christy minstrels."

which, like Stephen C. Foster's matchless "Old Folks at Home" with its wailing refrain and a harmony reflecting unutterable longing, are, perhaps, the nearest that we have come in this country to indigenous American music.

But whereas in the beginning the minstrels gave their concert as an interlude between two plays in a regular theatre, the popularity of the entertainment soon led to its expansion to the point where it occupied a whole evening. Thus it came about that the program of a Negro performance fell into three parts: "the first part," "the olio" and "the after piece." The "olio" division was really a small vaudeville show. There would be, for instance, a humorous sketch, a quartet of singers, a monologue by the chief comedian, something or other in two acts, and a miniature review. Then would come a hilarious "after piece" burlesquing all that had gone before.

Brander Matthews, writing in the London *Saturday Review* of June 7, 1884, records that the "first part" still "retains its name, to the present day being that portion of the entertainment provided by a single row of Negro minstrels seated on chairs with the grave interlocutor in the center, while at the ends are 'Bones' and 'Tambo,' the end men, known, oddly enough, in England as the 'corner men.'" He tells us that the row of minstrels had swollen at this period to "40 — count them yourself — 40" in the performance then being given at the Drury Lane Theatre by Haverley's Mastadon Minstrels.

The Romance of the American Theatre

J. W. McAndrews, who was known in this show as "The Water Melon Man," is distinguished as perhaps the only actor in history who successfully "kidded" Queen Victoria. And that he "got away with" this astounding feat is evidenced by the fact that he returned to America the proud possessor of a watch and ring which had been presented to him by Her Royal Highness! The bit of comedy which won for him these gifts is thus described by Marian Spitzer in an article entitled "The Lay of the Last Minstrels."[1]

"Reports of McAndrews' success with the Mastadons had reached the Queen's ears and she commanded him to give a performance at Buckingham Palace. He came, of course, and as he walked on the stage of the theatre in the palace he noticed that the Queen was seated in a stage box. He did his monologue and started to go into a song. It was part of the stage business of that song to remove his painfully ragged coat, fold it up carefully as though it was something infinitely valuable, and lay it down on the floor. He shuffled over to the side of the stage under the Queen's box, took off the coat, folded it with painstaking exactness, and laid it down with the utmost gentleness directly under the box and entirely within the royal reach.

"He started away, and then, looking back, returned to the coat, picked it up tenderly, carried it across the stage, indicating by every line of his face and body that it was far too precious to be left within her grasp, and put it down in a remote part of the stage.

"The Court was aghast. Such effrontery had never before been witnessed. They expected the outraged Queen to rise up and smite him. But she didn't. In-

[1] Published in the *Saturday Evening Post* of March 7, 1925.

stead she broke the horrified silence with one of her rare bursts of laughter. The tension relieved, the entire assemblage became hysterical."

We are fortunate in having a first-hand, delightfully vivid account [1] of the life of a Negro minstrel from the pen of Ralph Keeler who, in the last quarter of the nineteenth century, having some years since abandoned bones and make-up, made his mark in Cuba as correspondent of the New York *Tribune*.

Keeler's first contact with this lively art was through John T. Ford, in whose theatre President Lincoln was afterwards assassinated. There being then no Child Labor laws Keeler was able, at the tender age of twelve, to enlist as a minstrel after no more exacting preparation than was involved in buying a banjo, having pennies screwed on the heels of his boots, and then devoting himself to the practice of "Jordan" on the former and to the perfection of the "Juba Dance" with the aid of the latter. It was, however, not Ford, but Johnny Booker, minstrel impresario and hero of the then popular song "Meet Johnny Booker in the Bowling Green," who gave young Keeler his first real chance. For having subjected the lad to a hasty try-out in the barroom of the St. Nicholas in Toledo, Booker appointed him at once as jig dancer to his troupe with a weekly salary of five dollars and all traveling expenses. Keeler records that "the great Napoleon in the coronation robes which can be seen any day in the Tuileries was not prouder or happier than I when I made my initial bow before the footlights in

[1] "Three Years as a Negro Minstrel." *Atlantic Monthly*, July, 1869.

my small canton flannel knee pants, cheap lace, gold
tinsel, corked face and woolly wig."

The success of the youngster was so immediate that
within a fortnight he had the satisfaction of seeing hung
across the Toledo street near the theatre a large canvas
bearing a water-color representation of himself, with
one leg elevated in the act of performing "Juba" over
the heads and carts and carriages of the passers-by.
Keeler tells us that it was the habit of the minstrels to
lead the merriest of lives as they traveled from city to
city, through the country, staying from one night to a
week in each place, according to its size, and stopping at
the best hotels. In the troupe of which Johnny Booker
was the stage manager, Frank Lynch, who played the
tambourine and banjo and in association with "the
celebrated Jack Diamond" had been, as a young man,
among the first and greatest of dancers, also had a place.
Lynch had led the romantic life of a minstrel so long
and had so often sacrificed his trunks to "the rapacious-
ness of hotel keepers and the villainy of fly-by-night
managers" that he had hit upon the ingenious scheme of
carrying his stage and personal effects in two champagne
baskets, one of which, containing his stage wardrobe,
was always sent direct to the hall where the company
was to play, while the other, containing his linen, went
to the hotel and attracted no attention as a clothes re-
ceptacle because Lynch was the sort of man who had
been addicted to champagne baskets. Since the Booker
Troupe prided itself on its sobriety and gentlemanly
conduct and it was now the business of the four other

members of the company to keep poor Lynch straight, champagne baskets filled with linen fitted admirably into the plans of the group!

"There were so few of us that we could afford to go to smaller towns than were usually visited by minstrels," records Mr. Keeler. "The first part of our performance we gave with white faces and I had so improved my opportunities that I was now able to appear as a Scotch girl in plaid petticoats, who executes the inevitable Highland fling in such exhibitions. By practicing in my room through many tedious days I learned to knock and spin and toss about the tambourine on the end of my forefinger, and having rehearsed a budget of stale jokes, I was promoted to be one of the 'end men' in the first part of the negro performance. Lynch, who could do anything, from a solo on a penny trumpet to an obligato on a double-bass, was at the same time advanced to play the second violin, as this made more music and helped fill up the stage. In addition to my jig, I now appeared in all sorts of *pas de deux*, took the principal lady part in negro ballets and danced 'Lucy Long.' I am told that I looked the wench admirably.

"The Booker Troupe wandered all over the western country, traveling at all hours of the day and night and in all manner of conveyances from the best to the worst. The life was so exciting and I was so young that I was probably as happy as an itinerant mortal could be in this world of belated railway trains, steamboat explosions and collisions, and runaway stage horses."

When the Booker Troupe was disbanded Keeler played for a time with a company known as "The Mitchels." Then he had an interesting experience on The Floating Palace, a great boat built especially for show purposes and towed about from place to place by a steamer called the *James Raymond*, as this passenger boat made its voyage on the western and southern rivers.

Thackeray has preserved for us in his "Roundabout Papers"[1] a delightful description of just such a little group of show folk as this, people who carried on real domestic life while traveling on one of these Southern river boats for the entertainment of their fellow Americans. These were no less personages than the Vermont Giant and the famous Bearded Lady of Kentucky and her son; and they boarded at Memphis the boat in which the great English writer was then traveling.

The lady was wont in private life to cover most of her beard with a red handkerchief and sat much of the time on board the boat working with her needle. But while the Vermont Giant, as Thackeray observes whimsically, "was a trifle taller in his picture than he was in life (being represented in the former as at least some two stories high) the lady's prodigious beard received no more than justice at the hands of the painter."

The hirsute tendency of this remarkable person seems to have been inherited by her small son of three, for he had "a fine beard already, and his little legs and arms seen out of his little frock were covered with a dark down." But the bearded lady had another child, a little girl of some six years old, fair and smooth of skin, who wandered about the great cabin quite melancholy. No one seemed to care for her. "All the family affections were centered on Master Esau yonder. His little

[1] Charles Scribner's Sons, 1904.

beard was beginning to be a little fortune already. Whereas Miss Rosella was of no good to the family! No one would pay a cent to see her little fair face . . . But I do not believe that they were unkind to the little girl without the moustache. It may have been only my fancy that she repined because she had a cheek no more bearded than a rose's."

Though it may not have boasted a bearded lady coyly concealing her beard in a red handkerchief the *Palace* on which Ralph Keeler's troupe performed did contain a museum "with all the other usual concomitants of 'Invisible Ladies,' stuffed giraffes, puppet dancing, etc." And there was on the *Raymond*, beside the dining hall and state rooms of the employees, a concert saloon fitted up with great elegance and conveniences, and called "The Ridotto."

"In this latter I was engaged in conjunction with 'a full band of minstrels,' to do my jig and wench dances. The two boats left Cincinnati with nearly a hundred souls on board, that being the necessary complement of the vast establishment. We were bound for Pittsburg, where we were to give our first exhibition; purposing to stop, on our way down, at all the towns and landings along the Ohio . . . We saw a great deal of wild life in the country we visited and we steamed thousands of miles on the western and southern rivers. We went, for instance, the entire navigable length of the Cumberland and Tennessee.

"Our advertising agent had a little boat of his own in which he preceded us. The *Palace* and the *Raymond* would sometimes run their nose upon the banks of some of these rivers where there was not an inhabitant in view, but by the hour of the Exhibition the boat and shore would be thronged with people. In some places on the Mississippi, especially in Arkansas, men would come in with pistols sticking out of their coat pockets, or with long bowie-knives protruding from the legs of their boots. The manager had provided for these savage people; for every member of the company was armed, and, at a given signal, stood on the defensive. We had a giant for a door-keeper who was known in one evening to kick downstairs as many as five of these bushwhackers, with drawn knives in their hands. There were two other persons, employed ostensibly as ushers, but really to fight the wild men of the rivers.

"Besides these pugilists, we had in our company other celebrities. For instance, the amiable and gentlemanly David Reed, whose character in the song of 'Sally Come Up' made such a furore, not long ago, in New York, and, I believe, throughout the country. Also Professor Lowe, the balloonist, late of the Army of the Potomac, who was an ingenious, odd sort of Yankee with his long hair braided and hanging in two tails down his back. His wife, formerly a Paris danseuse, was my instructor in the Terpsichorean art. By the aid of a little whip, which she insisted was essential to success, she taught me to go through all the posturings and pirouettes of the operatic ballet girls. I was forced often to remonstrate against the ardor with which she applied her whip to a toe or finger of mine which would get perversely out of the line of beauty.

"Professor Lowe and Madame, his wife, conducted the performance of 'The Invisible Lady,' a contrivance which may not be familiar to all my readers. A hollow brass ball with four trumpets protruding from it is suspended inside of a hollow railing. Questions put by the bystanders are answered through a tube by a person in the apartment beneath. The imaginations of the spectators make the sounds seem to issue from the brass ball. It used to be amusing to stand by and listen to the answers of 'The Invisible Lady,' alias Madame Lowe, whose English was drolly mixed up with her own vernacular. But if responses were sometimes unintelligible this only added to the mystery and success of the brazen oracle . . .

"Madame Olinza was, I believe, the name of the Polish lady who walked on a tight-rope from the floor of one end of the museum up to the roof of the farthest galleries. This kind of perilous ascension and suspension was something new in the country then. It was before the time of Blondin, and Madame used to produce a great sensation.

"Now it may be interesting to the general reader to learn that this tight-rope walker was one of the most exemplary, domestic little bodies imaginable. She and her husband had a large state-room on the upper deck of the *Raymond*, and she was always there with her child when released from her public duties. One afternoon the nurse happened to bring the child into the museum when Madame Olinza was on the rope; and out of the vast audience that little face was recognized by the fond mother, and her attention so distracted that she lost her balance, dropped her pole, and fell. Catching the rope with her hands, however, in time to break her fall, she escaped, fortunately, without the least injury; but ever afterward her child was kept out of the audience when she was on the rope . . . "

Right in the heyday of the minstrels Miss Olive Logan was pleased to trace the ancestry of "Brudder Bones" back to the medieval minstrels whom one may find "sculpted" in bas-relief in the Norman churches of the eleventh century. To my mind, however, there is less interest in the thesis [1] she tried to prove in her article than in this description she has left to us of a typical minstrel show of her own day.

The minstrels are seated across the stage in a row. They are a bright-eyed, jolly-voiced set of men, all dressed in evening suits with exaggerated shirt frills, monstrous Brummagem diamond pins, heavy watch-chains, a great display of finger rings. They are 'blacked up,' of course, and their teeth are as white and their lips as red from the contrast as those of a genuine Negro. Each man holds the instrument upon which he is a more or less proficient performer, ready to play or sing when his cue comes. They all rise and bow to the audience as the curtain ascends, and then they reseat themselves to begin the concert . . . The fun of the performers upon the stage soon becomes animated. Brudder Bones has been singing the 'Sleigh-bell Polka' and during the chorus a 'larky' company of boys and girls are described as laughing and singing while the sleighbells are ringing and the horses prancing; that bright eyes are also dancing is, of course, in the bill, and it is no doubt their delightfully intoxicating effect to which is to be attributed the frisky capers of Brudder Bones.

" He stands upon his chair in his excitement rattling the bones, he dances to the tune, he throws open the lapel of his coat, and, in a final spasm of delight, as the last bar of music is played and the last stroke is given to the sleighbells by the others, he stands upon his head on a chair seat and for a thrilling and evanescent instant extends his nether extremities in the air . . . After the curtain has fallen and the first part of the program is over there is a busy interval behind the scenes while the per-

[1] *See Harper's Magazine* for April, 1879.

formers are hastily divesting themselves of their evening dress. The first part was made up principally of ballad singing, first one and then another of the performers taking a turn as soloist, with all the troupe joining in the chorus at the end of each verse. This chorus, it may be mentioned here, is usually sung twice as a finale, the second time in a sort of lugubrious and under-the-breath whisper, which is considered to add immensely to its success by admiring listeners in the gallery. Lugubriousness is also a very marked feature of part one of the program of the minstrel.

"The untimely death of his unusually attractive sweetheart is the customary burden of the 'genteel' minstrel song. Willows or cypress incessantly wave their melancholy boughs over the lone dank grave by the rippling river-side of a Cynthia Sue or Lily Dale; colored mothers, now in heaven, watch with what while in the flesh were saucer eyes, endued with a preponderous oversight of the romantic destinies of their off-spring, who survive and are wrestling like the rest of us with untoward events in this world of contrarieties, unfairly contributing, too, to the general sum of human unhappiness by wringing their hearts singing in mellow voices about the sadness of a mother's loss, white or black. These mournful ditties form the staple of the first part of the performances, speaking musically; but there is occasionally a rattling comic song by Brudder Bones and there is inevitably, after every ballad, some lively conversation between the 'interlocutor' or middle man and the comic men at the ends, or 'end men,' of whom Bones is ever one. To make these conversations novel and amusing is one of the most difficult parts of a minstrel's trade. Nothing so soon wears thread-bare as a joke. It is only after the curtain has fallen on the first part that the minstrels performance becomes really diversified. Then 'special-

ists' come to the fore : banjoists; men with performing
dogs or monkeys; Hottentot overtures; hamfatters;
song and dance men; the water melon man; persons
who play upon penny whistles, combs, Jew's harps,
bagpipes, quills, their fingers, and individuals who do
everything by turns, but nothing long, that the audience
will accept and laugh at.

"A great aid to comicality is now afforded by dress,
odd old rags being much in demand, while an eccentric
hat, be it as small as an egg or big as a bushel basket,
is a friendly assistant to a success of laughter. Sometimes the exhibit of an immense quantity of superfluous clothing elicits roars of delight, as when an affronted
darky prepares to strip for a fisticuff fight, and takes off
carefully, folding each one as he removes it, twenty-
six old vests, each raggeder than the other. Again some
daring aspirant for the success of novelty will enter,
almost devoid of the trammels of garments, to play upon
some strange device in the way of an instrument of his
own invention. Paganini's Variations on 'The Carnival
of Venice' are often attempted on the penny tin whistle,
and quite successfully achieved, too, if applause be any
indication. I used to know a minstrel, the Brudder
Bones of the first part, who made a very pretty melody
in the second by whistling through a bit of a quill upon
the strings of a violin, when attired as a plantation darky.
. . . A successful interlocutor or a desirable balladist who is not master of any instrument can always hold
a guitar in his hands and pretend to be strumming while
the others play. . . . Now on the stage our minstrels are
giving us the tinpanzee overture by the full blown band
with conducting *à la Jullian.* How the audience laughs
at the monstrous drums and the tremendous tin bassoon
into which Brudder Bones blows, in a fit of abstraction,
first at one end and then at the other, quite regardless

371

of the necessary laws of musical science in the real instrument! That is where the fun lies. It is always this mingling of the relics of barbarism with the last caprice in the refinement of civilization, which makes the most grotesque effect at the minstrels. The orchestra *à la Jullian* is outrageously false, played on the absurdest instruments, all tuneless, some dumb, yet it is related to the highest expression in music in such a curious way that to the modern audience it is more interesting, and, above all far more laughable, than a real concert given in all seriousness by the Negroes who inhabit the neighborhood of the course of the Nile, would be. . . . These musicians may be the progenitors, not of so near a race as the burnt cork Brudder Bones of our time, but of the far-away generations of blacks whose descendants live today to see their dramatical and musical art admired, through the medium of stage presentations of 'Uncle Tom's Cabin,' by the most cultured audiences of London and New York. . . .

"The spectators are rising now, for the plantation walk-around is almost over on the stage, the last feature of the evening. Every member of the minstrel company, from highest to lowest, must take part in the "hoe-down," each dancing in turn, and all singing the chorus and clapping their hands in time.

"To be able to do a good clog dance is a great ambition with the brethren of Brudder Bones and that the last act on the bill should be so bright and jolly as to send the audience away in high good humour is essential in the scheme of the success of the minstrel. Therefore any grotesquerie, so long as it is not indecent, is permissible in the walk-around. Children, dwarfs, 'wench dancers' — never women, always men dressed as such — take part in this chorus of song and dance. The ancestry of the wench dancer, that is, of the male dancer dressed in female costume, is at least as remote as Greek tragedy. The original representative of this sort of character in America, the "female impersonator" with a black face, was the late Barney Williams, who afterward left burnt cork altogether and made fame and fortune in playing Irish parts. Barney Williams originally sang the now obsolete Negro ballad 'Lucy Long' which set the New York of generations ago to humming and whistling its refrain for many a month after it was first heard on the minstrel stage. There is no member of a minstrel company who gets a better salary than a good female impersonator, the line being considered a very delicate one, requiring a high style of art, in its way, to judge where fun stops and bad taste begins, with decision enough on the part of the performer to stop at the stopping place.

"Some of the men who undertake this business are marvelously well fitted by nature for it, having well defined soprano voices, plump shoulders, beardless faces and tiny hands and feet. Many dress most elegantly as women, and in general the burlesque style of dressing in female parts on the minstrel stage has been abandoned by the balladist in skirts and relegated solely to the uses of the 'funny ole gal' sort of wench impersonator. It is this female, and not the ostensibly fashionable balladist of modern concerts, who takes part in the walk-around, from which the latter would naturally be excluded by the mere fitness of things alone, since no lady dances with plantation Negroes. Clad in some tawdry old gown of loud, crude colors, whose shortness and scantness displays long frilled 'panties' and Number 13 valise shoes, without corresponding views between themselves as to whether it is best to be laced, buttoned or held on by elastics, the ' funny ole gal ' is very often a gymnast of no mean amount of muscle, as her salutatory exercises in the breakdown prove. While she is indulging in a vigorous and prolonged attack of double shuffle, with various 'Hi's!' 'Hey's!' and 'Oh, laws!' as exclamations indicative of her hilarious state of mind, the rest of the company, including Brudder Bones, are chanting melodiously the wild bars of some plantation tune and striking together the palms of their hands to mark the measures. Sometimes they raise their hands over their heads while clapping; again they strike an elbow with a hand as a diversity.

"In every movement, however," insists Miss Logan, who out of extensive archeological research has assembled a number of interesting illustrations to substantiate her theory, "this is a repetition of what was done so many generations ago when the Assyrian populaces left their towns in processions, going forth beyond the gates to meet the conquerers returning from the nation's battles, to the sound of dulcimers and harps and double flutes. They clapped their hands in measure, even as Brudder Bones and his companions do on the minstrel stage to-day."

In launching her very interesting article [1] Miss Logan states that "for three years now a band of 'Christy's' have sung and danced in St. James's Hall, London, without the omission of a single night when they might legally be open" and that "for almost half this length of time the 'Mohawks,' another band of American minstrels, have repeated the experiment of the Christys in the suburb of Islington where, night after night, they take the chance of filling a vast hall wherein three thousand people may be seated and five hundred can stand."

As the years went on, minstrelsy gained almost as

[1] "The Ancestry of Brudder Bones," Olive Logan in *Harper's Magazine,* April, 1879.

strong a foothold in England as in the United States. Gladstone proclaimed it his favorite form of entertainment and used to rest himself from the cares of state by attending minstrel shows; and Thackeray has left his testimony that when "a vagabond with a corked-face and a banjo sings a little song and strikes a wild note," his heart was set thrilling with happy pity. The allusion here, however, is, of course, to the old-time minstrel who presented not caricatures, but genuine portraits of plantation Negroes in the South, — the type of minstrel which disappeared about the time of the Civil War.

But though in the later minstrelsy there was only the barest pretence at any imitation of plantation life, the banjo continued to play an important part in all the performances and was held to be the distinctive instrument of the plantation Negro. So there was great excitement when Joel Chandler Harris published in "The Critic"[1] an article in which he declared that though he was a very close student of the actual facts of Negro life he had never found a darky playing a banjo, the preference being wholly for the violin. He admitted that his personal observation of Negroes was limited to middle Georgia, but since many Negroes from Virginia and other parts of the South came to Georgia, he felt that he had ample ground for his statement.

Scholars of the type who browse in libraries immediately rushed into print, bent on counteracting this iconoclastic attempt to separate the plantation Negro from

[1] June 7, 1884.

375

his banjo.   One correspondent aptly quoted from Jefferson's "Notes on Virginia" a footnote (supplementing an assertion in the text that Negroes have an accurate ear for music), wherein the distinguished author explicitly states that "the instrument proper to them is the Banjar which they brought hither from Africa and which is the origin of the guitar, its cords being precisely the four lower chords of the guitar."

I have myself verified this quotation.   Therefore I feel that we may safely leave the Negro his banjo! More especially since we have the testimony of the late George W. Cable (who had observed Negro life in Louisiana as carefully as Mr. Harris had observed it in Georgia) that he "often spent half the night listening to the Negro picking the banjo in monotonous accompaniment to his song."   Whereupon there is reproduced for us a little Creole song [1] in which a slave seems to take his banjo into his confidence as he describes a passing dandy :

> "*Voyez ce mulet-là, Musieu Bainjo,*
>   *Comme il est insolent,*
>   *Chapeau sur côté — Musieu Bainjo,*
>   *La canne à la main, Musieu Bainjo,*
>   *Botte qui fait crin, crin, Musieu Bainjo.*"

One interesting thing about Negro minstrelsy is that the minstrels had to be jet black, whereas real colored men, as we all know well, are of various stages of blackness.   So that when the waiters at a Saratoga Hotel once put on a minstrel show in the dining room for the entertainment of the guests, they found it necessary to

[1] In the London *Saturday Review*, June 7, 1884.

N° 27.   MR T. RICE AS JIM CROW.   Price Halfpenny.

London. Pub. Jan. 1. 1837. by J.K.GREEN. 33. Salisbury Place. Walworth New Town.

THOMAS D. ("JIM CROW") RICE
From the Theatre Collection, Harvard University

TONY PASTOR, AFTER A CARICATURE BY W. J. GLADDING
From the Theatre Collection, Harvard University
See page 382

"black up," genuine Negroes though they were, in order to more closely resemble an authentic minstrel production!

Although organized Ethiopian minstrelsy was more closely associated with the Christy minstrels than with any other group, Thomas D. Rice, or "Jim Crow" Rice, as he was affectionately known, is generally conceded to have been the leading single figure in this interesting development of the American stage.

It was in imitation of Rice that the very distinguished Joseph Jefferson, at the tender age of four, made his debut on the stage [1] to the accompaniment of the couplet:

> "Ladies and gentlemen I'd like for you to know
> I's got a little darky here to jump Jim Crow."

Mrs. John Drew, who was present, has left the testimony that little Joe Jefferson instantly assumed the exact attitude of Jim Crow Rice and sang and danced in imitation of the ungainly, grotesque and exceedingly droll comedian who made the Jim Crow song famous.

There are conflicting reports of the way in which Thomas Dartmouth Rice found the original "Jim Crow." Edward Leroy Rice, son of William Henry Rice, another famous minstrel (not, however, a descendant of "Jim Crow" Rice), inclines to the version given by Edmund S. Connor [2] who was associated with Rice in the company at the Columbia Street Theatre, Cincinnati, in 1828–1829. Rice at this time was doing a sketch which

---

[1] *See* page 327 preceding.
[2] New York *Times*, June 5, 1881.

he had studied from life in Louisville the preceding summer.

Back of the theatre in Louisville, it appears, there was a livery stable kept by a man named Crow. And in Crow's employ was an old and decrepit slave who, following the custom of the time, had assumed his master's name, and called himself "Jim Crow." This old fellow was very much deformed, having a right shoulder drawn up high and a left leg which was stiff and crooked at the knee. Thus he walked with an extremely ludicrous limp and as he went about he had the habit of crooning to himself a queer old tune for which he had made some words. At the end of each verse he gave a peculiar step, "rocking to heel" in the manner his imitator made famous. The words of his refrain were:

> "Wheel about,
> Turn about,
> Do jis so,
> An' every time I wheel about,
> I jump Jim Crow."

Rice was quick to see that here was a character which would make a decided hit on the stage, and having written a number of verses and brightened and quickened the original air, he "made up" exactly like the old darky and scored an instant success with the Louisville audience before which he launched his act. The original words in his act were something like this:

> "First on de heel tap, den on de toe,
> Eb'ry time I wheel about I jump Jim Crow.
> Wheel about and turn about and do jis so,
> An' eb'ry time I wheel about, I jump Jim Crow."

Quatrains of topical and local interest were added as
time went on and soon not only everybody in Pittsburg,
but in every other city where Rice, originally a comedian
of only mediocre standing, was appearing to crowded
houses, was humming "Jim Crow." Theatrical managers sought out this figure who had introduced something altogether new to the American stage and Rice
was successively with Charley White's Serenaders, and
with Wood's Minstrels of New York. After his success
in this country was established he went to England,
where he repeated his triumphs with Jim Crow. In
this connection it is interesting to note that Rice must
have been that rare thing, a natural comedian. For
Joe Cowell, who was himself a man of no slight repute
in this field, records being present at the Park Theatre,
New York, when "Bombastes Furioso" was the bill
and the only man who got a laugh was a supernumerary
without a name who lost his job the next day for having
diverted attention from the real actors. This man was
none other than Rice, described by Cowell as "a tall
scrambling looking man with a sepulchral falsetto voice."[1]

With the development of the olio section of the minstrel show and the introduction of burlesque, there came
to be less emphasis on the Negro acts which first made
this form of entertainment unique. William Henry
Rice, though a popular minstrel, became really famous
for his burlesque impersonation of Sarah Bernhardt in
a travesty which he called "Sarah Heartburn." Once
Sarah herself, who was then touring the United States,

[1] "Thirty Years among the Players," page 86.

attended a special performance of this burlesque and is said to have laughed until she cried at some of the scenes which reproduced her rendition of Camille. Billy Emerson was another famous minstrel and made a great success, especially with the women, while traveling with Haverley's and heading his own company in tours not only of the United States but of England and Australia.

Famous also was George Evans, popularly known as "Honey Boy" because author of the popular song "I'll Be True to My Honey Boy." Evans survived until 1915 and was active until shortly before his death. Even my younger readers will remember his song "In the Good Old Summer Time." His career as a performer covered many, many minstrel shows, including repeated engagements with Primrose and West.

The George Primrose of this famous combination was John Delaney by birth, and began his career at the age of fifteen when he was billed in a minstrel show as "master Georgie, the infant clog dancer." He had a varied career with minstrelsy and circuses until in 1871 he joined fortunes with William H. West who was his partner for thirty years. Later he was associated with George Thatcher and with Lew Dockstader. Primrose and Dockstader were enormously popular in the "two a day."

Lew Dockstader, who is credited with having made more people laugh than any other man of his kind, was born George Alfred Clapp. His career began when he was a lad of sixteen and had a part in an amateur minstrel show. He organized his own company in 1866 and remained for many years in New York, attaining equal distinction as a comedian and as a manager. At the time of his death, in October, 1924, he was mourned, as the greatest "end man" in history,[1] by thousands who vividly recalled his ludicrous make-up with its huge coat and monstrous shoes. He had a perfect genius for mimicking men of prominence. Theodore Roosevelt used especially to enjoy Dockstader's burlesque of himself. Dockstader it was who, in 1908, started Al Jolson on his career as a black-face comedian; and Jolson is interesting to us in this year of our Lord, 1925, because he is the sole remaining minstrel of the days-before-the-Civil-War type. He succeeds not so much because of his minstrelsy, however, but because he has cleverly combined the traditions of the Ethiopian attraction with the appeal of the "girl show."

But if Al Jolson is the only outstanding player of our own time who is still a "minstrel," many famous players now living have been minstrels and are always glad to render tribute to minstrelsy as a stepping-stone in their careers.

Francis Wilson always felt indebted to minstrelsy for the wide acquaintance it gave him with the public. He is authority for a little bit of history which links many well-known names with this important "lively art."

"When a member of the 'All Star Rivals Company,' as we sat at table in the private dining car," he writes, "the subject of minstrelsy came up for discussion.

[1] Other famous Ethiopian organizations who had their own great "end men" were Buckley's Serenaders, Sam Bryant's, the San Francisco Minstrels, Kelly and Leon's and the Callender minstrels.

"'I suppose,' said Mrs. John Drew, 'there are few, if any, men in this company who have not at one time or another been connected with the minstrels.'

"Jefferson spoke up, saying, 'For years I danced "Jim Crow" in black-face, in imitation of Daddy Rice.'

"'I can vouch for that,' continued Mrs. Malaprop Drew, 'for I once sat in front and saw you do it.'

"'I was on the tambourine end of Pell's Minstrels,' added William H. Crane.

"'Francis Wilson knows that I was in the minstrel business and that he and I were in the same company in Emerson's Minstrels, in Chicago, in the fall of '85,' said Nat Goodwin.

"'Did Booth ever black his face professionally? I forget.' asked Mrs. Drew.

"'He did,' said Jefferson.

"'Indeed he did,' corroborated Crane. 'He told me so himself at Cohasset, when he was on a visit to Lawrence Barrett. He said that he had played a banjo in a minstrel company in which John S. Clarke was the "Brudder Bones."'" [1]

It was through minstrelsy that Tony Pastor, generally acknowledged to be New York's pioneer variety manager, made his way to the field in which he attained such distinction and success. Born in Granite Street, New York, in 1840, of a father who had for many years been a member of the Park Theatre in its earliest days, young Pastor while still a small boy, began to receive prizes for elocution. It fell to his lot to aid a temperance revival which

[1] Francis Wilson's "Life of Himself." Houghton, Mifflin Company.

was being carried on in a hall in Dey Street, New York. This appearance, he himself records,[1] constituted his début as a public entertainer. But he had previously seen the original Virginia Serenaders at the Park Theatre and so having secured for himself a tambourine and a Negro wig with a two-dollar bill which he had the good fortune to find in the street, he joined a party of minstrels who were giving concerts on the steamer then plying between New York City and Staten Island.

Thus he gained the preliminary experience of which he felt himself to be in need. Then he got a job with a minstrel band playing at Crotan Hall, and was well in the way of becoming a professional himself when his father interfered and sent him off to the country to cure him of this "nonsense."

The country, in those days, was exactly the place, however, for a lad like Tony Pastor to become confirmed in the entertaining line. He soon won great success as an amateur performer and his services were in great demand for parties and church affairs. "On one occasion," he writes gleefully, "while traveling a country road, a young farmer stopped me and asked me to mount a hay wagon and do a song and dance for the amusement of his haymakers, put a dollar in my hand and sent me on my way."

Such a lad was bound to tire speedily of the country and bound, too, to find a place no less speedily in the profession for which he yearned. P. T. Barnum (then of

[1] "A Group of Theatrical Caricatures with an Introduction and Biographical Sketches," Louis Evan Shipman. The Dunlap Society, New York, 1897

the famous Barnum Museum at the corner of Broadway and Ann Street) was his first manager. Then, though still only fourteen years of age, he was given an engagement by Colonel Alvan Mann, one of the proprietors of Raymond and Waring's Menagerie. His first chance to become a manager himself was obtained by the fact that, in those days, the menageries and circuses had no evening performances and when the country people had come to town for the afternoon they were glad to have something to do that same evening. So Pastor would hire the school or courthouse or hotel dining room of the town where the menagerie was showing for a kind of "concert" which it was his custom to advertise at the ring in the afternoon, And he was doing well, too, at this when the management put an end to the new departure, not relishing it that one of their underlings should make so much money.

An annex show in an extra tent owned by the circus proprietors, with a snake exhibit, a violinist and two clever circus children to help, offered the precocious Pastor his next opening. Here he was able to save money and so had a little capital with which to set up a show of his own when the outbreak of the Civil War gave a death blow to proprietors of circuses and menageries.

Pastor had the sense to see that there was a real opportunity in this new amusement field for the man who would disentangle songs and dances on the stage from the cigar smoking and beer drinking which, up to that time, had been the inevitable accompaniment of this

LILLIAN RUSSELL, "AIRY, FAIRY LILLIAN," AT THE HEIGHT OF HER RADIANT
BEAUTY
From the Theatre Collection, Harvard University

WEBER AND FIELDS IN "WHIRL-A-GIG"

From the Theatre Collection, Harvard University

type of entertainment. So with Sam Sharpley, who had been a manager in the minstrels, as his partner, he made the first bid in history for lady patronage at a show he put on at Paterson, New Jersey, March 21, 1865.

For some time the ladies were shy and failed to attend in any considerable numbers, but from Paterson he took his show to other towns, advertising fully, and everywhere promising that there should be nothing offensive in his entertainment. Thus on July 31, 1865, he and his partner were able to open, at 201 Broadway, New York City, what became famous as "Tony Pastor's Opera House." Here he remained for ten years, going thence to Number 585 Broadway for another six years and after that to the location on 142d Street, in connection with which he is perhaps best known.

It was Tony Pastor who first introduced to the public several performers who later became famous on our stage, among them Nat Goodwin, Evans and Hoey, May and Flo Irwin, Francis Wilson and Lillian Russell.[1] May Irwin and Francis Wilson are still with us, though Lillian Russell, whose radiant beauty was for more than two generations an American household word, died in 1921.

---

[1] It was Tony Pastor who gave this gifted woman her stage name of Lillian Russell. For she was born Helen Louise Leonard, in Clinton, Iowa, in 1861, her father being a country editor and her mother an early crusader for women's rights. Educated at the Convent of the Sacred Heart in Chicago, it was while being trained for choir work that she developed her exquisite singing voice. Her first stage appearance was with the chorus of Rice's "Pinafore." The following year she sang ballads for Tony Pastor at his theatre in New York. Her great reputation was made at the Casino, corner of Broadway and 39th Street, where she first appeared in "The Sorcerer," April 17, 1883.

These resplendent names, and many others which recall rare good times at the theatre, are, however, associated also with that other American institution, Weber and Fields.

To delight the old-timers to whom Weber and Fields have in the past brought so much of sheer joy, there has recently appeared a book made up of articles, previously published in the *Saturday Evening Post,* which reviews the entire career of these gifted comedians. A single quotation from this work [1] will serve to make clear the peculiar contribution which these famous partners made to the American theatre. As has been well said, America had no national theatrical institution individually its own when they started their career; and since their Music Hall, just south of Daly's Theatre on Broadway, at 29th Street, closed in 1904, after eight years of extraordinary success, there has nowhere in the country been a like personally intimate playhouse, a house devoted to clever nonsense, hearty burlesque and impromptu comedy which the audience particularly enjoyed because it played a part in it.

When Olga Nethersole in the spring of 1900 was playing "Sappho" at Wallack's Theatre, defying the police, who thought the play improper, the public looked eagerly to Weber and Fields for the burlesque certain to appear and so flocked by the thousands when it was announced that May Robson, whom Charles Frohman was glad to lend for the occasion, would burlesque Miss Nethersole

[1] "Weber and Fields," by Felix Isman. Boni and Liveright, New York, 1924.

386

as Sappho, with Peter Dailey, one of Weber and Fields' own stars, burlesquing the Jean of the original play. The thing must have been screamingly funny, — whatever else it was.

"The Music Hall merely reserved the character of the Daudet heroine and rechristened her 'Sapolio' in token of her having consecrated her life to the task of making Paris a spotless town morally. Dailey was Jean Gaussin, the unwilling victim of Sapolio's high moral purpose. Warfield had the rôle of Uncle Cæsaire, who ate mothballs to conceal his alcoholic breath from his wife. Fields was a comedy servant girl who, ordered to serve capon *en casserole*, cooked it in castor oil. Joseph, Fanny Le Grand's perfect little gentleman of a child, became in Weber's hands a kicking, brawling, tobacco-chewing little brat. Harry Morey, now a Hollywood hero, had the small part of a conciérge with an Irish brogue.

"'If you will only let me stay I'll black your boots,' Fanny, or Sappho, had pleaded, with Jean, in the original. Peter Dailey drags out a shoe-blacking stand and the curtain falls on the travesty of May Robson opening the bootblacking kit and beginning on Dailey's shoes." [1]

De Wolf Hopper was the successor in the Music Hall of Peter Dailey. He came to play here with Lillian Russell,[2] after having unsuccessfully set up his own company in the attempt to make a fortune (instead of losing

[1] "Weber and Fields," by Felix Isman, page 262. Boni and Liveright, New York, 1924.

[2] "Airy Fairy" Lillian was thirty-eight when she came to Weber and Fields Music Hall under a contract which assured her $1250 a week, a guaranty of thirty-five weeks to a season and all gowns and costumes paid for by the producer. For the Weber and Fields reunion in the spring of 1912 — which engagement also signalized their "farewell" as partners — she was paid $2000 a week.

one) with the fifty thousand dollars which came to him when his father died. Hopper is still on the stage and is still extremely droll and funny. David Warfield is another player of our own time who got his start in the Music Hall under Weber and Fields. A superb actor of burlesque, understanding thoroughly the importance of solemnity and finish to success in this line, Warfield might still have been making us laugh with his drollery instead of weep for the inadequacy of his Shylock, had not Belasco taken him from Weber and Fields to star him in "the legitimate."

Weber and Fields has now passed, alas! totally succeeded in public esteem by the Follies. Even Fred Stone, who perhaps comes nearest to being the artistic successor of these Music Hall stars, does not give us quite that proficiency in burlesque, with its pleasant personalities, its intimacy, and its local tang, which made a real American institution of the thing these men started and so painstakingly developed through the years.

For their success did not by any means come in a day. Not until 1890 did their work achieve the distinction of a press criticism, the variety stage having, up to that time, been for the most part dismissed as beneath notice. The paper which first reviewed their performance was the Chicago *Daily News* and the critic Amy Leslie. Miss Leslie had by chance strayed that spring afternoon from the beaten path of critics into the Lyceum Theatre in Chicago. And when the whisper that Amy Leslie was in the house ran back-stage it signified nothing to Joe and Lew. Their famous pool-room act went on as usual.

But the next afternoon Chicago's principal paper gave a column to the pool-room skit.

George M. Cohan has occasionally revived something of the spell of these gifted partners. But Cohan never depended solely on burlesque to make his successes. He had many "lines," about all of which he has fully told us in a snappily written, red-covered book [1] which, but for an inhibiting law, would probably have had an American flag on its cover. For the American flag has been almost a trademark with this highly successful fun-maker, who, besides being an actor and a dancer, is a composer, a manager, and a playwright.

In this last-named field he is acknowledged to be an expert craftsman but the success of his plays is probably due much less to his technical skill than to the fact that in all his work he represents the restless American spirit and dresses up with gay songs and twinkling dances whatever plot may for the moment engage his attention. In his book he explains with engaging *naïveté* how he has been able to achieve success in so many fields.[2]

I have elsewhere shown [3] that many good Bostonians became accustomed and reconciled to theatregoing through their childlike readiness to accept a certain early-Boston playhouse as a "museum," the curse of the stage being cancelled for them because there was a realistic portrayal, in a gallery of the theatre building, of a drunkard's

[1] "Twenty Years on Broadway." Harper and Brothers, 1924.
[2] His song, "Over There," composed when we entered the World War, is said to have earned royalties enough to have made its writer a rich man, if he had never made money in anything else.
[3] "Romantic Days in Old Boston," page 259.

family reproduced in wax. In the same way "Uncle Tom," because of the moral lesson it conveyed, was long accepted in many households where the theatre and play-acting were anathema. The play's pervading ebon hue, too, undoubtedly helped it. It partook of the prestige already being accorded to ministrelsy. Thus to the "Tom Shows" — to use the term in which actors spoke to one another of this type of entertainment — many of us who value our theatregoing privileges of to-day are far more indebted than we realize.

J. Frank Davis, writing in *Scribner's Magazine* for April, 1925, declares that, until he was thirteen, he had never seen a professional company of actors in anything but "Tom," but had already seen that sterling production five or six times. And Mr. Davis's experience in this connection is very like that of thousands of men and women, now of middle age, who were born and brought up in consciously pious homes.

"Uncle Tom's Cabin" had its first performance in America in 1852, and while no statistics as to the number of times it has been played are obtainable, it is probable that no play in the world ever had half so many productions. After the Civil War, and into the seventies, it was the chief stand-by of American drama. And in the eighties it became a part of the repertoire of every barnstorming company in the land.

There is an amusing story connected with one of these companies, the heroine of the tale being now an actress of well-established reputation. On this particular night she was playing Eva with a tent show, and while in the

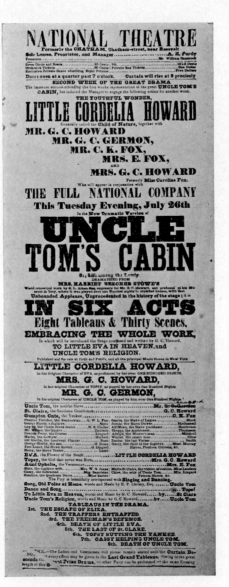

PLAYBILL OF "UNCLE TOM'S CABIN" AT THE NATIONAL THEATRE, NEW
YORK, IN 1853, WITH THE ORIGINAL CAST
From the Theatre Collection, Harvard University

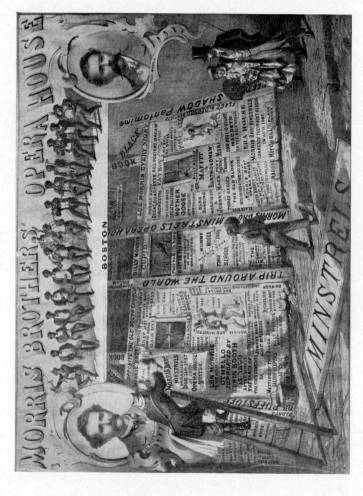

INTERESTING COPY OF A LITHOGRAPH POSTER ADVERTISING THE MORRIS BROTHERS MINSTRELS
IN 1867

Presented to the Theatre Collection, Harvard University, by Mr. Charles Taylor of the *Boston Globe*

midst of the death scene, and surrounded by her stage father, stage mother, Uncle Tom and the rest, a heavy shower came up. The tent, being old, offered no adequate resistance to the rain and a delicate stream began to trickle through the canvas and down upon her neck. But Tom Show actors had met greater crises than this, and with all solemnity, her weeping father rose from his knees, went out into the wings, returned with one of the property umbrellas and, resuming his place on the ground floor drawing-room of the St. Clair palatial residence in New Orleans, held it over Little Eva's head and "let her die dry."

"And will you believe it," this same little Eva added, when she told the story, "*not a soul in the audience laughed!*" [1]

By the time the nineties dawned, many little groups traveling in the West had adopted "Uncle Tom" as a steady means of livelihood. And it was not unknown as a headliner in the town halls of New England, after we had passed that epoch-making year which brought us into the twentieth century. I myself remember seeing a production, about 1900, in a little New Hampshire village with so crude a setting that between the acts a borrowed best sofa, on which little Eva was subsequently to die and go to heaven, was passed solemnly over the improvised footlights! As I write these lines, "Uncle Tom's Cabin" is being given its annual revival by a stock company in a city not ten miles from Boston,[2] thrilling

---

[1] J. Frank Davis, *Scribner's Magazine*, April, 1925.
[2] That "Uncle Tom's Cabin" is still "going strong" in certain western sections of the United States also is clear from a handbill to which

the unsophisticated theatregoer now no less than it did seventy odd years ago when it first blazoned its improbabilities across the footlights.

When I last saw the show it opened — as it often did, though there are infinite versions of the piece and the play was frequently acted in later years with no manuscript at all, being put together by word of mouth according to the extent of the cast and scenery, — with a tavern scene in which George Harris, who is on his way toward the river, reads on the wall the notice of a reward for his capture and, peeling off a kid glove, exhibits to a sympathetic friend his branded hand, making at the same time a speech in such language as no Negro and few educated Northerners could then command.

It was thus, however, that Mrs. Stowe made George Harris talk in the book and thus he was bound to talk in the play, even if every other Negro, except Eliza, always spoke with more or less of what they believed to be dialect. Uncle Tom, in my own cherished "last performance," wore a snow-white wig. This again was according to tradition, for though no Negro of forty ever has gray hair, Uncle Tom needed it in his business of winning tears from the audience.

my attention has been called just as this chapter goes to press. Apparently a "Tom Show" group out in Ohio, using as its base a floating theatre called *The Water Queen* finds that "Uncle Tom's Cabin" still draws! The handbill carries not only a picture of the *Water Queen*, of the death of Uncle Tom, of Simon Legree slashing his whip and of Topsy looking delightfully wicked, but it also points out that "'Uncle Tom's Cabin' has been played throughout the United States and is today the most popular drama in the land. The most exacting Christian people never hesitate to witness its rendition which they always do with great pleasure and delight as lessons of mortality (sic) and virtue may be learned from its teachings."

392

Eva, Topsy, Miss Ophelia, Shelby, St. Clair, and the unspeakable Simon Legree were all standardized in these "Tom Shows" and did their parts well enough. But the person to watch was Eliza, skipping across the floating ice, clasping her baby to her meagre bosom and being pursued by more or less vicious bloodhounds urged on from back-stage by various devices which nowadays would probably be suppressed by the Society for the Prevention of Cruelty to Animals.

The fashion in which heterogeneous actors and actresses were sent out to play in "Tom Shows" is delightfully described by Mr. Davis, who, one afternoon in the winter of 1888, in the company of an actor friend, climbed to the top floor of a loft building in Eliot Street, Boston, to seek out the office of "Stover's original Uncle Tom's Cabin." Mr. Stover was himself selecting a company to play in Gloucester not far away. Plenty of unemployed actors were already assembled, and the beasts, who, baying madly, were to follow Eliza across the ice, were also there. (But not Eliza herself. The bandana handkerchief which she would wear around her neck — now filled with meat — constituted the real interest of these bloodhounds, we are told!) The parts were distributed with scant ceremony, Haley and Legree being assigned to the same man and Topsy and Eliza to the same girl. The engagement was to be for one day only and the "salary" for the principals five dollars in cash, three meals, Saturday night's lodging and railroad fares from Boston to Gloucester and return. A street parade, for which the men were expected to produce high hats, as well as two shows, afternoon and evening, were demanded in return for this meager five dollars.

Yet no rehearsals were required, even though the members of this scratch company had never before worked together. Nor was it explained which one of the many current versions of the play was to be used or what scenes were to be left in or cut out! Apparently these things arranged themselves if one had had sufficient experience as a "Tom Show" actor.

The Eva represented in the book was supposed to be seven or eight years old at the time of her death, but the Eva of the stage was sometimes five and sometimes thirty-five. Just as Topsy, who should have been about nine, was almost never a child and frequently not even feminine! On one occasion, because of illness in the company, the stage manager blacked up and himself did Topsy, not at all deterred in his enterprise by the fact that he was endowed with a luxuriant mustache, which no one could possibly have expected him to sacrifice.[1]

"Uncle Tom's Cabin" was published in book form, May 20, 1852, and because Mrs. Stowe had not protected her dramatic rights, a version by Charles Western Taylor, which, however, was not a success, was put on the stage the following August, at Purdy's National Theatre, New York. It remained, however, for George S. Howard, the manager of the Museum at Troy, New York, who believed that his little daughter Cordelia would be a great success as little Eva, to stage the version, played first September 27, 1852, and presented to

[1] "Tom Shows." *Scribner's Magazine*, April, 1925.

delighted audiences probably unknown *thousands* of times since. This version was prepared by George L. Aiken and after running one hundred nights at Troy, and a long time at Albany, opened at Purdy's Theatre in New York, July 18, 1853, where it received three hundred and twenty-five performances, — an unprecedented run at that time. Twelve times, and finally eighteen times, weekly, the piece was given, the entire company being obliged to eat their meals in costume behind the scenes because there was not time between shows to dress for the street.

The original Little Eva, who is still living, tells me that her father's company subsequently appeared in "Uncle Tom's Cabin" as far south as Baltimore and St. Louis, where slavery still existed, and that they met with no opposition, in spite of the fact that Mrs. Stowe's book had caused much bad feeling in the South.[1] They played also in London, Dublin and Edinburgh;[2] and although other dramatizations had been produced, theirs

[1] "The Aiken version went to Philadelphia in 1853-1854, where Joseph Jefferson acted Gumption Cute, and was seen in Detroit in 1854 and in Chicago in 1858. Another version by H. J. Conway was first seen in Boston on November 15, 1852. In November, 1852 a version called "Slave Life," by Mark Lemon and Tom Taylor, was acted at the Adelphi Theatre in London. Two versions were enacted in Paris, one by De Wailly and Texier, at the Gayety Theatre, and one by Dumanoir and D'Ennery at the Ambigu Comique."

"History of American Drama," by Arthur Hobson Quinn, page 288. Harper and Brothers.

[2] The universal opinion was that Howard made an ideal Southern planter. On and off the stage he invariably wore a black broadcloth frock coat with brass buttons and he always had on lavender trousers. When he was around the hotels and on the streets of the towns, where the show was being given, people who had seen him at the theatre recognized him at once and exclaimed, "There goes Eva's father!" Hornblow's "The Theatre in America," Vol. II, p. 70.

was received with much favor. The acting of little Cordelia as Eva and of Mrs. Howard, her mother, as Topsy, accounted partly for the popularity of the play, but the Aiken version must have been one that the people liked in that it had a long life even after the Howards had ceased to act in it.

Occasional songs like "Eva to Her Papa," "I'se so wicked," "St. Clair to Eva in Heaven," all written and composed by G. C. Howard especially for his family, lent color and variety to this version. And after a series of effective and affecting scenes there came always a grand finale in the shape of an "allegorical tableau of Eva in heaven, a spirit of Celestial Light in the Abode of Bliss Eternal." Topsy and Little Eva were adored by their audiences. The former's "Golly, I'se so wicked" and Eva's angelic dying never failed to make a profound impression.

To the readers of to-day Aiken's play seems extremely melodramatic but so, for that matter, does Mrs. Stowe's book. The Aiken version sticks pretty close to the book. Divided into six acts and beginning with the Shelbys in Kentucky, it then takes Tom to New Orleans to St. Clair's plantation and brings him to his death under the persecution of Legree. Eva dies on the stage and is transported bodily by angels to a better world. From the standpoint of literary criticism every possible objection can be made to the story and to the drama. Yet "Uncle Tom's Cabin" in book and play proved itself the most powerful weapon ever forged to combat and conquer an appalling social evil.

CHAPTER XVI

DEALING WITH DRAMA ALONG OUR FRONTIER
AND IN THE THEATRES OF NEW YORK

BECAUSE our early American managers were garru-
lously inclined and, on retiring from active life, almost
invariably indulged in a plump volume of reminiscences,
a student of the theatre has ready to hand quite an assort-
ment of colorful memoirs, invaluable for the insight
they afford into pioneer stage conditions. One of the
most delightful books of this kind is from the pen of Noah
Miller Ludlow, who, when he wrote his account [1] of early
theatrical life in the West and South — particularly in
those cities then springing up along the Mississippi valley
— had been an actor for thirty-eight years and a manager for thirty-four.

Born in New York City, July 4, 1795, of a mother
who was "distinctly religious" and of a father who
"found no particular pleasure in the so-called amusements of the day," young Ludow none the less managed
to see the pantomime "Cinderella" on the stage of the
old Park Theatre at the tender age of twelve. From
that time until the year 1853, when he "professionally

[1] "Dramatic Life As I Found It." G. I. Jones & Company, St. Louis,
1880.

397

withdrew from histrionic duties," he was an intimate part of the theatre in this country.

The manager with whom he had most to do in his earliest years was Samuel Drake, Senior, who had been stage manager for John Bernard and who, in 1815, collected a company of young stage aspirants to take out West with him.

When this company decided to give Sheridan's romantic play "Pizarro" or "The Virgins of the Sun" in Pittsburg, great difficulty was experienced in providing the necessary complement of virgins; meaning, of course, stage virgins. Such supernumeraries were very difficult to secure in those days, for "seamstresses and shoe-binders would as soon have thought of walking deliberately into Pandemonium as to have appeared on the stage as 'supers' or 'corps de ballet.'" On the night of the performance the house, at a dollar a ticket all through (except for children), was crowded to capacity — the boxes with dark-skinned but beautiful ladies, and the pit with "foundrymen, keel-boat men, and sundry and divers dark-featured and iron-fisted burghers." And the virgins duly materialized! The first pair, and even the second pair, were quite personable and were received in respectful quiet, but when the third pair, consisting of an old Irish woman who cleaned the dressing room and the property man, a Pennsylvania Dutchman, made their appearance, the audience became unduly vocal.

"'Such Virgins!' the pit shouted as these two entered in all solemnity, singing the beautiful chant, 'Oh, Power

Supreme.' Whereupon Manager Drake, who was at the time standing in front of the altar as high priest of the sun, stepped to the front of the stage and roundly scolded those in front 'for insulting a company of comedians who have traveled hundreds of miles to contribute to their pleasure.' "

In those days the theatre was never open to the public more than four nights a week and often only three. So that strolling players had real opportunity to enjoy themselves in their travels if they were temperamentally fitted to make the most of such entertainment as offered. Mr. Ludlow recalls many a pleasant riding trip and tells us that while playing in Nashville, Tennessee, he had ample opportunity to woo "a small black-eyed widow" whom he subsequently married and from whom he was "never separated for more than six months at any time for over forty-five years and who became the mother of eight children, though she was almost constantly, notwithstanding this fact, on the stage."

Confronted with the prospect, as a Benedict, of having two — or more — to support, instead of one, young Ludlow (aged twenty-two!) now parted from his old manager, Mr. Drake, and, having obtained a set of traveling scenes, a wagon with horses, and saddle horses on which to ride, started out "on his own" as a manager and producer.

The journey that Mr. and Mrs. Ludlow and their fellow players took, soon after this, on a keel boat "purchased for $200 and previously condemned as not strong enough for heavy freight," from Nashville to New Orleans, via the Cumberland, Ohio and Mississippi rivers, was full of adventures. Natchez was one of the first stops made, and when they had convinced the leading inhabitants of this settlement that theirs was really a company of comedians and not "folks with a lot of niggers to sell," they were cordially urged to give a performance.

Already a nice theatre, which had been built by subscription and in which a band of amateurs had performed twice, was standing on the Natchez bluffs, and here for a fortnight five hundred people crowded in, at a dollar a ticket, while many others witnessed the performances through the windows, refusing to go away because they had traveled some distance from neighboring plantations and were determined to see a play.

New Orleans was ultimately reached on the keel boat and permission obtained from the mayor to give some American presentations in a theatre there which had previously been associated only with French drama. It is interesting to note that, notwithstanding the fact that manager Ludlow was strongly urged to make Sunday night a play-night in New Orleans, because the French theatre had always found that evening their most profitable one, he flatly refused so to desecrate the Sabbath! The training of his "distinctly religious" mother held!

The Ludlow company's performance on Christmas Eve, 1817, appears to have been the first production in the English language ever given in the city by a regularly organized troupe. At this time English was not a welcome tongue in New Orleans, there being a strong antagonism among the French and the Spaniards to any people who spoke this language. But on the other hand, New Orleans audiences had much higher theatrical standards than most audiences of that day. The population was cosmopolitan "and had seen good acting in New York, Philadelphia, Boston, England or France." So when the Ludlow company closed their books, in the spring of 1818, they found that, after paying all salaries and outstanding claims, and after the partners, too, had all drawn enough to pay the current expenses of their families, there was still three thousand dollars in the treasury as a result of a fifteen-week season. Not so bad!

A relative of Mrs. Ludlow's pointed out about this time that there had never been a theatrical company in St. Louis. Whereupon our players, nothing if not hopeful and suggestible, set out to extend the drama still further westward. Governor William Clark, of the celebrated Lewis and Clark Expedition, was very hospitable to them, and had it not suddenly turned so cold that the ladies of the town were unwilling to venture out and the men unwilling to go to the theatre without them, this first dramatic season of a professional company of comedians in St. Louis in the season of 1819–1820 might really have been a success.

Ludlow never lost his courage or his zeal, however. Once he journeyed down the Missouri River by canoe to give a scratch performance in Edwardsville. And as a traveler Mrs. Ludlow was scarcely less sporting than her husband. Sometimes when they set off together by carriage or steamboat for the remote spot where their

401

company was booked to play, she would be carrying in her arms a baby less than a week old! In the course of one such expedition [1] the couple encountered Junius Brutus Booth,[2] at Petersburg, Virginia, Booth having just made his first appearance in the United States as Richard III at near-by Richmond.

"On the morning of the day set apart (for the Petersburg performance) the large bills posted on the corner of the streets announced 'the first appearance of the great tragedian, J. B. Booth, from the London theatres, Covent Garden, and Drury Lane.' The play was called for rehearsal at ten o'clock, A. M.; at the proper time the rehearsal commenced, but without Mr. Booth. He had not arrived; but the manager said the rehearsal must go on, and he would have Mr. Booth's scenes rehearsed after he arrived. I think they had reached the fourth act of the play, and I was sauntering near the head of the stairs that led up to the stage, when a small man, that I took to be a well-grown boy of about sixteen years of age, came running up the stairs, wearing a roundabout jacket, and a cheap straw hat, both covered with dust, and inquired for the stage-manager. I pointed across the stage to Mr. Russell, who at that moment had observed the person with whom I was conversing, and hurried towards us, and cordially grasping the hand of the strange man, said; 'Ah! Mr. Booth, I am glad you have arrived; we were fearful something serious had happened to you!'

[1] During the autumn of 1821.
[2] Thomas Abthorpe Cooper was another player with whom the Ludlows were associated this same year. Priscilla Cooper, — who made a success as an actress, married Robert Tyler, son of President John Tyler, in 1838, and so became for a time mistress of the White House, — was the daughter of this actor by his second wife, Miss Fairlie, whose father had been Judge Fairlie of New York.

"I do not think any man was ever more astonished than I was just then in beholding this meeting. Is it possible this can be the great Mr. Booth that Mr. Russell says is 'undoubtedly the best actor living?' and I began to think Russell was trying to put off some joke upon us all. I observed, however, that when the small man came upon the stage to rehearse his scenes, he was quite 'at home,' and showed a knowledge of the business of the character that a mere novice or pretender could not have acquired. He ran through the rehearsal very carelessly, gave a very few special or peculiar directions, tried the combat of the last act over twice, and said 'That will do!' and the rehearsal was over. He told Mr. Russell then that he had been a few minutes too late for the stage-coach that left Richmond early in the morning, and that he soon after started on foot, and had walked all the way, — *twenty-five miles*."

Later that summer the Ludlows again ran amuck of the Drake company. Drake was one of the few pioneer managers who never wrote his own story, so we may as well at this point glean from the Ludlow book some account of this interesting family so prominent in the early drama of the West.

Samuel Drake, Senior, was born in England, November 15, 1768, and is said to have been apprenticed to the printing trade. But he ran away to be an actor and had toured many theatres in the west of England, and been manager of some of them, before coming to the United States. In England he married his first wife, a Miss Fisher, herself a member of a theatrical family. In 1813 the couple joined the company of John Bernard at Albany, New York; here Mr. Drake was stage manager and here

the following year Mrs. Drake died. Then Drake took
the remainder of his family West, having already made
arrangements to launch a theatrical circuit in Frankfort,
Lexington and Louisville. At the time the Ludlows
encountered him out West, Samuel Drake, Junior,
Alexander Drake and Julia Drake, all of whom had
been born in England, were members of the company.

The Mrs. Drake of whom we shall hear later from Joe
Cowell (another pioneer manager) was the wife of Alexander. She was a woman of considerable talent, who
afterwards established herself successfully as an actress
and played the leading theatres of Kentucky, Canada,
Boston, and New York. When Alexander Drake died
in 1830, his widow married a literary man, but this union
proved an unhappy one and she resumed the name of
Drake. During her latter years she made her home
on the farm of her son at Covington, near Louisville,
where she died September 1, 1875, at the age of seventy-
eight.

James H. Caldwell, the New Orleans manager, was
another theatrical potentate with whom Ludlow was
always making and breaking connections. The season
of 1824[1] was one of the periods when Mr. and Mrs. Ludlow were both with Caldwell, acting in the Camp Street
Theatre. That year the men parted bitter enemies;
two years later they were each trying to wrest a theatrical
success from reluctant Nashville.

The players of those days used to get a good deal of

[1] It was at this time that Ludlow helped Forrest to secure from Caldwell the chance his talents deserved.

fun out of their command of drama text, and Ludlow
describes with relish an experience of his company, on
the way to Montgomery, while being entertained at a
primitive place in which two Negro boys waited on table,
carrying each a torch of light-wood (pitch pine) in lieu
of candles. Ned Caldwell in the company had taken
two or three extra drinks of whisky, he tells us, and was
just in the humor to imagine himself some great potentate
surrounded by his court at a banquet.

"The first remark that he made was: 'This likes me
well! This is feasting in the Oriental, the Eastern style,
— Tippoo Sahib with his retainers on a foraging excur-
sion.' At the same moment his eye rested on the largest
Negro boy, who stood near him, and who was clad in the
most primitive kind of costume, namely a cotton shirt
scarcely long enough to be decent, over which was a
coarse woolen jacket, and this was all. Caldwell surveyed him from head to foot, then said in a pompous
tragic manner, 'Friend, what is thy name?' To which
the Negro replied, 'Sip, massa.' 'Sip,' repeated Caldwell, 'meaning Scipio?' The darkey smiled and nodded,
yes. 'Surnamed Africanus?' The boy nodded again.
'Scipio Africanus, stand further from the presence;
(with his hand waving him back) for, to say the truth,
I like not the contiguity nor the superfluity of the per-
fume of thy epidermis; it partakes not of the "Sabean
odors from the spicy shores of Araby the blest"; (then
drawing his chair nearer the table) nevertheless (quoting from King Lear) "I retain you as one of my hundred!" But I do not like the fashion of your garments;
you will say they are Persian attire, — let them be
changed!' During this harangue the company generally had paused and put on serious faces, in order to

humor the joke. The landlord and his wife stared in wonderment, and the darkeys tried to smile, but looked frightened rather than amused."

Curious presents were sometimes given to the players in the course of their wanderings. One day at Sandusky an Indian rode up bearing before him, across his pony, a very small and beautiful faun. Ludlow bought the faun for one dollar as a birthday present for his little daughter, who had just reached her seventh year. But when he got back to New York the faun developed a fancy for gnawing furniture and breaking crockery, and Ludlow passed the animal on to Thomas Cooper, to be given to his daughter, Mrs. Robert Tyler. The faun finally found a congenial home in the deer park of "Joseph Bonaparte, the ex-king of Spain . . . who when he returned to France took this deer with him."

Cooper was one of the men whom Ludlow always greatly admired, and he gives an affecting description of the great tragedian's rendition, in New Orleans, when an old man, of Wolsey's lines to Cromwell in Henry VIII:

" And when I am forgotten, as I shall be,
And sleep in dull, cold marble, where no mention
Of me more must be heard of, say I taught thee,
Say Wolsey, that once trod the ways of glory,
And sounded all the depths and shoals of honor,
Found thee a way, out of his wreck, to rise in;
A sure and safe one, though thy master miss'd it," —

He adds that as Cooper pronounced these words he was overcome with tears, weeping so copiously that his emotion was plainly visible to those who were acting with him on the stage.

The Romance of the American Theatre

In the summer of 1835, just before taking Sol Smith as a partner, Ludlow was able to establish a good theatre in St. Louis, Colonel Merriwether Lewis Clarke being one of the principal underwriters of this project. At the same time he was doing well with a theatre in Mobile. In connection with the opening of the Mobile house Ludlow introduced a reform which he says he adhered to and carried forward, in after years, in all theatres under his management. This was to refuse admission "to any female who did not come attended by a gentleman, or someone having the appearance of a man of respectability, not even in the third tier; women notoriously of the pavement were never under any circumstances admitted. The result of these rigid methods was that the third tier of our theatres was as quiet and orderly as any part of the house." Ludlow quaintly reminds us that there were then no matinees "as at the present day" (1880 when his book was published) which enable ladies to attend theatres "without gallants."

Madame Celeste was one of the stars at Ludlow's St. Louis theatre, and of her, as of Fanny Ellsler, he writes with the greatest enthusiasm. "Though not beautiful she was exquisitely formed," he tells us (speaking of the latter), "and when she danced she seemed to move through the air without touching the stage." Which makes one understand why Emerson, when he went with Margaret Fuller to see Fanny Ellsler dance in Boston, replied to Margaret's ecstatic whisper, "Ralph, this is poetry," with a fervent "Margaret, it is *religion!*"

Manager Ludlow was distinctly ahead of his time in

his adherence to truth in advertising. When he and his partner, Sol Smith, opened the new St. Charles, in New Orleans, January 18, 1843, he issued the following unique house bill:

"Being impressed with the belief that the public can very well dispense with play-bill puffs and extravagant eulogiums on the performers who enact the plays which are represented; believing that visitors to the theatre may possibly be capable of distinguishing the different grades of talent possessed by the several actors, without the aid of capital letters to enlighten their powers of perception; supposing that there are individuals attached to the dramatic profession who possess considerable merit, but are willing to form engagements for longer periods than six nights; and being convinced that the true interests of the drama call for reformation in the style and manner of making announcements, the management of the new St. Charles propose: First, to issue posting-bills, of a uniform size throughout the season, and printed on a single sheet. Second, to cause the names of the characters in the pieces represented, and the names of the performers appointed to enact them, to be printed on the bills in a uniform size. Third, to confine the notices emanating from this establishment to a plain and simple statement of the entertainments each night, the cast of the characters, and such other information relative to the performance as may be deemed proper to communicate to the public. Fourth, to make no statements whatever of *the great success* which has attended the representation of a play, or of the numerous requests at the box-office for its repetition. Fifth, to make no promises without the full assurance of being able to fulfil them, or to announce engagements with eminent individuals for limited periods, until they have actually arrived in the city; to advertise no pieces with 'new scenery, dresses and decorations,' unless such appointments are in readiness. And, finally, the management is resolved to make this new 'temple' now to be opened to the public, no party to the system of deception which has been generally practiced for many years throughout the theatrical world. . . ."

It was Ludlow, too, who insisted — despite the protestations of Macready, who seems always to have been looking for trouble — on his rights as a manager to advertise that the Honorable Henry Clay, then candidate for the presidency, would be in the audience at Mobile on the Englishman's opening night. Macready deeply resented the presence of Clay's name on the poster in type as large as that which heralded his own appearance.

Ludlow tells an amusing story of something that happened during the quarrelsome star's last professional tour in America. The Englishman always insisted that those acting scenes with him stand precisely at certain designated distances from him; so when at the rehearsal he told a young actor that he was to stand just on a certain spot the youth took the precaution to mark the spot on the stage with a piece of chalk. One may imagine Macready's wrath when, in the play, to the words, "Come nearer, sir, come nearer," the young man replied in firm tones loud enough to be heard by many in the audience, "*No, sir,* I'm standing on the mark."

Similarly amusing anecdotes concerning many other foreign attractions who early toured this country are to

be found in Ludlow's book (which, by the by, has plenty
of room for such things inasmuch as it consists of more
than 700 closely printed pages!). Such as the way he
put the fear of God into the heart of Madame Josephine
Weiss, the woman in charge of the Viennese Children,
forty-eight in number, who came over here to give entertainments. "These charming little creatures — forty-
eight pretty faces — with their tiny feet flitting about
the stage in graceful steps, and clad in flowers, forming
graceful figures and fantastic groupings, were to me the
realization of fairy dreams," writes our manager, waxing
lyrical. But Madame Weiss was rough with the "little
fairies," and it required Sol Smith's Yankee invention to
save the situation. Smith, without the slightest compunction, told the Madame that Ludlow was mayor of
the town, and this availed to restrain her temper and
her twitchings of the children while they were being
prepared for their performances. Apparently the lady's
knowledge of American political customs was too small to
cause her to regard it as at all strange that Mobile and
New Orleans should have the same mayor.

George Holland was another foreign-born actor with
whom Ludlow had to do. Not unnaturally, therefore,
our author recalls that incident connected with Holland's
death, December 21, 1870, which has given abiding
fame to "The Little Church Around the Corner."[1]

[1] Rev. W. T. Sabine, rector of a New York church, when asked by
Joseph Jefferson to read the funeral service for Holland, refused on the
ground that the man had been an actor. The clergyman added that
he had "always preached against theatres and actors," and that "offi-
ciating at the funeral of an actor would be inconsistent with his past

The Romance of the American Theatre

Sol Smith, who invented that story about the "mayor," was for eighteen years Ludlow's partner [1] in the management of western and southern theatres. But inasmuch as Smith's own life and activities cover at least half of the nineteenth century, he is of importance to our chronicle quite apart from his connection with Ludlow.

Sol Smith's father had been a volunteer fifer at the age of thirteen in the Battle of Bunker Hill, and, at the close of the war, received, as many Revolutionary soldiers did, a grant of land in Oswego County, New York, then almost a wilderness. Here in a log cabin Solomon was born (in 1801) and, there being a large family already, was "put out" to work for a farmer "when only four years old."

It was in Albany, when thirteen and a clerk in a store, that Sol first began to read Shakespeare and first made the acquaintance of a theatre. John Bernard was managing the playhouse on Green street that year and had in his company not only the Drakes, of whom we have heard from Ludlow's book, but Harry and Thomas

private and public denouncements of the profession." Mr. Jefferson in his dilemma inquired of the minister, 'Well, Sir, where can we go?' To which Dr. Sabine replied, 'Oh, there is a little church around the corner where they do that sort of thing,' referring to the Church of the Transfiguration at East 29th Street. The mourners went there and the Rev. Dr. George H. Houghton immediately consented to give the dead actor Christian burial in what, ever since, has been known as "The Little Church Around the Corner." Hornblow's "History of the American Theatre," Volume II, page 83.

[1] At the end of their partnership, however, their relations to each other were so far from cordial that each devotes considerable space in his book of reminiscences to vilifying the other! See Smith, page 116 et al.; Ludlow, page 423 et al.

Placide. Rather an unusually good company for that time. At any rate, so it seemed to Sol when he witnessed their performance of O'Keefe's comic opera "The Highland Reel." "The impression made upon my youthful mind was strong and lasting," he tells us, "and I remember the airs of that opera to this day. My heart was full of acting from that time forward; my tasks at the store became irksome to me; in brief, I became, as thousands had become before me and thousands will become after me, — 'stage mad.'"

Sol Smith's brothers had no mind to have an actor in the family, however, and they refused him permission to visit the theatre. But he had struck up an acquaintance with the Drakes and so managed to get behind the scenes. He earned his admission by "blacking up" and going on as a super in "Three Fingered Jack," but one night, having forgotten to wash his face, he nearly frightened to death the servant sent to arouse him next morning when he overslept. It looked as if the game was up when the word came back to the family that there was "a nigger in Sol's bed." Again he was forbidden to visit the theatre. But a lad so resourceful, and "stage mad" into the bargain, just could not be kept away from the enchanted land. When Bernard's company was succeeded the next season (1816–1817) by another company, which, making a failure, was obliged to move on to Troy, young Sol journeyed to Troy after them, feeling quite sure that having now learned the rôle of young Norval he would be given a part. There being no money for any one in the company, there was naturally none

SOLOMON FRANKLIN SMITH

PRISCILLA COOPER, THE ACTRESS WHO MARRIED PRESIDENT TYLER'S SON, ROBERT, AND SO BECAME MISTRESS OF THE WHITE HOUSE

See page 406

for this boy of sixteen. Stranded and afraid to return to his brothers, he thereupon walked to Saratoga.

Later, he learned that his brothers had forgiven him, and that one brother was about to try his fortune in Ohio. So Sol decided to go West also. But mails in those days were uncertain and the lads missed connections when the time came for them to leave together. Business of Sol purchasing a skiff at Olean Point, and setting out all alone to row and float down the Alleghany river to Pittsburg! After he had paid his tavern bill he, fortunately, had enough money left to buy a seat in the Pittsburg theatre.

The bill that night was "The Lady of the Lake" and it so moved Sol that he tried to get a part with the company. But failing in this, he cheerfully took a job on a flatboat and worked his way to Marietta, where he searched hard for his missing brother, living, the while, on apples and peaches and sleeping in barns. When the brother finally arrived, with others of the family, Sol joined them all in their "Ark" and together they moved on to Cincinnati. Eventually there were ten Smiths, each six foot tall, in Cincinnati! But the ten shrank to nine before long because young Sol apparently just *had* to be where he could go to the theatre. So he wandered on to Louisville and apprenticed himself to a printer, being welcomed back-stage the while by the Drakes, who were then playing in the Southern city. When the company left Louisville, Sol Smith left also. Eventually he reached Vincennes, Indiana, in search of a theatre in operation. Finding none he hoed corn for twenty-five cents a day and having secured a job as apprentice on "The Western *Sun*," joined the local Thespian Society. That held him for the winter.

Always in search of the dramatics which were his passion, he visited Nashville and St. Louis and Cincinnati in turn. His account of a winter passed in Cincinnati the year he became nineteen is interesting. He attended a series of law lectures; played the organ in the New Jerusalem Church three times on Sunday and every Thursday evening; performed the duties of a clerk in one of his brother's stores at a salary of eight dollars a week, and organized a Thespian Society. He records that these amateur Thespians did not do so badly in their representation of "Young Norval," considering that the youth who acted Lady Randolph "had a voice decidedly baritone and had not shaved for a week," and considering also that the meditative maid Anna was impersonated "by a tall lank carpenter who chewed tobacco and was obliged to turn aside every now and then to spit."

The professional companies with which this stage-struck youth had to do in Cincinnati and in Louisville are interestingly pictured. In the former town he made an earnest effort to study law and put in a year in a justice's office. But when Collins and Jones reopened their theatre in the winter of 1821–1822, with Thomas Cooper as the Hamlet of the company, Sol just could not resist the temptation to associate himself again with the stage and was very glad to obtain the post of prompter. At the close of that season our young friend married the daughter of a local music teacher, being possessed at the time of exactly $4.62, which he handed to the minister who performed the marriage ceremony!

In Philadelphia Sol Smith and his wife paid their expenses by giving concerts. His account of one musical entertainment they staged at Princeton is so interesting for the light which it throws on the Princeton undergraduates of that far-away day, that I cannot resist the temptation to quote it. Smith had presented letters of introduction to the president and now saw to it that:

"Notices were written and posted up about the college yard, announcing that 'Mr. and Mrs. Smith of Philadelphia would give a vocal concert,' on such a night, 'to consist of a great variety of songs and duets, sentimental and comic.' I had but nine cents remaining of my five dollars and with this sum I purchased oil sufficient to set a large lamp burning in the center of the school-room which I had rented for the proposed concert. I engaged boys to bring some additional benches from a neighboring church, promising them payment for their trouble in the evening. Having lighted my lamp about sundown, I waited for nearly an hour, doubtful whether a single individual would honor my concert by attending.

"Just as I was about to shut up the room in despair, one young gentleman came to the door, handed me a half dollar and walked in. 'What, nobody here yet?' 'Not yet.' 'Any tickets sold?' 'Don't know — probably — left some at the hotel.' 'Never mind, I'll go and rouse up the boys'; and off he went. I called a lad who was loitering about the door and dispatched him with the half dollar to purchase candles. The room lit up, I began to be haunted with misgivings that we should have no audience and that I should be required to refund the half dollar to the young man who had gone to rouse the boys. I was soon to be relieved from my suspense, however, for the young collegian returned with a dozen of his fellow-students.

"Seeing I had no door-keeper my first customer proposed to take this office, advising me to go and prepare for the performance, as the house would soon be full. Most readily accepting his services I retired to the little closet set apart for our dressing-room, where my wife was waiting my coming with trembling anxiety. Soon I heard a great stir in the room — moving of benches, rustling of silk, opening of windows, and all the indications of people gathering. At length our volunteer door-keeper came sweating to our closet and announced that he believed 'they had all come!' We commenced our concert and our eyes were gladdened with the sight of a room full of joyous looking persons of both sexes, fanning themselves for dear life. The concert went off finely notwithstanding it was exclusively vocal. When it was concluded our amateur door-keeper made his returns, and we found ourselves in the possession of the very handsome sum (in our circumstances) of forty-seven dollars. Quite a fortune!" [1]

Forty-seven dollars was a goodly sum in those days and availed to transport Sol, his wife and their child to Brunswick, New Jersey, where the aspiring actor-manager left his little family in the care of relatives while he made a determined effort to break into the New York theatre. When he found himself unable to do this he first kept a bookshop, then managed a telescope at the

[1] "Theatrical Management in the West and South for Thirty Years: interspersed with anecdotical sketches; autobiographically given by Solomon Franklin Smith, retired Actor," page 34.

corner of Broadway and Chambers Street, then acted as editor of a paper in Trenton, then gave concerts, and finally allied himself with a traveling theatrical company headed for western New York.

Varied experiences as a manager in Canada, where he made a very bad impression by addressing the Governor as "Mister" instead of as "Your Excellency," and as the guide, philosopher and general factotum for a company of players who were barnstorming in the upper reaches of New York State, now followed. In the town of Lewiston, New York, he was entertained by a man so fond of theatricals and so determined to enjoy a dramatic performance that he tore up his household linen to make wicks for candles, utilized for candle sticks half a dozen large potatoes, and arranged the net result on the floor in front of the improvised curtain to serve as footlights!

In these rude surroundings Smith actually gave a performance of "Lovers' Quarrels" to men and women from ten miles around who had come to the performance on horseback. The piece had to be cut short and the parties prematurely reconciled, however, because the lights began to go out.

One is not surprised, after this description of a "typical performance," to learn that when Sol Smith with his wife and son reached Cincinnati, two years and a half later, the managerial pocket was literally "without a penny in it."

It was about this time in Sol's career that we encounter his much-quoted experience of playing in a theatre erected on a lot where there had formerly been a graveyard. It was not at all difficult for him when digging the grave of Hamlet on the stage of this theatre to find bones and skulls to "play at loggats with!"

Sol and his brother Lemuel now proceeded to organize a company of their own. After playing Memphis, then a village of six hundred people, to receipts that averaged less than forty dollars a night, they started inland, traveling by wagon and playing in rooms or halls, often without any scenery whatever. "The people seemed to come out of the woods," Smith writes, "but they came in such numbers that at Jackson where we played in a log house twelve nights the box office drew $480."

The distances covered by the strolling player of those days were enormous. We learn that it was Sol Smith's custom to alternate between Natchez and Port Gibson, fifty miles away, and that he made the trip on horseback every day except Sunday for almost a month! Using relays of horses he could cover the distance in five hours. An extract from his diary for three successive days brings us a vivid picture of this feat:

"Wednesday. Rose at break of day. Horse at door. Swallowed a cup of coffee while the boy was tying on leggins. Reached Washington at 8. Changed horses at 9 — again at 10 — and at 11. At 12 arrived at Port Gibson. Attended rehearsal — settled business with the stage manager. Dined at 4. Laid down and endeavored to sleep at 5. Up again at 6. Rubbed down and washed by Jim [a Negro boy]. Dressed at 7. Acted the 'Three Singles' and 'Splash.' To bed at $11\frac{1}{2}$.

"Thursday. Rose and breakfasted at 9. At 10 attended rehearsal for the pieces of the next day. At 1 leggins tied on, and braved the mud for the fifty miles ride. Rain falling all the way. Arrived at Natchez at half past 6. Rub down and took supper. Acted 'Ezekiel Homespun' and 'Delph' to a poor house. To bed (stiff as steel-yards) at 12.

"Friday. Cast pieces — counted tickets — attended rehearsal until 1 P. M. To horse again and Port Gibson — arrived at 7. No time to eat dinner or supper! Acted in 'The Magpie and the Maid,' and 'No Song, No Supper,' in which latter piece I managed to get a few mouthfuls of cold roasted mutton and some dry bread, that being the first food tasted this day!"

"But I paid my debts!" declares Sol Smith triumphantly, after chronicling these hardships.

A theatre could apparently be put up under Sol's direction about as expeditiously as an efficient circus now sets up a tent. Something like this happened at Columbus, Georgia, if we may judge by the following paragraph in the local newspaper.

"Expedition: A theatre, 70 feet long by 40 wide, was commenced on Monday morning last by our enterprising citizen, Mr. Bates, and finished on Thursday afternoon, in season for the reception of Mr. Sol Smith's company on that evening. A great portion of the timber on Monday morning waved to the breeze in its native forest; fourscore hours afterward, its massive piles were shaken by the thunder of applause in the crowded assemblage of men."

Here "Pizarro" was acted one evening with real Indians for the Peruvian Army. The Indians (who were being paid fifty cents each and a glass of whisky), insisted

419

on making the war dance genuine — the whisky part of
their wages having inadvertently been paid in advance
— and were so realistic in their performance that the
"virgins" of the play fled to the dressing rooms and
locked themselves in. But episodes of this kind only
added zest and interest to life for Sol Smith, helping him
to accumulate experience and to develop to the point
where he became a manager of influence in large centers
and an actor very welcome, *at last*, to the boards of the
Park Theatre, New York.

In 1853 he retired from the stage, having paid all his
debts, and acquired a home in St. Louis in addition to
an income sufficient to live comfortably on for the rest
of his days. In 1861 he was elected to the Missouri
State Convention and by 1868 (the year before he died)
had reached the point where he was proclaiming with the
narrow-minded clergy of the day that "the legitimate
drama seems to have been nearly washed out by what
may be termed Black Crookery and White Fawnery,
consisting of red and blue fires, a fine collection of French
legs, calcium lights and grand transformation scenes."

Another early actor-manager whose recollections [1]
are full of interest and color is Francis C. Wemyss.
Though born in London (May 13, 1797) of a father who
was a British naval officer, Wemyss was half American
by birth (his mother first saw the light in Boston, Massachusetts) and almost wholly American in his career.
For considerable periods of time he was manager of the

[1] "Twenty-six Years of the Life of an Actor and Manager," by Francis
Courtney Wemyss.

Chestnut Street, the Walnut Street, and the Arch Street
theatres in Philadelphia, and of the Holiday and Front
Street theatres in Baltimore; besides which he had a
long managerial connection with the Pittsburg theatre
and acted both in New York and in Boston.

In his acting career before he left England Wemyss
was associated with a number of the most famous players
of his day. He once had a part at the Harrowgate
Springs theatre with Booth, then in the height of his
popularity (1815) and tells us that "The great man's
performance of Bertram was terrifically grand; his
mind was in its full vigor and a well cultivated soil it was.
A more delightful companion *'when not in his mood'* it
would be difficult to find. Gifted with powers of conversation the most agreeable, master of several lan-
guages, Junius Brutus Booth was born to control those
over whom he wished to cast a spell of fascination."

With Edmund Kean, also, Wemyss was associated in
England and he notes that this star of the British stage
was extremely kind to the youth suffering from stage
fright, even going to the length of asking him to supper
with him after the performance. Another well-known
English name which we find in Wemyss' "Recollections,"
about this time, is that of Joe Cowell, the comedian
whom we shall meet again in his own account of American experiences among the players.

In 1819 young Wemyss accepted an offer from Macready, lessee of the Theatre Royal, Bristol, to join his
company at two pounds a week "and the clear half of the
receipts of the benefit." But he did not stay long in

Bristol or in London, to which he soon found his way. For in 1822 an opportunity to sail for America presented itself. It was then a difficult matter to induce an actor to cross the Atlantic and no agent of American managers could be sure of his man until he had actually seen him on board the packet. The contract as a result of which young Wemyss boarded the ship "Robert Edwards," which sailed September 27, 1822, from the Isle of Wight for New York, is as follows:

"Dear Sir: I am favored with your letter, dated 1st May, and I agree without hesitation on the part of the proprietors of the Philadelphia theatre (Messrs. Warren and Wood) to secure to you an engagement for three years, at a salary of six guineas per week, with the accustomed benefits and advantages, on your engaging to play the light comedy of the theatre, and being with Messrs. Warren and Wood by the first of December, 1822, the time fixed for the opening of their new theatre. Should you require a more formal and detailed agreement, previous to your sailing, I engage to have it prepared and witnessed.

"I am, my dear sir, Yours truly,

(Signed) John Miller
(Agent to the Theatre)"

69 Fleet street, London
May 22, 1822

The young adventurer characterizes as "agreeable though very long" (seven weeks!) his passage to the new world. The pilot who came out to greet their boat at Sandy Hook advised them against venturing up to the city because yellow fever was raging there. Yet Wemyss went up just the same, took lodging at Niblo's

Hotel, went to see Matthews play Dr. Ollipod in "The Poor Gentleman" at the Park Theatre and then again took ship for the last lap of his journey.

Thomas Abthorpe Cooper was the first great name he encountered in his Philadelphia connection, and it is interesting to learn that at this time Cooper was described as "the flying actor" in that, in the most inclement weather, he often traveled a hundred miles a day over roads almost impassable in order to play on alternate nights in New York and Philadelphia.

From the point of view of actor opportunity, young Wemyss' first season seems not to have worked out well. Between December, 1821, and the last day of April, 1823, his services were called into action on twenty-two nights only, his manager, as he notes, having good-naturedly placed him on the shelf "to be used when and how he pleased." But for playing acceptably, those twenty-two nights, the sixteen parts assigned to him he received $602. And having had leisure to woo and marry, during this period, the youngest daughter of the sheriff of Philadelphia, he felt his winter had been well spent.

Especially as he now received the honor of a New York offer from Stephen Price, one of the most interesting characters in the early nincteenth-century theatre and the man who had originated what Wemyss calls "the bold idea of farming . . . the talent of those actors belonging to the London stage whom he thought might be available in the United States." Thus it was that Price acquired for himself in England the title of "Star

Giver General to the United States." Naturally the Park Theatre, for which he particularly sought his stars, became the first in the country.

Price's career had been inspired by the great success made at the Park by Charles Mathews (the elder), and Wemyss records that it is "to Mr. Price's exertions that the Americans are indebted for the opportunity of witnessing the performances of Mr. Kean, Mr. Matthews, Mr. Macready, Mr. Conway, Mr. Charles Campbell, Mr. Powers, Mr. Wood, Mrs. Wood, Fanny Kemble, Clara Fisher, Madame Vestris and Miss Ellen Tree, with a host of talented artists of minor importance." [1] A good friend as well as a good manager, and a man of honor though a strict disciplinarian, Price, after directing for years with profit and success the destiny of the theatres in this country, boldly seized the helm of the Drury Lane Theatre for one season and sustained himself in London against very great odds. Eventually, however, London proved too much for him.

For the jealousy between England and this country in matters having to do with the theatre showed itself in the managerial as well as the actor field. Earlier in this book we have seen various illustrations of such jealousy, but this may be as good a point as any to cite certain other examples which Wemyss has preserved. One of these has to do with the visit of Macready. During a performance of "William Tell" the star failed to be provided, through the negligence of the attendant, with the arrow which he had to break before Gesler in

[1] Wemyss' "Recollections," page 86.

the fourth act of the play. This compelled Macready to sacrifice from his own quiver the arrow so loaded and poised as to prevent the possibility of failure in the most critical situation of the play, — that in which the apple is shot from the head of the boy. Irritated at the loss of to him a valuable stage property, Macready said angrily to the property man who had failed him, but who was getting ready to apologize, "I can't get such an arrow in this country, Sir," which, because interpreted to mean, "I can't get in this country wood to make such an arrow," drew down on the head of the Englishman a flood of anonymous letters accusing him of having insulted America.

And again, when Fanny Kemble was visiting this country, she was accused of having spoken disrespectfully of the Americans in their own capital city of Washington. She was charged, for one thing, with having said Americans did not know how to sit a horse correctly and for another with the declaration that the passing to the left and not to the right, ought to be the rule of the road. "For this terrible crime of entertaining an opinion of her own and daring to express it, she was to be doomed and called upon to give an account at the bar of public opinion assembled within the walls of the Walnut Street Theatre, where placards were distributed with the intention of proving in this land of freedom that a lady's tongue, from time immemorial her weapon of offense and defense, must be bridled and not be permitted to wag in ridicule of anything American." [1]

[1] Wemyss' "Recollections," page 216.

Apparently there really existed behind the scenes of the American theatre such deep-seated jealousy of the foreign artist that every little word he uttered was construed into an intentional national insult.

Not only did the press of the day make trouble for visiting actors by malicious reprints of gossip and slander but also by failing to print the "puffs" (advance notices) then regarded as absolutely necessary for an actor's success. And only a brave man could show resentment for such neglect. When a Frenchman from overseas took the bit between his teeth and refused to grant passes to the representatives of a New York paper which had over-severely criticized a performance at the Chatham Theatre, which he was then managing, the paper printed the note in which Barrière took this stand, bad English, bad spelling and all.

"Sir: I sent you free admis to my theatur to prase my acturs, you no prase my acturs you shall not have free admis anymore."

The ensuing ridicule of Barrière humiliated him, of course. But visiting actors sympathized with the Frenchman rather than with the papers whose cheap critics could make or unmake artists by the ridiculous puffery of the time.

After Wemyss had taken a wife he found it necessary to make a larger income than could be derived from his theatre work. So he set himself up as manager of a lottery, lotteries being then as reputable as brokerage is to-day. But he had a passion for the playhouse, and was, therefore, extremely pleased when invited by William Warren of Philadelphia to accept the stage and acting management of his theatre and to cross to England and recruit Mr. Warren's dramatic company, acting under the following instructions:

"Dear Sir:

"In the mission you have so kindly undertaken for me, you will please to observe the following instructions — first, the performers:

"A gentleman capable of acting first tragedy or young men such as Harry Dornton, Claudio, Laertes, — as to Hamlet, Richard, etc. you know since they have seen Kean, Macready and such actors of the present day, to perform such plays without actors of that name and grade would be useless.

"A man capable of sustaining heavy parts, which I am obliged to confer at present on Wheatley.

"A young man who can sing, — on that subject you understand my views.

"A useful man to play low comedy, and if capable of playing Irishmen, the better; which will be four.

"A lady capable of leading in tragedy, Belvidera; also another lady who would perform Lady Macbeth. If a woman of the time of life who could undertake both, it would be better.

"The salaries not to exceed thirty dollars. I would rather have it not more than six guineas; but if an object is to be gained, two dollars will not make any difference.

"Passage and any advance you may make to be repaid by a weekly reduction.

"Every engagement for two years and the deduction shall be apportioned to the time. It may happen that some of the parties may be married. Any arrangement which you think necessary for their comfort will be acceded to by me, as I am well convinced that you will do the best you can for the concern.

"With respect to Mr. Miller, you will please to inquire what he has sent; and bring with you, what he has not, that you think will be useful; but I dont want anything else. He can draw for the amount by way of Carey and Lea."

Wemyss tells us that the first person he saw standing on the wharf when he docked at Liverpool, July 20, 1827, in search of his English trained players, was Stephen Price, at that time manager of the Drury Lane Theatre and still "considered the manager of the Park Theatre in New York." Price was collecting talent for the Park Theatre, and Doctor Hart of New York had engaged a strong reinforcement for the Bowery Theatre of that city. The Boston managers were also exerting themselves to meet the opposition which they knew would be offered by the erection in their city of the Tremont Theatre, of which William Pelby had been engaged as manager.

"The mania for theatrical immigration to America was at its height," comments Joe Cowell,[1] apropos of these expeditions to collect stage stars in England, explaining that the Wemyss undertaking had been directly prompted by the determination of the rival Philadelphia playhouse with whose management he, Cowell, was then connected, to bring over a group of players from England.

John Hallam was the man who had been dispatched by

[1] Joe Cowell, "Thirty Years Passed among the Players."

Cowell to perform this commission, Hallam being glad
to go because he had fallen in love back in England and
wished to marry the girl. "Of course he secured the
services of Mrs. Hallam, and her sister, Miss Rachel
Stannard, and her sister Mrs. Mitchell and her husband,
Mr. Mitchell. The rest of the family wouldn't come,
I suppose." The Hallam contingent was put up in New
York, at a hotel kept by Charles Irish, that they might
recover from the fatigue of the voyage and see the lions
of that great town. How they recovered may be inferred
from the following bill:

"Mr. John Hallam
　　　　　　　To Charles Irish
One days board and lodging for self and party 18.50
Refreshments at bar...................... 56.00!!
　　　　　　　　　　　　　　　　　　　　, 74.50

But too long have we left Mr. Wemyss in England to
cope with the difficult task of assembling for the Chestnut Street Theatre in Philadelphia a company which
would make that theatre a powerful rival of the Park
Theatre, New York. The Chestnut Street Theatre was
the fashionable place of entertainment for the Philadelphia
of that day, but Wemyss soon discovered, as many another
manager has, that the fickle public would go wherever
the entertainment they wished to enjoy was to be had,
and when Madame Vestris and her husband were announced for the Walnut Street Theatre, January 6, 1829,
Wemyss found the crowd diverted from his house and
was glad to undertake a season in Baltimore.

Managers in those days were always undertaking

seasons in Baltimore and, almost always, finding them utterly unprofitable. Wemyss' book describes a series of Baltimore failures and tells us, too, of many unsuccessful attempts, his own among them, to set up in Washington a theatre which should be made to pay.[1] Finally this actor-manager was obliged to abandon the Chestnut Street Theatre also and return to his old business of selling lottery tickets.

That year, 1830, was a particularly calamitous season in the theatre. Actors were seen walking the streets of Philadelphia with their toes protruding from their shoes, their elbows from their coats and wearing hats from which the brim had entirely disappeared. Apparently things had got so bad that they were bound to get better. Wemyss attributes the revival of the drama to the coming of the Kembles and declares that it was Charles Kemble and his daughter Fanny who once more made the theatre a fashionable place of amusement. He himself was back on the stage by this time (1832) having become connected with the Arch Street Theatre in Philadelphia.

Pittsburg was another town in which Wemyss had managerial experience. One extraordinary thing which he then did was to make the region behind the stage comfortable, not to say attractive. Every dressing room was carpeted and furnished. The green room was "equipped in the style of a modern drawing-room" with

[1] He is authority for the statement that even Forrest during the sessions of Congress could not draw more than $130 a night and that on one occasion in 1829, when Wallack's name graced the head of the bill, *not a single individual* presented himself to inquire whether the theatre was open!

piano, ottoman, chairs, looking glass, etc., the whole costing upwards of one thousand dollars. Fashion began to frequent his theatre. One night Tyrone Power drew a particularly big house in which there were many ladies, though the play ran amuck for the reason that two of the actors were so drunk that they had to be bodily removed from the stage.

But Pittsburg could not continue to hold Wemyss against the attractions in Philadelphia, and on December 22, 1834, we find him back in the town of his earlier affiliations in charge of a good company at the American Theatre on Walnut Street. One innovation he made at this time was to produce his new play on Saturday nights instead of Monday nights. Here he had some success, but when his three years' lease ran out and the stockholders were unwilling to equip the Walnut Street Theatre with the gas which was imminent at the rival house on Chestnut Street, Wemyss lost interest in his bargain.

Regarding the way in which his theatres obtained publicity from the press Wemyss is quite informing. With those newspapers in which he advertised he had an agreement to run daily an announcement from the Walnut Street Theatre for $60 a year! He was, therefore, not unnaturally a good deal disappointed when informed (April 2, 1835) that the charge in the future would be $2.00 a week for "bills of performance of theatres, circuses, etc. not exceeding one square per night . . . all puff communications to be charged the same as advertising, by the square at the same price." Temporarily, at least, puffs went into the discard.

Whereupon we are presented with an interesting résumé of the cost of the press tickets of that day: "the proprietor, a season ticket, valued at the minimum price of $15.00; the reporter, ditto, $15; the editor, ditto, $15; an order to admit four persons every Saturday — this to treat the devil and the journeymen at the management's expense. All this has been submitted to rather than provoke the ire of an editor; and these orders in the year amount to $104."

To Joe Cowell, who, it will be recalled, was a friend of Wemyss' — though he developed, as the years went on, into a formidable rival — we are indebted for a delightful supplementary glimpse of the theatre of this same period. Cowell was born in England in 1792 and, after some success on the provincial stage, went to London to become a member of the company at the Drury Lane Theatre. Then he was brought over here to play at the Park Theatre, New York, where until 1823 he continued to be a great favorite. Subsequently as acting-manager of Price and Simpson's Equestrian Company, at the Broadway Circus—with a traveling circuit that included Boston, Philadelphia, Baltimore, Washington and Charleston — and as a touring actor he saw a lot of theatrical life in *our* "provinces." His book was published in 1844, and, divided as it is into its author's dramatic experiences in England and in America, gives us much diverting information nowhere else to be found.

He tells us that under his management the demand to see Clara Fisher in Washington was so great that President John Quincy Adams's request for a certain box on a certain night had to be refused, and he adds that to the letter making the request for seats and addressed "Mr. Manager of the Theatre" he sent a reply directed to "Mr. Manager of the United States." It was about this time, too, that there developed in Philadelphia great interest in the erection of theatres. Cowell's explanation for this is that "building theatres was supposed not only to be an excellent investment of capital at that time but a good excuse for elderly, sedate Quaker-bred gentlemen to take a peep at a play or a look at what was going on behind the scenes in the character of a stock-holder."

Some of the most delightful passages in Cowell's book describe his encounters with the Drake family. There was always the feeling, among these early managers, that Cincinnati, "Queen City of the West," ought to be a good theatre town, and it was while acting on this illusion that Cowell stumbled on the Drakes and their performance of "The School for Scandal." Mrs. Alexander Drake had not then achieved the reputation afterwards hers, and the whole company were living in most squalid and hand-to-mouth fashion. When Cowell went to call on them at the theatre they were "huddled around the fire in what was called the green room. In one corner on the floor was a pallet-bed and some stage properties evidently used to make shift to cook with, such as tin cups, dishes, a brass breast-plate, and an iron helmet half full of boiled potatoes, which, I was informed, was the domestic paraphernalia of the housekeeper and ladies' dresser. She was a sort of half Indian, half Meg-Merrilies creature, very busily employed in

433

roasting coffee on a sheet of thunder and stirring it
around with one of Macbeth's daggers, for on the blade
and dudgeon gouts of rose pink still remained."

Yet in this setting Cowell had a delightful conversation with "the Mrs. Siddons of America," as Mrs. Drake
was later called, the lady seated the while close to the
fire on a bass drum. Then it was that the suggestion
was made that the comedian join the Drakes in giving
what they termed a "fashionable recitation" in no less
a place than Mrs. Trollope's bazaar. The author of
"The Domestic Habits of the Americans" in the course
of her wanderings had set up in Cincinnati an extraordinary structure "which was a kind of hodge-podge
architecturally of the exterior of a Harem and part of the
Pavilion at Brighton." Here, in front of the long counters and shelves, Cowell encountered an elderly lady in
spectacles, knitting, her shop assistant being, by a curious
chance, a man who remembered Cowell from having
sold gallery tickets at the Adelphi when the actor was
playing there.

"The old women thinks this 'ere will be a great go one
of these days," he told Cowell. "But she cant get the
Yankees to believe in it and they wont rent the stalls;
so any of her own country as apply she furnishes 'em
with a few things and gives 'em half the profit and a cold
cut, and a cup of tea, to try to get the place into notice.
But I think it is all in my eye. She'll never be able to
'melerate the manners of the Mericans, as she calls it.
D'ye see them 'ere spit boxes?" pointing to a row filled
with clean sawdust on the outside of the counters.
"Well, she can't begin to persuade 'em to make use on

'em; they will squirt their 'backer on one side which teazes the old woman half to death." [1]

It was in the same building with the counters and the "spit boxes," though in another room — an apartment equipped with a raised platform and a baize curtain — that Cowell and the Drakes gave a sort of variety show for the delectation of Cincinnati "fashion", and the Trollope family. Following the performance the hostess served refreshments.

Because these reminiscent managers all aspired to a New York career — and some of them, including Cowell, actually achieved their ambition — this may be as good a place as any to take up again the story [2] of New York's gradual development from a town no better, theatrically, than two or three other towns of the country, to the proud position it now holds as the acknowledged Mecca of plays and players in America.

For thirty years the John Street Theatre, [3] of which we heard much in an early chapter, stood without any important rival. Soon after it closed its doors — on January 13, 1798 — a number of rather ambitious amusement enterprises sprang up to take its place. At the head of the list must be placed the Park Theatre, which had a continuous and very interesting history from the day of its opening — January 29, 1798, in a somewhat unfinished condition, to present a performance of "As You

[1] "Thirty Years among the Players," by Joe Cowell.
[2] See also J. N. Ireland's "History of the Stage in New York," and T. Allston Brown's volumes of similar title.
[3] The John Street Theatre opened December 7, 1767, with the comedy "The Beaux's Stratagem."

435

Like It" — until the end of its career, a whole half century later. A very bare and ugly building was this first Park Theatre, with its pit (occupied exclusively by men and boys) equipped with board benches innocent of cushions, and its crudely constructed boxes which could be entered only from the rear and through a locked door carefully guarded by the box-keeper. In the wide space between the pit and the boxes gentlemen were wont to promenade between the acts. In the second tier a restaurant was to be found, while the third tier — set apart here, as in most theatres of the period, for the dissolute of both sexes — was accommodatingly supplied with a bar. Usually the house doors were opened by half-past six, the curtain being rung up an hour later. Almost always two pieces, a tragedy and a comedy, were offered, but sometimes there was a third piece with a comic song or a *pas seul* tucked in between the different parts of the program. Two thousand people could be seated in this first Park Theatre, and the house, for all its bareness, cost a very pretty penny — one hundred and thirty thousand dollars. It burned down in 1820.

Concerning the playhouse of the same name which replaced the first Park Theatre I cannot do better than to quote again from our friend Cowell when, by way of getting acquainted with the house, he viewed it first from the audience's side.

"Phillips, the singer, was the 'star' that night and the performance was 'Lionel and Clarissa.' The opera had not commenced but I took a seat with about twenty others in the second tier. The house was excessively dark; oil, of course, then was used in common brass Liverpool lamps, ten or twelve of which were placed in a large sheet-iron hoop, painted green, hanging from the ceiling in the centre, and one, half the size, on each side of the stage. The fronts of the boxes were decorated, if it could be so called, with one continuous American ensign, a splendid subject, and very difficult to handle properly, but this was designed in the taste of an upholsterer and executed without any taste at all; the seats were covered with green baize and the backs of the boxes with whitewash, and the iron columns which supported them covered with burnished gold!

"The audience came evidently to see the play and be pleased, if they possibly could, with everything; the men generally wore their hats; at all events they consulted only their own opinion and comfort in the matter; and the ladies, I observed, very sensibly, all came in bonnets, but usually dispossessed themselves of them, and tied them in large bunches high up to the gold columns; and as there is nothing a woman can touch that she does not instinctively adorn, the varied colours of the ribands and materials of which they were made, were in my opinion a vast improvement to the unfurnished appearance of the house. Phillips — as Lionel — and Mrs. Holman as Clarissa, shared equally the approbation of the audience, the current of whose simple unsophisticated taste had not been turned awry by fashion, obliging them to profess an admiration of the enormities of the German and Italian school, which in these days of humbug and refinement they alone pretend to listen to." [1]

Just before the first visit to America (in 1822) of Charles Mathews the elder, Cowell, who seems to have

[1] "Thirty Years Passed Among the Players."

been a many-sided genius, undertook the re-decoration of the Park. Glass chandeliers were then purchased to supply the place of the iron hoops; the proscenium was arched and raised, and the whole house dressed in gray and gold. Thus, when Mathews made his first bow to the American public, he found himself in a really attractive theatre with plenty of "fashionables." The proprietors at this time were John K. Beekman and John Jacob Astor, and that "all society" was glad to patronize their establishment is clear from the water-colour drawing made by John Searle for William Bayard, Esq., and showing "among those present" that night representatives of the most aristocratic New York families.

While the Park was thus growing in the favour of the fashionable, other houses, also, were coming to the front. Some of these, though quite humble in design and seasonal in character, soon attained great success, thus demonstrating that amusement was now in very definite demand in New York. Joseph Coree, who had been a cook to Major Carew, inaugurated a series of dramatic entertainments in his Mount Vernon Gardens, on the Leonard Street corner of Broadway, and here, in summer, members of the Park Theatre Company were wont to play while their own house was closed. The Hodgkinsons and Mrs. Susanna Rowson, author of "Charlotte Temple," were among the artists who here performed during the heated months. Castle Garden, too, was occasionally used as a theatre for many years.[1]

[1] Here on September 6, 1852, was held a "great dramatic festival" in commemoration of the supposed first introduction of the drama into

From the early twenties dates, also, the Chatham
Garden Theatre, of whose rise Joe Cowell gives the following entertaining sketch :

"A Frenchman, by the name of Barrière, had fitted
up a small garden at the back of a confectioner's shop
in Chatham Street, with two or three dozen transparent
lamps, and

'Seats beneath the shade,
For talking age and whispering lovers made.'

and, by selling 'sweets to the sweets' at a shilling a head,
had made a great deal of money; which, to rapidly
increase, he raised a platform, called it an orchestra,
covered it with canvas, engaged a French horn, clario-
net, fiddle and a chorus singer from the Park, with the
gentle name of Lamb, who bleated a song or two, and
with this combination of talent attracted crowds every
night, to the great injury 'in the springtime of the year'
of the theatre.   Price [manager of the Park Theatre]
put in force some fire-proof law, prohibiting all canvas
or skin-deep establishments within a certain limit, and
the old Frenchman was obliged to strike his tent; but
with the ice-cream profits he purchased brick and mortar
and built the Chatham Theatre." [1]

About this time, also, the Bowery was started.   Cowell
tells with similar sprightliness of its beginnings.   "While
this Chatham Theatre project was in embryo, Mrs.
Baldwin, a sister to Mrs. Barnes, turned the brains of
some half-dozen would-be-acting young men and women
and a private house in Warren Street into a theatre and

America one hundred years before.   In accordance with the dates and
data of William Dunlap, "The Merchant of Venice" and Garrick's
"Lethe" were then piously performed.

[1] "Thirty Years Passed Among the Players."

439

opened a show there. Tom Hilson had been seduced
away from the Park, where he had been a favourite in
my line of business, by Charles Gilfert, a German comedian who had married Miss Holman, and was, in consequence, manager of the Charleston, South Carolina,
theatre. On Hilson's necessary return to the North in
the summer, being shut out by me from the Park, he
accepted a star engagement at this old lady's concern,
and drew crowded houses. Gilfert, who was a very
enterprising talented man, with some powerful friends,
already began to talk of a theatre in the Bowery."

How this theatre was opened, in the fall of 1826, with
Forrest as chief drawing-card, we have already learned
in our sketch of that artist.

It was Gilfert of the Bowery who was responsible for
the introduction of French dancing into this country.
When Mlle. Hutin, who first distinguished herself in
this way, bounded on to the Bowery stage, February 7,
1827, her symmetrical proportions liberally displayed
by the force of a bewildering pirouette, every lady in the
lower tier of boxes immediately left the theatre, while
the whole audience crimsoned with shame. Joe Cowell,
in the course of his description of this "novelty," has a
realistic paragraph about the "poor half-dressed supernumerary women, now made for the first time in their
lives to stand upon one leg, who tottered bashfully and
looked as foolish and about as graceful as a plucked
goose in the same position." For a time after this, public opinion demanded that our dancing visitors should
wear Turkish trousers.

In 1828 the Bowery burned down, but it was rebuilt in the unprecedented space of sixty days and was opened with increased magnificence. *And* with a press agent, the first of his clan in America! Cowell writes:

"Agents had been dispatched to Europe for talent of every description, and the first good theatrical orchestra ever brought to America, Gilfert could boast of having congregated. William Chapman, an excellent comedian, was engaged, and George Holland, inimitable in the small list of characters he undertook, proved a deserved attraction, while Forrest, if possible, increased in public estimation. A very capable man, by the name of Harby, was employed at a handsome salary, to 'write up' the merits of the theatre, and such members of the company as the interest of the management desired to be advanced. This, being the first introduction of the system of forestalling, or rather, directing public opinion, had a powerful effect; and the avidity with which a large class of persons in all countries swallow, and implicitly believe what they read in a newspaper, is truly and quaintly enough described by Mopsa in the Winter's Tale: 'I love a ballad in print a-life for then we are sure they are true.' All these circumstances combined and the theatrical population of New York not being then equal to the support of more than one establishment of the kind, the tide of opinion sat full in favour of the Bowery while the Park was trembling on the brink of ruin."

Under the management of Thomas S. Hamblin, who assumed control in the autumn of 1830, this press-agent at the Bowery had plenty of material from which to spin his yarns. For it was here that Josie Clifton, the first native American actress to play in London, appeared;

here that Priscilla Cooper made her début in 1834; and here, in 1836, that Charlotte Cushman made her first New York appearance as Lady Macbeth.

Innumerable names of romantic association are also connected with the drama at the Bowery. For, though it burned down many times — before it was handed over, in 1879, to German playgoers and re-christened the Thalia — it ever pursued the tenor of its way as a people's theatre, and melodrama was not infrequently to be found in the private life of its cherished players as well as on its stage. This was especially true in the case of Adah Isaacs Menken, long a favourite here.

Chief exponent of the character of "Mazeppa," an equestrian drama in which the heroine made a thrilling flight about the auditorium bound to the back of a wild horse, Adah Menken was also extremely interesting as a woman. Before she began to act "Mazeppa" the performers used dummies in this scene, but she allowed herself to be tied to the horse and so naturally increased her reputation, already great. For no American actress had had such a varied and lurid career as this daughter of a Presbyterian minister of Louisiana, whose real name was Adelaide McCord. Born in 1835, she received so good a classical education that she could translate Homer at the age of twelve, and all through her life she showed marked literary tendencies. But when compelled to make a living she went on the stage as a dancer, first appearing at the French Opera House in New Orleans in 1855. (Already she had been married and abandoned by a man whose name is never mentioned in her list of

ADAH ISAACS MENKEN AND ALEXANDRE DUMAS, *père*, WHO SHARED
WITH SWINBURNE THE HONOR OF HER INTIMACY
A picture greatly in demand by collectors for its rarity

INTERIOR OF NIBLO'S THEATRE, "MASANIELLO, OR THE DUMB GIRL OF PORTICI," ON THE STAGE

husbands!) Soon after this she made her début at the New Orleans Varieties, taking the rôle of Bianca in "Fazio" and making a great success of it. Subsequently she supported Booth, Murdoch and Hackett and later became herself a star appearing not only in "Mazeppa" but in "The French Spy" and "Three Fast Men." While acting with the Nashville Stock Company she met and married Alexander Isaacs Menken, a musician, and adopted the Jewish faith, in which she died.

She had several other husbands, however, among them John C. Heenan, a well-known prize-fighter, from whom she was divorced in 1862, Robert H. Newell ("Orpheus C. Kerr") and James Barclay. She was also the intimate friend of Swinburne and of the elder Dumas. Between the Newell and the Barclay marriages she appeared in London at Astley's in her then-famous rôle of "Mazeppa," and after marrying Barclay, played in Paris where, one night, she was given no less than nine curtain calls. On the last night of her one hundred performances, Napoleon III, the King of Greece, the Duke of Edinburgh, and the Prince Imperial were all in her audience. It was in the French capital on August 10, 1868, that her extraordinary life ended. And she was then only thirty-three!

To Dickens, with whom she was on terms of close friendship, she dedicated her curious little book of poems, "Infelicia," and his graceful note, accepting the compliment, was printed as the book's preface. Henry P. Phelps, who as manager of the theatre at Albany, New York, knew Adah Menken well and greatly admired her pluck, as well as certain other of her many sterling qualities, records that she was "exquisitely beautiful in form and feature." Sala describes her as "a little black-eyed beauty with elegant legs."

Which brings us squarely to the "leg show" era and to Miss Olive Logan's delicious diatribes against legs. "A woman who has not ability enough to rank as a passable 'walking lady' in a good theatre on a salary of $25 a week," comments our strong-minded author, "can strip herself almost naked and be thus qualified to go upon the stage of two thirds of our theatres at a salary of $100 and upwards. Clothed in the dress of an honest woman she is worth nothing to a manager. Stripped as naked as she dare, — and it seems there is little left when so much is done, — she becomes a prize for her manager who knows that crowds will rush to see her and who pays her a salary accordingly." [1]

This outburst [2] was inspired not only by the "Mazeppa" kind of thing but by the tremendous success attained by "The Black Crook," which had its first performance September 12, 1866, in Niblo's Garden.

[1] "About Nudity in Theatres," p. 129 of her book "Apropos of Women and Theatres."

[2] The author of the most bitter contemporary comment that we have on the "leg show" was, interestingly, of player stock herself. Born in 1841, the daughter of an actor she herself became an actress when only thirteen. In 1857 she retired, married and went abroad, where she was introduced at the French Court and came to know many people who wrote current gossip for various Parisian papers. Following a brief interlude — after her return to New York in 1864 for her appearance on the stage of Wallack's Theatre in a play called "Eveleen" — she took up writing as a profession and also appeared much in public defence of woman's rights. That Miss Logan should have called a leg *a leg* at this period of America's development shows that she must indeed have felt very deeply about the current trend on the stage.

The Romance of the American Theatre

Niblo's, built on Broadway near Prince Street, within two years of the erection of the Bowery Theatre, was called, at first, the *Sans Souci* but soon became much more widely known under the name of its founder. William Niblo's amusement enterprise had originally been limited to a Summer Garden, but when the Bowery burned down, he shrewdly built an attractive little theatre in his garden and set up a coach service to bring his patrons from the Astor House to the play. Here the Ravels performed in 1837 and William E. Burton in 1839. Forrest, Charles Kean, E. L. Davenport, Mrs. Mowatt, John Brougham, George Holland, and the Falstaff of the elder Hackett were also seen at this first Niblo's Theatre before it burned down in 1848. Later, Charlotte Cushman, Dion Boucicault, Mr. and Mrs. Barney Williams, Mrs. John Wood, Maggie Mitchell and Margaret Mather here invited the plaudits of New York theatregoers.

It is, however, because "The Black Crook," a musical mélange notable as the first great success in the "leg movement" school of drama, here burst upon a gaping public, that Niblo's must for all time stand out in dramatic history. It is interesting to note that the production of this most unparalleled success in "spectacles" ever known to the American stage was entirely accidental. The firm of Jarrett and Palmer, who popularized the ballet in this country, had imported from Europe dancers, novel scenic effects and elaborate costumes to be used in a ballet for the opera "La Biche au Bois," which they were preparing to put on at the Academy of

445

Music. Just as the production was ripe the Academy burned down and Jarrett and Palmer found themselves with a ballet ready for production and no piece, or place, to make use of it.

But just before this time an actor named Barres had submitted to Niblo's the manuscript of a spectacular play called "The Black Crook," which Wheatley, the manager at Niblo's, had contracted to produce. Here was a chance to utilize the foreign ballet. The author of "The Black Crook" was placated by a check for $1500 for the necessary changes in his piece, though nothing of the original play remained except the title.

When the ballet from London made its first appearance, Niblo's was packed from pit to dome. Never before in this country had there been seen either scenery or costumes on such a scale of magnificence. But it was really the hundred girl dancers, all of whom wore the scantiest possible attire, which made the production a tremendous sensation and aroused a storm of controversy such as had never been known before in connection with the theatre. Preachers improved the opportunity offered by "The Black Crook" to denounce the stage and castigate its license, but this only served to increase the success of the show,[1] which ran for sixteen consecutive months and took in through the box office for 475 performances more than $1,100,000.

[1] From "The Black Crook" chrysalis, according to Oscar M. Sayler ("Our American Theatre," page 252), clambered, in 1907, the first "Follies" under the exacting wand of Florenz Ziegfeld, Junior. Since then we have had not only perennial Ziegfelds but John Murray Anderson's "Greenwich Village Follies," five in a row, J. J. Shubert's "Passing

The Romance of the American Theatre

Naturally a success of this kind meant the inundation of New York by English burlesque dancers who were not averse to a generous display of what had always before been known as "limbs" but which now for the first time became "legs" to the press of the day. Lydia Thompson, charming and gifted actress, for whom the younger Dumas wrote a play, is perhaps the best known of these English performers, though Pauline Markham and Eliza Weathersby were also very popular.

Lydia Thompson made an enormous dent in American stage history. Her burlesque company, engaged in England by Samuel Colville, made their American début on September 28, 1868, in "Ixion," preceded by "To Oblige Benson." Miss Thompson was thirty-two years old at this time and had long been a sensation at the Haymarket Theatre in London, but she attained tremendous success here and by the time her troupe had been transferred to Niblo's Garden (January 30, 1869) to appear in a burlesque of "The Forty Thieves," her work had become the subject of serious magazine articles.

Richard Grant White rationalizes the outbreak of burlesque acting over all the world. "No mere accident," he declares,[1] "has made so monstrous a kind of entertainment equally acceptable to three publics so

Shows," and half a dozen new Revues a year, including George White's "Scandals." Yet notwithstanding all of these and "studded though these are with dancers"; notwithstanding, too, the great contribution made in their own field by Isadora Duncan and Ruth St. Denis, "we still lack a native American ballet."

[1] The *Galaxy*, November, 1869.

different as those of Paris, London and New York."
The burlesque, "which casts down all the gods from
their pedestals," this serious-minded scholar and student
of the theatre then explains in Freudian fashion, as an
outlet for repressed feelings. "The temper of the time is
such that we cannot endure tragedy or even the ideal
presentation of life in high comedy . . . the next
step to the repression of manifestations of real feeling
is the caricature of such manifestations in art. Join
to this the craving for the enjoyment of material splendor
and sensuous beauty and the result is . . . 'The Black
Crook' . . . and 'The Forty Thieves.'

For Lydia Thompson herself with her "beauty and
saucy spritefulness" White has only the highest praise.
Where he had expected to find her coarse, he found her
"one of the most charming comic actresses it has been
my good fortune to see. She played burlesque with a
daintiness with which few actresses of note are able to
flavor their acting even in high comedy."

"She was doing hard work no doubt but her heart
must have been in it for she was the embodiment of
mirth and moved others to hilarity by being moved herself. Thus it was as if Venus, in her quality of the goddess of laughter, had come upon the stage. And if there
was a likeness to Venus in her costume as well as in her
manner I must confess that I saw in it no chance of harm
to myself or to any of my fellow spectators, old or young,
male or female. Indeed, it seems rather to be desired
that the points of a fine woman should be somewhat
better known and more thought of than they have been.
They seem to me quite as important and I think that they

are quite as interesting as those of a fine horse; and I should be sorry to believe that they are more harmful either to taste or to morals. Some of the outcries which we hear against the costumes which the burlesque actresses wear in the way of their profession have in them such a tone of personal injury that it might come from mammas and papas who have a very poor article of young woman lying heavy on their hands and are indignant that there should be so good and so easy an opportunity of trying it by a very high standard."

This scholar and critic of the theatre even declares that he finds Lydia Thompson in "Sinbad" better than much high tragedy that he had seen — Mr. Forrest, for instance, in "Hamlet," further pointing out that "if the ladies of our most cultured society need an excuse for attending the performances at Niblo's . . . they may find it in the benefit which they might derive from listening to Miss Thompson, Miss Markham and their companions." For the beautiful manner in which these women spoke English, particularly Miss Pauline Markham — "she who has found the lost arms of the Venus de Milo and whose speech is vocal velvet" — White, who certainly knew what good English was and how it should be pronounced,[1] had only the most enthusiastic praise.

During the same visit to America in which the English burlesquers were thus praised in high places Miss Thompson's company gave "Pippin, the King of the Gold Mines" at Niblo's, and on May second produced

[1] Richard Grant White, born 1821, died 1885, was Dramatic and Art Editor of the Riverside Shakespeare.

449

for the first time on any stage "Mosquito," [1] the piece Dumas *fils* had written for Miss Thompson. The gifted burlesquer made several subsequent visits to America. During one of these (in the fall of 1877 when she was on the bills at the Eagle Theatre, New York, with quite a different company from that of a decade before) she appeared as "Robinson Crusoe." She had attained the mature age of fifty-five when New York saw her for the last time (January, 1891) at the Standard Theatre in "The Dazzler."

The truth of the matter concerning "leg shows" and the kind of thing which Lydia Thompson brought to a delighted public seems to have been that they raised to quasi-respectability the vogue for *tableaux vivants* which had for some twenty years been rife in New York. Many of these had been degrading spectacles. Such things as "Venus Rising from the Sea," alternating with "exhibitions of naked Negroes" were shown at peep shows until indecency became so flagrant that the New York *Herald* called upon the Common Council for the suppression of these exhibitions as a menace to morality. Thus it was that, in the May of 1848, we find a writer in the *Sunday Mercury* asking "Where are the Model artists gone?" —

> "Those nice tableaux vivants
> Of beautiful young ladies, sans
> Both petticoats and pants,

[1] In the playbill for the "Mosquito" production, one rather surprisingly finds the name of McKee Rankin, remembered by many playgoers still in the early forties for his tutelage of Nance O'Neil, with whom he often played the heavy father in Sudermann's "Magda."

LYDIA THOMPSON AS ROBINSON CRUSOE

JAMES W. WALLACK

Who, scorning fashion's shifts and whims,
Did nightly crowds delight
By showing up their handsome limbs
At fifty cents a sight."

Obviously New York had now become a full-sized town theatrically. Because during the same decade that indecent exhibitions were being suppressed by the Common Council, Joseph Jefferson and Jenny Lind [1] were making their appearance at the New National Theatre (formerly the Chatham Square) and a formidable rival to the Park Theatre was being launched in the Second Broadway Theatre, now generally known as the old Broadway, situated between Pearl and Anthony (afterwards Worth) streets.

This large and elegant edifice opened in September, 1847, with "The School for Scandal," John Barrett being the stage manager. The first night of this house marks also the initial appearance in the United States of Lester Wallack in the farce "Used Up." The bills of the evening give Wallack's name as John Wallack Lester, which he had assumed on the other side of the Atlantic in order that he might not seem to trade on the renown of that very gifted player, James William Wallack (1795–1864), who was his father.[2] Four years be-

[1] This was the Swedish Nightingale's third visit to New York, in June, 1851. On her first visit she broke her contract with P. T. Barnum rather than sing in this very place; the theatre had then just been used as a circus and seems to have needed purging. At any rate Miss Lind, who disliked the odour of horses, flatly refused to sing in the "stable," as she called it.

[2] Thackeray once declared that the elder Wallack's Shylock was the first rendering of the part which he had ever seen that gave him any idea what an ill-used man this Jew was.

fore his New York début, Lester Wallack had been pronounced "the coming young man" by Charlotte Cushman, who had been led to this prophecy by his superb work as Mercutio when she had been playing Romeo in London to her sister's Juliet. To the youth himself she said in her straightforward way: "There is a great future before you if you take care and do not let your vanity run away with you." For young Wallack was very good-looking, even as his father — who shared with Byron the distinction of being one of the handsomest men in England — had been before him.

It was at the Old Broadway that there occurred (December 29, 1851) the sensational première of Lola Montez about whose extraordinary career a very interesting book has recently been written.[1] This notorious woman was born Elizabeth Gilbert, her father being a British officer and her mother a beautiful Irish woman who was fond of fancying that she was descended from a Spanish grandee. When Lola was nineteen, in order to escape a marriage with an elderly Indian judge, which her mother was arranging for her, she eloped with a young Irish officer. The young couple had a brief triumph at the Vice-regal Court in Dublin, but Lola soon compromised her reputation beyond repair, and, having become an outcast from society, went on the stage as a dancer. Apparently she *could dance* but her husband's friends were determined that she should not find an opportunity to do so, and a number of engagements which she had suc-

[1] "Lola Montez," by Edmund d'Auvergne. Brentano, New York.

ceeded in securing at Her Majesty's were cancelled and she was compelled to leave London.

All over Europe she traveled, visiting Brussels, Paris, Warsaw and St. Petersburg, establishing in the last-named place a close intimacy with Czar Nicholas I. From Russia she went to Dresden, where she met Franz Liszt, and without the slightest compunction shattered his relationship with Countess d'Agoult, who had borne him three children.[1] In the spring of 1844 Lola and Liszt travelled together to Paris. In the French capitol this dancing demi-mondaine promptly made her bow (March 30) to the Parisian public and, almost as promptly, became the mistress of Dumas *père*.

Her greatest triumph, however, was in winning the passionate devotion of King Ludwig of Bavaria, when she danced before him in Munich, and though his scandalized ministers threatened to resign — and did — he refused to give up Lola, and she appointed their successors. The king created her Countess of Landsfeld and Baroness Rosenthal and granted her a large annuity. Because some of the students espoused her cause and others attacked her, it was necessary to close the University, as the controversy concerning her waxed hotter and hotter. But not until the opposition became so strong that even the king could not stand out against it was he willing to banish her from his court.

More scandalous episodes in England and Spain followed. Though her first husband was still alive, she contracted, in 1849, a marriage with another army

[1] One of whom became the wife of Richard Wagner.

officer, and after being prosecuted for bigamy went with him to Madrid, where she deserted him.[1] Coming to this country in the same vessel with Kossuth, she gave performances from New York to New Orleans and San Francisco, making a particular sensation in a drama called "Lola Montez in Bavaria," in which she herself depicted her own career as *danseuse*, politician, revolutionist and fugitive. Then she went to Australia but subsequently returned to the United States and died in New York, June 30, 1861, in utter poverty. Her distinction as a stage figure seems to have been that she acted modestly and danced gracefully, so disappointing those who thronged the playhouse, avidly expecting a prurient performance.

The Chatham Square Theatre, however, not the Old Broadway, supplied the setting in 1848 when young Wallack played Edmund Dantes in "Monte Cristo," [2] and he distinguished himself a year later in this same background by acting D'Artagnan in some versions which he had made of "The Three Guardsmen." During the next two years he was connected with Burton's Chambers Street Theatre, after which, for nearly ten years, he was closely associated as actor and manager with the theatre on Broome Street, which his father controlled and which had formerly been known as Brougham's Lyceum. This house derived its name from the John Brougham who, in 1842, saw "The School for Scandal" given at the

[1] Afterwards, in California, she married a Mr. Hull — both previous husbands having finally died.
[2] This was one of the first plays in dramatic history that rivalled "Richard III" and "London Assurance" by a run of one hundred nights.

Park to an audience which numbered not more than fifteen all told. "But to make up for the scarcity of spectators," Brougham declared, "there was an inordinate number of rats, so admirably domesticated that they sat on the ledge of the boxes and looked you squarely in the face without moving a muscle."

John Brougham must never be taken quite literally; yet that his wit was often not wide of the mark is clear from his observation to William Winter concerning Dion Boucicault, who tried to cheat him out of his rights in "London Assurance." "If Dion had to play a second-old-man," testified this fellow Irishman, "he would scalp his grandfather for the wig."

At the Park Theatre in 1845 Mrs. Anna Cora Mowatt's "Fashion" was produced. "Fashion" is interesting not only because it was one of our first social comedies but also because Anna Mowatt, who wrote it, was the first American woman of birth [1] and breeding to identify herself with the fortunes of the stage. She has written delightfully of her own career in a book called "The Autobiography of an Actress," and from this work we learn that she was born in Bordeaux, France, in 1819, during the sojourn there of her mother, and of her father, Samuel G. Ogden, who was tried for his part in the Miranda Expedition to liberate Venezuela and Colombia. Even as a child she had stage experience, for, when only five, she took the part of a Judge in a French version of "Othello"! When she was seven she came to New

[1] Her father was the son of an Episcopal clergyman, her mother great granddaughter of Francis Lewis, Signer of the Declaration of Independence.

York to live and by the time she was ten she had read all of Shakespeare's plays. At an early age she began to write verse and at fourteen put on the stage at her home in Flatbush, a translation of Voltaire's "Alzare."

The following year she was married to James Mowatt, a New York barrister, who had fallen in love with her when she was only thirteen and who now persuaded her, at sixteen, to marry him secretly and tell the family afterward. Seventeen found her writing verse which showed the influence of Byron. One is not surprised to learn that, at eighteen, she was threatened with tuberculosis.

But with the decision and enterprise which always characterized her career she refused to be discouraged by this setback in health, and sailed for Liverpool, thinking a sea voyage would prove beneficial. Apparently it did, for she spent a gay week in London and saw Madame Vestris at the Olympia Theatre. Then she went on to Hamburg, where she was joined first by her sister, who had just been married, and later by Mowatt, who had come over for medical treatment.

A revealing glimpse of the future author of "Fashion" is given in a letter which Mrs. Mowatt wrote about this time, from Paris, and in which America's tendency to imitate social forms without any conception of the spirit behind these forms is criticized. It will be remembered that it was just this failure to understand the meaning of certain Paris customs that makes Mrs. Tiffany in the play such a delightful characterization. In Paris Mrs. Mowatt also saw Rachel.

MRS. ANNA CORA MOWATT, THE FIRST AMERICAN WOMAN OF SOCIAL STAND-
ING TO BE CONNECTED WITH THE THEATRE
Mrs. Mowatt was the author of "Fashion" as well as an actress of distinction

DION BOUCICAULT AS CON, IN "THE SHAUGHRAUN"
See page 462

So not only did this clever young woman recover her health during this visit abroad but she received a fresh impetus to dramatic expression. The return to her home in Flatbush was marked by the composition of her first play "Gulzara, or The Persian Slave" (published in the *New World* in 1840). Under the name of Helen Berkeley, she now contributed to many of the American magazines of the day articles which were copied into London periodicals and even translated into German. Often she would write several articles for the same number under different names.

It was at the suggestion of Epes Sargent, who recognized that Mrs. Mowatt's gift was essentially a dramatic one, that "Fashion" was prepared definitely as an acting play for the Park Theatre. It was promptly accepted by Simpson, the manager, and put into rehearsal. At one of these the author was present, hidden in a private box, and so unseen by the actors, "a rehearsal so solemn that I began to fancy I had made a mistake and unconsciously written a tragedy." [1]

Mrs. Mowatt ruefully describes her emotions at her play's first night, March 24, 1845, and at the "cutting" on the stage next morning. She likewise explains that Mrs. Tiffany, wife of a newly rich business man of New York, who is the central character of the play,[2] was only

[1] "Autobiography of an Actress," by Anna Cora Mowatt. Ticknor, Reed and Fields, Boston, 1854.
[2] Recent opportunity to see "Fashion" has been afforded theatregoers in New York by the New York Drama League, in Chicago by the University of Chicago Dramatic Club, in Philadelphia by the Zelosophic Society and in Boston by the Copley Theatre Players under the direction of E. E. Clive.

457

a composite and not meant to be a caricature of any individual, as the critics tried to make out.

The great success attained in its day by "Fashion" is easily understood. For here we have that rare thing, a social satire, based on true knowledge of the life it depicts yet all done with a light touch and in entire good humor. Edgar A. Poe, then dramatic critic for the *Broadway Journal*, regarded the piece of such importance that he went to see it several nights in succession in order to determine the full extent of its merits and demerits.[1] The play ran three weeks in New York, and while still occupying the boards at the Park Theatre was taken to the Walnut Street Theatre in Philadelphia. Here the author was given a most enthusiastic ovation when she appeared in a box.

The publishing business in which Mr. Mowatt had been engaged failed about this time, and as Mrs. Mowatt had attracted managers by the success of her play, she was strongly urged to go on the stage. This she finally decided to do (having with difficulty converted the members of her family to a belief that this step was the right one for her) and made her début at the Park Theatre, New York, June 18, 1845, as Pauline in "The Lady of Lyons." After scoring a distinct metropolitan success

[1] Poe should have been glad to do what any review of his could for this woman so pluckily making her way on the stage. His own mother had similarly endeavored, it will be recalled; but she was not similarly successful. Just before her death she advertised, November 29, 1811, through the newspapers of Virginia:
"To the Humane
"On this night Mrs. Poe, lingering on the bed of disease and surrounded by her children, asks for your assistance and *asks it perhaps for the last time*."

she played the part of Gertrude (in "Fashion") at Philadelphia and this rôle she repeated in Charleston, Mobile and New Orleans. Then she began what proved to be a brilliant season at Niblo's Garden, acting, among other things, Katherine in "The Taming of the Shrew," — and even Juliet. The next season, having secured E. L. Davenport for her leading man, she wrote "Armand, the Child of the People" especially to fit his and her powers, and the play was produced both at the Park Theatre, New York, and in Boston.

In the fall of 1847 Mrs. Mowatt, still with Davenport as co-star, sailed for England, and together they played "The Lady of Lyons" at the Theatre Royal in Manchester as well as a number of pieces (including "Armand") at the Princess', the Olympia and Marylebone in London. "Fashion" too was given at the Olympia and ran for two weeks. It is interesting to observe the review in the *Sun* the following morning:

"America has within the last three years given us Miss Cushman, the greatest tragedian at present on the stage, Mrs. Mowatt, the most interesting young tragedian, the most lady-like of genteel comedians . . . besides a host of excellent delineators of Yankee peculiarities. But America has *not* given us until last night any play that would stand the test of representation before a London audience. . . . Last night this reproach was wiped out . . . there was presented at the Olympia Theatre with the most deserved success an American five act comedy the scene of which is laid in New York and which delineates American manners after the same fashion as our Garrick, Colman and Sheridan were accustomed to present English manners, and which as regards plot, construction, characters or dialogue is worthy to take its place by the best of the English comedies." [1]

A very serious illness interrupted Mrs. Mowatt's career for four months after this great London success. In January, 1851, she went to Dublin and after that to Scotland, where the news came to her that her husband had died. Early in the summer she returned to America and again had a successful engagement at Niblo's Garden, following which she made another tour of the country. The pluckiness, which was a part of her indomitable character, was again demonstrated when, expected in Philadelphia by December 30 to put on a performance, she left St. Louis in extremely cold weather; and though the trip, which usually occupied seven days, stretched to seventeen, the steamboats and the Ohio River froze up, the primitive stagecoaches of Indiana and the railroads of Pennsylvania failed to work on schedule, she won the race and arrived at her destination on time. Similarly in March, 1852, when she fell from a horse in Boston and broke a rib, she pursued her career unflinchingly. Finally in June, 1853, she had to take a holiday and this she spent in writing her "Autobiography," a book which makes very delightful reading. That same year she retired from the stage and married W. F. Ritchie of the Richmond *Inquirer;* at her farewell appearance in Niblo's Garden she played the part of Pauline, in which she had made her début. During the latter years of

[1] Quoted in "Autobiography," page 326.

her life Mrs. Ritchie lived much abroad; she died in London, July 28, 1870.

Apart from her great contribution as the author of "Fashion" this remarkable woman did much for the American stage, then still suffering from the disapproval of the Puritan element in our society, by proving that an American gentlewoman could succeed as an actress while at the same time adhering to her own high standards of personal life. I am glad to be able to quote here, as bearing on her ideals for players, the "farewell to the profession" with which her book closes:

"I would beg them to believe that I sympathize in their toils; and their sacrifices; I appreciate their exertions, I respect their virtues; and I cherish the hope that in ceasing to rank among their number I shall not wholly be forgotten by them." [1]

Laura Keene is another woman whose name stands out in the history of New York drama. Laura Keene's Theatre was built for her on Broadway, near Houston Street in 1856. The opening bill was "As You Like It," Laura Keene herself playing Rosalind. For eight years this very able woman was the controlling factor at this house. Tom Taylor's "Our American Cousin" was first produced here and made a very great success by reason of the skill with which E. A. Sothern built up the part of Lord Dundreary. Jefferson has declared that the first night of this play — in which he acted Asa Trenchard — was the turning-point in three careers, his own, Miss Keene's and Sothern's.

[1] "Autobiography," page 448.

461

Miss Keene's success made possible, too, the great success of Dion Boucicault, who supplied her with plays in something the same facile fashion with which Clyde Fitch later met the demands of Charles Frohman. "The Colleen Bawn" was turned out on a rush order from Miss Keene to take the place of "Vanity Fair," which had failed. Upon leaving the theatre, the dramatist was quite without inspiration concerning a new play, but, chancing to buy at a bookstore on the way home a novel by Gerald Griffin, called "The Collegians," he read it that night from cover to cover and, in the morning, wrote his manager:

"My dear Laura: I have it! I send you seven steel engravings of scenes around Killarney. Get your scene-painter to work on them at once. I also send a book of Irish Melodies, with those marked I desire Baker to score for the orchestra. I shall read act one of my new Irish play on Friday; we rehearse that while I am writing the second, which will be ready on Monday; and we rehearse the second while I am doing the third. We can get the play out within a fortnight.

"Yours,
"D. B."[1]

Such was the speed with which "The Colleen Bawn" was prepared for its production under Laura Keene, March 29, 1860. It was, in many ways, typical of the method used by Boucicault in writing, adapting, and translating the four hundred plays which came from his pen in the course of his almost fifty years of labor

[1] Quoted in Montrose Moses' "Actor Families of America."

as a dramatist.[1] The play with which Boucicault is most intimately associated is "The Shaughraun," which was first produced at Wallack's Theatre, November 14, 1874, the playwright himself acting Con.

We have now reached the period of the uptown trend in the building of theatres, a movement with which the Wallacks had much to do. Having abandoned the playhouse on Broadway near Broome Street, which had formerly been Brougham's Lyceum, they built, in 1861, the second Wallack's Theatre at Broadway and Thirteenth Street; here for twenty years the best old and modern English comedies were presented. The star of this theatre was handsome Lester Wallack, and in his company, from time to time, were John Gilbert, John Brougham, Henry J. Montague, Dion Boucicault, the second Charles Mathews (who was willing temporarily to cease being a "star" for the sake of playing at Wallack's), Fanny Morant, Madame Ponisi, and Rose Coghlan — to mention only a few of the most familiar names. At Wallack's Theatre on Broadway and Thirtieth Street, built under the auspices of Lester Wallack and opened January 4, 1882, with the "School for Scandal," the splendid traditions of the earlier theatre were for a time perpetuated. Then the managerial genius of Augustin Daly began to assert itself in a rival house,

[1] Dion Boucicault, dramatist and actor, was born at Dublin, December 26, 1822, was educated at University College, London, and died in New York, September 18, 1890. "Arrah-na-Pogue" (1864), "Flying Scud" (1866), "Formosa" (1869), and "The Jilt" (1886) were, with "London Assurance" — in which he collaborated with John Brougham — among the best known of his plays, besides those to which reference has already been made in this book.

and this, added to the fact that Wallack's had definitely lowered its artistic standards, brought it about that "what is pretentiously called the leading American theatre is not an American theatre at all . . . but a cheap copy of an English theatre from the stage of which American writers and plays are rigorously excluded." [1]

Augustin Daly, who did more than any other American of his generation to maintain the dignity of the stage and to make its possibilities and purposes manifest, first emerged from journalism in 1864, when his "Lorlie's Wedding," an adaptation from the German, was produced in the Winter Garden Theatre. Other translations and adaptations marked these juvenile days, but his individual powers as a playwright were first revealed in the strong and ingenious melodrama "Under the Gaslight," notable for its stagecraft and its vivid character drawing. From some points of view this play was pretty poor stuff, but it helped its writer to find himself, and when the Fifth Avenue Theatre fell into his hands in 1869, he was ready to regale New York with such a balanced menu of classic and poetic comedy, romance and French social drama, as could be enjoyed at no other playhouse in the city. Every detail of a production — the acting, the setting, the music, the costumes, and the lighting — were under Mr. Daly's personal direction, and it thus came about that his

[1] L. Clarke Davis in *Lippincott's Magazine* for October, 1883. Point was given to this criticism by the fact that Mrs. Langtry had made her début at Wallack's November 6, 1882, playing "An Unequal Match" and supported by her own English company.

William Gilbert   Charles Leclerq   John Drew   May Fielding
John Moore   Mrs. Gilbert   Ada Rehan   Virginia Dreher
James Lewis   George Parkes   Augustin Daly   Charles Fisher

THE DALY COMPANY IN 1884

JAMES A. HERNE IN HIS OWN "MARGARET FLEMING"
See page 484

JAMES H. HACKETT AS COLONEL NIMROD WILDFIRE
See page 481

theatre, by day as well as by night, was the most wonderful school of dramatic art in the country.

How a man so burdened with the details of theatrical management could find time to turn out plays as often as Daly did, was a profound mystery. His "Under the Gaslight," "Article 47" (written for Clara Morris), and "Pique" (for Fanny Davenport) were some of his successful original works, while from the German and the French he made adaptations without number. No branch of theatrical activity, indeed, was alien to the dynamic brain and broad human sympathy of Augustin Daly, and every player who ever had the luck to be associated with him looks back to the experience with a heart full of gratitude. To the early period of Mr. Daly's managerial activities belong Agnes Ethel, for whom he adapted "Frou-Frou," Clara Morris, Fanny Davenport, Kate Claxton, Linda Dietz, Sara Jewett, Mrs. G. H. Gilbert, James Lewis, George Clarke, George Holland, Louis James, Mrs. Scott-Siddons, Mrs. Jennings, E. L. Davenport, and Charles Mathews. By 1880, Ada Rehan and John Drew had been added to the company, and a theatre bearing its manager's name opened on Broadway, near Thirty-first Street. Miss Rehan was now the central figure in the brilliant stock company, having served a valuable apprenticeship as a member of Mrs. John Drew's company at the Arch Street Theatre, Philadelphia.[1]

Ada Rehan was essentially a comedian, but one of the

---

[1] It was the printer here, who, by a typographical error, caused her to be called Rehan; her real name was Crehan.

great successes of her career was as the strong yet tender
Kate Verity in "The Squire," a piece filched in large
part from Hardy's novel, "Far from the Madding
Crowd," · Clarke Davis has declared that some of the
noblest acting he ever saw occurred in the two scenes
of this play which Miss Rehan shared with Charles
Fisher,[1] that gifted comedian of an earlier generation
who had been one of the props of the Wallack theatres,
and whose Dandy Dinmont divided with Meg Merrilies
the honours of Miss Cushman's greatest performance.
The whimsical, quaint humour of James Lewis and the
dry, crab-apple humour of Charles Leclerq [1] were also
seen to very good advantage in this play.   The tragic
foil to Miss Rehan, in the Daly company, was Miss
Virginia Dreher, while John Drew was uniformly clever
and capable then as now — especially so, perhaps, when
playing *vis-à-vis* with Miss Rehan.   Mrs. Gilbert, who
had begun her career as a dancer, was another valuable
member of the Daly company.   She came to it first
in 1867 and so was able, for many years, to present the
antiquated dames or fine old women of legitimate comedy
in the impressive manner made famous before her time
by Mrs. Vernon and Mrs. John Drew.

It was, of course, a very great advantage which this
theatre enjoyed in being managed by a gentleman who
was his own playwright.   When Shakespeare or the old

[1] Charles Fisher and Charles Leclerq were both brothers of distinguished actresses.   Leclerq's sister supported Fechter during his earlier
seasons in America, and Fisher's sister was the celebrated Clara, about
whom the gilded youth of the period raved long and loud, and after
whom everything, from cakes to omnibuses, was named.

English comedies were not holding the stage, farces were put on which Mr. Daly had himself cleverly adapted from the German. For ingenuity, variety, and unflagging fun there never were such farces, and as given by James Lewis and Mrs. Gilbert, by John Drew and Miss Ada Rehan,[1] by Otis Skinner and Miss Dreher, they kept their public laughing night after night and so contributed greatly to the success and prestige of their gifted author. Moreover, the manager could recoup by means of a German farce the enormous expense sustained in putting on Shakespeare and the old comedies in lavish style.

Beginning with 1884, Mr. Daly took his company to England every second year for some time, and though London, as might have been expected, did not show itself very enthusiastic over the German-American farces, the critics could not find the adjectives to praise adequately the "Taming of the Shrew" as these players presented it, beautifully set with charming scenery, with appropriate dresses and grouping, with the Induction retained and with good musical effects. Ada Rehan was pronounced "the only really adequate Katharine seen upon the stage in the memory of middle-aged enthusiasts."

[1] Ada Rehan was born in Ireland in 1860, educated in Brooklyn, New York, and made her first appearance on any stage at Newark, New Jersey. But her first *opportunity* came when she was with Mrs. John Drew's stock company at the Arch Street Theatre, Philadelphia, which she joined in 1875. Daly first engaged her to do a small part in his adaptation of "L'Assommoir" (produced at Mrs. John Wood's Olympic) and she remained a member of the Daly company until the manager's death in 1899, her humour, high spirits and charm enabling her to make a pronounced success in the nearly two hundred parts she essayed during this period.

When Augustin Daly died, in 1899, American drama, scarcely less than the men and women intimately connected with Daly's Theatre, sustained an almost irremediable loss. For Daly knew the literature of the theatre and had collected one of the finest dramatic libraries in America, as well as many articles of great interest to theatregoers. Garrick's writing desk, which he also used for a make-up table, and the scales, bond, and knife employed by Kean in "Merchant of Venice" were among the treasures of his wonderful collection.[1]

After Daly's death, Daniel Frohman acquired the lease of his theatre and sustained for several years the prestige of the Daly stock company; but the day of "regular stock" was now over. For many years there had been reproduced at this theatre the methods and standards of the Comédie Français; but the end had to come.

The old order, indeed, had already begun to change when, in 1886, Daniel Frohman organized his Lyceum Theatre stock company and proceeded to make theatrical history at the little playhouse on Fourth Avenue and Twenty-third Street. This theatre was the inspiration of Steele MacKaye, and the first play put on was "Dakolar" with Robert Mantell, John Mason, and Viola Allen in the cast. Miss Helen Dauvray was a manager for a short time during these early years, and David Belasco served as stage manager.

How Belasco grew from this beginning to his present

[1] The Kean relics are now in the possession of Harvard University, cherished items of the Theatre Collection in the Widener Library.

position of great influence on the American stage has been so well told by Montrose Moses in his book, "The American Dramatist"[1] that I need not do more here than outline briefly this man's very interesting career. Belasco's father, of English-Portuguese-Jewish stock, was a harlequin in a London theatre but came to America in response to the lure of the gold discovery in California and settled in San Francisco. Here, in 1859, David was born. The lad was educated in a monastery and, perhaps as a result, has all his life affected a kind of clerical attire which, with his handsome face and now white hair, gives him a very striking appearance. Young Belasco wrote his first play when only twelve and his initial appearance as an actor was in 1871 at the California Theatre. Then followed years of barnstorming in California and in Nevada, where he met Dion Boucicault, from whom he learned much about the art of play-writing. Thus varied experience as house playwright, actor and manager had all been Belasco's before he made his first appearance in New York in 1880. His career since then as playwright and as a leader of stagecraft has been one of almost continuous success.[2] But in all this he owes much to the early opportunity given him by Daniel Frohman,

[1] "The American Dramatist," Little, Brown, & Co., Boston. Because this book very admirably presents the history of native drama in America, I have touched very lightly on this subject.

[2] Belasco's first important production came in 1895 when he starred Mrs. Leslie Carter in "The Heart of Maryland." The piece and the players made an enormous success and, after three years in this country, Mrs. Carter went to London, where she appeared at the Adelphi and was presented to King Edward VII. Blanche Bates, Henrietta Crossman, David Warfield, Frances Starr, Ina Claire and Fay Bainter are other stars for whom Belasco achieved success.

himself an interesting member of a most interesting family.

Henry Frohman, father of Daniel, Gustave and Charles, all of whom have played a big part in American stage history, came to this country from Germany and began life here as a peddler, finally settling in Sandusky, Ohio, where he opened a small cigar factory. He had always aspired to be an actor, and one of the first things he did in his new home was to organize an amateur theatrical company whose members were, like himself, of German birth or descent. This little company gave performances, in the original, of Schiller and other classical German dramatists, and as the Frohman cigar business grew and its head built up trade in the adjoining countryside, he was wont to rehearse his own amateur parts while driving along in his buggy with a load of samples strapped on behind, one of his sons, whom he had taken along with him for company, serving as prompter.[1]

Sandusky soon proved too small for these boys. Gustave, when still quite young, achieved a theatrical connection in New York; after serving an apprenticeship selling "Books of the Opera" at the old Academy of Music on Fourteenth Street, and souvenir books of "The Black Crook," then having its sensational run at Niblo's Garden, he became advance man for a minstrel show. Next Daniel [2] broke into the theatrical business by way of

[1] "Charles Frohman, Manager and Man," by Isaac F. Marcosson and Daniel Frohman, published by Harper & Brothers.
[2] When the Frohman home was removed to New York and Father Frohman set up a cigar store at what was then Number 708 Broadway,

journalism (his first New York job was in the circulation department of the *Tribune*), and in due time Charles, destined to be the most successful of the brothers, was also launched on a theatrical career, begun by selling tickets in the box office of Hooley's Theatre in Brooklyn.

Charles Frohman proved himself to be a veritable genius as a producer, a theatrical promoter, and an inspirer of budding American dramatists. Clyde Fitch is commonly accorded first place among the playwrights whom he stimulated to success (though, unfortunately, he imposed his own mental limitations on Fitch!); and Maude Adams is usually conceded to be the most distinguished of his native stars.

Maude Adams was born November 11, 1872, in Salt Lake City, where her mother was leading woman of a stock company, and first appeared on the stage in children's parts. At sixteen, she played with E. H. Sothern in New York. Subsequently she was leading lady in various companies and supported John Drew for five years. Her career as a "star" began in 1897 when she achieved very great success as Lady Babbie in "The Little Minister," the author himself having chosen her for this part. She also created the rôle of Peter Pan in Barrie's play of that name, so becoming not only the most successful but the most beloved American actress

the boys made the acquaintance of many theatrical personages because Number 708 Broadway was almost in the heart of the theatrical district and Tony Pastor and other well-known stage lights of the time used to come to this shop to buy cigars. Moreover, since the Frohman store had a large window in which the playbills of the day could be displayed in exchange for tickets, the whole family had free access to all the theatres.

known to playgoers of our day. Her elfish charm particularly lent itself to Barrie's parts.

It was, however, "Joan of Arc," which Frohman staged at the Harvard Stadium, June 22, 1909, which marked the crowning artistic success of Miss Adams's career. The text used was Schiller's "Jüngfrau von Orleans," the music Beethoven's "Eroica." No one of the fifteen thousand persons present that night will ever forget the beauty of the production, with the haunting melody of the sheep's bells as the Maid's flock wandered about the huge stage, nibbling at the grass which, with a proper regard for realism, had been grown especially for them, the exquisite lighting, and above all the superb acting of Maude Adams. This performance netted fifteen thousand dollars for the building fund of the Germanic Museum at Harvard University, and Charles Frohman, having had a complete photographic record made of the production (which had attracted great attention in Germany), saw to it that the resulting volume was magnificently bound in vellum and presented to the German Kaiser. The unconscious irony of all this is very striking in view of the fact that it was the Germans who were responsible for Frohman's death, May 7, 1915, on the ill-fated *Lusitania*.

It is extraordinary that a man who had made so much money for other people and often, too, for himself, fairly earning by his boldness and enterprise the nickname of "Napoleon of the Drama," should have died a poor man. But this was because Charles Frohman experienced great business losses as well as great successes. In the

Photo. Sarony, New York

MAUDE ADAMS

Photo. Sands, Providence, R. I.

E. H. SOTHERN AS HAMLET

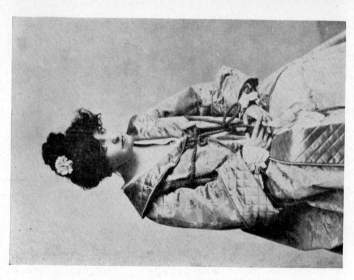

MINNIE MADDERN FISKE AS BECKY SHARP

fascinating book about his career, written after his death, some of the risks he took as well as the personality which lay behind his work are vividly pictured. He wove a great deal of himself into the character of his "stars," we there read. In other words, the personal element counted enormously in the friendly relations which made all the men and women he managed feel that he was much more than their manager. As Sir James Barrie has put it: "He regarded his women stars as his children. If they were playing in New York they were expected to call on him and talk personalities three or four times a week. On the road they sent him daily a telegram; these were placed on his desk every morning and were dealt with in person before any other business of the day." [1]

Sir Henry Irving once sent Frohman a message that he wished to be under his management in America "because Frohman always understands; he is always fair." Apparently this manager who so loved the theatre that he made it the first interest of his life attracted and held the right kind of stars because, as he himself put it, "my ambition frankly centers in the welfare of my actors. The day's work holds out to me no finer gratification than to see intelligent, earnest, deserving actors go into the fame and fortune of being stars."

The element of chance in star-making always fascinated Charles Frohman and he was keen for the adventure. He met his last, and the greatest, adventure of

[1] "Charles Frohman, Manager and Man," by Isaac F. Marcosson and Daniel Frohman. Harper & Brothers.

them all with the same courage that had characterized him throughout life.

E. H. Sothern was one of the "stars" developed by Daniel Frohman, the play through which this talented actor first came to public notice being "The Highest Bidder." One factor used in bringing immense audiences to this attraction, night after night, was sensational publicity of a kind then new to America. A messenger boy was sent to Europe to deliver addressed souvenirs of the play to all the leading actors over there, and a member of the company, who was a strong swimmer, appeared alongside an ocean liner, near the Atlantic Highlands, and astonished the officer in charge by answering to the inquiry if he wanted a life-preserver, "I only want to know if the passengers on this boat have seen 'The Highest Bidder.'"

Richard Mansfield [1] and Mrs. Fiske (then Minnie Maddern) were also among the gifted artists whose development Daniel Frohman advanced notably back in the middle eighties.

Minnie Maddern Fiske, born in New Orleans in 1865 of parents who were both players, has contributed more than any other American woman still on the stage to the prestige of the American theatre. She was prac-

[1] Richard Mansfield was born in the island of Heligoland, May 24, 1857, and was educated in the University of Jena. He was prepared for the East India civil service, but came to this country with his mother, Madame Rudersdorff, a famous teacher of singing, and opened a studio in Boston. Returning to England he studied art, but later chose the theatrical profession. In his time — he died in 1907 — he played many parts, none better than the dual leading character of "Dr. Jekyl and Mr. Hyde." He is especially well remembered as the poet-hero in Rostand's "Cyrano de Bergerac."

tically brought up on the stage, her début having occurred as the Duke of York in "Richard III" when she was only three. Various child rôles followed, but in 1892, when sixteen, she developed that sprightly and arch quality which has always distinguished her acting. It was not until her reappearance on the stage in 1894, however (after temporary retirement following her marriage in 1890 to Harrison Grey Fiske), that there was to be noted in her work what William Winter has described as "impetuous volubility commingled with intensity of repressed emotions." She now became the exponent of the Ibsen drama, then made an enormous impression as Tess in "Tess of the D'Urbervilles" (1897) and, two years later, followed up the Hardy rôle with her extraordinary characterization of Thackeray's heroine, Becky Sharp. In these early successes Mrs. Fiske was strongly supported by George Arliss, the English character actor, whose "Disraeli" has since been greatly enjoyed and whose work in Galsworthy's "Old English," during the past winter, has added notably to a growing reputation.

Critics have always differed violently as to Mrs. Fiske's rank as an actress. Alexander Woollcott is on record in the New York *Tribune* to the effect that she has "instinctively and surely identified herself with the best in the theatres of Europe and America," and has placed her characters "among the unforgetable things alongside of Ada Rehan's 'Katherine' and the Hamlet of Forbes-Robertson!" On the other hand, John Ranken Towse declares that "in all her 'creations' she presents her own identity without any substantial modification

or special gesture, look or manner. The deeper notes of
passion she could not sound and her pathos was hard
and hollow without the true ring." [1] My own feeling is
that while Towse is quite right in declaring, as he goes
on to do in this same critique, that Mrs. Fiske's elocution . . . is faulty and does not "lend itself readily to
emotional expression," he is wrong in denying her great
power in deeply passionate scenes. None the less she
is happiest in light comedy which has a little bite in it,
and her Becky Sharp will, I think, be remembered when
all her other parts are forgotten.

Several English dramatists of nineteenth century note
were brought prominently to the attention of the American public by Daniel Frohman, among them Pinero
and Henry Arthur Jones, R. C. Carton and Anthony
Hope. "The Second Mrs. Tanqueray," which Ethel
Barrymore has latterly revived with considerable success, was regarded in 1887, it is interesting to note, as
meat too strong for anything except afternoon audiences. [2]
"Sweet Lavender," "Lady Bountiful," and "The Amazons" were more nearly the kind of thing regular theatre-
goers in New York then desired.

Albert M. Palmer was another New York manager
who contributed notably to theatrical history in New

[1] "Sixty Years of the Theatre," by John Ranken Towse. Funk and
Wagnalls Company.
[2] To be sure it was eventually given a regular New York production
by Madge Robertson Kendal. Daniel Frohman, who had a hand in
this matter, tells us that because Mrs. Kendal had previously been widely
known as the "British matron" of the drama — by reason of the purity
of her domestic life — she was greatly criticized in the New York press
for undertaking a rôle so at variance with her career as a woman and an
actress.

York,[1] not only through the Union Square Theatre, opened on East Fourteenth Street, September 11, 1871, but also through the playhouse at Madison Square. The original intention was to make the Union Square a variety theatre, and during its initial year it was run on that basis. Thus it was that the Vokes family here appeared for the first time in America,[2] and so helped establish "vaudeville" in this country. This family was made up of English specialty performers, and Rosina was its most gifted member. Their "vehicle" at the Union Square was a farcical absurdity entitled "Belles of the Kitchen," in which singing, dancing, pantomime and burlesque acting all had a place. They were followed by a swarm of imitators who made possible on the legitimate stage the kind of thing which had previously been confined to the variety theatres — not then considered a proper place for ladies to attend. But some ladies found this new species of entertainment attractive, and so, of course, there arose managers who were glad to provide them with it.

Palmer's other theatre — the Madison Square — opened on February 4, 1880, with "Hazel Kirke" by James Steele MacKaye — also played an important part in the theatrical history of New York. The Rev. G. S. Mallory and Marshall Mallory were the business backers of this house, finding financial relationship with the drama

[1] Space limitations make it impossible to treat this branch of the subject adequately. T. Allston Brown has devoted three huge tomes to the history of the New York stage and then brought his chronicle only as far as 1903.

[2] The exact date of their American début was April 15, 1872.

477

not at all incompatible with the publishing of the *Churchman*. When A. M. Palmer assumed control, in 1884, however, there was no more of the "milk and water" drama with which the Madison Square had previously been associated. Instead, "The Private Secretary" was almost immediately produced and ran more than one hundred and fifty nights. T. Allston Brown comments that this was "a screaming farce with a low comedy clergyman as the hero" and seems to wonder that Dr. Mallory offered no protest to it. The fact, however, that Gillette[1] showed himself able in this play to write a farce which did not sacrifice the essential qualities of humanity — and that the public took heartily to such a farce — seems to me quite as noteworthy as that a clergyman failed to protest because mild fun was here poked at another clergyman. Two fetishes were now demolished at one blow: first, that "the cloth" is sacrosanct; second, that a piece needs to be grossly overdrawn and de-humanized in order to be thoroughly amusing. Later, this house was intimately associated with farce that had little or nothing except ridiculous situations to make it theatrically effective; for, in 1891, Charles Hoyt became one of its lessees and so was able to produce "A Trip to Chinatown," "A

[1] William Gillette was born in Hartford, Connecticut, in 1855, his father being the United States Senator from Connecticut, and received a good academic education. His first stage experience was at the Globe Theatre in Boston. It was in 1880 that he turned his attention to play-writing and on June 1, 1881, that he made his début in New York in the dual rôle of actor and dramatist, taking the part of Professor Hopkins in his own play "The Professor." Since then he has appeared in his own pieces almost exclusively ("Held by the Enemy," "Secret Service," "Sherlock Holmes") though he has also been successful latterly in two plays written by Sir James M. Barrie, "The Admirable Crichton" and "Dear Brutus."

478

Temperance Town," "A Texas Steer," and various other Hoyt perpetrations.

Steele MacKaye, Bronson Howard,[1] William Gillette, and Charles Hoyt were all *American* playwrights, however, and were now giving *American* types of character to our stage.[2] In an analysis of the plays presented in New York between 1884–1888 — when Wallack's, Daly's, the Madison Square, and the Lyceum were all equipped with permanent companies playing serious drama — it was observed that every one of the enduring successes were plays of American character. The Jonathan in Royall Tyler's "Contrast" had been succeeded by Hackett's Colonel Nimrod Wildfire, Chanfrau's Mose, Jefferson's Rip Van Winkle, Frank Mayo's Davy Crockett, Florence's Judge Slote, and the Joshua Whitcomb of Denman Thompson — characters true, in each instance, to certain phases of American life.

To James H. Hackett credit appears due for placing on our stage a character which, to the American theatre, supplied the place occupied in English comedy by the Yorkshire clown. This was his conception of a "down-east" Yankee, Solomon Swap, and may well stand at the head of parts generally described as those of the "Yankee type." Francis Courtney Wemyss was ap-

[1] Bronson Howard's "The Young Mrs. Winthrop," first produced at the Madison Square Theatre, October 9, 1892, ran for more than one hundred and fifty nights.
[2] Irish-American types were being set forth at the so-called Theatre Comique managed by Harrigan and Hart and devoted exclusively to the reproduction of scenes of New York life, as lived by amusing types of local characters. Here it was that the adventures and misadventures of the Mulligan Guards were originally presented.

parently of the opinion that Hackett owed something for this character to Colman's play "Who Wants a Guinea?" For with the comment "set a thief to catch a thief," he gives in his book, "The Life of an Actor and Manager," the following letter of indignation sent to him by Hackett:

"Philadelphia 5th November 1833
"My dear Wemyss:
"During my absence in England, *Mr. Hill* has had the impudence, as well as injustice, to perform, without my permission, my best Yankee character, Solomon Swap (well known as unpublished, and of my own originating) at the Park (some dozen times) and elsewhere. I have, of course, a remedy at law against him and the managers who permit it, but a resort to it would be looked upon, perhaps, by the public (who don't understand these matters) as a kind of ill nature on my part, and beneath me; and therefore to prevent my property being thus further hacknied, after being taken down from my mouth, or otherwise surreptitiously obtained, I have notified managers generally of the fact, and shall consider their permitting such an infringement of the most unalienable of literary rights (the spinning of one's own brains), an act of open hostility to me, and proceed accordingly. Mr. Hill has characters enough of his own without carrying on that species of Yankeeism; and if I cannot protect myself from having my character made stale by such depredations, I will resort to rigorous measures against both him and managers wherever the infringment transpires.

"Of course, I do not fear *your* countenancing such dishonesty, but I thought I would drop you a line, as you might be ignorant of the fact of Solomon Swap being, in every respect, my own exclusive property. I have stopped him in Boston, New York, and here, but understand that he has been trying it in Albany; and though he will not attempt it again there, if I can catch him in New York, where I am returning tomorrow, I must clap 'Grace' upon him, for example's sake.

"Wishing you all success and hoping to have a chance with you next season, I remain

"Yours truly
"Jas. H. Hackett

"N.B. I shall esteem it a personal mark of friendship, if you will inform me of any attempt at keeping up this Yankee piracy coming to your knowledge in the course of Mr. Hill's projected peregrinations in the West, this winter.

"J. H. H.

"What a farago of nonsense."

Hackett may well have cherished whatever rights he had [1] in plays of the Yankee type, for such plays have been immensely popular ever since the far-away days when Royall Tyler made a Yankee the outstanding character in "The Contrast," America's first comedy. Hackett's Jonathan Ploughboy and Lot Sap Sago were other rôles that endeared him to audiences everywhere, and he had already made a great success as Colonel Nimrod Wildfire in "The Lion of the West," a drama of

---

[1] Joe Cowell, who was a rather shrewd observer, describes Hackett as starting in business "with a very small lot of goods but their variety was suitable to many markets and with great tact and shrewdness he made everybody believe that they could not be obtained at any other shop . . . Who but Hackett would have thought of using Colman's excellent but seldom acted play 'Who Wants a Guinea?' as a vehicle for introducing such a sketch of humanity as Solomon Swap; and although whittling a stick and cheating a man out of a watch are not very complimentary characteristics to select for a Yankee portrait, they were highly relished by the audience."

frontier life in this country which James Kirke Paulding had written especially for him.

Wildfire, afterward put into a drama called "The Kentuckian" by Bayle Bernard, wore buckskin clothes, deerskin shoes and a coonskin hat, and he represented to city-bred lads their idea of "the real thing" from the great open spaces right up to the day that Buffalo Bill came along with actual cowboys and bona fide Indians. From Paulding's life, written by his son, we learn that when Hackett took "the Colonel" to England in 1833 it made an enormous success at Covent Garden and again at the Haymarket Theatre, the play of which this character was a part being then called "A Kentuckian's Trip to New York in 1815."

It was the character of Nimrod Wildfire in this prize play, written especially for Hackett, which carried the piece into fame. At the end of the play the colonel introduces his intended wife, Miss Patty Snap of Salt Licks, in this fashion, "There is no back-out in her breed for she can lick her weight in wild cats and she shot a bear at nine years old." London had an enthusiastic response for Hackett in such a part, as did also America.

For, outside of the classics, your old-time actor courted a really bad play, for the chance it gave him through eccentricity in acting to vivify his rôle with characterization. Thus it was that Mose, the tough fire-boy, in "A Glance at New York," provided a marvelous vehicle in the far-famed forties for F. S. Chanfrau. Volunteer fire companies were well-known institutions in those days, and by blending in the play, as the fire-boy did in

DENMAN THOMPSON AS JOSHUA WHITCOMB IN "THE OLD HOMESTEAD"
See page 484

RICHARD MANSFIELD AS CYRANO DE BERGERAC
See page 474

real life, social and political forces with the job of putting out a fire, there came a chance for scenes of most extraordinary appeal. One of these introduced a visit to a "Ladies Bowling Club" where presumably respectable women were seen dressed in male attire, smoking large cigars! Yet another "Glance at New York" spread before us the "loafers' retreat," a bar and lodging house of the lowest kind where Mose is given a priceless opportunity to fight and a fire scene is introduced for the express purpose of providing the hero with a chance to drag a hose across the stage. The appearance of Mose, as Chanfrau played him, in the red shirt, plug hat, and turned-up trousers of the fireman, was always a signal for a wild ovation.

Tame enough by comparison with this, though unquestionably to be included in any grouping of plays having to do with the distinctively American type in drama, was Jefferson's "Asa Trenchard," the rough, kind-hearted Yankee who afforded so sharp a contrast to Sothern's "Lord Dundreary" in Tom Taylor's "Our American Cousin." It was at about this same period that the amusing character of Colonel Mulberry Sellers, that stage American from the Southern States, which "Mark Twain," John T. Raymond, and Dudley Warner jointly endowed with life for us, came into being. And at least mention must be made of W. J. Florence as the Honorable Bardwell Slote, in Benjamin E. Woolf's "The Mighty Dollar," Slote, with all the vices of the vulgar politician, yet with the amiable qualities too, which some of us know to-day as an intrinsic part of the private character of many a public official not otherwise admirable.

These examples of the Yankee type on our stage lead us straight on to Denman Thompson as Joshua Whitcomb in "The Old Homestead" and to James A. Herne as Joe Fletcher in his own "Margaret Fleming."

America, being the native land of the Indian, we have, naturally, suffered a good deal from the Indian type of play. Of "Tammany," written by the sister of Mrs. Siddons, mention has already been made, though since this lady was not an American, precedence here should be given perhaps to "The Indian Princess," a work musical in its character, of which James N. Barker of Philadelphia was the author, and which was produced at the Park Theatre, New York, June 14, 1808. Several other successful plays, written around this theme, as well as John Brougham's clever burlesque, "Pocahontas," also utilized Indian life as a leading motive. The most noteworthy production of this kind was undoubtedly "Metamora," a prize drama for which Forrest paid its author, John Augustus Stone, five hundred dollars — considerable money in those days — and which the leading American tragedian long kept in his repertoire.

Another American subject, the Revolution, has furnished material for the playwright from the days of "Bunker Hill; or the death of General Warren" (written by an Irishman, John D. Burke, and played at the theatre on John Street, September 8, 1779), to the "Major André" and "Nathan Hale" written by the late Clyde Fitch. Our Civil War has also inspired several dramatists, although the most successful play written around this subject, John Drinkwater's "Abraham Lincoln," is the product of an English, not of an American, playwright. Boucicault's "Belle Lamar, An Episode of the Late American Conflict," written for John E. McCullough and first produced at Booth's Theatre, New York, August 10, 1874, was one of the least successful of the many plays turned out by the prolific Irishman.

The opportunities presented to the playwright by the frontier life of the west were first realized clearly by Augustin Daly, who, in 1871, brought out at the Olympic Theatre "Horizon," a piece suggestive of Bret Harte at his worst, or of Nick Carter at his best. A much more artistic piece of work was the "Davy Crockett" of Frank Murdock, as played by Frank Mayo. Lawrence Hutton has called this drama of an American Lochinvar — who, because he is brave, strong, and capable of sacrifice, wins the deep love of a young woman much his superior in station and education — "almost the best American play ever written." This dictum preceded, however, Mayo's own dramatization of Mark Twain's "Pudd'nhead Wilson," a piece which, as Mr. Mayo played it, was entirely worthy to be classed with "The Old Homestead," "Alabama," "Kit, the Arkansas Traveller," and "M'liss," [1] as real American plays of wide-reaching appeal.

Thus it will be seen that Dion Boucicault was treat-

[1] It was in this piece that Annie Pixley made her New York début, March 22, 1880.

485

ing the exact truth with characteristic carelessness when, in 1890, he declared of the American stage that it could best be described, in Hamlet's lines, as "an unweeded garden that grows to seed — things rank and gross in nature possess it merely."

To take a gloomy tone concerning the theatre in America seems, however, to have been a kind of habit with us ever since we began to have a theatre. In a country so cosmopolitan and heterogeneous as this one we must necessarily have many different kinds of plays, for the simple reason that we have many different kinds of public, but the critic with cultivated tastes usually shuts his eyes to this fact, and, focussing his attention on some one of the fifty-seven varieties of "Follies," proceeds to declare that the theatre is hopelessly bad. Thus the *Dial* of Chicago asserted in 1905 that the drama in America was "little more than a low form of stage-craft," whereas, in every continental country, the theatre was being regarded as a vital mode of expression and was enlisting in its service the most penetrating intellects and the highest creative ability. On the continent, it was pointed out, the stage "shrank from the envisagment of no serious relation."

England shared America's disgrace in the eyes of the *Dial's* essayist, for Phillips, Pinero, and Jones were the best men that country could then show, even as Augustus Thomas and Clyde Fitch — whose concern was still with the trivial and the superficial only — then headed our own short list of dramatists. Things are considerably better with us now, our new dramatists

486

EUGENE O'NEILL
See page 491

ETHEL BARRYMORE
From the portrait by Frances Houston
See page 493

being men and women who deal so earnestly with important contemporary aspects of human life and human thought that their work is being printed as well as played, and played as well as printed! Our commercial showmen have come to see that the public intelligence and public capacity have too long been underestimated.

Playwrights are asserting, and the play-going public is glad to concede, that social movements and social ideals have a claim to dramatic representation. A vast number of Americans to-day are in earnest about life, and playwrights who appeal to our social interests and who, by skilful dramaturgic presentation of a "Vision," help us to see clearly the things we have been puzzled about, are assured of immediate success.

At last, too, we seem to have concluded that the problems of the plain people are worthy of dramatic treatment. Molière and Shakespeare were always thinking, as they wrote, of the plain people who were to constitute the bulk of their audiences. And the God who demonstrated His love of the plain people by making so many of them — and who has always blessed with immortality the work of authors able to pass on to succeeding generations the hopes and fears of the plain people of their day — shows Himself consistently gracious to social-minded playwrights of our own time. Of course contemporary critics are often very slow to acclaim the merits of men and women who paint the thing as they see it for the God of things as they are; apparently many of them are as shocked at a drama which is not primarily "literary" as was M. Jourdain when he made the appalling discovery that he had all his life been talking "prose." In the field of the novel we came long ago to accept realism as a valuable contribution to our understanding of life. On the stage, however, fustian and bombast still lingered; it was expected that, at the theatre, triviality and improbability should prevail. Otherwise no intelligent person could have read such a novel as "The Ordeal of Richard Feverel" in the afternoon, and sat through a play like "Rosedale" in the evening.[1] But at the time that "Rosedale" was written, it was not thought necessary that any dramatist, except Shakespeare, should deal with the eternal verities. When Shakespeare was not being played, the theatre was regarded as a pleasant place in which to "have a good time." Conflict, even sentimental heartache there might be, briefly, but it must all "come out right"; the day of the "Doll's House"[2] was not yet. To-day, however, we demand that our plays shall, above all else, tell us the truth; the successful comedy of manners must be a comedy of morals as well.

That the consummation of the "intimate" theatre has had a great deal to do with the multiplication of plays whose appeal is direct and forceful, there can be no doubt. The plays of Shakespeare, as we all know,

[1] For this penetrating observation, and for much that is helpful and suggestive in regard to our developing dramatic intelligence, I am indebted to Clayton Hamilton's article in the *Bookman* of June, 1913.

[2] The production of Ibsen's "Doll's House" in London, in 1889, has been characterized by G. B. Shaw as a knockout blow to the British drama of the eighties. Not that the public liked Ibsen, but that, after Ibsen, no modern manager could be expected to have courage enough to give Byron or Tom Taylor or Sardou.

were frequently performed in buildings open to the sky, with only the crudest of scenery. The pieces of Molière, on the other hand, were given by candlelight in a closed hall, so making scenery possible. By the time of Sheridan there were theatres much like ours externally, but huge in size, badly lighted with oil lamps which smelled to heaven, and having a stage which projected far beyond the proscenium arch. On this space beyond the curtain and close to the flickering footlights it was necessary to act those vital episodes which require a sight of the actor's face to be understood. Consequently, these episodes occurred but rarely; only one, indeed, was considered essential to every play — that which committed the heroine to the hero's embrace as the final curtain fell. One very important step in the history of the American Theatre was the introduction of gas in the playhouse.

Something could now be done in the way of creating real illusion on the stage. Wemyss records that credit for this step should be given to Madame Vestris (Mrs. Charles Mathews) and that "to her the American theatres are indebted for the improvement so apparent in the arrangement of the stage; carpets, ottomans, grates, fenders, center tables, etc. in the drawing-room; gravel walks, beds of flowers, hot-house plants in gardens, all were her work."

Not very long after it had become possible, by means of gas, to give to a play all the light necessary to make its action completely visible to the audience, another step scarcely less important was made feasible. This

was such use of electricity as enabled the playwright
to create atmospheric effects on the stage. Who can
forget the impressiveness of James Herne's final "cur-
tains?" Which of us failed to respond to the true
psychology of that utter darkness which marked the
confession episode in "The Climbers?"

When realism had done all that it could for us and
electricity had made the ultimate possible in the way of
atmospheric effects the time was ripe for a revolt against
realism and for the emergence of the new stagecraft.

It is interesting that we owe to Ellen Terry's son,
Gordon Craig, the most revolutionary ideas that have
come to our theatre since Ibsen. From 1889 to 1896
Craig was content to play in the company of his mother
and Henry Irving. Then leaving the actor's profession,
he turned to the study of stage management and has
since contributed notably to the new stagecraft, for which
Adolphe Appia and Max Reinhardt have done so much
in Germany, which Jacques Copeau valiantly pushed
forward in Paris, which Stanislavsky has steadily fos-
tered, through the years, in the Moscow Art Theatre,
and to which Norman-Bel Geddes,[1] Lee Simonson,
Robert Edmond Jones,[2] and others, have made notable
contributions in America.

[1] Francis Wilson, commenting on "the new stagecraft" and fully
realizing its value, too, in that Norman-Bel Geddes made the beautiful
set for Wilson's famous "Erminie" production, declares, *not wholly in
fun*, that some people fear in this new movement the substitution of
scenery for drama!

[2] Jones as designer, no less than O'Neill as author, owes much to Arthur
Hopkins, "a manager with ideas," whose own career has been full of
color and variety. Born in Cleveland of Welsh blood, after the briefest
of schoolings, Hopkins met the world as a newspaper reporter and vaude-

WALTER HAMPDEN AS HAMLET
Declared by many critics to be the best Hamlet of this generation

See page 493

To my friend John Barrymore
John S. Sargent 1923

JOHN BARRYMORE AS HAMLET
From John S. Sargent's sketch made during Christmas week, 1923, while Barrymore was
playing in Boston
See page 493

The Romance of the American Theatre

The important thing for us about the new stagecraft is that it is developing a new type of drama, aided and reinforced by the new theatre.[1] Eugene O'Neill and his co-workers, having abandoned the limitations of a photographic realism, which would tend to make them mere limitators of life, are pushing on to the task of *illuminating* life.[2]

Eugene O'Neill has gone so far in this direction that many critics are calling him in these days "*the* American playwright." His career is certainly full of interest and in him promise has already developed into performance by reason of his "Beyond the Horizon," "Emperor Jones," "Anna Christie" and "Desire Under the Elms," to name only a few of his productions. Born in New York in 1889, the son of James O'Neill, who was then at the height of his fame as star of "Monte Cristo," this lad was early exposed to all kinds of stage influences. Private school prepared him for Princeton, but since he was expelled during his freshman year, college cannot be said to have counted much in his development. What did count was his vagabond career as gold prospector in

ville press agent. He had done some unusual work as a producer before going to England in 1913, but after his return he seems to have definitely conceived of the theatre as a place in which the people could be stirred and moved, as nowhere else, to an appreciation of what life really is. In 1918 he opened his own theatre in New York, the Plymouth.

[1] See "The Theatre of To-morrow" by Kenneth MacGowan (Boni and Liveright, 1921) for much that is suggestive and illuminating on this subject. Also Oscar M. Sayler's "Our American Theatre."

[2] "Miss Lulu Bett" by Zona Gale, produced at the Belmont Theatre, New York, December 27, 1920, and "Icebound" by Owen Davis, produced at the Sam H. Harris Theatre, New York, February 10, 1923, both of which were awarded Pulitzer prizes, are plays emphatically in this category.

491

Honduras, as able seaman on a ship of the American line sailing to divers distant points, and as newspaper handy man in New York. All of which culminated in an attack of tuberculosis that brought to. the wanderer his first leisure to write. Following a winter (1915) devoted to Professor George P. Baker's English 47 at Harvard University, O'Neill began to produce those remarkable plays which have already earned for him two Pulitzer prizes as well as universal acclaim.

Thus we come to the place where we stand to-day, with a new theatre, a new stagecraft and Eugene O'Neill to head the new dramatists. The moving pictures[1] and all counter interests to the contrary notwithstanding, appreciative audiences are being developed too, for good plays as they arise. Not only can New York boast about sixty theatres devoted to what is usually described as "the legitimate" but there are "little theatres," theatres in our colleges and repertory groups in many cities to back up the Theatre Guild of New York in its espousal of worth-while drama.

Nor should we feel at all hopeless regarding our actors. Many of the successfully established already mentioned or indicated in this book are still rendering yeoman service, among them William Gillette, Ferdinand Gottschalk, Mrs. Fiske, Blanche Bates, Margaret Anglin, Lucile Watson, Effie Shannon, Otis Skinner, Fred Stone, George Arliss, E. H. Sothern, Will Rogers, Ethel Barry-

[1] The moving picture first reared its head as a formidable rival to the theatre in 1910. Not until then, though this form of entertainment was introduced to the United States in 1896, were stars of the legitimate stage engaged as players and the vast possibilities of the business realized.

The Romance of the American Theatre

more, and numerous others whom only lack of space prevents me from naming. In addition, Walter Hampden and John Barrymore[1] have recently given us highly creditable Hamlets, and Jane Cowl and Rollo Peters have presented us with a superb "Romeo and Juliet," the latter demonstrating in the remarkable setting supplied for this immortal love story that he is endowed with authentic gifts as a stage designer also.

Meanwhile Lionel Barrymore, Frank Craven (writer as well as actor), Arnold Daly, Roland Young, O. P. Heggie (from England), Richard Bennett, Charles Gilpin, Ina Claire, Fanny Brice, Ruth Chatterton, Claire Eames, Jean Eagles, Helen Hayes, Eva Le Gallienne, Winifred Lenihan, Elsie Ferguson, Pauline Lord, Mary Nash, Laura Hope Crews, Martha Hedman, Emily Stevens, Katherine Cornell, Leonore Ulric, Laurette Taylor, Margaret Wycherly, Edith Wynne Matthison (she of the golden voice!), Alfred Lunt, Lynn Fontanne,

[1] Son of that sterling actor, Maurice Barrymore, and the brother of the well-beloved Ethel Barrymore, "Jack" Barrymore, who had played parts of the lighter sort acceptably in London, in Australia and all over this country, became *John* Barrymore and an actor to be reckoned with when he began to play Hamlet. He shares honors for bringing us a new interpretation of this rôle with Walter Hampden, whom many critics declare to be the best Hamlet of our generation. Hampden was born in Brooklyn, New York, June 30, 1879, the son of John Hampden Dougherty. Harvard University and the Polytechnical Institute in Brooklyn supplied him with his education, and the year after his graduation from the latter he made his first stage appearance (1901) with F. R. Benson's company in England, playing classical rôles. For three seasons he was the leading man at the Adelphi Theatre, London, and in 1905 acted Hamlet there, succeeding the younger Irving in the part. Soon after his return to the United States, in 1907, he made a great impression as Manson in Charles Rann Kennedy's "The Servant in the House." His most recent success has been as the poet-lover of "Cyrano de Bergerac," a part which, it had been generally supposed, died with Richard Mansfield.

493

Frank Reicher, Robert Milton, Charles Coburn, Joseph Schildkraut, Arthur Byron, Wallace Eddinger and others are also doing highly meritorious work in their several lines to delight ever-widening audiences.

And as prejudice against the theatre is disappearing in the world at large, jealousies within the theatre are likewise melting away! It is now recognized that all the arts of production — painting, lighting, machinery, and spectacle — no less than the art of player and playwright, belong here; that our stage, besides being the heir of all the ages in the realm of dramatic expression, is the heir of all that has ever helped to make for art in any field. So the American theatre presents to-day, as never before, an open door of opportunity to members of every race, every craft, every creed and every calling — to depict and advance every Cause.

THE END

INDEX

INDEX

"ABRAHAM LINCOLN", 485
Adams, Abigail, 104, 105
Adams, Edwin, 322
Adams, John Quincy, 340, 432
Adams, Maude, 471, 472
Adams, Samuel, 110, 114
Addison, Joseph, 47
Adelphi Theatre, 469, 493
"Admirable Crichton, The", 478
Advertising and Publicity Methods, 431–432, 474
Aiken, George L., 395, 396
Ainsworth, William Harrison, 161
"Alabama", 485
Aldrich, Louis, 322
Aldrich, Thomas Bailey, 324, 326
Alger, William R., 188, 199
Allen, Viola, 468
"Amazons, The", 476
America's first comedy, 481
Ancient and Honorable Society of Free and Accepted Masons of Charleston, Virginia, 79
Anderson, D. C., 322
Anderson, John Murray, 446
Anderson, Mary, 345, 346
André, Major, 88, 89, 90
Anglin, Margaret, 492
"Anna Christie", 491
Annapolis, 18, 66, 68, 69, 70
Appia, Adolphe, 490
Arch Street Theatre, Philadelphia, 421, 430, 465, 467
Arliss, George, 475, 492
"Armand, the Child of the People", 459
Arnold, Matthew, 235

"Arrah-na-Pogue", 463
"Article 47", 465
"Asa Trenchard", 483
"Assommoir, L'", 467
Astor, John Jacob, 438
Auvergne, Edmund d', 452

BAINTER, FAY, 469
Baker, Professor George P., 492
Baldwin, Christopher Columbus, 232, 253
Ballet in America, 445, 446, 447
Baltimore, 71, 72, 73, 74, 75, 76
Banjo, a native negro musical instrument, 375, 376
Barclay, James, 443
Barker, James N., 484
Barnum, P. T., 333, 383–384, 451
Barnum Museum, 384
Barrett, George, 225, 336
Barrett, John, 451
Barrett, Lawrence, 195, 298, 314, 323, 343, 345–349, 382
Barrett, Wilson, 207
Barrie, Sir James, 471–472, 473, 478
Barrière, 426, 439
Barron, Charles, 322
Barrymore, Ethel, 476, 492, 493
Barrymore, Lionel, 493
Barrymore, Maurice, 322, 493
Bates, Blanche, 469, 492
Bayard, William, 438
Bearded Lady of Kentucky, 365
Beauvallet, Léon, 272, 273, 274
Beekman, John K., 438
Belasco, David, 388, 468–469

497

Index

"Belle Lamar, An Episode of the Late American Conflict", 485
Belmont Theatre, New York, 491
Bennett, Arnold, 493
Bernard, Bayle, 482
Bernard, John, 125, 173, 176, 398, 403, 411, 412
Bernhardt, Sarah, 279, 301–305, 379, 380
Betterton, Mrs. Thomas, 2
"Beyond the Horizon", 491
"Biche au Bois, La", 445
Bispham, William, 326
"Black Crook, The", 444, 445, 446, 448, 470
"Bombastes Furioso", 379
Bonheur, Rosa, 343
Booker, Johnny, minstrel impresario, 362
Booth, Edwin, 169, 172, 287, 292, 298, 299, 310, 326, 327, 347, 348
Booth, John Wilkes, 319
Booth, Junius Brutus, 164–172, 211, 216, 311, 312, 313, 402, 421, 443
Booth, Junius Brutus, Jr., 313
Booth's Theatre, 321, 344, 485
Boston Theatre, 274, 275, 288, 337
Boucicault, Dion, 329, 330, 445, 455, 462, 463, 469, 485
Bowery Theatre, 185, 186, 216, 230, 334, 428, 439, 440, 441, 442, 444
Bracegirdle, Anne, 2
Brereton, Austin, 300
Brice, Fanny, 493
Broadway Circus, 432
Broadway Journal, 458
Brougham, John, 322, 454, 455, 463, 484
Brougham's Lyceum, 208, 454, 463
Brower, "Frank", 358
Brown, T. Allston, 20, 269, 477, 478
"Brudder Bones", history of, 368, 369, 370, 371, 372, 373, 374
Bryant, Dan. *See* O'BRIEN, DANIEL WEBSTER
Bryant, William Cullen, 201

Bryant's Minstrels, 358
Buffalo Bill, 482
"Bunker Hill — or The Death of General Warren", 484
Burgoyne, John, 82, 83, 84
Burke, Edmund, 17, 140
Burke, John D., 484
Burke, Master Joseph, 231, 232, 233
Burlesque, introduction of, 379, 380, 447, 448
Burton, W. E., 328, 445
Butler, Pierce, 242
Byrne, Henry Herbert, 334
Byron, Arthur, 494
Byron, Lord, 97, 129, 452

CABLE, GEORGE W., 376
Caldwell, James H., 183, 184, 191
Caldwell, Ned, 405
Campbell, Charles, 424
Camp Street Theatre, New Orleans, 404
Carter, Mrs. Leslie, 469
Carton, R. C., 476
Castle Garden, 438
"Cato", 20, 47, 48, 71
Céleste, Madame, 229, 230, 231, 407
Chanfrau, Frank, 479, 482, 483
Chaplin, Charles, 355
Chapman, William, 441
Charleston, 55–65, 76–79, 442
Chatham Theatre, 358, 426, 439, 454
Chatterton, Ruth, 493
Cheer, Margaret, 40, 41
Cheney, Arthur, 284
Chestnut Street Theatre, 91, 102, 176, 421, 429, 431
Child Labor in the Theatre, 362
Chlapowski, Charles Bozenta, 296
Choate, Rufus, 172
Christy, Edwin P., 359
Christy, George. *See* HARRINGTON, GEORGE
Christy Minstrels, 359, 374
Cibber, Charlotte, 42
Cibber, Colley, 2, 3, 5, 28, 42, 67

Index

Cibber, Mrs. Theophilus, 67
Claire, Ina, 469, 493
Clapp, George Alfred. *See* DOCK-STADER, LEW
Clapp, Henry Austin, 282, 283, 326, 340, 341
Clark, Governor William, 401
Clarke, Asia Booth, 312, 318
Clarke, Colonel Merriwether Lewis, 407
Clarke, George, 465
Clarke, John S., 382
Claxton, Kate, 465
Clay, Henry, 409
Clifton, Josie, 441
"Climbers, The", 490
Coburn, Charles, 494
Coghlan, Rose, 463
Cohan, George M., 355, 389
Colden, Cadwallader, 34
Coleridge, Samuel Taylor, 129
"Colleen Bawn, The", 462
"Collegians, The", 462
Collier, Jeremy, 62
Collins, William Wilkie, 283
Colman, John, 280, 284, 480, 481
Columbia Street Theatre, Cincinnati, 377
Colville, Samuel, 446
Congreve, William, 62
Connor, Edmund S., 377
"Contrast, The", 37, 91–94, 98, 113, 479, 481
Conway, H. J., 395
Conway, William Augustus, 159–163, 183, 424
Cooke, George Frederick, 97, 111, 119–129, 170, 177, 188, 214
Cooke, John Esten, 46, 48
Cooper, Priscilla (Mrs. Robert Tyler), 402, 406, 442
Cooper, Thomas Abthorpe, 118, 123, 173, 175, 176, 177, 225, 240, 310, 402, 406, 414, 423
Copeau, Jacques, 490
Corcoran, W. W., 225
Coree, Joseph, 438
Cornell, Katherine, 493

Covent Garden, 482
Cowell, Joe, 128, 379, 404, 421, 428, 431–433, 434, 436, 437, 439, 440, 441, 481
Cowl, Jane, 493
Crabtree, Lotta Mignon, 248
Craig, Gordon, 490
Crane, William H., 382
Craven, Frank, 493
Crawford, Ann, 2
Creole song, 376
Crews, Laura Hope, 493
Crossman, Henrietta, 469
Crotan Hall, 383
Cushman, Charlotte, 310, 315, 322, 334, 337, 340–345, 442, 445, 452, 459, 466
"Cyrano de Bergerac", 474, 493
Czar Nicholas I, 453

DAILEY, PETER, 387
"Dakolar", 468
Daly, Arnold, 493
Daly, Augustin, 60, 311, 339, 352, 353, 463, 464, 465, 467–468, 485
Daly, Charles P., 20, 44, 55, 326
Daly's Theatre, 386, 468, 479
Dana, Charles A., 201
Dauvray, Helen, 468
Davenant, Sir William, 3
Davenport, A. H., 328
Davenport, E. L., 310, 315, 322, 336–340, 349, 445, 459, 465
Davenport, Fanny, 334–339, 465
Davis, J. Frank, 390, 393
Davis, L. Clarke, 464, 466
Davis, Owen, 491
"Davy Crockett", 485
"Dazzler, The", 450
"Dear Brutus", 478
Delaney, John, 380
D'Eon, Chevalier, 42
"Desire Under the Elms", 491
Devlin, Mary, 315, 316, 328
Diamond, Jack, 363
Dibden, Charles, 16, 42
Dickens, Charles, 282, 443
Dietz, Linda, 465

Index

"Disraeli", 475
"Dixie", first rendering of, 358
Doche, Madame, 335
Dockstader, Lew, 380
"Domestic Manners of the Americans", 251
Doran, Dr. John, 7
Dougherty, John Hampden, 493
Douglass, David, 28, 29, 34, 36, 37, 40, 66, 76, 98
Douglass, Mrs. David, 25, 29, 31, 42, 49
"Dr. Jekyll and Mr. Hyde", 474
Drake, Alexander, 404
Drake, Mrs. Alexander, 404, 433, 434
Drake, Samuel, Sr., 398, 403
Dreher, Virginia, 63, 466, 467
Drew, John, 62, 322, 465, 466, 467, 471
Drew, Mrs. John, 328, 339, 377, 382, 465, 466
Drinkwater, John, 385
Drury Lane Theatre, London, 360, 424, 428, 432
Duane, William, 180
Duff, John R., 214, 216, 218
Duff, Mary, 210-221
Dumas, Alexandre, the elder, 443, 452
Dumas, Alexandre, fils, 447, 450
Duncan, Isadora, 447
Dunlap, William, 19, 34, 48, 87, 95, 96, 97, 98, 99, 101, 106, 222
Durang, Charles, 89
Duse, Eleanora, 294, 295
Dwight, Pres. Timothy, 24

Eagle Theatre, New York, 450
Eagles, Jean, 493
Eames, Claire, 493
Eddinger, Wallace, 494
Edinburgh, Duke of, 443
Ellsler, Fanny, 231, 407
Emerson, Billy, 380
Emerson, Ralph Waldo, 407
Emmett, Daniel, 358, 359
"Emperor Jones", 491
"Erminie", 490

Ethel, Agnes, 465
"Ethiopian Operatic Brothers", 359
Evans, George, known as "Honey Boy", 380
Evans and Hoey, 385

Faneuil Hall, 82, 83, 84
Farquhar, George, 2, 20, 60
Farren, Elizabeth, 105, 106
"Fashion", 455, 457, 458, 461
"Fazio", 443
Fechter, Charles Albert, 122, 235, 280-285
Federal Street Theatre, 114, 115, 116, 215
Fennell, James, 118, 173, 174, 175, 176
Ferguson, Elsie, 493
Fielding, Henry, 86
Fifth Avenue Theatre, 464
Fisher, Charles, 322, 466
Fisher, Clara, 232, 424, 432
Fiske, Harrison Grey, 475, 476, 492
Fiske, Minnie Maddern, 474, 475, 476, 492
Fiske, Stephen, 298
Fitch, Clyde, 462, 471, 484, 468
Floating Palace, The, 364, 366
Florence, W. J., 479, 483
"Flying Scud", 463
"Follies, The", 446
Fontanne, Lynn, 493
Forbes, R. B., 225
Forbes-Robertson, Sir Johnston, 475
Ford, John T., 328, 362
Foreign Actors, jealousy of, 422, 423, 424, 425, 426, 427
"Formosa", 463
Forrest, Edwin, 173-207, 211, 225, 226, 227, 228, 310, 315, 341, 350, 351, 356, 440, 441, 445
"Forty Thieves, The", 447, 448
Foster, Stephen C., 360
Fox, Charles J., 17
Francis, Dr. John W., 129, 142
Franklin, Benjamin, 27, 28, 77, 78
French dancing, Introduction of, 440

Index

French Opera House (New Orleans), 263, 442
"French Spy, The", 443
Frohman, Charles, 386, 462, 470, 471, 472, 473, 474
Frohman, Daniel, 468, 469, 470, 474, 476
Frohman, Gustave, 470
Frohman, Henry, 470
Front Street Theatre, Baltimore, 421
"Frontier type", plays of the, 485
"Frou Frou", 465
Fuller, Margaret, 407
Furness, Horace Howard, 326

Gaine, Hugh, 76, 86
Gale, Zona, 491
Galsworthy, John, 475
"Garden of Allah, The", 346
Gardiner, John, 109, 110
Gardiner, John Sylvester, 111
Garrick, David, 2, 9, 12–18, 84, 86, 118, 235, 306, 344, 345, 459, 468
Garrick, Mrs. David, 2, 16, 17
Geddes, Norman-Bel, 490
Georges, Mademoiselle, 190
Germany and the German Kaiser, 472
Gilbert, Mrs. G. H., 465, 466, 467
Gilbert, John, 211, 322, 463
Gilfert, Charles, 440, 441
Gillette, William, 478, 479, 492
Gilpin, Charles, 493
Gladstone, on minstrels, 375
"Glance at New York, A", 482
Globe Theatre, Boston, 478
Godwin, Parke, 201
Goldsmith, Oliver, 17, 308
Goodwin, Nat, 382, 385
Gottschalk, Ferdinand, 492
Greece, King of, 443
Greeley, Horace, 211, 218
"Greenwich Village Follies", 446
Griffin, Gerald, 462
Grillo, Marquis Capranica del, 286
Grossman, Ignatius R., 324
Grossmann, Edwina Booth, 315, 324

"Gulzara, or The Persian Slave", 457
"Gustavus Vasa", 72, 94
Gwyn, Nell, 7

Hackett, James A., 479, 480, 481, 482
Hackett, James H., 322, 339, 443, 445
Hackett, James K., 339
Hallam, Beatrice, 49, 66, 68, 69
Hallam, John, 428, 429
Hallam, Lewis, 19, 22, 26, 27, 48
Hallam, Lewis, Jr., 25, 28, 29, 100
Hallam, William, 19, 27, 81
Hamblin, Thomas S., 334, 336, 441
Hamilton, Clayton, 488
Hampden, Walter, 493
Hancock, Governor, 113, 114
Hansson, Laura Marholm, 294
Hardy, Thomas, 475
Harman, Mrs. Catherine Maria, 41, 42, 67
Harned, Virginia, 332
Harper, Joseph, 107, 112
Harrigan and Hart, 479
Harrington, George, 359
Harris, Henry, 123
Harris, Joel Chandler, 375
Harris Theatre, Sam H., 491
Harrison, Gabriel, 206, 210
Harrison, William Henry, 182
Harte, Bret, 485
Hatton, Mrs. Anne Julia, 106
Haverley's Mastadon Minstrels, 360, 361, 380
Hayes, Helen, 493
Haymarket Theatre, Boston, 116, 447
Hayne, Julia Dean, 337, 347
"Hazel Kirke", 477
Hazlitt, William, 161, 227, 234
"Heart of Maryland, The", 469
Hedman, Martha, 492
Heenan, John C., 443
Heggie, O. P., 493
"Held By the Enemy", 478
Henry, John, 99, 100
Herne, James A., 484, 490

501

Heron, Matilda, 298, 329, 333–336
"Highest Bidder, The", 474
"Highland Reel, The", 412
Hilson, Tom, 440
Hind, Thomas J., Jr., 322
Hodgkinson, John, 100, 101, 102, 310
Holiday Street Theatre, Baltimore, 421
Holland, George, 410, 441, 445, 465
Hooley's Theatre, 471
Hope, Anthony, 476
Hopkins, Arthur, 490
Hopper, De Wolf, 387, 388
"Horizon", 485
Houghton, Rev. George H., 411
Houssaye, Arsène, 298
Howard Athenaeum (Boston), 314, 333, 337, 349
Howard, Bronson, 479
Howard, Cordelia, the original "Little Eva", 394
Howard, George S., 394
Hoyt, Charles H., 478, 479
Hunt, James Henry Leigh, 60, 120, 246
Hutin, Mademoiselle, 440
Hutton, Lawrence, 344, 355, 485

Ibsen, 475, 488, 490
"Icebound", 491
"In the Good Old Summer Time", 380
Incledon, Charles Benjamin, 123, 125
Indian plays, 484
"Indian Princess, The", 484
"Invisible Lady, The", 366, 367, 368
Ireland, Joseph N., 211, 212, 231, 239
Irish, Charles, 429
Irving, Sir Henry, 305–309, 323, 348, 472, 490
Irving, Washington, 221, 224, 329, 330
Irwin, May and Flo, 385
Isman, Felix, 386, 387

Itinerant acting and barnstorming, 401, 417, 418, 419, 420, 432
"Ixion", 447

Jackson, Andrew, 166, 195
James, Louis, 465
Jameson, Anna, 240
Janauschek, Madame, 297
"Jane Shore", 8, 9, 215
Janin, Jules, 277
Jarrett, Henry C., 302, 328
Jarrett and Palmer, 445, 446
"Jealous Wife, The", 140
Jefferson, Joseph, 77, 326, 327–332, 337, 382, 395, 410–411, 451, 461, 479
Jefferson, Thomas, 376
Jennings, Mrs., 465
Jewett, Sara, 465
"Jilt, The", 463
"Jim Crow" Rice. See Rice, Thomas D.
"Jim Crow" song, origin of, 377–379
"Joan of Arc", 472
Johnson, Eastman, 326
Johnson, Dr. Samuel, 12, 14, 15, 17, 160, 163, 237
John Street Theatre, 37, 39, 91, 95, 100, 435, 484
Jolson, Al, 381
Jones, Henry Arthur, 476
Jones, Hugh, 45, 46
Jones, Robert Edmond, 490
Jordan, Dora, 120
"Juba Dance", 362, 363
"Jüngfrau von Orleans", 472

Kean, Charles, 122, 129, 136, 138, 139, 140, 141, 235, 322, 445
Kean, Edmund, 122, 128, 129–139, 165, 184, 185, 188, 211, 215, 234, 421, 424, 468
Kean, Thomas, 21, 27
Keeler, Ralph, 362
Keene, Laura, 314, 329, 461, 462
Kehew, Mrs. Mary Morton, 324
Kemble, Charles, 177, 193, 225, 233, 238, 239, 240, 241, 430

Index

Kemble, Fanny, 424, 425, 430
Kemble, Frances Anne, 105, 132, 218, 225, 231, 238–245, 279, 288
Kemble, John Philip, 120, 122, 126, 188, 233, 234, 235
Kemble, Roger, 234
Kendal, Madge Robertson, 476
Kennedy, Charles Rann, 493
"Kentuckian, The", 482
King Edward VII, 469
"Kitchen Minstrels", 358
Kynaston, Edward, 3, 4

"LADY BOUNTIFUL", 476
"Lady of Lyons, The", 458
Lafayette, 90
Langtry, Lily, 464
Lawrence, Sir Thomas, 234
Lawrens, Henry, 90
Leclerq, Carlotta, 141, 284, 375
Leclerq, Charles, 466
"Leg Shows", 420, 444, 445, 446, 447, 450
Le Gallienne, Eva, 493
Lemon, Mark, 395
Le Moyne, W. J., 337
Lenihan, Winifred, 493
Lennox, William Pitt, 121, 123, 140
Leslie, Amy, 388
Lewes, Georges Henry, 129, 278, 290
Lewis, Francis, 455
Lewis, James, 63, 465, 466, 467
Lincoln, Abraham, 319, 362
Lincoln, Benjamin, 91
Lind, Jenny, 231, 266, 451
"Lion of the West, The", 481
Liszt, Franz, 453
"Little Church around the Corner", 410
"Little Minister, The", 471
Logan, Olive, 368, 374, 444
"London Assurance", 455, 463
Longfellow, H. W., 245
Lord, Pauline, 493
"Lorlie's Wedding", 464
Lowe, Professor, the balloonist, 367

"Lucy Long", famous colored song, 364, 373
Ludlow, Noah Miller, 397–410
Ludwig, King of Bavaria, 453
Lunt, Alfred, 493
Lusitania, SS., 472
Lyceum Theatre, 468, 479
"Lying Valet, The", 18
Lynch, Frank, 363

McANDREWS, J. W., 361
Macaulay, Thomas Babington, 157
MacCullough, John, 205, 285, 297, 322, 332, 345, 346, 347, 349–351, 485
MacGowan, Kenneth, 491
MacKaye, James Steele, 468, 477, 478
Macready, William Charles, 119, 120, 122, 162, 163, 193, 196, 197, 198, 199, 226–229, 235, 336, 341, 409, 424, 425
McVicker, J. H., 320
McVicker, Mary, 320, 321
Madison, James, 127
Madison Square Theatre, 477, 478, 479
"Major André", 484
Mallory, Rev. G. S., 477, 478
Mallory, Marshall, 477
Mann, Colonel Alvan, 384
Mansfield, Richard, 474, 493
Mantell, Robert, 468
Marcosson, Isaac F., 470, 473
"Margaret Fleming", 484
Markham, Pauline, 447, 449
Mark Twain, 483, 485
Marlowe, Julia, 332
Martin, Sir Theodore, 279
Marylebone Theatre, 459
Mason, Edward Tuckerman, 290
Mason, John, 468
Mather, Margaret, 445
Mathews, Charles, Sr., 142–158, 161, 424, 437
Mathews, Charles James, 245, 246, 247, 248, 463, 465
Matthews, Brander, 236, 360
Matthison, Edith Wynne, 493

Index

Mayo, Frank, 322, 479, 485
"Mazeppa", 442, 444
Menken, Adah Isaacs, 442, 443
Menken, Alexander Isaacs, 443
Merington, Marguerite, 343
Merry, Mrs., 91, 176, 177
"Metamora", 189, 206, 484
"Mighty Dollar, The", 483
Milton, Robert, 494
"Miss Lulu Bett", 491
Mitchell, Maggie, 248, 445
"Mitchels, The", 364
"M'liss", 485
Modjeska, Helena, 295–300, 324
Montague, Henry J., 463
"Monte Cristo", 454, 491
Montez, Lola, 452, 453, 454
Moore, Thomas, 212, 213, 214
Morant, Fanny, 322, 463
More, Hannah, 17
Morey, Harry, 387
Morris, Clara, 298, 352–354, 465
Morton, Robert, 88
Moscow Art Theatre, 490
Moses, Montrose J., 331, 462, 468
"Mosquito", 450
Mt. Vernon Gardens, 438
Moving pictures, 492
Mowatt, Anna Cora, 278, 336, 445, 455
Mowatt, James, 456, 458
Murdoch, James E., 314, 322, 443
Murdock, Frank, 485
Music Hall of Weber and Fields, 386

Napoleon III, 443
Nash, Mary, 493
Nash, Thomas, 3
Natchez Theatre, 400
"Nathan Hale", 484
National Theatre, Boston, 206, 209, 230, 333
Navarro, Antonio de, 346
Nazimova, Alla, 294, 295
Negro Minstrels, 355–382; first organized, 358
Neilson, Lilian Adelaide, 300

Nethersole, Olga, 386
New National Theatre, 451
New Orleans French Theatre, 400
New Orleans Varieties, 443
Newell, Robert H. ("Orpheus C. Kerr"), 442
Newell, Timothy, 85
Niblo's Theatre, 444, 445, 446, 447, 459, 460, 470
"Notes on Virginia" by Jefferson, 376

Oakes, James, 187, 188, 189
O'Brien, Daniel Webster, 358
Ogden, Samuel, 455
Old Broadway Theatre, 452
"Old English", 475
Oldfield, Nance, 1–6, 9, 118
"Old Homestead, The", 484, 485
Olinza, Madame, the tightrope walker, 368, 369
"Olympia Theatre", 459, 485
O'Neil, Nance, 450
O'Neill, Eugene, 490, 491, 492
O'Neill, James, 491
"Oroonoko", 74, 75, 357
Osgood, Rev. Samuel, 315, 316
Otis, Harrison Gray, 110, 113
Otway, Thomas, 80
"Our American Cousin", 461, 483

Palmer, Albert M., 326, 476, 477, 478
Park Theatre, New York, 107, 124, 129, 165, 176, 186, 192, 216, 222, 225, 239, 251, 382, 397, 420, 423, 428, 429, 432, 435, 436, 438, 451, 455, 457, 458, 459, 460, 484
"Passing Show", 446
Pastor, Tony, 382, 383, 384, 385, 471
Paulding, James Kirke, 482
Payne, John Howard, 125, 214, 221–225
Peale, Charles Wilson, 68
Pelham, "Dick", 358
Pepys, Samuel, 7, 9
"Peter Pan", 471
Peters, Rollo, 493

Index

Phelps, Henry P., 443
Phillips, Stephen, 486
"Pinafore", 385
Pinero, Sir Arthur, 476, 486
Piozzi, Mrs. (Mrs. Thrale), 160, 161, 162, 163
"Pippin, the King of the Gold Mines", 449
"Pique", 465
Pittsburgh Theatre, 430-431
Pixley, Annie, 485
"Pizarro", 398, 419
Placide, Henry, 328
Placide, Jane, 183, 191
Placide, Thomas, 328, 412
Players' Club, 324, 325, 332, 348
Plumstead, William, 27
Plympton, Eben, 322
"Pocahontas", 484
Poe, Edgar Allan, 458
Ponisi, Madame, 463
"Poor Gentleman, The", 423
Porter, Charles, 179
Powell, Charles Stuart, 112, 114, 116
Power, Tyrone, 225, 250-265, 431
Press agent, first in America, 441
Price and Simpson's Equestrian Company, 432
Price, Stephen, 125, 145, 177, 217, 247, 423, 424, 425, 439
Primrose and West, 380
"Princess, The", 459
Princeton undergraduates help the early drama, 415-416
Pritchard, Mrs., 237
"Private Secretary, The", 478
"Professor, The", 478
"Pudd'nhead Wilson", 485
"Puffs", attitude of press towards, 426
Pulitzer Prize Plays, 491, 492
Purdy's National Theatre, 394, 395

QUINN, ARTHUR HOBSON, 395

RACHEL, 122, 129, 191, 266-280, 281, 456
Randolph, Peyton, 66

Rankin, McKee, 450
Ravels, The, 445
Raymond, John T., 483
Raymond and Waring's Menagerie, 384
Reade, Charles, 14, 307
"Recruiting Officer, The", 20, 59, 79
Reed, David, 367
Rees, James, 220
Rehan, Ada, 61, 351, 352, 465, 467, 475
Reicher, Frank, 494
Reinhardt, Max, 490
Revolutionary Plays, 484, 485
Reynolds, Sir Joshua, 236
Rice, Edward Leroy, 377
Rice, Thomas D., 327, 377-379
Rice, William Henry, 377, 379
Rich, John, 11
"Richard the Third", 475
Richmond Hill Theatre, 218
Ristori, Adelaide, 286-289, 324
Ritchie, W. F., 460
Robertson, Agnes, 141
Robertson, Thomas W., 16
"Robinson Crusoe", 450
Robinson, Henry Crabb, 120
Robinson, "Perdita", 71, 72
Robson, May, 386
Rogers, Samuel, 15, 235
Rogers, Will, 492
Roosevelt, Theodore, 381
"Rosedale", 488
Rostand, 474
"Roundabout Papers", 365, 366
Rowe, Nicholas, 8, 9
Rowson, Susanna, 438
Rudersdorff, Madame, 474
Russell, Lillian, 385, 387
Ryan, Dennis, 73, 74, 75, 90

SABINE, REV. W. T., 410
St. Charles Theatre, New Orleans, 408
St. Denis, Ruth, 447
Salvini, Tommaso, 122, 289-293, 307
Sands, George, 248

Index

"Sans Souci", 445
"Sappho", 386
Sargent, Epes, 457
Sargent, John Singer, 309
Saunderson, Mrs., 3
Savannah, 71, 76
Sayler, Oliver M., 446, 491
"Scandals", 447
Schildkraut, Joseph, 494
"School for Scandal, The", 75, 76, 433, 451, 463
Scott-Siddons, Mrs., 465
Searle, John, 438
Seaver, Joel G., 219, 220
"Second Mrs. Tanqueray, The", 476
"Secret Service", 478
Sedley, Henry, 209
Seilhamer, George O., 19, 20, 34, 36, 39, 48, 71, 72, 75, 97
Seldes, Gilbert, 355
"Servant in the House, The", 493
Shannon, Effie, 492
Sharpley, Sam, 385
"Shaughraun, The", 463
Shays, Daniel, 91
Shelley, Mary Godwin, 176, 221, 224
Shepheard, Charles, 58
Sheridan, Richard Brinsley Butler, 76, 235, 489
"Sherlock Holmes", 478
Shipman, Louis Evan, 383
Shubert, J. J., 446
Siddons, Sarah Kemble, 120, 122, 210, 217, 235, 236, 237, 238
Sienkiewicz, Henry, 297
Simonson, Lee, 490
Simpson, Edmund, 128
"Sinbad", 449
Sinclair, Catherine Norton (Mrs. Forrest), 194, 199, 200, 201, 202, 203, 207, 208, 209, 314
Skinner, Otis, 63, 299, 322, 467, 492
Smith, Mark, 322
Smith, Solomon Franklin (Sol Smith), 356, 407, 408, 410, 411–420
"Sorcerer, The", 385

Sothern, Edward Askew, 129, 249, 322, 329, 332, 333, 461, 483
Sothern, Edward Hugh, 332, 471, 474, 492
Southwark Theatre, 88, 94, 102, 103
Spectacles, 445
Spitzer, Marian, 361
Spottiswood, Governor, 44, 45
"Squire, The", 466
Stanislavsky, Constantin, 490
Stanley, Thomas, 82, 86
Stark, James, 322
Starr, Frances, 469
Stedman, Edmund Clarence, 354
Stephens, Leslie, 164
Stetson, John, 293
Stevens, Emily, 493
Stewart, A. T., 272
Stone, Fred, 388, 492
Stone, H. D., 170
Stone, John Augustus, 484
Stowe, Harriet Beecher, 392, 394, 395
Strong, Rev. Paschal N., 147
Stuart, William, 329
"Sweet Lavender", 476
Swinburne, Algernon Charles, 443

"TABLEAUX VIVANTS", 450
Talfourd, Serjeant, 193
Talma, François Joseph, 190, 191, 223
"Taming of the Shrew, The", 459, 467
"Tammany", 106, 484
Tarleton, Colonel, 72
Taylor, Charles Western, 394
Taylor, Laurette, 493
Taylor, Tom, 395, 461, 483
"Temperance Town, A", 479
Terriss, William, 323
Terry, Ellen, 141, 305, 307, 308, 309, 323, 354, 490
"Tess of the D'Urbervilles", 475
"Texas Steer, A", 479
Thackeray, William Makepeace, 365, 375, 451

Index

Thatcher, George, 380
Theatre Guild of New York, 492
Theatre Royal, 459
Thespian Societies, 414
Thomas, Augustus, 486
Thompson, Denman, 479, 484
Thompson, Lydia, 447, 448, 449, 450
Thorne, Charles R., Jr., 322
"Three Fast Men", 443
"Three Guardsmen, The", 454
Tompkins, Dr. Orlando, 319
"Tom Shows." *See* "Uncle Tom's Cabin"
"Tom Thumb", 86
"To Oblige Benson", 447
Tony Pastor's Opera House, 385
Townshend, Charles, 17
Towse, John Ranken, 475, 476
Tree, Ellen, 122, 139, 140, 424
Tree, Maria, 140
Tremont Theatre, Boston, 428
"Trip to Chinatown, A", 478
Trollope, Mrs. Frances M., 251, 434
Tyler, Robert, 402
Tyler, Mrs. Robert, 406
Tyler, Royall, 37, 91, 92, 98, 479, 481

Ulric, Leonore, 493
"Uncle Tom's Cabin", 372, 390–396
"Under the Gaslight", 464, 465
"Unequal Match, An", 464
Union Square Theatre, 477
Upton, Thomas, 22, 23
"Used Up", 451

Vandenhoff, George, 121, 129, 208, 209, 340, 343
"Vanity Fair", 462
Vaudeville, establishment of, 477
Vauxhall Garden, 358
Vermont Giant, 365
Vestris, Madame, 246, 247, 248, 424, 429, 456, 489
Victoria, Queen, 361
Viennese Children, 410

Vincent, Mrs. J. R., 333
Vining, Fanny, 337
Violante, Madame, 10
"Virginia Serenaders", 358, 383
Vokes, Rosina, 477

Wagner, Richard, 453
Walenski, Count, 279
Wallack, J. W., 225, 284, 328, 451
Wallack, James W., Jr., 322, 329, 339, 454
Wallack, Lester, 328, 451, 452, 463
Wallack's Theatre, 386, 444, 463, 479
Waller, Mrs. Emma, 322
Walnut Street Theatre, Philadelphia, 421, 425, 429, 431, 458
Warfield, David, 387, 388, 469
Warner, Charles Dudley, 483
Warren, Sarah Isabel, 331
Warren, William, Jr., 91
Warren, William, Sr., 91, 176, 427
Washington, George, 73, 94, 95, 96, 103, 105, 164, 356, 357
Watson, Lucile, 492
Weathersby, Eliza, 447
Weber and Fields, 386–388
Weiss, Madame Josephine, 410
Wells, Mary, 322
Wemyss, Francis Courtney, 420–432, 479–480, 489
"Wench dancers", 364, 366, 372, 373, 374
West, Benjamin, 97, 223
West, William H., 380
Westminster Abbey, 2, 9, 306
Wetmore, Prosper M., 185
Wheatleigh, Charles, 328
White, Charles T., 357, 358
White, George, 447
White, Richard Grant, 447, 448, 449
White's Serenaders, Charley, 379
Whitelock, Mrs., 233
Whitlock, "Billy", 358
Whitman, Walt, 170
"Who Wants a Guinea?", 480
Wignell, Thomas, 91, 92, 93
"Wildfire, Nimrod", 479, 481, 482

507

Index

Williams, Barney, 359, 373, 445
Williamsburg, Virginia, 19, 44–55
Willia, Eola, 79
Wills, W. G., 308
Wilson, Francis, 381–382, 385, 490
Winter Garden Theatre, 316, 318, 320, 464
Winter, William, 284, 310, 325, 326, 331, 335, 344, 348, 455, 475
Woffington, Peg, 9–15, 63
Wood, Mrs. John, 445, 467
Woods, Mary Ann Paton, 121

Wood's Minstrels, 379
Woolf's, Benjamin E., 483
Woollcott, Alexander, 475
Wright, Mrs. Mabel Osgood, 316
Wycherly, Margaret, 493

"YANKEE TYPE" CHARACTERS, 479, 480, 481–484
Young, Charles Mayne, 122
Young, Roland, 493
"Young Mrs. Winthrop, The", 479

ZIEGFELD, FLORENZ, JR., 446